CAROLYN KIRBY's  er
debut *The Conviction* es
from the Historical W t/
Specsavers Crime Fict n
by the *Times* and *Sunday Times* as one of the Best Novels of the Year and has been translated in Polish.

Born in Sunderland, Carolyn studied history at St Hilda's College, Oxford and she now helps run Hilda's Crime Fiction Weekend, a world-renowned literary festival held every year in the college.

Find her at carolynkirby.com or X/Twitter @novelcarolyn

Also by Carolyn Kirby

The Conviction of Cora Burns

When We Fall

Praise for *When We Fall*

A TIMES AND SUNDAY TIMES HISTORICAL NOVEL OF THE YEAR 2020

'A gripping novel about the moral choices faced during times of great peril.' - **Antonia Senior,** *The Times*

'A poignant story of love, betrayal and impossible moral choices.'
– **Nick Rennison,** *Sunday Times*

'A terrific World War II novel, which deals with complicated matters of love and loyalty... Tense and tender, it captures the terrifying frailties of truth and trust in brutal time.' - **Eithne Farry,** *Daily Mail*

'Engaging and elegantly written... Highly recommended.'
– **Roger Moorhouse, author of** *First to Fight*

'Powerful and moving... a tale of tragedy and brutality, with characters that are so well-drawnthey practically get up and walk from the page.' – **Jenny Quintana, author of** *The Missing Girl*

Praise for *The Conviction of Cora Burns*

'A spirited gothic adventure ...Kirby writes with skill and gusto.'
– **Antonia Senior,** *The Times*

'Even at its darkest it is beautifully written.... A great historical novel with bite.'
– **Deirdre Brien,** *Sunday Mirror*

'This richly woven Gothic tale is an atmospheric treat' – *Heat*

Ravenglass

Carolyn Kirby

Northodox Press Ltd
Maiden Greve, Malton,
North Yorkshire, YO17 7BE

This edition 2025

1

First published in Great Britain by
Northodox Press Ltd 2025

Copyright © Carolyn Kirby 2025

Carolyn Kirby asserts the moral right to
be identified as the author of this work.

ISBN: 978-1-915179-71-5
This book is set in Caslon Pro Std

This book is a work of fiction. References to real people, events, establishments, organizations, or locales are intended only to provide a sense of authenticity, and are used fictitiously. All other characters, and all incidents and dialogue, are drawn from the author's imagination and are not to be construed as real.

All rights reserved. No part of this publication may be reproduced, stored in a retrieval system, or transmitted, in any form or by any means, electronic, mechanical, photocopying, recording, or otherwise, without the prior permission of the publishers.

This book is sold subject to the condition that it shall not, by way of trade or otherwise, be lent, re-sold, hired out or otherwise circulated without the publisher's prior consent in any form of binding or cover other than that in which it is published and without a similar condition including this condition being imposed on the subsequent purchaser.

Credit for the ballads quoted in the novels goes to English Broadside Ballad Archive. Ref EBBA 32526, Huntington Library shelf mark HEH289784 and titled: "A song, on the confession anddying words of William Stevenson, Merchant, late of Northallerton in the County of York aged 27 years who was executed at Durham on Saturday 26th August 1727 for the barbarous murder of Mary Fawden near Hartlepool…"

the

first part

–

in Whitehaven

the first chapter

What I first remember of my life is the forced removal of my skirts. This was during my fifth or sixth year, when I was small enough, at any rate, to be held down and stripped by two strong women. I can still feel the grip of their hands raising me aloft, the sudden emptiness of air beneath my flailing feet, the bubbling of snot from my indignant nostrils. One of the women pins me against the floor-cloth whilst the other pulls at the fastenings about my waist. But a howl is gathering in my chest. I know what they are doing and I will use all the force of my considerable infant will to stop them.

Beside me, a fire sparks in the grate but that is no indication of the season in which this undressing takes place. In our wind-blasted town, planted between the English mountains and the Irish Sea, it is as like to be July as January. Above me, the wainscot is olive green so this is certainly the dining parlour of our new house in Queen Street. Even at a distance of five and thirty year, I can still bring to mind that room's perfume of meat juice and coal smoke. And I can still hear the cooing of Poll, my nurse, and the more shrill injunctions of my Aunt Ravenglass as both women wrestle with the strings of my beloved petticoats.

I was a spindly child, fair like my sister but agile and strong, and so my disrobers huff at their work. Fliss, my sister, is also there, hopping from one foot to the other. With her white apron and flaxy hair, she lights up the corner of the room like a sconce. If I am four or five year old, she will be nine or ten. I picture her toying with a pink ribbon that covers the foul scar across her neck, for throughout our childhoods, or at least the part of hers that I can remember, her fingers were never far from that stripe of angry, puckered flesh.

Years would pass before I learnt how this injury was inflicted. But Fliss, being older, could not escape the daily recollection of a Tragedy too awful to be spoke about, though it ravaged our small family forever.

On this day, though, Fliss is laughing as she presents me with the cause of my anguish, namely, my first pair of breeches.

'Come Kit!' she says, raising them like a prize. 'How grown-up you will seem if you put these on.'

At that, I cast up a furious, dripping eye. God in Heaven! They are brown! And not a velvety doe-brown nor a silken tawny, but the same hue as a dirty corner of the harbour, or of fell-tops in November drizzle. Had the breeches in Fliss's hands been lavender or vermilion or gold my objection might have weakened. But brown!

I suppose the females must, that day, have squeezed my thrashing legs into the itchy breeches. My father, although he makes no appearance in this episode, would not have allowed me to keep on my baby-skirts a moment longer than necessary. He believed that the son of a would-be gentleman should be dressed, as soon as his dribbling infant pizzler would allow, like a man. For, more than anything, my father wanted me to be manly. And so it was my fate to always let him down.

I realise now the torments that must have broiled beneath my father's wildbore waistcoat. I understand too that when disaster lapped at his feet Henry Ravenglass would cling to manliness like a drowning sailor to an empty barrel. But his efforts, perhaps intended as solicitude, to make his son into a masculine manikin of himself, only drove me to vexation. For there was never the merest possibility that Christopher Ravenglass would grow into the heavy-wigged, Loyal-Toasting, ship owner and charitable benefactor that Henry Ravenglass did his best to be, as my father might himself have realised had he witnessed on that breeching-day the depth of his son's passion for the wearing of skirts.

the second chapter

Next, comes the sea. Even before the boom of my father's voice, the roll of the waves might have been the first sound I ever heard. For the narrow house on Tangier Row where I was born was so close to the shore that maggoty turnips and cabbages could be dispatched from a back window directly into the surf.

Thankfully, before I was sensible of this low birth-place, my father moved us to Queen Street and the new abode built to his own specification upon a parcel of land purchased from Sir James Lowther. This solid, double-width residence, with cellar, stable-yard, strong-room and counting-house, was set three streets back from the sea. But even in a stiff westerly with the windows tight shut we could still hear the harbour. There was never any true respite from the crack of sailcloth, the creaking of hulls and the disquieting growls of the shipmen.

As a child, I would cover my ears and imagine that our town with its tidily frontaged houses and straight modern streets was reclining landlocked in some distant mid-shire with fields on all sides. But of course, our new town would not have existed without the presence of the sea. And close by Whitehaven's civilized heart, the harbour was its rumbling, pulsing, shit-slopping belly.

My father would have had it no other way. From an early age, the world of ships and the sea had gripped his masculine fancy. At fourteen year old he took the bounty offered by Queen Anne and joined the *Breda*, a full-rigged, seventy gun ship-of-the-line. I fear that this was the proudest moment of his life.

Ravenglass

My father owed everything he had to the sea, or rather to Admiral Sir George Byng whose audacity in capturing Spanish vessels during the Battle of Cape Pessaro benefited every Briton serving upon the *Breda*. Prize money from that day was distributed in lowering amounts down to the littlest cabin boy. But my father had by then bettered himself to become the armourer's mate and after the battle he was presented with a prize of fifty seven pounds which enriched him beyond the imaginings of any previous Ravenglass in history.

He might have stayed with the *Breda* and enjoyed more good fortune and manly excitement had he not, one morning of his shore leave, been walking past the Meeting House on Scotch Street and there spied my mother. His passion for her was powerful enough to break my mother from her kin and himself from the service of the King. And thereafter my father diverted his considerable shrewdness and energy towards the investment of his prize-money in the sea-vessels and burgeoning industries of our town.

By the time of my breeching-day, which was ten year or so since he had left the *Breda*, my father was one of Whitehaven's rising merchants. His interests extended from the sugar-house to a white-smith's yard beside the harbour. His foremost income, however, came from shipping. He had become the leading share-holder and ship's husband of the *Resolve*, a newly-fitted slaver, and he was soon to own the coal brig *Swallow* outright.

There must have been a time when I didn't despise my father but I cannot remember it. I suppose as a babbling infant I wouldn't have noticed him picking at his ears or eating without a fork. But once I had reached sensibility about my own manners I couldn't ignore my father's low habits. It never occurred to me that he had been brought up in immeasurably harsher circumstances than my own and that the pleasantries I enjoyed in our spacious, comfortable house were entirely the product of my father's sea service and canny investments. For most of my childhood, I had little interest in these investments and certainly no moral qualms about them. His spitting into the fire and whistling in the street were enough to kindle my contempt.

If my father noticed my childish disrespect he never chastised me for it. Though he was a big man with black eyes beneath black eyebrows and quick to anger, his blows were rare. The beatings that came my way were more usually delivered by his sister, my Aunt Ravenglass. I once asked her why she had no husband and got a clip to my forehead as a reply. She was too old to marry, I assumed. In fact, she did not pass thirty until I was sent to serve upon the *Swallow*, and she was, I realise now, a goodly looking woman.

Once I was civilized enough to wear breeches, I was allowed into the ware-house, a counting-house and strong-room, which adjoined our Queen Street house. My father no doubt intended this to be an education in commerce but I stayed out of his way, or at least out of earshot from his common utterances and throat clearings. So the hours that I spent arranging goose-quills into fans or constructing nutshell shoes for the cat provided very little instruction in the ways of trade.

Other boys of my station, by the time they got to six or seven year old, would be at a school of one sort or another. But I continued to while away the hours doing very little. Perhaps looking back, my father was ashamed of our family's situation and did not wish me to be exposed to the gossip of the town at a young age. Or perhaps, given the uncommon sort of child that I was, he was ashamed of me.

But I did not mind my daily sojourns in the ware-house. New diversions constantly arrived, especially if my father was amassing cargo for a Guinea voyage. From the unheated strong-room below the counting-house, I would savour the odours of Cheshire cheese, gunpowder and gin. Sometimes, my father would let me handle the muskets and pistols and count the iron trinkets that began to load the shelves as each departure of the *Resolve* grew closer.

Although I remember no teacherly instruction, I managed during this time in the counting-house to learn my letters and, more inevitably, how to count. The rest of my education was entirely neglected. My father never doubted that his son would one day share his own passion for the glorious possibilities of an empty ocean and a ship in full sail.

My father sometimes bade me accompany him as he paced about the bulwarks and tongues of the harbour pointing at the vessels.

'See,' he would say, 'the topman is clapping a sheepshank to the mizzen,' or 'Mark you, Christopher, what tonnage of ballast is needed to steady yon sloop?'

I grew to regard these attempts at maritime education with dread.

Following my father along the piers, I would wrinkle my nose at the odours of excrement, tar and coal-dust, and stop my ears against the roaring hulls that strained at their ropes like bulls at a fair. Worse still were the sailors. Upon an inland street, the seafarer, with his short coat and gee-gaws is an object of curiosity or even ridicule but when clustered together at a harbour or inside their own particular vessel, seamen become strange and awful to behold. On my harbour visits, I tried neither to hear their mysterious expletives nor look at their gurning, winking faces.

Once, when I was around seven year old, I remember standing with my father on the Merchants' Tongue beside the *Swallow*. This vessel was an elderly coal-brig with a tar-slopped hull and patched sails, but being in his sole ownership my father regarded her with the pride of an admiral for his just-launched flagship.

My father shouts up. 'Captain Power!'

The master gives us a nod and a sour look as we wait for a gap between the black-grimed porters who are filling the *Swallow*, sack by sack, with Whitehaven coal. My father urges me up the plank before him but stepping on to the deck, I am sideswiped by the unaccustomed lurch of the vessel and something slick underfoot. I fall, almost instantly, on to my behind.

My father claps a hand on my shoulder and yanks me up while nearby two boys throw back their heads and laugh. They are not much bigger than me but they wear the knotted neckerchiefs and ruddy complexions of seamen. As we pass these boys, my father slaps each of them soundly on the head but they seem not to notice. My own complexion, I know, has turned carnation.

Before he descends to the master's cabin my father directs me to wait by a capstan on the deck. 'Watch, and learn the mariners' business,' he says. 'And grow yourself some sea legs.'

'But Father…'

His frown allows no argument. So I try to stand firm on deck as my eyes go upward to the rigging where boys scuttle across the ropes like spiders on a web. The bosun shouts mysterious commands through a screech of gulls and at the stern, a line of seamen hauling cable sing The Sailor's Complaint with surprising power and sweetness.

Ropes slither across the deck like serpents. On the boards beside me are a pair of bare feet attached to naked legs that disappear into the loose white folds of a sailor's petticoat breeches. I struggle to raise my eyes from this strangely feminine garment that reminds me of my much-missed baby-skirts.

Wearing it is a thin-faced young sailor who sits upon an upturned barrel and bends over the work on his knee. A skinny pigtail drapes almost girlish across his shoulder as his needle flies in and out of a red waistcoat, but the silken thread indicates that this is decorative work rather than repair.

I edge closer to see his embroidery and he looks up, a smile widening around his grey teeth. His breeches hitch back to reveal a hairy thigh as he lifts the waistcoat to show me what he has sewn. I blink down at a plump green-tailed mermaid with bare fly-stitch bosoms each topped by a brown French knot for a nipple.

My mouth falls open. I have never in my life seen a female

breast. But the main cause of my surprise is that a man has produced such delicate embroidery. For some moments, my mouth fails to close and the sailor's lips, mirroring and mocking my own, turn into an open O. Still I stand, gormless and staring.

Then the sailor lifts a forefinger towards his mouth, licks it and runs it around his lips. I cannot pull my eyes away. Softly, teasingly, he pushes the tip of the finger into his orifice. In it goes, a little further, then out again, and then firmly in, right to the hilt. The sailor's face flushes and his eyes roll back in apparent ecstasy.

I know that he is jeering at me, though for what reason I cannot say. Yet I can't take my gaze from his face. That finger, in and out, and in again. That look of pleasure! And inside me, at that moment, something stirs. My breeches seem to tighten and I feel a surge of joy laced with horror. It is a feeling that I wish fervently would continue, yet just as strongly I yearn for it to end.

Laughing, the sailor shakes his head and roars some words, which I cannot, thankfully, make out. Hastily, I button my coat which is still too large for me, down through the skirt.

My father, when he returns, glances at the leering sailor and then at me. His black eyes narrow and he opens his mouth as it to exclaim, but then closes it again. I prayed that, in the hubbub of the decks, no-one but the sailor had noticed my shame, but I had took my first taste of the fruit, so dangerous yet delicious, that has delighted me ever since.

the third chapter

Well before that lewd episode upon the *Swallow*, my fingers were already aflame for needle-working which not only indulged my swelling love of fashion but also afforded me the best opportunity to admire my sister. For Fliss, in my eyes, was a goddess.

As a small be-skirted boy, my chief delight had been to stroke her pale hair and kiss the white skin of her forearms. Once in breeches, I tried to restrain such pawing but still I followed her about like a spaniel pup, asking her to play with me or to let me rest my head on her knee. She also regarded me as a pet, to be slapped and ignored or coddled and stroked according to her mood.

Needle-working restored me to the feminine orbit of our house and whenever my father departed for the coffee house or the tavern, or occasionally for Lancaster or Liverpool, I would join the world of women beyond the ware-house door.

I don't think I was ever so content in my early life as those winter evenings in the upstairs parlour with my aunt and sister and Poll circled about the tea-table, all of us leaning in toward the glass bowl of water that magnified light from the candlesticks as we chattered and stitched. And my eyes, when lifted from the needle, always went to Fliss.

For I yearned to make myself like my sister in every way. In private, I mimicked her movements and way of speaking. More than once I took from her satinwood box one of the silk ribbands she used to hide the scar on her throat and, whispering to myself in a voice that I thought made me sound like Fliss, put this ribband about my own neck.

I remember once asking Fliss, in my childish prattle, how she had come by her scar.

'You are so tiresome,' she replies.

'Did you fall over?' I persist.

She is quiet for a moment pursing her lips. 'It came from a… a lapse.' Her eyebrows wrinkle to a delicate frown. 'Now shush.'

I had no sense of what 'a lapse' might be but assumed it was a type of trip or tumble. Poll told me when I asked her that it meant *blunder*, so I assumed I was right.

My occasional questions to Fliss about our mother received even brusquer replies although my curiosity was essentially frivolous. To me who had never known one, a mother seemed a mythical creature like a centaur or a mermaid, a character useful in a story but redundant in real life. For I was perfectly supplied with the benefits of a mother from the three females in our house; Aunt Ravenglass disciplined me, Poll loved me and saw to my bodily wants, and Fliss was the object of my devotion. Any mention of my actual mother was as rare as a black sun.

When I was nine or ten year old, on a wet Saturday afternoon (of which there seemed to be many more in Whitehaven than any other place I have lived), my heart skipped when Fliss invited me into her chamber for some 'trying on.' This would allow me to wear any of my sister's clothes as long as I engaged with the elaborate play-lets she liked to invent. Whatever the script of these tableaux, I was always the girl.

Sometimes, wearing only a lace-edged shift, I would be Hepzibah, a maiden stole from her family by gypsies. Or, in a flowered bed-gown with a silk handkerchief over my head, I would become Tanitha, a harem-slave who tended the concubines before their nightly visits from an imaginary Sultan. But mostly, swamped in Fliss's Sunday frock of green shalloon, I would be the imagined person that my sister and I both called Stella.

We thought of Stella as our darling cousin from Ireland who had come on an extended visit. She was older than Fliss and more worldly, Dublin having such superior society to our own isolated nook of the British Isles. And Stella knew a great deal about the opposite sex. Fliss would quiz her about them as we stood together at an attic window watching young men stride along Queen Street.

'He is a fine fellow,' Fliss might say, pointing out some swarthy type in buckskin breeches and tall boots.

'Oh, no,' I'd say in Stella's voice that was deeper than my boyish fluting and full of womanly confidence. 'Him with the laced cuffs is far more the gentleman.'

Whenever I spoke in my 'Stella' voice, my sister paid me more heed and pride glowed within me. Perhaps this accounts for the persistence my urge to wear skirts. I would have told myself that I preferred feminine apparel simply because it was more fetching but this was not entirely so. I remember giggling at the window with Fliss and seeing the ghosts of our faces in the glass. With my light hair scraped back beneath a lace cap, we were hard to tell apart. *We might be sisters*, Fliss said and at that moment I wished more than anything that we were.

On this particular wet Saturday, my father must have been away for Fliss put on a pair of his breeches and then smeared coal-dust from the scuttle over her chin and top lip.

'Will you not have me, darling Stella?' she says in a voice gruff with male passion.

Sitting on a tapestried stool in the green robe, I half-turn my face away and flutter my eyelids. 'No, I cannot countenance it, dearest... .' For a second, my voice jumps from Stella's back to my own. 'What is your name again?' I whisper.

Fliss rolls her eyes. 'Horatio,' she hisses.

'...dearest Horatio,' Stella says.

Then, as Horatio, Fliss strides forward and grasps my bare forearm, raising me up to stand before her. 'I am mad with desire for you.'

Stella flutters her lids. 'But I cannot love you whilst you are a soldier.'

We stand frozen, eyes locked.

'What's next?' I murmur.

Fliss sighs. 'I told you what to say.' She gathers herself and looks to the distance as if remembering, 'You must desist from this hateful trade.'

I nod and Stella returns. 'You must desist from this hateful trade.'

'No,' Fliss says in her own voice, 'say it with passion and fury as if the thought is sending you mad.'

I was not entirely convinced about this scene that Fliss had conceived for Stella and her lover. To me it seemed far-fetched. But I knew better than to argue.

'You must desist from this hateful trade!'

Fliss nods with satisfaction at my pretended tears. 'Then I shall leave the army...' she says, as Horatio. 'What I do matters not, as long as we are together.' Fliss pulls the fan from my face. 'Darling Stella, we are meant to be as one. Let me show you the strength of my passion.' She begins to plant small frantic kisses over my forehead and cheeks but I pull away for fear of becoming covered in coal-dust.

'Nay, my love.' I say, tussling myself from her embrace. 'I could not countenance the danger. There is nothing for it. We must part.'

With an ankle-flick of my gown, I turn and go to the window. Raindrops drizzle the panes.

'Then I shall learn an honest trade,' Horatio's voice booms as Fliss follows me. 'We should be poor, but happy.'

'No, no, that would not do,' Stella replies with a titter. 'You will not love me for long if I am wearing rags.'

'Oh yes, I should!' Fliss takes hold of me from behind pulling her to me.

I wriggle free, keeping her dirty face well away from mine. 'You say that now, but how could you love someone dressed plain and ugly, like… like,' I pull a disgusted face and look down through spattered raindrops to the street where a Quaker woman and her child are passing, '…like one of yon dissenters?'

Here, I cannot suppress a titter at the Quaker woman's dull and formless garb. As if she hears me, her white moon-face turns to stare at us from beneath her grey cloak. The stare goes on for several moments though she does not slow her pace.

'You should not laugh at them.' Fliss has turned away, her Horatio voice forgotten.

'Why not?' I remain stubbornly Stella. 'Those Quaking folk should not go around looking so hideous if they don't want people to stare and laugh.'

'You should not speak of them nor have anything to do with them.' Fliss's voice is quiet but furious.

'You are too serious my pet, they are nobodies…' I put up a hand to stroke Fliss's hair but she bats it away.

'Idiot!' Her face is red now and her brows furrowed. 'Do you not know? They are Salkelds.'

For a second I cannot speak. The name, so rarely uttered, poleaxes me.

'Our mother's folk?' I blink, all pretence of Stella abandoned, and look outside but the formless females have gone. 'I didn't know she was a Quaker.'

'You don't know anything about her.'

'Because you won't tell me.'

Fliss says nothing but sinks down on to the stool. Beneath the coal-dust beard her face is white as death.

I am afflicted by a sudden stab of jealousy. Why should Fliss know so much about our mother but keep it all from me just because of her five extra years? I have an urge to slap my sister out of her silence but when she looks up the emptiness in her eyes tells me that nothing I could say or do would make her speak of this further. The special silence that followed any mention of our mother, Verity Salkeld, had descended across the attic room like a pall across a coffin.

the fourth chapter

My urge to imitate my sister in speech, manner and dress did not abate as I grew older but rather became more covert and tinged with envy. This feeling was never sharper than during the Michaelmas of the year that Fliss was fifteen year old and due to make her first entrance at the Assembly Rooms, for it was then that she was allowed a mantua-gown.

I was gobbled up by desire at the thought of that new gown. How I yearned to feel its silky slither along my own arms and to weight my hips with the heavy swish of a petticoat boned by hoops. And when it came to walking within a pannier-cage or tolerating the restriction of tight stays, I was the more accomplished follower of female fashion.

It seemed to me particularly unfair that so much expense and trouble was being expended upon Fliss' gown, when the best I could hope for that Christmas might be a new linsey-woolsy coat in some dull colour. It was unjust in general, I thought, that the shelves of Mrs Cleasby the mantua-maker were groaning under a vivid array of cloths that had started their journey to Whitehaven in a Carolina cotton field or a cocoonery of Italian silkworms, whilst Mr Borrodale, the tailor, rarely traded in anything that had not begun its life on the back of a Westmorland sheep.

However, I realised that if I suppressed my resentment, I could at least join in with the creation of the wondrous garment. Fliss was eager for my involvement.

'You must help me, Kit,' she beseeched, 'for I cannot trust our aunt or Poll. They look only for modesty and economy whereas you will advise me about the current modes.'

Already, my gifts were becoming apparent.

'Gladly,' I replied, 'as long as, when it's ready, you'll let me try it on.'

She answered with a coy smile and the blowing of a kiss from her palm.

And thus encouraged, I helped Fliss choose from the snippets of stuff sent by Mrs Cleasby, always using my Stella voice to flatter and cajole her and making sure her taste was moulded to mine.

Despite the cost, we together persuaded Aunt Ravenglass that the gown should be a sack-back with a not inconsiderable train, all in sky-blue satinett. I was allowed to accompany the women for its final fitting on a foggy December fore-noon at Mrs Cleasby's shop.

Aunt Ravenglass leads the way along King Street with a basket on her arm. Behind her, Fliss in her fur-lined cloak links arms with Poll while I weave betwixt them chattering with excitement. Despite the dank weather, the morning is lively with tradesmen going in and out of the taverns and hawkers calling their wares. A ballad-seller booms out the contents of her newest sheet. It is the story of a fellow hung at Durham for the murder of a girl he got in the family way and then pushed off a cliff into the sea. The tune is gaily sung. Fliss stops to listen.

But I dash on, as I always do, to admire the display at the peruke-shop. Each wig in the window, whether curled long in traditional style or short and tied youthfully back, is mounted upon a wooden head. Mr Pratt, the peruke-maker enjoys painting and repainting these heads with a myriad of expressions; jolly, winking, blushing, asleep. Their novelty makes me laugh out loud and as I stand to look, the scent of lavender seeping from the shop briefly masks the yeasty broth of the street.

Today my eye is drawn to a new wig. The hair is powdered dazzling white and tied back into a black silk bag. The wooden head is white too, apart from the bow of rosy lips and black arching eyebrows. It could be male or female or both. And upon the cheek just below the corner of the eye, is a black beauty patch in the shape of a perfect crescent moon. I have read that a patch thus placed signifies the wearer's passionate nature. But in Whitehaven powdering and patches are rarely seen beyond Mr Pratt's window.

'Fliss! Look!'

I turn to her, pointing, but the Ravenglass party has walked on ahead.

Darting across the cobbles, I almost collide with a hat-box seller, and as I grab my sister's arm and pull her back towards the peruke-display, triangular boxes swing about on strings hung from the pole across his shoulder.

'Oi!' The hat-box man shouts.

Fliss's hood falls away from her face as she turns to look, and the man's protests wilt as his eyes follow her.

At the window, I point out the whitened head. 'See!'

'What of it?'

My aunt and Poll are out of earshot so I can speak as Stella. 'Face powder would so compliment the blue of your Assembly gown.'

'But that's the face of a man.' Fliss grimaces. 'And a French one at that.'

'But why not wear a beauty patch, dearest? They are easy to make and apply.'

Fliss tuts and walks off.

I run after her, dodging a pie-lass until we are all halted by a sudden crashing, as loud as ballast tipped into a ship's hold. Up ahead, a wheel-barrow has overturned and spilled its heap of coal on the cobbles. Beside it, a man and a woman raise angry voices. A crowd is gathering.

I catch up with Fliss and we hurry to see the commotion,

but coming nearer we both slow and then stop. For at the heart of the bad-tempered shouting is Aunt Ravenglass.

The aggrieved barrowman makes no effort to clear the obstruction of upturned barrow and coal but instead holds up the wrist of a small girl and shakes it at Aunt Ravenglass like a weapon. Clutched in the girl's fist is a lump of wet coal.

'See,' he says, 'there's the proof. You hoity do-goods are raising up thieves!'

Pushing through the small crowd, I see that the girl is between Fliss's age and my own and she wears a red broadcloth cape badged upon the breast with a black velvet R. My heart pounds a heavy beat, for this R, I know, stands for Ravenglass.

For several years, through the auspices of King George's Church, my father had provided a portion of his profits from the Guinea trade to be spent on winter capes for poor girls. I was unsure why my father had endowed a charity for pauper children for he never tried to instil into his own children any sympathy for the poor. Fliss and I grew up in a house of plenty while all around us children were in rags. And whilst sometimes moved to pity, we were never encouraged to consider how these wretches actually lived. Perhaps my father's endowment was his way of giving thanks for the wealth that had followed his own humble childhood. Or maybe he simply liked to sit in church each Sunday and see the name *Ravenglass* prominent amongst the Charitable Benefactors listed on the wall.

Whatever the reason, there were soon many of these red Ravenglass capes to be seen scuttling around the gutters of our town. Sometimes their wearers, recognising my father or other members of our family, would curtsy their thanks, a gesture which caused me intense awkwardness, partly because I must acknowledge these displeasant girls, and partly because I wished very much to be wearing one of those striking hooded capes myself.

My aunt is in pressing conversation with the red-caped

pauper-girl but my view is obstructed by a passing covered chair. A woman's head leans out of the chair's window and instructs her porters to turn around. When they depart, my aunt is still interrogating.

'Explain yourself, girl.' Her tone makes me wince.

'I did not steal the coal.' The girl's reply is high-pitched but steady.

'Then why are you holding it?'

'I saw it fall from the barrow, and was going to put it back.'

'That's a lie,' the barrowman says. 'She reached in and took it and so caused me to drop my load.'

'Only because you pulled her to the ground,' my aunt retorts sourly.

'Either way, she owes me,' the barrowman goes on, 'for the coal and for my time clearing up the mess.' He still holds tight to the girl's wrist.

'Well,' says my aunt. 'You may have the coal back.' She glares at the girl who then opens her hand and lets the lump drop.

The barrowman does not loosen his grip. 'I should deliver this sneak direct to the House of Correction, and save this town's traders from future thievery.'

'No,' the girl says with a hint of panic.

'So,' my aunt turns to her. 'Will you confess?'

'No, for I always speak plain truth.'

My aunt frowns at her dissenting turn of phrase as much as at her insolence.

'Why, you are a saucy wench. What is your name?'

'Hannah Salkeld.'

My aunt seems to blanch. Hairs shiver down my neck. It is not an unknown surname in our county but far from commonplace. My aunt is still for a moment then she fumbles beneath her cloak and into her pocket. Two silver coins drop from her fingers onto the barrowman's outstretched palm.

'It will take me a deal of time to pick all this up,' he says, his hand still open.

More coins fall before his fingers close over them. Reluctantly, his other hand releases Hannah and my aunt straightaway grabs her cape. She does not let go of the red broadcloth as they move around the corner to stop beside the shuttered window of Mr Snell's Pawn-brokerage. Fliss and I follow but hang back, torn between curiosity and embarrassment.

'Well, Hannah Salkeld,' I hear my aunt say, 'I just spent more than a shilling to preserve your freedom. What do you say to that?'

'I did nothing wrong.'

'As if!' My aunt scoffs, outraged.

'If you don't believe me, why did you give him your money?'

'Only to preserve the good name of my brother's charity.' Aunt Ravenglass gives an angry tug on the cape. 'And so you must pay me back.'

'I have nothing…'

'With your labour.'

Hannah lowers her head.

'Well?' My aunt persists.

'Aye. All right.'

'Is that the best you can say?'

My aunt's scowl makes me quiver for the girl.

'Aye. Thank you, madam,' she says again but quieter. 'What shall I do?'

'We have a mess of windfell apples rotting in our orchard and attracting vermin. You should come up to the house between now and Christmas and clear them onto the bonfire.'

Hannah nods.

'You know our house, in Queen Street?'

'Aye.'

'If you don't come, you'll not keep that cape this winter.'

Hannah shoots a narrowed look at me and Fliss as we stand like a cheap-row audience behind our aunt, but then she dips a brief curtsy. I am suddenly ashamed by my thick knitted stockings and stout shoes. Hannah's feet are black and bare on the wet pavement.

I cover my mouth with my hand before putting it to my sister's ear.

'Is that girl our kin?'

Fliss shrugs and turns away, pulling her squirrel-lined hood close over her throat-ribband. But as Hannah Salkeld turns toward Lowther Street, and goes to raise her cape's red hood, I see for a second the white outline of her face and it gives me an indisputable answer to my question.

the fifth chapter

On the evening of the unfortunate Assembly, I was allowed to help with the ladies' toilet. The blue satinett had turned out perfect for a sack-robe, being light enough to cascade in folds from Fliss's shoulders and heavy enough not to crease. The gown was worn with a saffron-coloured Florentine stomacher which added greatly to the cost, being trimmed with silver ruffles. But I had persuaded Aunt Ravenglass that for economy the ruffles could be detached and used elsewhere, and the stomacher re-trimmed for Fliss's future outings into society, though as things turned out, the only person to again make use of the fancy stomacher was I.

But on the night of the Assembly, Fliss stands in her finery in the upstairs parlour shining like the Light-House across the dark harbour. I hop around her adjusting ribbands and pins. And though I would have given anything to be wearing the wide-hooped mantua-gown instead of my sister, I summon Stella to coo her admiration.

'Oh! But you could not look finer!' Stella claps her hands.

'Are you sure?' Fliss's fingers go, as they always do when she is worried, to her throat.

'Except perhaps…' Stella's head tilts to one side.

'What?'

'Your old pink ribband will not do tonight. You must wear the black.'

'No.' Fliss is determined. 'It is not sufficiently wide.'

'Come, dearest,' Stella says holding out the velvet strip. 'This is so much more elegant.'

'The colour doesn't matter.'

'Oh child,' Stella laughs with disdain, 'what an outlandish notion!'

'Now then, Kit,' Poll says coming into the room. 'The pink is perfectly clean and nice.'

The parlour door had opened without me hearing. I blush into my hair but if Poll heard Stella speak from my mouth, she gives no sign.

'And pink compliments the shoes,' Poll goes on.

Fliss lifts her skirts and we all peer at the new shoes. Dark pink brocade, almost red, is topped with silver-plated buckles. The heels are at least two inches high. I lick my lips with desire.

'But no one will see them unless you dance.' I say in my own peevish voice.

'Then no one will see them.'

'Of course you'll dance, pet.' Poll strokes a wisp of stray hair under Fliss' lace pinner.

'Who will ask me?' Her hand goes to the pink ribband at her neck.

'You will be beating them back,' tuts Poll.

Fliss flings her a look of disdain.

'Especially if you wear this,' I say again holding out the black ribband.

Without a word, Fliss snatches it up. As she turns her back to remove the pink ribband, a gust of rain hurls itself against the shuttered window. Our eyes all go from Fliss's shoes to window and back to shoes.

Fliss's brow wrinkles as she ties the black velvet into a bow. 'Where are my pattens?'

Poll frowns. "Tis only two steps out to the chair.'

My father has wisely ordered three covered chairs to convey the Ravenglass party, in their Christmas finery, the five-minute walk to the new Assembly Rooms in Howgill Street. But Poll's voice is almost swallowed by a blast of the December gale outside the painted shutters.

Then, there is a rustle of silk at the parlour door and the sight that appears turns all our heads. Aunt Ravenglass is wearing her sand-coloured wrapping gown to which she has added new lace cuffs and pearls at her throat. Coils of dark hair drape on to her shoulders. She looks, it must be said, splendid, though her voice is unchanged.

'Where is the boy?'

'What boy?' I say, not having heard of any boy being involved in the evening's preparations except myself.

My aunt goes to the window and unlatches the shutter, though there is nothing beyond the black glass but the lash of rain.

'Fliss's attendant,' she says, as if this explains the matter. 'He should be here by now.'

'Her attendant?' I say, perplexed. 'What for?'

'For holding my train as I make my entrance into the Assembly Rooms,' says Fliss, not the least ashamed that she has withheld this outrageous information from me until now.

'Why can't I do it?' I plead. 'Then I could accompany you.'

'Because,' says my aunt as there is a distant opening of doors and footsteps on the stairs, 'you are the wrong hue.'

And with this, Aunt Ravenglass steps back and we all turn to stare at the boy-attendant loitering at the threshold. He is an inch or two shorter than me although older, I imagine. His coat of green velvet is badly worn and his buckled shoes so large they are clearly not his. Under his arm, he holds a pink silk turban with extravagant tassels. I have never before seen an African boy this close.

'Make haste, lad,' says my aunt to him, 'come in and let us show you how to hold the gown.'

He says nothing but comes forward, his eyes wary.

'Here, come round.' My aunt indicates the blue satinett train that flows down Fliss's back to pool on the floor behind her heels. 'You should pick up the end with both hands, but not carry it too high. We may see the shoes beneath the gown but nothing above them. Do you understand?'

The boy blinks which she takes for an assent.

'Right then. Show us.'

The boy doesn't move.

'Don't dither, lad. Put on your hat and pick up the gown.'

The boy raises the pink tasselled turban to his head. Then he stoops to take hold of the train.

'That's it,' says Aunt Ravenglass. 'Now, Fliss, walk round and around the tea table until you both get the hang of it.'

With a glance over her shoulder, Fliss throws the boy a small smile. He blinks back at her then lowers his eyes, and they both set off at a stately pace.

The boy-attendant's task is not as easy as might be imagined by a person who has never tried it. He must shadow Fliss's pace at all times and concentrate on the correct leverage of the satinett from the floor; neither too high nor too low. The boy is engrossed in this duty, his steps careful and his eyes, apart from an occasional glance at Fliss, are fixed on the train.

But my gaze is consumed by him. He walks with effortless grace, his dark skin a gorgeous contrast against the luminous pink of the turban. And the candle-lit vision before me, of Fliss fair and lovely in a shining blue gown with the darkly beautiful boy, stops my breath. I had never in my life seen a sight so glorious.

'Lower,' commands my aunt. 'Keep the train from the floor but let it always cover the lady's ankles. Yes. That's right.' She nods to Poll. 'Will you get the cloaks?'

And then, in a crush of hoops and fur and satinett we are in the passage by the front door. My father descends, already a little unsteady but resplendent in heavy cuffed velvet and best wig. He gives Fliss a queer look then takes her hand and kisses it. I believe there are tears in his eyes. Fliss looks away, tight-lipped.

Poll opens the door and with a blast of wet air, the party is gone down the front steps to the waiting line of covered chairs. Just before Poll pulls me from the threshold, a link-boy's torch illuminates the boy-attendant's turban into a small pink moon. How I wish that I could, just for one night, change places with him!

'There now,' Poll closes the door and wipes her hands on her apron. 'At least we don't have to go outside into that!' She smiles at me and pats my cheek. 'Come, I'll warm us some posset.'

I follow her to the indoor kitchen where she pokes the fire and lifts the saucepan from the trivet, pouring the warm winey milk into a tankard. I take a swig and collapse onto the stool by the fire. It is all I can do not to blub.

'Don't fret,' Poll ruffles my hair. 'There'll be Christmas revelries for you too. The mummers are coming soon.'

I try to smile but she is making me feel worse. Watching ugly youths cavorting in their mothers' hats is no substitute at all for an outing to the Assembly Rooms in hooped satinett or a tasselled turban.

Poll sits in the fireside chair.

'Who was that boy?' I ask her.

'He belongs to Captain Littlewood of the *Resolve*. His cabin boy, I believe. The captain offered him to us for tonight to increase the grandeur of our party. They made a fine sight, him and Fliss, did they not?'

I hide my wobbling chin behind the tankard. Jealous tears threaten to flow.

'I wish I was he.'

'Oh tush, Kit! No-one in their right mind should envy his state.'

'Why not?'

'I daresay he was plucked bawling from his mother's breast and then thrust into a life of servitude far from home.' Poll's eyes shine with tears.

'Father says that the slave's life is no different from that of a bonded servant or a 'prentice serving their time.'

Poll gives a small shrug and I see from her face that she does not agree, although she would never say anything against my father.

'Will the boy sail with the *Resolve* to Africa?' I ask, trying in vain to quell my envy of an enslaved child.

'Aye. I expect.'

'So he may there find his mother again.'

Poll pats my leg. 'That I doubt, my pet.' She wipes her eye. 'But they shall meet in heaven.'

The cat jumps upon my lap and purrs as I stroke her grey fur. She has forgiven me the earlier torments I visited on her with a toasting fork from the pile of metal-work in the strong-room. Along with the bolts of broadcloth, tallow candles and closed kegs, all this cargo will go into the hold of the *Resolve*. Then, with the first fair spell in January, the brig will leave Whitehaven for Dublin, load more provisions and, with luck, make landfall on the Guinea Coast before the tornadoes of April.

I stare into the fire wondering how many weeks the brig will spend buffeting grey waves before the water around her turns to blue.

'Should you like to see Africa, Poll?'

'That I would not!' She laughs and bats her dishcloth across my knees.

'Why not?'

'It's full of dangers.'

'Crocodiles?'

'Aye.'

'And cannibals?'

'I daresay.' She laughs again but then strokes her pinny with a melancholy look.

We both stare into the fire and I take a sip of posset as Poll starts to sing.

"I used my whole art, till I stole her heart,
And swore to befriend her and still take her part,
Thus being beguiled, she soon proved la la,

Which made her weep sorely but I only smiled."

It is the new ballad about the Durham hanging. Poll *la-la*'s the parts which she deems unfit for my childish ears, but I know from hearing Fliss sing, that the line ends '*with child.*' Poll's features, as she sings, are hollowed by shadows from the dying fire.

"We then took our way to the brink of the bay,
And there like a fury to her I did say
You la la la la, that covets my store,
I'm fully resolv'd you should plague me no more…"

'What's an impudent whore?' I ask, having heard the words in Fliss's version. Although I am pretty sure I can guess.

Poll tuts and gives my knees a playful tap. Still singing, she rises to pour the last of the posset into my tankard. Although I know what is to come, the dreadful story of the young merchant and his mistress enthrals me, especially the part where, whip in hand, he drives her to the sea shore and there she plummets from the cliff edge to lie sprawled in blood on the strand below.

Poll is so engrossed in the awful tale that when she comes to the worst part (or to my mind the best) she forgets her *la-la*'s.

"And to blacken my crime, the babe that was mine,
I could perceive stirring within her some time."

Here, she leans toward the fire and gives the iron of the poker a superstitious stroke.

The soothing fumes of posset rise into my jaw-cracking yawn, and even before Poll gets to the ballad's hanging scene, I slump to a doze. Perhaps Poll dozes too for some while after both of us are roused by a violent commotion in the passage.

Poll's hand goes to the poker as she sits bolt upright then rises from the chair. Even at my young age I wonder if I should take the weapon from her and play the man. But then we both hear voices that are undoubtedly female and, dropping the poker, Poll picks up the lighted candlestick instead. The orange flame drags past me and I follow in its wake towards the front door.

When I picture the scene that greeted us there, I still feel a sink of despair in my belly. Illuminated by the candle's glow, Fliss's face is white-pale and streaked by tears. Behind her, Aunt Ravenglass' countenance is hardly less disturbed. Her sand-coloured gown is drenched and spattered below her short cloak. Both of their hair arrangements are dishevelled and Fliss seems to have lost her lace pinner. There is no sign at all of her boy-attendant. The mantua-gown's train is slathered in filth.

Fliss looks down to the brown trail that has followed her in snail-like across the parquetry. A turdy smell laces the confined air and from the colours on the floor, I guess that at least two different helpings of dog-manure must have lain steaming in her path on the unlit pavement. The woven pink shoes are ladled with foul orangey sludge.

'Pooh!' I shout, pointlessly.

This brings forth a wail from Fliss and she lets her cloak fall onto the floor beside the stinking shoes. Dark stains dapple the blue satinett. I see then that her neck-ribband has come off and her scar, throbbing red, is on full show. A rib of cane hoop presses into me as she flies past and we all stand in the passage listening to her stockinged feet patter up the dark staircase.

Poll lifts the light toward Aunt Ravenglass. 'What has happened?'

My aunt purses her lips and shakes her head. 'Something and nothing.'

But her disquiet is as glaring as my sister's.

'Let me take that candle,' she says and grabs the stick from Poll.

I think, although I cannot be sure, that as she pushes past us to follow Fliss up the stairs, I hear my aunt mutter, 'Too much of the wrong one in her.'

Poll and I fumble back to the kitchen.

'Rest you here a while.' Poll lights another candle from the fading fire. 'I'll settle your sister to bed before you come up.'

'What's amiss with her?'

With her back to me at the door, Poll's silhouetted shoulders shrug. I think of the ballad.

'Has Fliss been wooed by a bad'un?'

Poll huffs and shakes her head. 'Don't you pay any heed to those ha'penny tales.'

But even with Poll's omissions, the song's villainous story has infected my thoughts. I can almost see my sister at the cliff edge, about to be pushed over it by a glowering figure with a *la-la* in his hand.

'Is she in danger?' I ask, my voice cracking.

'No, child, of course she's not.'

Poll's voice does not waver but as she whisks the candle's orange flame through the black air, I catch a glimmer of doubt in her eyes.

the sixth chapter

For many days afterwards, Fliss could not bring herself to speak, even to Stella, about what had transpired at the Assembly Rooms. Then on the morning after the bloated indulgences of Christmas, when the house was quiet, Fliss at last bade me come into her chamber.

'May I do some trying on?' I ask, thinking of the mantua-gown.

'Not now, Kit,' says Fliss heavy-lidded but restless as she subsides on to the bed. 'Read my fortune.' She hands me *Dorinda's Gift*.

My sister and I both heartily believe in Dorinda as a real person who informs ladies, through her feminine almanac, of noteworthy events in the forthcoming year, the movements of the heavens, race meetings and royal birthdays. Dorinda also includes receipts for the kitchen and notes on fashionable dress as well as poems, riddles and mathematical equations.

But the new edition of *Dorinda's Gift* includes a novelty which we are yet to work out. Again, I read the preamble aloud.

'Hail! Happy ladies of the British Isle
On whom Fortune's Face does smile,
Whate'er questions you care to supply,
Dorinda's Finger of Fortune will make reply.'

'Yes, yes,' says Fliss, wearily.

I frown at the instructions. *Dorinda's Finger of Fortune; Being an insight into futurity by gifting every answer to many various questions.* But the grid of letters, stars and questions has me flummoxed.

'Tell me again Fliss, what to do.'

Fliss props her head upon her elbow and pulls *Dorinda's Gift* from me. 'Here, see, there are tiny stars arranged in different constellations. You must close your eyes then let your finger fall on one. The constellation that your finger chooses will guide you to the letter on the chart corresponding to the question of your choice.' Her eyes widen. 'And at the intersection of letter and constellation will be your answer.'

'Oh, yes, I remember, let me try!'

'Do not fidget so, Kit! Consider each question before you choose.'

But I am too excited and I select the first I see. '*Shall I obtain my wish?*'

'What is your wish?'

I frown, knowing exactly but too ashamed to speak my deepest desire aloud.

'Can I whisper it to Dorinda?'

Fliss smirks. 'Why so sheepish?'

I shrug one shoulder. 'Maybe it won't come true unless kept secret.'

She gives a dubious laugh. 'Let's see, then. Whisper away.'

Holding the open almanac close against my face, I turn from Fliss and mumble into the pages. 'I wish to have my own mantua-gown.'

Fliss is leaning my way but I don't think she has heard.

'Now close your eyes Kit, and let your finger fall upon the stars.'

Squinting, I let my finger range over the page. It lands on stars in the shape of a cross. Fliss turns the page and finds the same shape on the chart.

'*Your wish will be granted but only at the expense of ANOTHER.*' She blinks up at me. 'Who do you think is '*ANOTHER*'?'

I shrug but cannot help my smugly spreading smile. For I suddenly have no doubt that someone, someday, will provide me with a gown as majestic and extravagant as Fliss's own. How blissful it will feel to wear it, even if I'm seen only by a looking glass.

Fliss starts laughing at the silly grin on my face. I thrust the almanac toward her. 'Stop it, Fliss, and take your turn.'

As she looks down at the page of questions, her face darkens. 'Which is it to be Fliss?'

She points. *Shall I be lucky or unlucky this day?* Eyes closed, her fingertip drops on to a *Y* of stars. Then her finger follows the line on the grid to its intersection. I look over her forearm as she reads the answer; *There is sorrow AND danger before you.*

Fliss says nothing but drops back down to the bed, staring up.

'Don't accept the first answer,' I say, trying to inject her with some cheer. 'Have another turn.'

She frowns, her face pale. 'Can you not read? Dorinda instructs that to try the same question twice in one day is unlucky.'

'But it's just a game.'

Fliss shrugs and closes her eyes. 'Dorinda speaks the truth. I am not a person who attracts good fortune.'

What she means by this, I can't imagine. Nor can I think of any reply. Her words seem to proceed from the same gloom that has encased her since the night of the Assembly. I realise, belatedly, that it is time for Stella to make an appearance.

Sitting upright as if wearing a pair of stays, I untie my neck-cloth and smooth it over the top of my head into an approximation of pinner and lappets.

'There, there, dearest. What ails you?' Stella strokes Fliss's cheek. 'You may tell your cousin.'

Fliss sighs and turns to me with a heartfelt look. 'How I wish I were a boy.'

'A boy? But why?' Stella and I are both aghast.

Fliss looks away. 'Because on a boy, a scar would not matter.'

'Oh?'

'On a boy, such a blemish would be accounted a trophy, a proof of bravery and manliness.'

I have to allow that she is right and it takes me a moment to consider my reply. I lower Stella's voice a notch. 'But your blemish is hidden. No-one knows of it.'

'Oh, but they do.'

'Not many, then.'

'You are wrong.' She closes her eyes.

'Who?'

'All those who were at the Assembly.'

'No, sweetest. You had on your ribband.'

'The black one was too thin and slipped down without my knowing. My brother should not have bade me wear it.'

My stomach twists. 'Maybe nobody paid any heed.'

Fliss laughs, nasty and quick. 'One at least did.'

'Who?'

And then my sister tells me what had transpired at the Assembly. At first, she says, all was gaiety and excitement. The grandly appointed Rooms at Howgill Street were a-glitter with sconces and even, in the principal gallery, a chandelier. A small orchestra played as Fliss and Aunt Ravenglass went about, greeting townsfolk of their acquaintance and being introduced to others they did not know. Whitehaven's best people were gathered in their brocaded finery. Most excitingly, a small party of Lowthers (though not Sir James) was in attendance.

Despite all this, my father had gone straight to the tables in the card room and was not seen again that night. Perhaps his presence would have prevented the misunderstanding which ensued when Mrs Westray, a harbour trustee's wife, introduced a young kinsman of her husband's.

This young Mr Westray seemed most taken by the conversation with Aunt Ravenglass and Fliss that ranged from his interests in maritime underwriting to his desire to explore the mountainous interior of our county. This last, most peculiar suggestion should by itself have made the ladies wary. Fliss said that despite thinking him under-dressed for the occasion in a plain brown suit, she found her breaths quickening at the prospect of taking the hand of a man, even this man, in a dance.

But as the intercourse with Mr Westray grew longer, my Aunt Ravenglass lost her patience and asked him outright if he had any intention to dance.

'Indeed I do,' replied he, all smiles.

'Excellent,' said my aunt. 'My niece is a most accomplished dancer.'

The young man turned then to Fliss and she realised that he had not, until that moment paid her any heed at all. And still, he did not look at her face. Instead, his eyes went to her neck with a look, fleeting but unmistakable, of pure horror.

Recovering himself, Mr Westray returns his eyes to my aunt. 'But you, dearest lady, would you not do me the honour..?'

By this time Fliss had touched her neck and felt the loose velvet ribband languishing far short of the blemish it was meant to cover. She understood then, with a surge of woe, that for all her youth and beauty she was, in the eyes of the male sex, damaged beyond repair. There might never be a suitor who would see beyond the badge of shame across her neck.

At this, I give a start but Stella comes to my rescue. 'Do not dwell upon it, child.' My fingers caress Fliss's arm. 'Tell me instead how you escaped from the ghastly Mr Westray.'

'I simply set off down the stairs and out of the door to come home.'

My eyes widen but Stella's voice remains composed. 'What did your aunt say to that?'

Fliss shrugs. 'She did not catch up with me until I was almost in Irish Street. By then there was no turning back for either of us. The wind and water had already done their worst.'

'Did you give no thought to your shoes, or your gown?'

'No.'

Stella tuts and shakes her head. My outrage is real. I could not imagine ever being so overcome by passion that I would pay no heed at all to those gorgeous pink shoes.

Fliss drags a palm fiercely across her cheek. 'Easy for you

to censure, but what does your sex ever understand of the tribulations endured by mine?' Her face is suddenly scarlet. 'Look, look! See what is happening to me just from thinking on all this. Tears! And I never weep!'

It was true. No matter how hard her tumbles nor how sharp her disappointments, Fliss's eyes always stayed dry. Now though, at the memory of her humiliation, they were brimming.

'Oh, I wish I could strike all of it from my mind!' she wails.

'There, my sweet. Let it not prey upon you.' Stella recovers herself. 'Think instead of the entertainments to come this very night.'

Fliss looks blank.

'Have you forgot, my dear,' Stella coos, 'about the mummers?'

I had recently begun to wonder if mumming should be considered a coarse entertainment suitable only to infants and uncouth types, but later that day I could not prevent my excitement stirring as preparations for this Yule festivity began.

I helped place candles in each pane of every window that overlooked our courtyard and come dusk, lights dotted the dark buildings like grids of stars. By the back-kitchen door, a brazier of hot coals glowed and Aunt Ravenglass, in apron and rabbit-fur hood, oversaw an ales-bench laden with half-full tankards and squares of Christmas parkin baked with ginger and molasses.

Our rear courtyard was enclosed on all sides by the house, ware-house, back-kitchen and stable and at my father's invitation it had become the mummers' main stopping place on Queen Street. Once it was properly dark, our neighbours of the lower sort, shoemakers, stonemasons and butchers, started to come into our yard through the covered carriageway from the street and gathered, laughing and calling out festive greetings.

My father, only too happy to play the host to common folk, stood to one side of the ale table. His coat was left open to display the polished hilt of his cutlass, a weapon which he wore partly as a decorative reminder of his sea service and partly to deter the mumming show from descending into a brawl, which sometimes it did.

Though Fliss had told me that she had no heart for festivity, I hoped that once she heard the fiddle and the drumbeat she would not resist. And as the gay procession comes dancing through the carriageway, I see her slip out of the back door to stand on the step. She is dressed in her silver-buttoned blue riding-coat and tri-cornered hat with a flounced lace stock covering her neck. Her face is a-glow between two flaming torches as she gazes out upon the mummers.

At the heart of their troupe is a sailor with an un-cocked hat festooned with ribbands. In flowing white breeches and short blue coat, he beats time for the fiddler by thumping the ground with a holly-topped broom. His face is daubed coal-black.

Surrounding him, and holding up their skirts to weave a dance around the blackened sailor, is a gaggle of molly-dancers. Their faces are painted white and rouged but there is no mistaking their true sex. Wadding seeps out of bosoms as bodices sag and their movements are so clod-hopping they cannot be other than male. Yet, for all the crudeness of these fake-females' appearance, I yearn to don one of Fliss's petticoats and join them in their japes.

The pretended women proceed around the yard, poking at the crowd and laughing to each other. Then, on the word of the black-faced sailor, the fiddle is stilled and the molly dancers take up a low humming note, *mummm… mummm*. They join hands in a ring then step backwards, widening the circle and forcing the crowd against the walls.

In the dark corner of the yard, I notice a small figure in a hooded red cape come through the archway from our orchard to loiter behind the ale bench. Her eyes seem too large for her face as they follow the merry crew around the yard. My aunt offers her a tankard and a square of parkin but the girl shakes her head and I'm struck with a type of awe that the pride in

Hannah Salkeld's belly is fiercer than the hunger.

Edging towards the ale-table, I grab two squares of parkin and hold them out to Hannah. 'You can take these with you if you like.'

She looks down at the dark, moist cake in my hands and then at my face. Without a word, she takes the parkin and folds her apron around it.

'Take more if you have brothers and sisters.'

She shakes her head. 'Only my mother. But thank you.'

'I'm Kit.'

'I know.'

'I'm your kin, I think.'

She nods. 'My cousin.'

This information astounds into silence. But the mummers' humming has started up again. *Mummmm, mummmm*. The sound deepens and grows more solemn. And then, at the tap of the sailor's stick, the molly-men begin to sing. It is the usual wassail song, but inside the harmonious melody is a voice so pure that I feel sure one of the molly dancers must be a real female.

The circle of dancers around the sailor widens, sweeping me away from Hannah. The fiddler dives into jaunty beats of The Keel Row which sets everyone clapping along. Skirts are lifted high above hairy knees as the molly dancers cavort across the circle, swinging their partners and clutching at home-made breasts. I join in the clapping and laughter that urges them on.

The circle widens. Men who look like men alternate with men who look like women. One molly-man, in a bird-nest wig, makes a play for my father, swaying toward him and beckoning with a lascivious wink. But Henry Ravenglass lunges at him and half-pulls the cutlass from his belt. There is a playful smile on my father's lips, but a sharp look in his dark eye. The bewigged molly dancer retreats.

At the centre of the circle, the sailor is twirling about and about, pointing his stick as he goes widdershins to the rotating dancers. Beside him is the source of the truly female sound. This girl is tall and well-made. Her bed-jacket is leather-belted over her petticoat and a wide-brimmed straw hat tied with a bow beneath her chin. Her face is as comely as her voice but she has a naughty look. And as the wassail song closes, she gives a lusty call, one hand to the side of her mouth for someone to join her in a dance. She loops her thumbs in her wide leather belt and looks brazenly about. And her eye lands, of course, on Fliss who stands on the step above the rest of the crowd, resplendent in her silver-buttoned riding habit.

Climbing on to an upturned barrel, I see the dancer push through the crowd towards Fliss with a hand outstretched. And, after a glance at our father, Fliss takes it. Even in the dimness of the candle-lit courtyard, Fliss's face glows as they make their way inside the ring of men and then, begin to dance. Fliss is a head shorter than her partner but their strides fall easily into step.

The jig becomes faster. Fliss and the straw-hatted girl link elbows and press palms as they twist and skip, the onlookers clapping and shouting their encouragement. Torch flames dip and leap in the churn of air. As the couple whirl, my sister careens to one side but is steadied by her partner's firm hand. The wide straw hat falls backward on its strings and my mouth falls open. For this dancing girl wears no cap beneath her hat, nor is her hair arranged. Instead, her face is framed by short brown locks tied back like a man's. And there is no doubt now that this she is, in fact, a he.

Dismayed, I slump down from the barrel. How was I so fooled by a rough molly dancer? Now that he is unmasked I cannot understand how I ever thought him female. For the brown haired youth is handsome and robust. He has not the slightest shame in his woman's dress and Fliss returns his brazen smile with no hint of surprise. Had she known his sex all along? Was it only I who was blinded by his voice and his womanly guise? I look around for Hannah to ask if she was also tricked by his sweet singing, but she has gone.

The fiddler scrapes his bow across the final, triumphant chord of the reel and Fliss and her partner come to a halt, beaming and breathless, amidst the claps and whoops of the crowd. Fliss makes a deep curtsy and the molly-dancer gives a flourishing bow. As his head rises, I take a long look at this boldly smiling young man. I do not yet know that his name is Daniel Bragg but I already wish that I had never in my life laid eyes upon him.

the seventh chapter

Fliss, I soon discovered, was already acquainted with Daniel Bragg, who shortly afterwards took up residence in my father's counting-house as his apprentice. The lad belonged Penrith way but had kinfolk in the butcher's on Whitehaven Market Place. Their dried meat provisioned to the *Resolve* had acted as payment for his apprenticeship and the butcher assured my father that Daniel, though of farm-stock, was well-schooled and already showing a keen eye for profit.

I could not see any purpose in my father having an apprentice. He seemed until then to have managed his affairs perfectly well with his own penmanship and the brawn of John, our manservant. If there were small errands to be run about the town or checks to be made on the strong-room stock for mould or mice, I myself would be called on.

But a merchant-apprentice was a signal of my father's ventures' growing success. The stable part of his income came from the voyages of the *Swallow* to Dublin and back with coal, but the best, though riskiest, opportunity for profit came from his five-sixteenths share in ownership of the *Resolve*. For this brig, at some time around the year of my birth, had been fitted out with cannons, cauldron stoves and a deal of the assorted ironmongery that made her into a slaver.

By my eleventh year, the *Resolve* had completed three successful voyages to the Guinea coast and thence to Barbados. The profits from these long and risky voyages varied but my father had thus far never made less than a sixty percent increase upon his investment. However, the necessity of sharing *Resolve's* gains with other part-owners meant that she had not entirely bore my father the riches for which he hoped. His expectations were fuelled by stories of Africa merchants in Liverpool and Bristol building marbled mansions out of their investments in Guinea-men, and endowing not only hooded capes for poor children but churches, hospitals and schools.

With Daniel Bragg in it, the counting house seemed suddenly to shrink. He was a well-made youth of seventeen, handsome in his new brown suit and buckled shoes. Once he had brought his small chest of belongings into the counting-house and was given a pallet bed to unroll in the back-kitchen each night, my own usefulness to my father seemed to evaporate.

Soon, Daniel slyly took over the tasks that had given me most satisfaction.

'But I always unpack the bundles from Mr Harrison.' I protest to him on a biting January afternoon a week or two after his arrival.

Daniel pays no heed and unties the bundles that have come in from the Newcastle carrier. My father has told his agent in that city to buy up anything from the rag-men that may serve as cargo for an Atlantic voyage. The contents of these bundles are often smelly and worn but I can happily spend the whole of a winter afternoon spreading petticoats and embroidered shifts over the warehouse floor to examine them and, if there is no chance of my father seeing, to try them on.

Daniel smiles. 'Your father said I'm to do it.' He has not so far been rude to me but his manner grows haughtier by the day. 'There is no time to waste, you know. The *Resolve* will set sail as soon as the weather looks fair.'

'I know that.' I say, irked by his condescension.

Vexation grows as I climb the ladder up into the counting-house and march up to my father at his table. One of his hands is on his bare scalp, fingernails itching, as the other writes with a goose quill.

'Father?'

'Mmmm.'

'Am I not to sort the bundles from Mr Harrison?'

He doesn't look up. 'Daniel will see to it.'

'But I want to.'

His goose-nib moves away from what seems to be a very long sum. Laying down the inky end of the feather, he opens his enamelled snuff box. The fingernail that had been scratching his scalp takes up a wedge of the clay-brown dust inside. I try not to grimace in disgust. My father gives me one of his dark-eyed stares.

'How old shall you be this year, Christopher?'

'Eleven in May, sir.'

'And have you ever given any thought to your schooling?'

I shake my head. But that single word has weight enough to squeeze the breath from my chest. My father puts fingernail to nostril and inhales. Then he wipes his eye and flicks his fingers. A puff of mushroomy dust floats in the air.

'Well then, 'tis high time for it if you wish to become a midshipman.'

My pursed look doesn't dampen my father's enthusiasm.

'So,' he continues with a satisfied sniff, 'I have enrolled you in Captain Nathaniel Bravery's Nautical Academy.'

My mouth falls open like a mackerel unhooked. 'What?'

'You'll be with other lads. And 'tis just at the other end of Queen Street. You'll be home each night.' He frowns a little.

'But I like… I like to be here.'

'Fie, lad.' My father sits back in his chair and looks at me as if noticing my appearance for the first time in a while. His black eyes glint. ''Twill do you good. Make you more… robust.'

There is an edge of distaste in his voice. I wonder for the first time if I may be as much of an embarrassment to my father as he is to me.

'Come now, Kit, muscle up. Don't you want to run around

with your fellows?'

I shake my head, perhaps a little too vehemently and my father's brows furrow. Fliss and I had rarely had any playfellow except each other. The middling sort of family who might have supplied us both with company, did not, for some reason, seek out our society, nor we theirs.

'You have become too used to womenfolk.' My father rasps a hand across the stubble on his chin and sighs. 'You should by now be learning your ropes and latitudes, instead of slavvering over fancy clouts from Newcastle.'

Here, my stomach spins like a moth caught in a spider's web as I suddenly realise that he must have seen me trying on petticoats from Mr Harrison's bundles.

'Anyways, 'tis all settled.' My father reaches across the table for his second-best wig and claps it upon his head like a judge passing sentence. 'You'll go up to Bravery's on Monday next and commence your studies.'

I turn away to hide the frustrated tear slipping from my eyelash but I am met with the smirking face of Daniel Bragg coming up through the trap door from the strong-room below.

His smirk was all the wider the following Monday morning when I set off along Queen Street toward the Nautical Academy. The bustling southern part of the town around our house was as familiar to me as my own palm, but I had rarely ventured north of the old church. The churchyard behind it had a melancholy air and beyond that, the houses became sparse. In those days, Queen Street did not rise very far up the hill before it was stopped up by the fence of the rope-walk which formed the northern boundary of our town.

On that January Monday, my mind was a-stew with childish worries. I recall my hand in my coat pocket fidgeting between two boiled eggs, still warm from the kettle, as I wonder how to find the right house, how to introduce myself to my fellow pupils. Mainly though, I hope that this will not be the day when the *Resolve* finally sets sail. She is due to leave at any time and I should be sorely irked to miss her departure.

The final portion of Queen Street is a short jumble of new buildings and half-built parcels between garden-land. Thankfully, unmade roadway is frozen to hard mud ruts as it climbs the steepening bank. I scan the newly built house-fronts for one that looks like a Nautical Academy. None seem likely. Then, unexpectedly, I come to a stone gable-end set back from the street. A heavy feeling I cannot explain chills the pit of my stomach. There is a dankness to this tawny-stoned windowless wall that fills me with dread. Beside the wall is a gateway and looking through it into a yard I see that the building stretches long and low away from the street. High windows are shuttered and barred with iron. There is a smell of damp and night-soil.

In the frosty greyness of the morning no one is about and yet the building seems to give out a murmur of movement. Behind the barred windows people, perhaps many people are stirring. Then I see the sign above the central doorway; *WITHIN AMEND, WITHOUT BEWARE*. The peeling paint is faded but the words send a sudden coldness through my whole body. Surely this place cannot be a school for boys?

Losing courage, I step backward into the street. If this is the Academy, I will run home, swallow all pride and beg my father not to make me enter it. Turning on my heel, I see across the street a sign above a black-edged doorframe in the new terrace of white-painted houses. It is a single word that reads like an exhortation, *BRAVERY*.

A sudden gale of boyish laughter bursts from the half-open door beneath the sign. Quietly, I slip into the passage. It is a tall, narrow house. On each floor, are two rooms to the side of the stair-passage or landing. In the front room on the street floor, the laughter is quieted but there is another worrying sound that pulls me closer. It is a sound that I fear could emanate from a human only in a fit of vomiting or worse. Yet as I listen, there are, amidst this bodily cacophony, words.

'Bend. Over. Boy!' The verbalisation burps out. 'And. I'll. Give. You. Some of. My. Black. Puddin'!'

At this, the room erupts into roaring laughter and provides my cover to enter.

On the bare floor of the dining parlour that smells of new carpentry and wet washing, a small boy stands upon a chair, hands on hips. He smiles down at eight lads of different sizes who shudder and stamp as they clutch at stomachs and mouths while straining, red-faced, to control themselves. The performing boy on the chair throws me a sideways look as again he speaks in a torrent of belches.

'Now. You. Knaves. Look. What. Is. Here.'

The faces, wet and whimpering with mirth, all turn towards me.

'Another. Boy. To. Be. My. Slave.'

This last word ends with the loudest, longest burp I have ever heard before or since. And all in the room, except me, dissolve into howling, spitting laughter.

It is some hours after this arrival before I meet Captain Bravery. Although his classes are advertised to begin at nine, our master takes his time to rise of a morning and rarely appears before eleven. Until then, the boys entertain themselves about the house, sometimes carrying out the chores allotted by the captain who keeps no servants apart from his pupils, but mostly enjoying the various nasty amusements in which any group of boys, if left to themselves, will engage.

Singly, my fellows were not bad sorts. Most of them boarded at the Academy, having been sent there from various parts of Cumberland, Westmorland and Lancs. Their nautical instruction was intended to help them, at some future date, find a mid-ship position on a merchantman or pass their lieutenant's certificate for the sea service of King George. Captain Bravery's custody would keep them until then out of their parents' or guardians' hair. Only myself and Neville

Stewardson, the little burper, were day-boys from the town.

Stewardson had quickly learnt to ingratiate himself with the tight and sometimes vicious pack of boarders by making constant use of his special skill, namely the recitation of witticisms and skits in the school-boys' favourite language of belch. I soon realised that I would need to find a similar talent to amuse. Either that or grow a layer of protective skin about my person and over my ears.

On that first morning the boys treated me with caution, not being quite able to work out whether I had some connection to their schoolmaster but once Captain Bravery appeared it became obvious that he would have the same blind disregard for me as he did for every other boy in his care.

The captain was a man of about my father's age but one whom life had treated, physically at least, more harshly. His left arm was absent below the elbow, and his gait was so comically peculiar that it seemed a lower leg must have been also mislaid. When, later on my first day, I asked Stewardson if this was so, he replied (for once, without burping) that it was not. The odd manner of the captain's walking, in which his right knee appeared to bend in both directions, was probably the result of a shattering and poor repair of his leg aboard some vessel. But the truth of the matter was buried beneath a confusion of instructional narratives. For the captain's various explanations regarding the infliction of his wounds were, I soon learnt, deployed as surprisingly effective educational tools.

Captain Bravery delivers one such nautical lesson on my first day.

'Now boys, what is this?'

The captain stands in the upstairs parlour that passes for a school-room and pulls back his coat sleeve to hold up what remains of his left arm. The scholars, not quite controlling their smirks, stay silent. I do my best to follow their example and stare at a patch of the peeling yellow distemper on the wall behind our master's head.

'Ravenglass!'

Horrified, I look up.

'Well, boy, speak! What is this?'

I swallow. 'A stump, sir?'

The vicious rap of leather on wood lifts my behind from the bench.

'No, boy,' Captain Bravery raises his padded horse-whip, which I already know to be called 'Black Pudding,' and points it at Dixon, the fleshiest boy in the room who seems older than any of us although this may be on account of his size.

'Sir, a lesson, sir!' shouts Dixon, jumping up from his shared bench and then bobbing back down.

'Indeed.' Captain Bravery folds Black Pudding behind his back. 'A lesson in what?' He looks around the room at nine young faces displaying varying degrees of interest. 'Fletcher?'

A narrow-eyed, black-haired boy gives a movement that may, from some angles be interpreted as a shrug. I don't see the tail of the whip but only hear its crack as it licks the top of Fletcher's head. To my amazement and unbound admiration Fletcher smiles. Then, lazily, he stands.

'Sir, the dangers of the armourer's trade, sir.'

'No, Fletcher. It is not. Not today. Today I shall tell you of my time aboard the *Terrible* frigate, when I was aloft on the fore topsail yard and paid the price of an errant midshipman's slippery bowline knot by leaving my left hand in the shallows off Antigua. And so, to prevent any of you lubberly wretches severing the limbs of your fellow sailors, today's lesson will be in the tying of knots.'

With that, he picks up a sheaf of waxed cords and throws them with frightening accuracy and speed at each boy in the room. This must be a regular occurrence, for without the need for further instruction the scholars split into pairs, one holding an end of cord as his partner creates the specie of knot chanted from the front by Captain Bravery.

Being new, I am charged to watch Jonathan Muncaster and George Guy who, I soon learn, are accounted the best sailors-in-waiting amongst us. Their hands fly so fast on the cord-work that I am hard put to see the difference between a bowline and a sheepshank. Then Captain Bravery commands me to try for myself and throws me a length of cordage.

Perhaps my needle-working has paid off for the captain seems surprised by my progress, and I soon discover a satisfaction in the complex symmetry and perfect strength of a well-tied knot. So deep is my absorption in this work that before I know it, Captain Bravery has called an end to morning lessons. Before re-mounting the staircase to his attic chambers, he announces that the afternoon shall be spent in an examination of the construction of rope. At this, the boys give a cheer. Only after I have eaten my boiled eggs and watched my fellows swoop upon every edible scrap in the pantry do I understand why.

Our teacher, as I was to discover, favoured practical education of the sort which allowed him to retire to his chamber each afternoon and rest his mangled limbs. So we were often sent on nautically themed excursions into the town.

As we leave Bravery's for our visit to the rope-walks on that first afternoon, I glance at the fearsome stone edifice across the street and now see, *House of Correction* clearly chiselled beside the gateway. How could I have mistook such a place for a school?

George Guy throws me a sideways look as we climb the hill toward Brackenthwaite.

'What do they call you, then?' he asks.

'Ravenglass,' I reply warily.

'I know that,' says George Guy, somewhat vexed. 'We all heard Natty address you. But what else?'

'Christopher,' I say, noting how they refer to our master. 'But mostly,' I continue, trying to show confidence, 'I get Kit.'

Will Fletcher looks up, interested. 'Kit.' He says, rolling the word around his mouth.

I follow as the boys climb over the fence and into the first of two rope-walks that stretch, dead-straight, along almost the entire northern edge of our town from the saltiness of Tangier Row to the verdant boundary of Lowther parkland. The full length of this fenced off lane is required for the twisting, back and forth and back again, of the finest Whitehaven rope.

'Kit,' says Will again, leading us through crisp winter air toward the cluster of labourers in the landward distance. 'No. 'Tis not enough.'

'For what?' say I, perplexed.

'For us.'

I stare, empty-faced.

'For what we all call each other,' Will continues. He points at the boys around us. 'Dixon there is Bloater. I don't need to tell you why.'

The other boys hearing this, laugh. It seems surprising they continually wring such amusement from Dixon's weight given that he is rarely out of their sights.

'Muncaster,' Guy goes on, nodding at the sandy-haired lad, 'is Monkey, which will make yet more sense when you see him let loose in a ship's rigging. Our belching friend is Stew-breath. And Guy gets Bonny.'

The others laugh even more cruelly at this and I allow myself, despite a whiff of guilt, to join in. For George Guy, with his pock-scarred face and crooked teeth is the very opposite of handsome. He leans over and gives me a punch in the ribs which briefly robs my lungs of air.

'Which is solely on account of my name,' Bonny growls.

I blink and try not to rub my side. 'Your name? Why?'

'Where does the guy go each fifth of November, you dolt?'

'Oh, aye. The bonfire,' I say.

By now, we have caught up with the roping-gang who are walking backwards away from the sea-end of the rope-walk each with an unfeasibly long hempen strand tied about their waist. As they make this reverse progress, they lay their rope-strand over the series of wooden hurdles designed to keep the cordage clean and separate. We Bravery boys lean our backs against the fence to watch what will happen next.

One of these ropers, indeed the one who seems to be in charge, is a sturdy young woman. She is swathed in leather stays and an indigo camlet petticoat so short that we can see the mud spattering her red stockings right up to her knees. I wonder, from my classmates' avid glances, whether her calves may be the true focus of their interest in rope-making.

With a nod from this wench, the three lads in her gang tighten the knots at their waists. Then she raises her arm in the air and gives a throaty shout of *handle turn!* At the far-off extremity of the lane, the four strands of tarred cordage are attached, through a dolly, to a turnstile. Unseen hands rotate the turnstile handle, twisting the cords into one thicker cable. The ropers lean back and take out the slack from each strand, thereby transferring their strength into a new rope which any of us ship-destined boys might one day depend upon for our lives.

As the twisting of the thickening rope pulls the roping-gang gently toward the sea, my fellows soon lose interest in the short petticoat. Muncaster climbs atop the narrow fence between the two rope-walks and somehow balances his way along its narrow summit.

Will Fletcher turns his eyes to me with a half-smile. 'We could call you Kit, but it tells us nothing about you. What can you do?'

I sense that a moment of great jeopardy has arrived and I must tread with care.

'I can run pretty fast,' I say, but Will is not impressed.

'What else?' he demands.

I shrug and look across the smoking rooftops of the town. In the distance, a large brig is setting sail out of the harbour. Already well away from the shoreline, she is passing beyond the Light-House and the Main Pier. The brig's new sails gleam white as more of them unfurl into the breeze.

This, I realise, is the *Resolve*, now fully cargoed for Guinea with forty ells of plain linen cloths and ten of striped, a deal of Halifax broadcloth in bright colours, fourteen hundredweight of wrought iron and copper bars, a parcel of gunflints, fifteen bundles of old clothes, seven dozen felt hats, a heap of rusting blades, ninety kegs of gunpowder and thirty barrels of Lancashire cheese.

My father gave me no word that the *Resolve*'s departure would be today. As ship's husband, he will have been on deck this morning when Captain Littlewood said a prayer for the vessel's speed and I have no doubt that Daniel Bragg will have been there too standing in the place that should have been mine had I not, this day, been sent to school.

With a prickle of regret, I picture the African cabin-boy who was Fliss's attendant also there on deck. Is he glad to be going at last to the land of his birth? Or is his handsome face solemn, fearing the perils of the sea. Does he, perhaps, look around for me?

A blur comes to the edge of my eye and my chin crumples. I cannot look at Will Fletcher nor hope to answer his question without my voice betraying my distress. I shrug with one shoulder and turn away to brush a teardrop from my lashes.

But I am too late.

'Looks like you can weep well enough,' says Will with a glint of victory in his eye, 'as good, in fact, as a girl.'

Boyish laughter explodes around us. Bloater laughs so hard he falls over onto the half-thawed ground.

'Fear not,' says Will Fletcher, his triumphant smile widening. 'We'll call you not Kit, but Kitty. And we shall treat you like a lady.'

the eighth chapter

And so, amongst my schoolmates, I become Kitty. At first their teasing is gentle. They flutter their eyelashes at me sometimes and talk in girly voices when I come into the room. *Oooh, here's Kitty!* they might say, *what has SHE been up to?* I try to laugh along so as not to rile them. I even play up to their caricature of me, speaking sometimes in a too-high voice and shortening my steps. I hope that this comic entertainment will endear me to them in the same way as Stewardson's burps.

In an ordinary school, the boys might have humiliated me further by giving me the womanish tasks about the place, but in Bravery's Nautical Academy, as in a ship at sea, all the domestic work was done by men or boys. And Bravery's scholars displayed their acceptance of the nautical life by showing not the slightest shame at engaging in feminine tasks, even laundry and needlework.

One April afternoon, when spring air through the open school-room window softens occasional noxious wafts from the House of Correction, the boys bring out their sewing bags and settle down to work with surprising eagerness. Being the newest amongst us, I am given a worn bed-sheet to be cut in two and re-sewn ends to middle. This is dull fare and I eye Hartley patching a quilted coverlet with envy.

The boys chatter like women until, for no obvious reason, they fall silent. Glances shift about the room. Then Bloater pipes up.

'Say, lads, who shall we have for our Fell Faery this year?'

'The faery?' says Will Fletcher with perhaps excessive awe.

'You know that every year it must be the most handsome and elegant amongst us. So,' his needle halts in the air, 'why need you even ask?'

His gaze moves around the room before fixing on me.

'What? What are you on about?' I ask.

'Tis a tradition of the Academy for bringing in the May,' says Will, easily. 'Each year, one of us is chose to be the Fell Faery and dressed in greenery then shown off through the streets. The more lavish our faery's appearance, the more pennies we get from passers-by. Natty gives us the whole morning to do it as long as we pass him a cut of the lucre.'

'Oh,' say I, my heart quickening.

For a few seconds, nothing fills the silence except the thudding from across the street. This sound, Bonny has told me, comes from the hard labour done by the convicts, vagrants and dissolutes who are incarcerated at the House of Correction. Every day except Sunday, the prisoners beat piles of raw hemp with mallets before it is sent the conveniently short way up the hill to be twisted into rope. Most of the prisoners, he says dribbling with glee, are women.

'What say you, Kitty? Shall you do it?'

I swear Will bats his lashes at me.

'Yes,' I reply, like a fool. 'Gladly.'

There is a flutter of something between the boys but only when I think back do I realise it was laughter.

'Capital,' says Will, his face straight. 'We shall go up on the fell at dawn on May morning to gather the green for your garland. You bring the apparel. Shall you find some all right?'

'What sort of apparel?'

'That's the thing,' a twitch of a smile plays about Will's lips, 'you won't object, will you, to dressing as a girl?'

Bloater's sudden coughing drowns out my reply but I shake my head vigorously and then nod, for good measure, to make clear my wholehearted assent. And as I go back to sewing the bed-sheet, I am already thinking of which of Fliss's garments might best suit a May faery. So engrossed am I in these thoughts that I hardly notice the boys' sideways glances passing foxily around the schoolroom.

The day before May Morning, I confide to Fliss the plan for the morrow and she looks at me askance.

'Are you sure, Kit?'

'Sure of what?'

'That they do it every year?'

'Why, yes. 'Tis an honour to be chose as the faery.'

'Who was it last year?'

'Why, Stewardson, I think.'

This is a lie. I know nothing of last year's Maying and whether Stewardson was part of it or not.

'And did he wear a petticoat?'

'Aye.'

She lifts an eyebrow but says no more and we look through her presses for garments that might suit a faery. After a pleasant trying on, we agree on her lace-edged shift, a sprigged silesia petticoat and her second best stays. I am getting close in height to Fliss and if all the strings are pulled tight and the edges overlapped her old clothes almost fit me.

Next morning, I wrap them into a bundle along with an old lawn cap and a printed silk handkerchief. Fliss is still in bed as I come from her closet but she sits up with a start.

'Don't go yet, Kit,' she says, her face flushed and furrowed with concern.

'Why not?'

'Ask Dorinda first.'

'Ask her what?'

'Whether this dressing-up is a good idea.'

'Why should it not be?' I say, trying to sound jaunty, but I submit my finger to Dorinda's charts.

Be cautious THIS day, lest TROUBLE befall you is her advice.

'See?' says Fliss.

'But that is true for every day,' I reply.

Fliss sighs and shakes her head. 'Don't let them taunt, will you, Kit?'

I give a dismissive laugh. 'The Fell Faery is held in highest regard.'

Fliss reaches out and strokes my hair in a rare caress. But her fearful expression brings a nervous pinch to my stomach.

Outside, the first of May has dawned with clear cool air and a riot of birdsong. Although it is early, the streets are already clacking with clogs. Two milkmaids pass by me giggling, their straw hats threaded with hedgerow blossoms. Not far off, in the Market Place, a fiddler and a hurdy-gurdy man start up a jig and the milk-lasses run toward the sound, pails swinging on their yokes.

It is not quite seven when I reach the far end of Queen Street, but already Bravery's boarders have returned from their daybreak expedition to Bransty Fell. The parlour is filled with whitethorn, marsh marigolds and green yarrow. When I come in they all stop talking as if a secret is afoot. This should give me cause for caution but I am too eager to be dressed in my faery garb to think of anything else. Only Stew-breath, as I now call Stewardson, is not there.

'Here he is, our Fell Faery,' says Will arms wide and beckoning. 'Have you your girly slops?'

I nod and open up my bundle. Will and the other boys crowd round to caress the glazed petticoat and slightly frayed stays. They blush and stroke the garments hungrily as if they are made not of linen and whalebone but female flesh.

'Very good,' says Will, red spots burning on his cheeks. 'Is he still abed?' He points at the ceiling.

Falling quiet we look upward until, from high above us, comes a juddering snore.

Will smiles. 'Let us begin.'

As they surround me in a circle, heat rises in my throat.

'Shall I undress?' I ask, suddenly uncertain.

'Aye,' says Will. 'Take it all off.'

On the floor beside me I fold my coat, waistcoat, shirt and stock, and then look at the faces circled around. All eyes are intent upon my lower parts.

'I can leave on my breeches…'

'No,' Will says firmly. 'The petticoat will not sit right. And anyway, faeries don't wear breeches.'

He is right, I suppose. I undo the knee buttons and ease the breeches over my stockings and shoes, so that these last garments are now all that I am wearing. For a moment I stand before them, naked above my knees. As all my fellows look with eager fascination at the inevitable place, I cover my little member with my hands, but must reveal it again as I untie my bundle. Foreheads gleam with sweat. Their gazes do not waver until I pull Fliss's lace-adorned shift over my head.

Will's lips part as I tuck my hair beneath a lawn cap. 'What a very comely wench you make, Kitty.' The others burst to a raucous laugh but Will hushes them with a scowl, eyes indicating the ceiling. 'Quiet lads. Let us help this lady gently with her toilet.'

Smirking, they jostle around me, Bloater pulls tight the strings of my stays, Bonny and Monkey hold open the sprigged petticoat for me to step inside while Will festoons my bosom area with posies.

As the boys step away from me, I feel everything change. They have transformed me from an awkward boy into a creature who is dainty yet suffused with power. The glorious swish of sprigged linen around my legs and the tight pull of the stays fill me with grace and strength. And, like magic, the boys' demeanour towards me becomes respectful, perhaps even admiring. They know I am not female yet the splendour of my feminine appearance tricks them into imagining that I am.

'Look, dear Faery,' says Bonny with a little bow, 'look what we have made for you.'

He brings forward a wicker pyramid about a yard high that is fastened down on to a basketry lid. Clearly, in the past week, once Stewardson and I have departed for the day, the boarders have been busy. Monkey is decorating the wicker frame not just with greenery but also with pewter tankards and a brass plate that are all tied to the structure with yellow and pink ribbands.

'What's that?' I ask, impressed.

'That,' says Will proudly, 'is your hat.'

I blink and almost laugh, but this is not a jest.

'Are we right lads?' says Will, lowering his voice conspiratorially. 'Bloater, have you the money-box?'

Bloater fixes a hastily-made wooden box to the end of a broomstick. There is a single word, *PENNIES*, written in charcoal on the side the box. Will takes my elbow and guides me out onto the street for the hat-fitting. There, Bonny and Bloater together lift up my garlanded headdress and place it, metal-ware clanking, upon my head.

I buckle under the weight.

'It's too heavy!' I protest.

'Fear not,' says Will. 'We'll walk alongside and help you.'

After a few paces, with both hands clutching the wicker edge of the structure, I gain some balance and realise, for the first time, the skill and strength of the coster-girls and fishwives who port their heavy loads on their heads as if they were no more than a laced bonnet.

Once we are down the hill and on to Duke Street, the boys start up a chant.

Salute! Salute all ye,
Our garlanded Fell Faery
Spare her, Good Sir, a May Day penny,
And all summer long, your joys shall be many.

The rhyme is so rough, the boys must have devised it themselves but as we begin to meet with townsfolk it has the desired effect. A collier, black from the mine and tumbling drunk, plops a coin into Bloater's box. But then, to my horror, he slurringly demands a faery-kiss in return. Thankfully, the boys crowd protectively around me and hurry us away. I cling to my garland headdress as it sways dangerously from side to side, the collier's rants floating across the Churchyard. *Let's see your whore-pipe, you little molly!* I have no notion of what he means.

As we head toward the strains of fiddle, drum and pipe coming from King Street, the throng thickens and the competition for pennies grows. Boy-sweeps holding chimney brushes sing from behind their masks of new oak leaves. Coins fill the hat held out by their master for even in Whitehaven's bitter clime, May heralds the lean months for chimney-sweeps.

But on this gay morning, revellers are feeling merry enough to toss a good crop of pennies even into the begging-box of a gang of well-fed nautical scholars. I feel that these coins must come as applause for my attire. It matters not to me whether the men who wink or the women who blow me a kiss regard me as male or female. I care only that they should admire my appearance. The few laughs aimed in my direction seem good-natured and the further we go, the more I feel myself basking in the smiles that are turned my way. I wish I might be a Fell Faery every day.

The Market Place is thronged with Mayday revellers. To the lilt of a rasping fiddle, pit-lasses with primrose posies weave a circle dance with sailors in flapping breeches. All about them call and whoop and clap. A salty, beery perfume hangs in the warming air.

Passing along Tickell Lane, I look into Queen Street with a pang of nervousness and pull the handkerchief up from my throat to cover my mouth. But this would serve little purpose if Aunt Ravenglass is already out and about on her morning messages, for she would know me straight off by Fliss's petticoat and stays. Even my father might recognise these garments. Should he see me, could I pass off my faery garb as a form of mumming? But I know he would still be outraged to see me in skirts. Sudden dizziness at the thought of his fury threatens to topple my garland hat but the boys crowd around me to steady it. And with a wash of relief I hear Will declare that it is time to retrace our steps to Bravery's.

On the way back, streets are quieter but more odorous. Early morning revelries have dissolved into wayside puddles of vomit and piss. Wives going about their morning business step around effluent and scowl at drunkards slumped against walls. And as our gay little party turns on to Duke Street, my innards jolt as I meet the gaze of one of these wives.

'Oh!' says Mrs Cleasby, her face surprised and then aghast. 'It is you!'

I dip an unsteady curtsy then stand for a moment, perplexed and fascinated. The mantua-maker seems a walking advertisement for her wares in a garish concoction of pink tabby and black Mechlin lace. I feel I must explain to her the tradition of the Fell Faery but before I can speak, my classmates sweep me away and up the hill to the Academy.

At the door, the boys relieve me of my grandiose hat and Bloater counts up the pennies in his box which come to four shilling and eight pence. And so it is in a state of high excitement that we re-enter Bravery's Nautical Academy and josh into the parlour. The sight we meet there washes away all levity for Captain Bravery is already up, fully dressed and awaiting our return. Beside him is Stewardson, whose mouth falls slack when he sees me. For a few moments, we are all frozen in Captain Bravery's thunderous scowl, but the stillness is smashed, suddenly, with a hard thwack against the bench of Black Pudding.

'What, in God's name, is this?'

Natty addresses the question to the room in general but its subject, I have no doubt, is me. I feel duty bound to reply.

'I have been chose as the Fell Faery this year, sir.'

'The what?'

Despite the cloud of Captain Bravery's rage that has descended upon the room, I sense around me an array of suppressed sniggers.

'The May Day faery, sir. It is my honour to be her this year, sir.'

'Your... honour?'

Even at ten year old I am no dullard and it takes only a second for me to compute that what has thus far been told me of the Fell Faery is a great clanking lie. Ignorance seems my best defence.

'Aye, sir.'

'And what do you boys know of this outrage?' The captain peers blackly around the room.

All is quiet until Bloater's snigger finally escapes.

Again, Black Pudding comes crashing down.

'Silence!'

Stewardson and all the other boys apart from Will Fletcher, look suddenly chastised.

Then, in a movement faster than I imagined his waggling knee would allow, Captain Bravery leaps toward me. With a thump, he claps Black Pudding to my back and uses that fearful object to push me to the far end of the room. There, as I stand in Fliss's clothes, I'm drenched by the horror what might follow. It is all I can do not to collapse on the floor.

'And what, you saucy youths, do you call this?' Natty presses Black Pudding against my corseted belly.

Silence reigns.

'C'mon you dolts. What is it?'

Bloater, the colour drained from his face, pipes up. 'A lesson, sir?'

Natty nods grimly. 'That it is. A lesson about the most heinous crime a naval man may commit, worse even than murder. It is a lesson I learnt when I was serving upon the *Blonde* sloop in the tepid waters off Maroc. Two ratings on that otherwise tidy vessel were found engaging in an act so vile it gave our good captain no choice but to sentence the rogues to his harshest sentence, namely one thousand lashes. By six hundred lashes, both queer plungers were dead, but the sentence required completion. At the end, their corpses were no more than slices of flesh to be sluiced off the deck.'

Bloater's face has drained of colour. Both of Stewardson's hands are across his mouth. I have no notion of the crime that the ratings on the *Blonde* may have committed but the description of their punishment is enough to unleash a piddle of piss down my leg. Mercifully this shame is hidden by the sprigged petticoat.

'And so, to ensure that you boys are never again tempted to practices from the realms of Sodom or Mollydom, you shall today stand and witness the flogging of your fellow.'

'Sir, if you please, sir.' This is Stewardson, a hand raised from his mouth into the air.

'What?' Natty glares.

But Stewardson has thought better of whatever he was about to say and his hand descends. 'Nothing, sir.'

Natty's gaze rotates to my bowed head. 'So, Ravenglass, you shall take ten strokes of my whip and take them like a seaman. Come here to the bench.'

Hardly able to move with terror, I shuffle forward.

'Now, bend over,' Natty booms.

Kneeling, I rest my whale-boned middle against the bench. Cold air rushes in as my sprigged petticoat is lifted from my bare arse. I close my eyes. They are all looking, I know, at my nakedness. Dread quivers through my belly. Vomit threatens to gorge.

Yet the first blow, when it strikes comes almost as a relief. Natty, I realise, is using the most puddingy end of his whip, so there will be bruises but, if I'm lucky, no blood. The next hit is harder. Each fresh pain worsens in the wait for the next. My body curls from the blows, water smarting from my eyes but I don't make a sound.

At the tenth strike, Natty stands up. 'And may that be a lesson to you all.

He points Black Pudding at his charges before folding the whip behind his back.

'Now boy,' he says, with his good hand on my elbow to help me up, 'put on your rightful clothes and swear that never in your life shall you again sport womanly garb.'

Even in my distress, this last is something I cannot bring myself to do. Indeed, I can't wait to defy the unjust cruelty I have just suffered by again wearing skirts. But my mumbling of *yes, sir* and *no, sir* seems to satisfy the captain.

As I pull on my breeches, Stewardson seems to teeter more closely to the edge of tears even than I. The other boys look about awkwardly, and for the rest of the day they remain sheepish. Natty, perhaps abashed at his own outburst, decrees that being May Day we may take the afternoon for leisure. And at the end of the morning, once Natty has clumped up the stairs, I wearily gather my sister's things into a bundle and wipe the hem of the shift across my nose. I am determined not to blub.

As I approach the door, I hear Stewardson in the passage, whispering. I am not sure who he is addressing, but I guess by his tone it is Bloater.

'You should have more pity,' Stewardson hisses, 'because of his mother.'

'Why?' It is Will Fletcher, indignant, 'what did she do?'

'She was found...' I press my head closer to the door but cannot hear his mumbling, '...and is buried in yon House of Correction,' is all I hear him say.

For a moment, I cannot quite make sense of these words. Then, stunned but dry-eyed, I slip into the passage and out of the front door without looking at either lad. Only once outside and faced by the dread bulk of the House of Correction, do my tears overflow.

the ninth chapter

I did not tell Fliss about the horrid outcome of my incarnation as the Fell Faery, nor about the slur that I heard cast by my school-mate on our mother. My mind remained in a stupor of humiliation and confusion. But the lingering ache in my buttocks was enough to persuade me that I must, once and for all, do away, with 'Kitty.' And so, the following Sunday, on our walk to King George's Church, I resolved to change my ways.

My father, in his best wig, leads the walking procession of our household the short distance along Queen Street and Roper Street to the church. Poll, John the manservant and Daniel Bragg follow behind my father with Aunt Ravenglass on his arm, then me and Fliss. All of us are dressed in our spring finery.

I walk in silence, brooding on my school-mates' ill treatment of me and I vow to myself that from now on, I shall move and speak and think in the most male fashion I can muster. As we cross the road to the church and Daniel Bragg comes forward to hand Fliss on to the pavement. I take in his broad, manly outline and decide to use my father's apprentice as my masculine pattern book.

To be like Daniel, I shall lengthen my strides and keep my arms straight as I walk. I shall try not to swish my body nor cross my legs when I sit. If I turn to look at anything, my neck shall stay stiff. My movements must all become more deliberate and more centred around the bundle of appendages at my crotch. I see that it will pay me to keep Daniel's mannerisms always in mind when I am with my fellows. Like him, I shall not giggle nor exaggerate my facial expressions. I shall even do my damnedest to produce a confident squirt of spit.

Inside the stone gateposts, a throng of respectable townsfolk has gathered across the entrance to the church. Many of Whitehaven's better sort who attend King George's Church had subscribed to the cost of its building during the reign of Queen Anne. I don't know what name was originally intended for the church but by the time that the elegant stone-faced edifice was complete, the Queen was dead and German George was on the throne. Indeed, the new Church received its singular name during a rebellion provoked by the debatable royal succession that followed the old Queen's death.

Even in Loyal Whitehaven, a mob had gathered waving cudgels and calling for Queen Anne's closest relative, her Catholic half-brother, to be crowned as King James III. This 'Pretender' was then trying to invade England but this limp rebellion of 1715 was easily put down. Whitehaven's Jacobite rebels were written off as Scotch pit-men, some of them Papists but all of them devoted to their national sport of brawl. Nevertheless, the town felt thereafter obliged to proclaim its loyalty to German George by the naming its new church, not for some Popish saint, but for a Protestant King.

My father had little time for religion of any sort and regarded his attendance at Church as a purely civic duty, but he had conceived a fierce dislike for anyone of a Jacobite tendency. He held to the view that King James the Second, the Pretender's father who was deposed for his Catholicism, had been the enemy of English sea-traders. King James, whilst Duke of York, had created The Royal African Company to be a monopoly and thus kept independent merchants out of the Africa trade. Only when King James was banished to France was the monopoly ended and the slave trade opened up to small ship-owners. My father feared that James, the Pretender, if he ever became King would also seek to keep all profits from the African trade to himself.

So my father, from his commitment to slave-trading, was always the first in any party to raise his glass in a Loyal Toast. Indeed, it became his habit on the birthday of the second King George each November to donate a rum barrel to the Indian King Inn on Roper Street and himself lead the drinkers' Loyal Toasting throughout the day.

As we join the throng of worshippers funnelling through the open door of King George's Church, I cannot avoid Mrs Cleasby. Even in my depressed state, my eyes bulge at the mantua-maker's emerald swansdown skirts widened by side-hoops. Her stomacher drowns under silver ruffles and bows as she glides toward us like a milliner's wheeled display.

'Miss Ravenglass,' she says to my aunt with an incline of the head, 'and Mr Ravenglass.' She dips a curtsy.

My father and aunt give a nod and a friendly *how do?* in her direction. We shuffle forward, taking care not to tread on any of the petticoats around us, and especially not on the emerald swansdown.

'And Miss Felicity,' says the mantua-maker, her smile bending down the wrong way as she turns to my sister. 'I see you are recovered from your Maying.'

Fliss bobs respectfully but looks puzzled. As she opens her mouth to reply, Aunt Ravenglass steps between them.

'On the contrary, Mrs Cleasby,' my aunt puts on her best voice, 'I do not think Felicity went out at all on May Day. The streets can be so rough, even later on.'

'Oh no, I saw her quite distinctly on King Street. She had on her head a most elaborate garland of hedge-blossom and pewter-ware, and she was being squired by a gang of jolly boys.'

Colour glows in my aunt's cheeks. She has risen a considerable way in the world from the village forge at Distington where she and my father grew up but I sense, in this moment, her urge to revert to the ways of her childhood and to give Mrs Cleasby a good clout.

She straightens herself to her full height. 'You are mistaken, madam. Good day.'

Fliss then shoots me a look of piercing accusation. I glance away, mortified and for a second catch Mrs Cleasby's eye. In that second, she too seems to understand the origin of her mistake over the Fell Faery's true identity and purses her lips. My face, I have no doubt, is puce as beetroot stew.

'That's the last time you'll be wearing my things,' Fliss hisses beneath the babble echoing through the light-filled, balconied church. I pretend not to hear and she budges into me, scowling, to make space on the pew for her flowered chince petticoat.

During the litany, Fliss continues fidgety. She touches again and again at her neck ribband and then at her lace lappets, pulling them to the back and then the fore of her shoulders and looking around as if she has lost something. Then, when the congregation sings *Awake my soul with the sun,* a fine contralto rises above other voices and Fliss finally turns her head toward the servants' pew behind us. There she catches Daniel Bragg's eye and cannot entirely suppress her smile. Strange that when I first heard him sing with the mummers I thought Daniel a girl, but now he is dressed as a man, his voice, though fashionably high, does not sound female at all.

Parson Carr stands silent for a moment in the white-painted pulpit and then commences his sermon. I shift my bruised behind on the pew and, in boredom, read memorials and the lists of charitable donors on the wall behind his head. *AN ACCOUNT OF THE SEVERAL BENEFACTORS TO THE CHURCH AND THE POOR OF THIS PARISH... Mr Henry Ravenglass on the 22nd of November in the year 1728 gave the sum of TWO POUNDS for cloaks for poor girls to be given out each year upon that day...*

I have read this board many times, of course, but I have not before thought about why my father made his bequest. I was two year old in 1728 so I have no recollection of that time nor what prompted my father's generosity. The size of the gift is greater than any he might make now. Was it perhaps my mother's idea? Or was she by then already buried, if Stewardson is to be believed, in the House of Correction?

With a thud of shame and dismay I realise that I do not know anything of my mother's death, not even the date. The horror of Stewardson's words come afresh into my mind. Why would a respectable merchant's wife ever cross the foul threshold of the House of Correction, let alone meet her death there? Was she a lunatick, or had she committed some disreputable crime? Surely this cannot be. But Stewardson, of all Natty's boys, is the most truth-telling. And, I think with a sudden intake of breath, that my mother's moral state, indeed her character itself, is a mystery to me.

A cold shiver tickles my spine. Clasping my hands together I insert my own murmured entreaty into the State prayer.

'*Most heartily we beseech thee with thy favour to behold our most gracious Sovereign King George...* and, God, if my mother is not buried in Whitehaven House of Correction, I promise I shall never again dress in anything but breeches ... *through Jesus Christ our Lord. Amen.*'

And then as I stand, a simple idea comes to me and with it a sense of my prayer being answered. From the curving balcony above, the organ's retiring anthem swells through the nave and the congregation begins a stately departure with nods and tight-lipped smiles to neighbours. But I can't delay. Pushing myself into the aisle and weaving around the company I begin to run. Aunt Ravenglass is already in deep communication with Mrs Arnott, the apothecary's wife and does not notice me. From the servants' pew, Poll casts a disapproving glance but I will not let her stop me. For I am on my way to search the churchyard for my mother's grave.

The walled plot to the rear of the church is grassed but bare of trees. Away from the lee of the church-walls, two straight rows of headstones finish in coffin-shaped mounds of brown soil. I cannot think why I haven't looked for my mother's grave before. Even at my young age, I begin to see how peculiar it is that no-one has ever told me where my mother lies and, even stranger that I have never asked. But now there is a flame of passion inside me; a passion to know that my mother rests in a respectable burial place that befits a virtuous life, a passion to rid myself of shame.

Thumb-tip in mouth, I walk the first row of memorials and stare at the lives carved into Yorkstone.

Bridget Gibson aged 21
Departed this life
With her unborn child
20th December 1725

Thomas Strickland, Mariner
1698 - 1727

Here lieth ye body of Sarah Grove
Born 3rd June 1722
Died 10th August 1722

In the farther row of headstones, some are carved with cherubs' cheeks and angels' wings. But there is no stone for any Verity, whether Ravenglass or Salkeld.

Some graves, it is true, are indicated only by a dip in the grass or a patch of raw earth. But my mother must have a stone. My father would, surely, have spared no expense, and he had no shortage of money then as his bequest of pauper capes showed. Perhaps she is buried not here but in the yard of the old church, although I cannot think why she would lie in such an inferior place. In death, as in life, the best church to be seen in is King George's.

Then, on a rounded raise of limestone, I spot, with a tumbling in my belly, the word *Ravenglass*. Crouching before it, my trembling fingers trace the letters that are starting to fill with lichen. But this is a child's stone.

Isaac Ravenglass
5th January 1728
Aged 3 years and 10 months
Safe with God

My heart pounds. I know we have some estranged kin in Distington who share our name, but we are the only Ravenglass family in Whitehaven. This little dead lad must be some relation to me.

A sudden peal of laughter rings from the hum of conversations spilling outward from the church door. I look up. Protruding from the bend of the curving apse wall is a familiar swell of hooped chince.

'Fliss!'

The skirt is hastily pulled out of sight but I set off toward it.

'Fliss! I found a Ravenglass!'

She steps forward then, but too late to hide the departing outline of Daniel Bragg striding away toward the front of the church.

I pretend that nothing is amiss. 'I found our name. On a stone. It must be one of our kin. Come and see.'

I take hold of her hand and start to pull but she wrenches it free.

'Come on! There is a stone for someone called Isaac Ravenglass.'

She takes a step back. 'I know.'

'You do?'

'I've seen it before.'

I am confounded. 'Do you know who he was?'

'Aye.'

'Who?'

'Our brother.'

'Our brother? What do you mean? Have I a brother?'

'It is plain enough that you have one no longer.'

'But I know nothing of him.'

Fliss shrugs.

'Do you remember him?'

'Of course,' she says with a flick of her gloved hand. 'He was my little brother.'

A wave of envy swamps through me. I am her little brother. I always have been. Why should this dead boy usurp my place? Vexation, hot and itchy, rises through my innards. What else does my sister know that she has never told me?

I step toward her, my voice rising. 'And does our mother also lie in some nearby tomb that you and everyone else have forgot to show me?'

'No.'

'Where is she then?'

'Why do you care all of a sudden?'

'I heard it said that our mother is buried in the House of Correction.'

Fliss's face transforms into a mask of hard indifference. 'I'll speak no more of this.'

'That's not fair, Fliss. Just because I'm younger I'm kept ignorant.'

Her eyes flash. 'And you should thank the Lord for it.'

With that, she turns her back on me and swishes her chince petticoat away.

I huff and pivot about, vexed tears pricking at my eyes, and I'm drawn back to the lichened stone that records the life of Isaac Ravenglass. I stand before it, stunned and shaking. A brother. Can I remember naught of him? When he died, I was an infant barely walking, I suppose. But still…

Indignation blooms inside me. It is not fair that I've been lied to. For these omissions of elemental facts are as good as lies. Gathering all the righteousness I can muster, I resolve to confront my father about the manner of my mother's death and the location of her grave. This thought brings a flutter of apprehension to my belly, but the time has come, I decide, for me to be given the courtesy of truth.

Then, from inside the church, like a message from the Almighty, comes the unmistakeable sound of my father's voice.

I look up at the plain glass panes that form the elegant curve-topped window and I hear it again. The words are unclear but this is certainly my father. And he is exclaiming in anger.

Heart thudding, I move from the graveside and creep along the exterior walls of the church to the open front door. Here, my father's words reverberate out of the nave and into the lofty entrance hall.

'What in God's name, girl, did you mean by it?' he is saying.

Keeping close to the wall, I slip inside the entrance and bound up the sweeping staircase that leads up to the balconied gallery. The organist has departed, and the seats in the airy balcony are empty, as are the pews in the nave below.

Crouching down, I clutch my fingertips on the smooth painted edge of the rail and peep above. My father stands before the altar with Parson Carr at the far end of the aisle. His legs are planted wide apart, one hand on his waist and the other leaning on his ebony cane. His best wig gives him greater height than he really possesses. The parson, in his billowing black and white Sunday vestments, also appears more daunting than the small man inside them.

Standing before them is a girl. Her back is to me and from my high perch in the gallery, I can see her struggle of mousy hair and bare feet but I cannot tell her age. She is wearing a short, hooded red cape that I would wager is one supplied from the Ravenglass benefaction.

'But you must have known that it was a wicked act,' Parson Carr is saying in his whining voice as he looks intently at the girl.

She does not seem to reply.

My father leans toward her. 'Did it make you feel ashamed, was that it?'

The girl says something in quiet reply.

'You're happy enough to wear the warm cloak though, aren't you?' the parson says.

'It was the name Ravenglass that you couldn't stomach,' my father says.

I feel my heart quicken with the sense of his anger rising.

Again, the girl's muffled response escapes me, but my father's face reddens.

'Then why did you pull our initial from your cape?' his voice is edging toward a shout. 'If you cannot tell me, I must take this act of yours as an insult to me and my family.'

Parson Carr lifts a wary eye to my father then turns back to the girl. 'Come, child. Do you feel no gratitude towards your benefactor?'

My head, I fear, has risen more than it should above the rail but I am intent on knowing more of the girl's misdemeanour.

Then, her voice rings out, reedy but clear and steady.

'Here, take it back. You don't own me.'

With this, she pulls the strings at her throat and lifts the hooded cape from her shoulders. But before she has quite finished disrobing, Parson Carr snatches the woollen cape away from her causing the girl to stumble forward. Beneath this outerwear she has on little more than a threadbare shift and a petticoat. She clutches at this greyish linen as she rights herself. The parson then holds up the cape in front of her face to show that the place on the breast which should be adorned by a black velvet R, has only a discoloured patch and a fray of threads.

'And now,' says the parson, folding his hands, 'stand you there still to take your punishment.'

I don't think I breathe as my father steps forward and raises his ebony cane. He has never hit me with it. A slap on the legs is the worst I can remember. Yet he has been in a black mood for weeks due to the delayed return of the *Resolve*. He had borrowed heavily against her return in order to establish a new copperas works which was yet to turn a profit. The hairs on my neck bristle at the thought of what he might do to this girl.

The cane comes down with an audible thwack against the girl's thigh. Once, twice, three times it strikes. My jaw slackens in horror as I watch but the girl hardly flinches. I wince for her, knowing well how each blow hurts sharper than the last and my own bruised buttocks ache afresh. By the fifth blow, my eyes are watering and I'm ready to put my head above the rail and shout *stop!*

But then, my father steps back and leans on his cane as if fatigued. I stare at his red sweating face and my resolve to confront him over my mother's demise shrivels.

Parson Carr looks down his nose at the girl. 'Do not expect to benefit from any further charitable endowments in this parish. Now go.'

The girl in her scanty shift hesitates, as if ashamed to be seen in the street without the cape that was her only decent clothing. But then she turns and I see her face clearly for the first time. Too late I drop down my head below the rail but Hannah Salkeld's eyes, full of tearful defiance, have already met mine.

the tenth chapter

In the year that followed my May Faery humiliation, I did my damnedest not to behave or speak in any girlish way. On becoming twelve year old, I hoped my body might become manlier, though there were no signs of such as yet, and the boys of Bravery's Nautical Academy still called me Kitty. But my constant, unspoken refrain, *ACT LIKE DANIEL BRAGG* helped me rein in my natural inclination to the feminine.

It also began to occur to me that whatever upsets lay in my family's past, it would not be manly to enquire about them. Men, it seemed, had little time for sentiment and though I remained curious about the fates of my brother and mother, I could not imagine Daniel Bragg having much interest in such things in his own family. Therefore, I tried to keep my own eyes, like Daniel's, fixed firmly on the future.

At home, I spent less time in Fliss's chamber and wore her clothes guiltily, and only in secret. When Fliss and I were together, Stella was absent and I wondered, with some regret as well as relief, whether she had departed back to Dublin for good. Then, in the summer after my twelfth birthday, my resolve to maintain a lad-like habit was sorely tested when I became smitten by a sulphur-yellow Quilted-Petticoat.

When I first spied this treasure hanging in the window of the Indian King tavern on Roper Street, my mouth drooled as at the smell of a hot venison pie. It was amongst the garments put up by the innkeeper to be prizes at Lammas Fair, the most celebrated day in Whitehaven's calendar when folk would come from miles about for the sport and diversions. As I stood outside the inn, gawping, I tried to berate myself. If Daniel Bragg were to win a race, he would choose as his prize the gold-laced hat or the moleskin breeches or the coat of Exeter serge. I should pin my hopes on one of those. But I could not drag my eyes from the Quilted-Petticoat.

This skirt was fashioned of strong silk padusoy in a colour between yellow and green with two wide bands of cream above the hem. The quilting was of such intricacy that I imagined it must have been done in foreign parts and its padded heft gave the petticoat, even without hoops, a fashionable shape.

My desire to wear this garment, to feel its warmth and weight moulding my body into female form, became a physical ache inside my chest. And as I was accounted the quickest runner at the Natty's Academy I hoped I was in with a chance. The Fair was on the minds of the other Bravery boys as we floated in a jolly-boat on one of those rare Whitehaven days when the sea was blue and topped with diamond-glitter. That summer, Captain Bravery had took loan of the jolly-boat with six oars and a mast for the use of his charges. The boat was kept at the head of the strand below Brackenthwaite and if the day was reasonable, or even if it wasn't, the captain would send us out to accomplish a task of his choosing.

Sometimes, we would be instructed to sail to Parton and back in a high wind with a new creel for the fish-wife, sometimes to row a hogshead of ale to Saltom pit. We were meant to take some learning in sea-faring from these short voyages but I have no doubt that our teacher was taking payment for his scholars' labour as ferrymen.

On this day, however, we had no commerce to perform, but were charged simply to sail our way to St Bees Head and back without use of the oars. To ensure we did not cheat, Captain Bravery watched our departure from the strand whilst sat upon a pile of the said oars. On three hundred and fifty days of the year, our task could have been completed within an hour or two, but on this sparkling windless afternoon, we had travelled out of the harbour only as far as Tom Hurd Rocks.

The jolly-boat easily accommodated the nine of us boys. Will Fletcher quipped that it was our good fortune that Bloater had long since departed as a rating aboard *HMS Basilisk* or our progress today should have been even slower. I laughed loudly at this, raucous laughter being one of my most confident masculine affectations. But I felt little mirth. The *Basilisk* frigate had gone to the coast of Georgia where Spanish outrages against British shipping were growing more numerous and violent by the day. Since his departure six months before, we had heard only once of Bloater in a rumour, at second or third hand from a petty officer briefly ashore, that Hugh 'Bloater' Dixon was dead. How he had died no-one knew. We soon pretended we had never heard this news so that our departed companion could live on as the butt of our jokes.

The new boy in the Academy was Jim Whillans, a thin lad with flame-red hair and a Scotch twang who became known as The Pope despite us never having any evidence about his religion. Jim took his new name in good part and did his best to endear himself to us through lewdness, a tactic which worked exceedingly well.

Indeed, his special talent is displayed in the jolly-boat as he stands suddenly upright, unbuttons his breech-flap and pisses to an extravagant distance in the direction of the grassy cliffs. The cries of wheeling gulls are briefly drowned by peals of rude laughter, mine being the loudest. My months of practice have made acting in a boisterous, Daniel Bragg-like manner almost natural. And the sight of the water-jet being disgorged from The Pope's generous appendage causes me, almost without conscious thought, to leap up and start throwing my weight from one side of the jolly-boat to t'other in order to jostle the piss-stream. The wayward shapes drawn by yellow water on blue cause even greater hilarity amongst the boys.

'Quit that, Kitty!' The Pope cries, but without anger.

Then with a broad smile on his red face, and clutching hard on the source of his squirting, The Pope swings round to face me and unleashes his nozzle's last shots across my white shirt. Roaring laughter sweeps the boat. But my eyes are transfixed by the sight of the item in his hand. I am not alone.

'That's a fine instrument you have there,' says Will Fletcher when the laughing subsides.

'Why, thank you, sir.' The Pope replies sweeping back his free hand to make a bow but keeping his pizzle in full view with the other. 'Would any of you gentlemen care for a closer look?'

I glance around then and see that it is not just I that wants to say *yes*. Only Will Fletcher leans forward to peer.

'It seems a waste not to put such a creature to its natural purpose.'

'What would that be?' The Pope's grin wavers and his member seems to shrink at the thought.

'Why,' says Will Fletcher, "tis a gift, of sorts, for a lady.'

'Not any lady I know,' says The Pope, putting himself away and buttoning his breeches. We all laugh again but less heartily.

'Well then,' says Will, 'you and your little man must not have been mixing in the right sort of female company. We must put that to rights.'

All eyes in the jolly-boat fix, then, on Will Fletcher. The distant thump of the coal-pit Fire Engine beats into the salt-air stillness as we wait, rapt, for him to say more.

Will lowers his voice as if the fish might overhear. 'There is bound to be a likely lass at Lammas Fair who will not be missed while The Pope here gives her some enjoyment.'

The jolly-boat lurches and for a moment there is silence. Then George 'Bonny' Guy clears his throat and speaks.

'Why should The Pope have all the pleasure?'

'Why indeed?' says Will, sweat glistening beneath the line of his hat. 'We can all have a turn after him.'

Bonny frowns. 'But I should go first, being the eldest.'

'All right,' says Will, 'then The Pope, and then me and then anyone else that wants her.'

'Wants who?' Stewardson pipes up.

'Does it matter?' Will shrugs. 'Whoever we choose, will be of no consequence, except for being a she.'

The boys snigger.

'But you should not force her to anything,' Stewardson persists.

'I see.' Will gives a laugh. 'She can expect no enjoyment from you, then, Stew-breath?'

I laugh too, though not so enthusiastically and Will's eyes light on me. 'And what of you, Kitty? Shall you sniff the air like a stallion when the little filly flicks up her tail, or hang back like a gelding?'

Laughter starts again but I shout it down. 'Why should I not do as well as any of you with the lass?'

Smirks and sideward glances pass between my school-mates as the boat tilts in the unexpected swell of a wave although no actual jibes are spoken. Yet as I gaze out across the sparkle of water and the twinkling blue emptiness of sky, a grey gloom seems to descend. How have I become an accomplice of these nasty boys in their plan to defile an innocent girl? I am now a prisoner of their dismal code of masculine excess and I can see no possibility of escape.

As a breath of wind jabs at our single limp sail and the jolly-boat makes a small lurch forward, I suddenly see, rounding the headland of St Bees, the outline of full-rigged sails.

'Look!' I shout, glad to move the boys excitement to a new object. 'A brig. Coming this way.'

The vessel is making good progress and so cannot be relying on wind alone. We hear then the distant lilt of a song and see, below the flap of limp grey sails, a splash from two jolly-boats like our own that are pulling at the brig's bow. The rowers bark out The Keel Row in time to their strokes as they tug the becalmed ship toward the port.

'Is it a Whitehaven vessel?' Cries Stewardson, whose father is master of the *Sally and Susan Galley*, a Virginia merchantman that has already been gone a few months too many.

I strain to see. There is a familiar lilt to the brig and I squint into the salty light to make out her shape. Then my innards give a leap. Is this, could this possibly be, the return of the *Resolve*?

We had heard almost nothing of the *Resolve* since she set sail for Barbados by way of Guinea, on that frosty morning when I made my first entrance to the Nautical Academy more than a year and six-month before. The following summer, my father received a report that the vessel was still wandering along the Gambia River, being unable to buy sufficient cargo, that is to say, people, at a fair price. Rumour was that Captain Littlewood had been swindled out of his goods by accepting the false coinage from the sharp native traders of the African coast. But this report came from an untrustworthy source. In the spring, word was that the *Resolve* was tied up at Bridgetown, but this could not be confirmed.

Standing up in the jolly-boat, I squint at the approaching brig. Her squat proportions mark out her origins as a collier, but as the sailors' voices grow louder and I see two broadside gun-ports, not quite in line, I know, heart pounding, that this is indeed the *Resolve*.

'Ahoy! *Resolve* of Whitehaven, ahoy!' I call out, waving my hat like a lunatic, 'Have ye profit or loss?'

Some faces aboard the *Resolve* turn our way as the brig creeps past us toward the outer harbour and I find myself searching for the striking countenance of the African cabin-boy who attended Fliss at the Assembly. But he is not there.

My fellows on the jolly-boat, perhaps also glad to forget Will Fletcher's unsettling scheme for Lammas Fair, cause a dangerous lurching as they join in my cry of 'Profit or loss?' Jumping and calling, they waggle their thumbs from up to down in a cacophony that makes it hard for me to make out the answer from the *Resolve*.

But amidst the waving hands on the brig's main deck, thumbs are raised and with the other jubilant cries, there is a shout of *profit!*

And by the time I get home on that balmy August evening, our yard is filled by a line of salt-bleached mariners with curved elephants' tusks of such size and weight it takes three men to carry each one. In total, sixty-eight elephant ivories are that day stored in our strong room. They are the most valuable portion of the *Resolve*'s returning cargo, although still in her hold are hogsheads with five tons of muscovado sugar and at least fifty sacks of coconuts. And that is without the coin and Bills of Exchange the captain had secured in the slave-markets of Bridgetown that will now be offered up to the shareholders of the *Resolve*.

Later that evening, I am called to sit beside Captain Littlewood at a celebratory supper in my father's dining room. Aunt Ravenglass presides over a spread of cold meats, pease pudding and fruit jellies that fill the table for the short-notice feast. But all that Captain Littlewood consumes as he tells us of the voyage is a full bottle of my father's finest Madeira wine.

'So reports of your delay on the Gambia River were untrue?' says my father as he carves off a slice of beef. The windows to the yard are fully open but there is still no breeze and the air is clammy with whiffs of market waste.

'Well, I would not call it a delay,' says the captain. 'I had heard tell of a stock of elephants' teeth upriver, the price depressed on account of excessive supply. It was an opportunity that could not be ignored, and as you saw, they make a fine addition to our cargo.'

'Indeed,' my father beams as he forks the beef on to Captain Littlewood's plate where it lies untouched. 'And the slaves, were they plentiful too?'

Fliss looks up, ice-pale in her blue mantua-gown against the room's dark-painted wainscot. The gown was made serviceable after the dreadful night at the Assembly Rooms two year before by cutting off the dirtied train. Today the gown hangs loose over her everyday stays. I have never seen her wear again the costly silver-ruffled stomacher. Her eyes go to Daniel Bragg who is placed as far from her as the length of the table will allow.

'Well,' Captain Littlewood leans back with a well-satisfied smile, 'they are never especially plentiful. Getting them is mainly a case of cunning negotiation and patience.'

'And your losses on the middle passage were not excessive this time?'

The captain shrugs with one shoulder. 'Tolerable.'

'So there must have been a good price in Bridgetown for those that remained?'

'Deplorable.'

'Oh?' My father's black eyebrow rises as he tucks an over-large square of linen into his neck cloth.

'Three fully-laden slavers out of Topsham, Falmouth and Lyme had just arrived from Guinea. As a result of this over-supply of cargo, the plantation men could name their price for any of the specimens in our hold.'

The captain is dressed in a light grey velvet coat and a black tye-wig. Despite the superficial fineness of his appearance there is an odour of bad meat that must be emanating from his person rather than from the choicest cuts of my aunt's pantry.

'So what is the main source of your profit?' Daniel Bragg asks boldly.

My father's apprentice is now grown to the strut of full manhood. He is handsome too, though I hate to acknowledge it, and at the far diagonal of the table Fliss struggles to take her eyes from him though he does not once return her gaze.

With a whiff of rottenness, Captain Littlewood turns to look square at Daniel.

'Well, lad, we mainly have our sovereign King George to thank for the size of it.'

'How so, sir?'

'Well,' the captain leans back as he takes a swig of Madeira from one of our best goblets. 'Most vessels moored at Bridgetown were not merchantmen but men o'war.'

There's trouble brewing with the Spanish, and when I spied the impress men striding about the Careenage, I saw a clear way to profit.'

Daniel looks perplexed. 'A profit from the press gangs?'

''Tis a question of manning, Daniel.' My father leans into the table. His face, beneath his best wig is shiny with sweat. 'A human cargo requires more manpower to tend it than any other. But once the middle passage of the vessel's journey across the Atlantic is done and the hold is filled only with sugar and elephant teeth, the need for labour is much less.'

The captain smiles. 'And a sly nod to a Naval impress officer who can require any sailor to join their service will greatly increase the profits made by any master of a slaver with a surfeit of sailors.'

My father and the captain together raise their goblets and burst into a peal of manly laughter.

'So withholding the sailors' wages has inflated your profit?' asks Daniel, concentrating.

'Well,' the captain replies, a little defensive, 'some of the men pressed from the *Resolve* were in fact glad to join a man o'war. Their victuals are superior to ours, you see. Only a few of the fifteen had to be coerced.' He takes a long draft from his goblet.

My father nods and chews his meat. His mouth is open and I can see the brown flesh turning to mush in his mouth. My father's low table-habits fill me with embarrassment and disgust.

'Tell me, Captain,' my father licks his lips and turns serious, 'what say you to my idea of the *Swallow* following the same route the *Resolve* has just trod?'

'As a slaver?'

'Aye.'

The captain's bad scent swills about him as leans back in his chair.

'Well, she is a solid Whitehaven collier as the *Resolve* once was.'

Our coal-brigs are well-suited to the Guinea trade, their double-hull being padded with oakum and tar to carry a hefty weight of coal whilst also taking the ground upon Whitehaven's harbour sands at every low tide. This design, by coincidence, also makes them resistant to the teeth of the teredo worm which infests the waters around the Gambia River and can chew a death sentence into the hull of a weaker vessel.

'She would need refitting with platforms and chains,' says the captain, 'a stove pan to cook up horse-beans and such, but you know all this from the *Resolve*. The success of the venture depends mainly on her master. He must have a sharp eye and a shrewd nose in the market, whether that market be a jungly riverside in Africky or a fancy-painted auction house in Bridgetown. Sailing the vessel, even in a tropical storm is the easier part of a slaver-master's lot!'

At this, both men sit back and a knowing look passes between them. It was plain even to me that Captain Power of the *Swallow* was a very different breed of man to Captain Littlewood of the *Resolve*. Captain Power was a surly Dubliner, respected for his reliable knowledge of the Irish Sea-bed and for his expertise with canvas and rope. Seamen would count a lash or two of Power's discipline a fair exchange for his confident profile at the wheel amidst a raging January gale. But Captain Power's trading expertise was rarely put to the test upon these British journeys. Exchanging Cumberland coal for Irish ballast required no great intelligence to produce profit. On far-flung voyages though, the intricacies of trading with the caboceers of the Guinea coast and the auctioneers of Bridgetown were quite another matter.

Daniel puts both elbows on the table to address my father. 'You might always send a man to act as supercargo on the *Swallow*,' he says. 'Someone who would do the trading and leave Captain Power free to think only of sailing.'

A smile creeps across my father's face. 'Aye. That I could.'

Fliss's knife shrieks across her plate as she cuts her meat into smaller and smaller morsels but she eats none of them.

'Before any decision is made on re-fitting the *Swallow* as a slaver,' says my Aunt matter-of-factly as she reaches to re-fill the men's goblets, 'a voyage to the James River might be a prudent test for the vessel. She could go next spring once the coal season slackens. A good clean is all that she'd need to carry Virginia tobbacie instead of coal. And she might take servile passengers on the outward passage.'

Daniel's eyes flit from my aunt to my father. 'A supercargo could prove his worth on such a voyage.'

'No!'

Fliss cries out, but not in protest at the idea of Daniel travelling on the *Swallow*. A dark flapping shadow has invaded the dining room and Fliss stares wild-eyed at the sudden thrashing of feathers between open window and tabletop. A goblet is knocked over. Cruets scatter across the white linen cloth. All of us are frozen as our eyes try to understand this rude and unnatural commotion. At the centre of it, standing on the dining table directly before Fliss with his wings half-spread, is a fine adult magpie.

His tail-feathers are oiled blue-green. His breast is white as new snow. The bird puts his heavy-beaked head to one side and seems to weigh up many things in our dining room; the glint of salt in a pewter bowl, the opals at my Aunt's throat, a white-carved mutton bone. But it is my sister's face that draws his bead-black eye. Then, his beak opens and the bird speaks.

'Repent ye! Repent ye!'

The voice has a Welsh lilt to it.

Fliss, aghast, throws a beseeching look to Daniel but even now he will not meet her eye. He seems, in fact, to be cowering toward the door. Captain Littlewood is first to act. Pulling the cloth from his collar, he pushes back his chair and cracks the linen at the magpie.

'Away with you, damned carrion!'

But the magpie only hops closer to Fliss.

'Leave me be,' she cries, her voice thick with fear.

My father is up now, trying to defend his daughter from the beast, but with one eye on the protection of his tableware.

Too quick, Fliss stands up and her chair falls back against the wainscot. The magpie flies up then, the mutton bone clutched in its black beak. As inky wings beat toward the light, they seem to stroke Fliss's face, and with an anguished wail my sister runs from the room, sky-blue satinett flashing.

Aunt Ravenglass rushes after her and the men sit down, chuckling awkwardly and throwing each other amused looks which are meant to convey male fortitude in the face of womanly weakness. But, in truth, all of us have been disturbed by the bird's strange visitation.

Soon the concealed half-door beside the chimney breast opens and Aunt Ravenglass returns from the indoor kitchen below holding a dark bottle. Poll comes after her up the twisting corner stairs. Together they clear the soiled plates and spills. Then Poll sees a black-green feather on the tabletop. Twirling herself around three times on the spot, she incants, *Mercy. Mercy. Mercy.* My father and the captain exchange raised eyebrows and smirks but I am still perturbed and I imagine Fliss will be even more so. Most folk account a bird in the house unlucky, especially a magpie. And even the most rational mind would be unnerved to receive a Godly instruction from a pyet's beak.

'Is Fliss all right?' I ask my aunt.

'Yes, yes,' she replies, lifting a clutch of walnuts that drip with spilt wine.

'Shall I go to her?' This I address to my father.

'Aye,' he says, 'All of you, if you please, go now and leave the captain and I to our private business. You an' all, Daniel.'

Daniel, in the midst of helping himself to another cube of

quince jelly, looks affronted but he bows to the men before quitting the room.

I go first to Fliss's chamber but she is not there. Her hooped pannier-cage lies collapsed where she must have untied the waist strings and stepped out of it. As I eye the cage of basketry and tapes, desire licks at my innards. How I long to tie those strings about my waist and feel the swing of hoops against my own hips! There is no other sign of my sister elsewhere in the attic, nor in any room in the house.

Then, standing at the bottom of the main stairs, I hear, in the cool waft of air from the cellar, a hiccup. Surely Fliss would not descend in her finery into the black-dusted hollow that stores kindling and coal? But there comes another hiccup and then, the murmur of her voice.

Softly, I descend the tread of the stairs. Cool dank air envelopes me like a breath of winter. I stay unseen behind the brick partition though I can see the tall mouse-proof cupboard which is empty of potatoes and apples at this time of year. A cascade of satinett tells me Fliss is standing against the side of this cupboard.

She speaks again though I can't hear the words. Then another voice murmurs in reply. I creep to the edge of the partition better to hear Fliss and Daniel whispering in the dark.

'But why did you not help shoo away that foul creature?'

Horror amplifies Fliss's words.

'Your father was there…'

'But you stayed as far away from me as you could…' Fliss makes a sound that turns into a sob. 'And you did not even look at me. Not once.'

'You know I am your slave, sweetheart.'

'Then why will you not prove it?'

'Fliss, Fliss…' There is a silence here, or rather a shuffling and slight banging of the mouse-proof cupboard. Fliss gives a small whimper like a dog. I stand transfixed.

'Don't stop,' Fliss whispers.

'My heart…' Daniel's voice is low and breathy too. 'Let us be married first.'

I knew before this, of course, that my sister admired Daniel Bragg. The first hint of it showed even as she saw him dressed as a girl with the Christmas mummers. But I didn't imagine that this admiration could become serious. He was little more than a Westmorland cow-herder. So the mention of marriage hit me like a slap.

Fliss says something I cannot hear.

'Perhaps after I have proved myself to your father on a Guinea voyage…' Daniel replies.

'No!' Fliss's voice is shrill with emotion. 'You must never, never go on such a venture. It is the Devil's work.'

His sigh is loud enough to sound false. 'How else are we to be married?'

'Daniel…' Fliss's voice is low and breathy. 'Please…'

'Without marriage it would be a sin.'

'We have already sinned. The magpie knew…'

Daniel snorts. 'It was just some old sailor's bird taught to speak whilst in a cage.'

'But why did it pick on me?' Her voice cracks. 'It thought me a worse sinner even than the captain of a slaver.'

'No, no, my Felicious, how could that be?'

'Because it knew.' Fliss's voice cracks. 'It knew all about me.'

Here, there is a rustling of satinett. Sweating and red-cheeked, I listen harder. The rustling is accompanied by soft moans and lovers' whispers. And too ashamed to take a peek, I tip-toe back up the cellar stairs and out of the coal-damp air.

the eleventh chapter

On the morning of Lammas Fair, I awake to a pelt of water against the pane and a knot of foreboding in my stomach. My school-mates, or rather Will Fletcher, won't leave off about the plan to procure a girl at the fair for their wicked undertakings. Should I shy away from it, I know my position in the Academy will be no higher than an arse-rag in the necessary-shed.

Yet also inside me, as sleep melts away, is a heart-skip at the thought of the sulphur-yellow Quilted-Petticoat. I reach beneath my bed for *Dorinda's Gift* to ask her prediction *Will this day be lucky?* I close my eyes and let my finger hover above the stars before it falls. *This day is NOT lucky, rather the reverse,* is my reply.

I stand up, chest thudding. But the thought of seeing someone else wear the petticoat only inflames my passion to win it. Buttoning my best waistcoat, I resolve to prove Dorinda wrong. Somehow today, I shall obtain my heart's desire.

The rain has eased as I leave the house and climb the hill above the harbour. Black-grey clouds hang low over Harras Moor but it takes more than thunderclouds to keep Whitehaven folk from the most riotous day of their sporting year. Gulls wheel and screech above folk ribboning up the hillside toward Saltom.

All are in their gayest attire. Even the lowliest shepherdess wears flowers on her cap. The steep path affords a fine view out to sea, but neither the full-rigged ships in the offing nor the distant prospect of Scottish mountains can hold my interest as firmly as the flame-stitch poppies on a dairymaid's hat.

Four ha'pennies given me by Aunt Ravenglass clink in my

pocket and kindle the excitement in my belly. A swell of music and voices pull me toward the stalls and entertainments that have overnight appeared beside the bowling-green on Saltom Tops. The green itself has been cleared for races. 'Prentices and servant-girls, all in their best holland coats and camlet petticoats, crowd around peddlers of trinket-toys and ribbands.

I hope to stay clear of Natty's boys and their nasty prank by hiding in this throng.

But at the very entrance to the fair-field, I'm lured from the crowd by a bushy-eyed fellow playing bagpipes. A string leads from his foot to a board upon which a miniature lord and lady bow and twirl. Beside them, a tiny hound wearing a cape and tri-corner hat stands on his hind legs and appears to beat time by thumping a little polished stick on the ground.

Then comes a sharp punch on my shoulder.

'Kitty!'

My spirits sink. It is Bonny.

'Have you seen the others?' he asks.

But I have no chance to answer before he pulls me by the arm toward the bowling-green where a boxing bout is in loud progress. In loose, bloody shirts, a wiry sailor is pummelling a brawny collier as their mates from ship and mine shout along to the punches. The air is laced with beeriness.

'Look!' says Bonny, 'there's Will!'

Will Fletcher has seen us too. From his place amongst a press of men's coats, he beckons us closer, a greedy look on his face.

'Come on,' says Bonny breaking into a run but not letting go of my arm.

Not just Will is there but also Stew-breath, Monkey and The Pope. The press of men about them is so great that I cannot see the source of the great attraction in their midst, but only hear excited male braying pierced at intervals by the screams of a fowl.

'What's this?' asks Bonny as we push into the onion-breathed scuffle.

'A challenge,' says Will, pressing between broadcloth-ed bodies. '£5 is on offer to anyone who can eat a whole live cock. There must be nothing left though, not a feather nor a claw.'

'But that is impossible,' I gasp.

'Perhaps,' says Will, 'but for £5 yon collier would likely eat his own cock.'

I laugh with the other boys but I am fascinated and appalled in equal measure.

'This we must see,' says Bonny, piling in behind Will and pushing to the front.

I dip down and crawl on hands and knees between coat flaps and stockings. A few kicks to my ribcage are a reasonable price for a good view of this spectacle and I stay crouched down at the front of the cleared circle so that none of the jeering men will bat me out of the way.

A showman in faded velvet lifts aloft a black and grey cockerel in one hand and in the other, he holds up the arm of a hefty collier, as wide as he is tall.

'A final call then,' shouts the showman. 'Any more wagers in this battle of man against cock?'

The pitman smiles blackly. I can't imagine how his few teeth will be sufficient to the task in hand.

'Very well, let the challenge commence,' says the showman, 'and bon appétit!'

With that, he hands the screaming cock to the pitman who takes it with confidence. Then he opens his mouth as wide as he may. The bird's beaky head, eyes, coxcomb and all, disappears inside the pitman's orifice where, with a single crunch, it is bitten off and spat out.

With the spurt of blood, a great cheer goes up from the crowd. But now the pitman's hard work begins. Starting with the soft parts of the belly, he chews through downy feathers, skin and entrails with a look of sly satisfaction. But the bird's severed head still lays on the ground and the clawed feet dangle, dangerously sharp from the extravagantly plumaged body.

I glance at the circling crowd. Though it is still morning, some spectators are already drunk but all are aroused by a spectacle so foreign to their everyday existence. Many are disgusted but all wish they had the pitman's courage to attempt something so remarkable.

On the other side of the ring, I see Captain Littlewood, in pink laced brocade talking earnestly to the man next to him. Money changes hands between them. Bets are still being laid on the progress as well as outcome of the pitman's feat. Shall he go next to the wings or the feet? Or shall he attempt to ingest the head? All are worth a wager.

The crowd starts to bray for their preferred body part. A great whoop goes up, part cheer, part boo, as the collier bites into the rooster's tail-feathers. He chomps but his face darkens and, for the first time, he gags.

The watchers, whether their money is on failure or success, all gasp. But the pitman swallows hard and opens his mouth wide as he pivots in a circle to prove to all that the feathers have gone down. The spectators on the pitman's side give a loud *huzzah*.

Then, the pitman picks up the cock-head. Throwing it into the air, he catches it, to a great cheer, in his mouth and starts to chew. Clapping whips up amongst the audience in time to the pitman's crunching.

Heated by the frenzy of expectation around me, I join in. But then I see a certain face in the crowd and my eyes cannot be drawn from it, not even by the cock-eating collier. It is an African. He is wearing the short blue jacket and knotted red neckerchief of an able-seaman, but how much better these garments become him than any of the other, sallow-faced sailors in the crowd. And, though there is only a remnant of resemblance, I would lay a wager that this handsome lad is the cabin-boy from the *Resolve* who served as boy-attendant to

Fliss at the ill-fated Assembly.

I stare at him, trying to map the face of that boy on to the calm, strong features of this young man. The spectacle of feather, blood and spit is, for a moment, forgot and I can see only the singular beauty of his face.

But then, after much gurning, the pitman takes a final gulp of cock-head and grins, opening wide to show the absence of fowl in his mouth. The crowd erupts, those who have won their bet cheering while the losers bellow with dismay.

I glance back at the African and, for a second, his eyes find mine. Our expressions, I realise are identical. Both of us are amazed and delighted by the pitman's preposterous feat. For it seems to prove that no matter how difficult, nay impossible, an enterprise may appear, it can with sufficient determination, be done.

Then commotion in the ring moves and blocks my view of the sailor. I shift as far as the pressing crowd will allow to try again to make connection with those calm black eyes. But the African has disappeared amongst the hubbub of men clamouring for their winnings and I find myself pulled away by Bonny and Will Fletcher.

'Where are we going?' I ask.

'To find us a likely girl,' says Will.

My stomach sinks.

'Oh,' I say, trying to sound bored by the venture.

Will's smile turns sly. 'What, Kitty? Do you have no fancy for our dare?'

Pulling myself to full height, which is taller than Will, I snort. 'I can roger as well as any.'

'Aye?' Will sneers. 'But can you roger a girl?'

Even after a year and a half of smutty talk I have no real notion of what any of this means and can only shrug.

'Well,' Will says, gripping the shoulder of my coat, 'we shall soon find out once we have our girl. And you're going to help in the search, aren't you?'

I blink and try not to nod.

'Where shall we look first?'

We all follow Will's roving gaze. Rapiers of sunlight cut through black clouds over the sea. On the fair-field, patches of brightness illuminate the coloured bolts of cloth on the pedlars' stalls. And then I see raised up on crucifix poles between beer tent and ribband stall, and shining yellow as an earth-bound sun, the Quilted-Petticoat.

'Let's try the lasses' race,' I suggest casually and hope that whilst my school-mates ogle the runners they will not notice me slip away.

The Bowling-Green is now cleared and the race is getting ready to be run. A gaggle of wenches wait at the start in loosened leather stays and short petticoats. They are hearty creatures, farm, pit and fish-girls, as strong as many a man. Coming toward them, and directed to the field by a young shepherd wielding a crook, is a small flock of this year's brown-fleeced lambs.

Bonny eyes the field nervously. 'Should we try for one of these?'

'What? A ewe d'ye mean?' says The Pope and guffaws.

Their laughter gives the boys courage to edge closer to the terrifying maidens.

'That red-head looks like she'd be willing.' Bonny says covering his mouth with his hand as if there is the slightest possibility that the girl will either hear him or take any notice.

'That little fat one, for me,' says The Pope loudly. 'With such good handfuls of udder, my entry cannot fail.'

Will and Bonny laugh excitedly at the thought of this striking tableau. I try to join in and appear eager but I could no more touch one of these buxom sweating lasses than eat a live hen. The abject look on Stewardson's face mirrors the sinking feeling in my own innards.

Then there is a shout and the shepherd looses the lambs.

The girl-racers, with cries of *out me way!* and, *fuck you an' all!* are off too, running headlong towards the scattering sheep. The lambs, not long parted from their mothers, are nimble with terror and their unshorn fleeces are slippery with the grease that protects them from Cumberland rain. So even when a pit-lass, in a flurry of bare shins and dirty under-skirts grabs a little shearling, she cannot keep her grip and the lamb runs off, white-eyed and bleating.

In the end, a farm-wench triumphs, seizing a lamb by a firm bite to its fleece. She then clamps a hold on its legs, front and back, before carrying the creature upside-down across the grassy square towards the prizes.

As she nears the yellow Quilted-Petticoat, my heart cavorts in my chest. Surely, given a choice, she will choose the marvellous petticoat above breeches, coat, or smock? But I let out a breath of relief as the girl strides forward to exchange her lamb for the frock coat of Exeter serge.

The farm-wench waves the coat in the air and gestures rudely at her defeated opponents who stand panting and scowling amidst scattered grazing lambs. Then triumphantly, the winner puts on her man's coat and looks, it must be said, both fetching and invincible.

'We must find fresher meat than that,' says Will with disdain.

I follow his gaze from the hurdy-gurdy man, to the children swinging in hanging chairs, to the bare-chested wrestlers. But every female is either escorted by a male companion or is part of a giggling breathless gaggle. Perhaps the boys' foul design will remain no more than a fantasy. The tightness in my shoulders loosens at the thought.

'Well,' I say. 'I'm away to race.'

'You?' says Will.

'Aye. Why not?'

He sneers and shakes his head. 'Come back and find us when you've lost…'

But I am already running toward the start-line.

At the beer tent beside the bowling-green, the innkeeper's man stands with an open leather bag.

'How much to run the lads' race?' I ask.

'A penny.'

I feel the ha'pennies in my pocket. 'What is the prize?'

'Take your pick,' he says. 'But you'll have to beat that lot first.'

He nods to the well-muscled collier-lads, 'prentices and sailors milling about at the start. They all look older than I. Amongst them I recognise Ben Moorhouse the chandler's tall son, as well as another who cannot be missed, the dark-skinned African sailor.

I take out my ha'pennies then go to the start-line to undress.

'Ha!' Says a grinning plough-boy, pointing as I lay down my coat, stockings and shoes. 'We'll have no fear of this girly runt!'

But they do not know how fast I am, nor how slippery. As the shout goes up and we all lurch forward, hands reach from all quarters to pull me down but none are quick enough. Some runners are floored by this tussle at the start but I keep to the fore of the pack, my bare feet speeded by the cold, wet grass.

By half way there, only the African is ahead of me, although long-legged Ben Moorhouse is hard up behind. Ben makes a grab at my shirt but then stumbles and lets go.

Then to my left, the yokel is gaining on the African. Perhaps preferring to lose rather than let the African win, he makes a lunge for the sailor's heels. And as I reach the finish, both lie grappling on the field.

The landlord of the Indian King raises his tankard as I approach the beer table.

'Young Ravenglass.' He winks. 'The winner, eh?'

Beside him, a bearded sailor laughs and slurps beer from a mug.

'Aye. I've come for my prize.'

Various garments are still strung up on poles, but I see only the Quilted-Petticoat.

'Got your eye on something, have you?' The innkeeper has a jovial face but narrow, foxy eyes. 'Is it the hat you fancy, or the breeches?'

'Neither,' I reply. 'I want the petticoat.'

The sailor spits a spray of beer through his roaring laugh.

'Oooh,' says the innkeeper with his head to one side. 'Just your colour.'

'Tis for my sister,' I protest but my cheeks flush.

The innkeeper wipes his eyes and reaches for the shining yellow skirt. Laughing he holds it up against my waist before handing it over. I grab it from him and fold the fat skirt into as small a bundle as I may before wedging it under my arm. And then I stride off, smiling smugly to myself that Dorinda has got her prediction for the day so entirely wrong.

But I do not get far before Natty's boys come jostling toward me with shouts and leers and evil in their eyes.

'Blow me, Kitty, you chose a petticoat!' Will Fletcher claps me on the back.

'Pretty Kitty,' croons Bonny.

As we walk towards the pie stall, they start to hop about me touching my face and hair.

'Get away with you,' I say, unable to contain my vexation. 'It's for my sister.'

'Oh aye, of course, it is,' Will says, winking. 'But why don't you put it on and see how it looks on you?'

I know I should join in with their laughter and make a joke of it all but I can only scowl. Why should I even try to fit myself into this company of oafs? I wish only that they would find someone else to bait. And then, as if a gift from the malignant gods, I see The Pope approaching and at his side is a thin girl in a dirty apron. A shawl is wrapped tight about her shoulders and a wary frown contorts her features, but there is no disguising who she is.

I had not seen Hannah Salkeld since her humiliation in King George's Church and I'd begun to wonder, given the iciness of the winter, whether she might be dead. That fleeting thought had brought with it an unexpected wave of sadness for my proud pauper-cousin.

Now, as she approaches I have a strong urge to hide. But I can't escape her quick gaze. When she sees me, her hands loosen from her shawl as if she is reassured by my presence. Already in a quandary, I stay blank-faced as my bowels begin to tie themselves into a series of tightening knots.

Jim Whillans puts out a hand toward Hannah. 'I was just telling this lassie about the pies,' he says and directs a meaningful look at Will Fletcher.

'Ah, the pies…' Will says.

'Aye, the *free* pies,' Jim says and his hand moves to the small of Hannah's back.

She stiffens and I see the new swell of her breasts. I know I should step forward now and usher her away, braving the boys' angry taunts. But their punishment of me would continue. My school hours would become a torment. So, I stay blank-faced and unmoving, telling myself that the boys won't go through with their vicious plan and that Hannah won't be fooled by their trickery.

But she looks wide-eyed from The Pope to Will.

'Are they meat pies?' she asks.

My heart sinks.

'There's mutton and a few beef,' Will smiles at Hannah with no hint of anything but kindness, 'though we'll have to be quick.'

'At the mine they are, you say?' The Pope's acting voice is over-loud and stilted.

'That's it,' Will says, his eye not leaving Hannah.

She looks to me, but I keep my face turned toward a distant conjuror who has just released a dove from beneath his hat. I will her to turn around and leave now but she speaks with a calm, almost womanly voice.

'And they're free to all for Lammas Fair?'

'Well,' Will puts his head to one side. 'Not to all exactly, but if you stick with us we'll get you one.'

Hannah's eyes narrow. 'Why would you get me a pie?'

'You're a friend of The... Jim here, aren't you?'

'This is nonsense!' We all turn as Stewardson strides within dangerous arm-reach of Will Fletcher. 'Why would anyone give out free pies?'

Will's handsome features darken as he thrusts his face into Stewardson's. 'If you don't want one, just get lost. Now.'

For a moment, neither boy moves and I wonder if Stewardson, though a head shorter than Will, is prepared for a fight. But then he steps back.

'I don't want any part of this,' he says, shaking his head.

'Well, be off with you then.' Will waves a dismissive hand in the manner of a Lord Chamberlain, 'and don't expect any more favours from me.'

Stewardson throws me an angry glance as he strides away and Hannah stiffens. 'Who's paying for these pies?'

'They are a generosity from Sir James Lowther,' says Will, 'for passing colliers going to Lammas Fair. But my uncle is the Mine Overseer and he said that me and any of my companions may also have one. So, shall you come with us?'

Hannah tightens her shawl. 'Are all of you going?'

I know she is looking at me.

'That we are,' Will says. 'And growing increasing peckish! So, shall we?'

With a slight bow that to me seems an insult, he extends his arm and lets The Pope and Hannah lead the way.

Will, Bonny and Monkey follow but I hang back, not sure if I can bear to go with them. Then a rough hand grabs my elbow.

'Are you going along with this?' Stewardson asks me, indignant.

I shrug. 'They'll not hurt her. They don't have the bottle.' But my voice quavers.

'I think they do.'

'Don't fret.' I try to give Stewardson a confident nod. 'I'm going with them and I'll see she comes to no harm.'

But I can tell by his expression that he has no faith in me. And as I start down the wagon-way, with clouds thickening over Scotland's distant hills, I have no faith in myself. How shall I find the courage to divert the lads from their purpose?

Ahead, Will Fletcher, Monkey, Bonny and The Pope seem to box Hannah in and shuffle her along. Hannah lifts her skirt to cross the wagon rails and I see she is barefoot.

Further down the hill, by the wooden hurries where coal-wagons tip their loads to the harbour-side, Will Fletcher stops and puts his hand to his brow. He points at the cliff face behind the harbour and the brick-arched entrance to the mine.

On most days, even in summer, this cavern would be alive with blackened pitmen and basket-laden ponies. But today, because of Lammas Fair, it is deserted.

'Just in yonder archway,' I hear Will say.

Hannah stops. 'What? In the Bear Mouth?'

'Aye.'

I squeeze the quilted petticoat to a smaller bale under my arm.

Hannah takes a backward step. 'Surely the pies aren't inside the mine?'

'I thought I told you,' Will's voice has a rough edge. 'They're for the colliers. And that's the place they have their bait.'

Hannah goes to turn away but Will catches her elbow.

'Here,' he fumbles in his coat pocket, 'take this penny and if there are no pies left you may keep it instead.'

Even from some yards behind, I see that Bonny and Monkey are struggling to stifle their laughter but Hannah is looking at me as she reaches out a thin arm to take Will's coin. I wonder if it is only my presence that stops her seeing him for a liar.

Rarely have I been so close to the Bear Mouth and never inside the dirty, noisy place that is usually crowded with black-faced colliers swearing and hawking spit on to the ground. But today the pit cave, though reeking of coal-dust and horse-piss, is quiet. The ponies are at grass and the miners at the fair, their equipage locked away in the tunnels.

I hang back unnoticed by the brick arch in the cliff as Will leads the others inside.

'Where are the pies?' Hannah says looking around the walls of dank rough-hewn rock.

'They should be here somewhere,' Will says pushing Hannah onward. 'Come, help us look in these crannies.'

He spots me at the threshold and beckons like a conspirator. I go forward trying to keep Hannah in my sights. Further in are the locked wooden gates that bar access to the mine and beyond them is the labyrinth of tunnels and shafts that descend for mile upon countless mile far under the sea.

'But there's nothing here,' Hannah says.

A circle of boys has formed around her. I see Bonny and Monkey exchange a dark look. Bonny bites his lip.

'Well, never mind,' Will says. 'You may keep the penny and buy yourself a pie…' The girl starts to turn to walk away but he places a firm hand on her shoulder, '…if that is, you do something for us.'

'What?' Hannah's voice wavers.

'Not much.' Will takes a small step closer and puts his other hand on her, gripping the top of her arm. 'It will be quick.'

'No!' Her voice is strong now. 'Where is Christopher?'

I step forward into the circle but the Pope's firm arm is thrown against my chest.

'No, no. You'll not be going first. I'm the one who found her.'

'Let her be.' My voice is so thin even I can hardly hear it.

'Christopher! Help me!'

Hannah struggles but Will holds on to her. 'Come on lads! Get her down.'

'No, let me go!' Hannah's eyes fly across the faces, one to another before her gaze settles on me. 'You, Kit Ravenglass, Help me! For your father's sins, you owe me.'

Is she talking of what happened in King George's Church? The red cape with the black R ripped from it and the thwack of an ebony cane? As I squint, recalling the scene, The Pope looms in front of me and punches a hard palm into my shoulder.

'If you're not with us, then you must be against us.'

His face pulses red and his eyes are black with excitement. Sharp, manly sweat wafts from inside his coat.

I back away.

'Kit, please!' Hannah beseeches.

But Will is already exerting his considerable strength on her scant frame.

'Get her on the ground,' he says.

The others step forward, but are unsure what to do. Then, Monkey takes hold of a foot and Hannah buckles backward. Her shift and apron fly up past her white thighs.

I freeze, horrified, and again she catches my eye.

'You… Ravenglass,' Hannah spits, ''tis no wonder your mother wanted you dead.'

Do the others hear this? Or have I just imagined the words? I am floored by her venom, numbed by her strange accusation. My urge is to flee but The Pope, a sneer on his sweaty face, blocks my way.

Perhaps, had I been more determined, I could have pushed past him and raised an alarm. But Hannah's words had left me too limpid and distracted to take on the straining, stoked-up youths who were now pinning her to the ground.

As Will fumbles with the buttons on his breeches, I creep backwards from the dreadful scene, retreating further into the coal-heavy air at the back of the cave. A recess in the rock shields me from the sight of what the boys are doing. And I know to my core, that if this is what men do, I don't want to become one.

Taking the sulphur-hued Quilted-Petticoat from under my arm, I shake it out. Even in this dark hole, the silk ripples with golden light. Carefully keeping the hem from the dirt, I step inside and pull the waist strings tight. The skirt balloons around my legs and I sense myself clothed in richness. Instantly, I am transported to a better place, a place that values beauty and elegance, a place where people treat one another with gentleness and civility.

From the other side of the stone partition come the sound of scuffles and grunts. Before I can hear anything of Hannah, I clamp my hands to my ears and start to twirl and twirl about, humming an old cradle song to keep the nastiness out. The Quilted-Petticoat glows. Faster and faster I go, air inflating the skirt like a bell about my legs until I am drunk on the swish of padded silk.

And then the Bear Mouth is filled with the boom of a man's voice that penetrates even my padded ears. Twirling halted, I stand panting and stupefied. The voice comes again.

'What in God's name is this?'

My heart drops in my chest. It is my father's voice. I shrink back, breathless, toward the rock wall.

Unseen around the corner, there are scuffles. Will, I think, protests and my father shouts again.

'Let her up, you scoundrels.' And then, 'is Christopher here?'

I try to shrink back further. But around the rocky corner comes Daniel Bragg. His eyes widen then he sneers with satisfaction as he casts a look back to my father.

'Sir! He is here.'

I have no choice now but to step forward and face my father who is standing over the gaggle of shame-faced boys. As I come into the open and his eyes fall upon the Quilted-Petticoat, I see in his face a sudden turmoil of emotions. There is shock, anguish, dismay and perhaps, though I hate to acknowledge it, love.

He takes a quick breath. 'Christopher.'

Disappointment oozes through his voice and despite my disgrace, a shiver of exhilaration goes through me. Shock has given me a power over him. A power to wound. I am almost glad that he has found me.

From the ground, Hannah Salkeld scoots up to her feet and dashes out of the cave. I blink into the light but she has gone. The Pope is panting and dishevelled, and Will Fletcher is stuffing his shirt into his breeches. But as I appear, all the boys' eyes are drawn to only one place, my sumptuous, shining petticoat. Their mouths fall open. And at last, my father shakes his head.

'Well,' he says with a heartfelt, weary sigh. 'I think it's high time that all of you disreputable lads were straight away put to sea.'

the second part

—

at Sea

the first chapter

There is a brief moment on my first climb up the foremast when, stopping to catch my breath, I look around and wonder if my father is right about the lure of the sea. The mast lurches dizzyingly downward. Grey waves rise up. But the sailors are scuttling easily around the rigging and the yards. Sail-cloth unfurls purposefully into the stiffening November wind, and the *Swallow* seems speeded along by the lively cries of mariners. Having already climbed to the height of a full-grown tree, I can see the cliffs of St Bees Head receding behind us. Ahead, the distant Lancashire sands look as vast and tranquil as a desert of Araby.

Perhaps the voyage will not be so bad, I think. I might even enjoy the adventure of a crossing and the opportunity to view Dublin's urban delights. Perhaps, as my father has always hoped, the sea will make me into a man.

'Ravenglass!' The voice from below is full of rage. 'Get yersel' up to that topgallant. Now!'

This is Riddle, the bosun and mate, a black bearded Yorkshireman who has instructed me to free the topgallant sail from the braces, a task which requires me to climb the foremast up to the highest yardarm. Only once before have I climbed into high rigging when the boys of the Nautical Academy were tasked with scraping and cleaning the cordage of a vessel. This was to give us a taste of the dizzying heights at which a sailor must work, though Natty was no doubt well paid for our labour. But that lesson was undertaken on a brig tied up at the Tongue, and on a day when there was hardly a breeze.

'Get up there, or I'll come mesel' with a lash.'

I glance down at Riddle's face, red behind his beard. There is something familiar about him though I can't think what.

Pressing on, the climb is not difficult. The cables are sturdy in my hands and the ratlines beneath my feet are strengthened with wooden slats. But soon I find my way barred by a top, the wooden platform around the mast to which the shroud-ropes are anchored. This top blocks my view of the full height of the foremast and presents an overhang which, even close up, offers no obvious route around.

Perched beneath the top's wooden boards, I reach outwards and upwards to feel the unseen surface above for some secure handhold that will allow me to climb onto the platform. But there seems nothing on to which I can get a good hold. The mast dips forward wildly and I almost lose all grip.

Below, Riddle and a couple of the crew stand, heads back and hands on waists. Wind-blown instructions are shouted in my direction. *Stand on the futtock shrouds! Grab the halliard!* I can hear their words all right but they might as well be in Chinese.

Hot tears of frustration prickle. But I will not let myself fail at the first obstacle. There must be some way up. And my pride, it turns out, is at least as strong as my fear. I lean the full weight of my body backwards into the wind and again reach out and up to pat at the unseen surface of the top for anything that can become my hand-hold.

Then, the whole brig makes a violent downward shudder, as if we have hit a rock or another vessel. Wind blasts my face and my bare toes slip from the ratlines. One desperately grasped hand-hold is all that prevents me tumbling to the deck. Heart pounding, I haul myself back into the fold of the rigging and I cling to it, cold and breathless below the top. I blink down at Riddle's beard. It opens and closes around his mouth but his words are lost to the wind. Up here, the gusts are stronger as the *Swallow* slaps into deep crevices of the rolling grey sea.

A fall, even from this height, might kill me. Yet if I don't go further aloft, I may feel more than just the lash of Riddle's tongue. Frozen, I cling to the ratlines.

Then, from below, there is a tensing in the cordage. Someone is coming up. I look down and see a black head and a blue short jacket ascending at speed. The sailor is suddenly beneath me. I feel the warmth of his body and brush of his petticoat breeches as he rises across me and into my ear, he whispers encouragement.

'Stretch your hand over the top and I will guide it.'

The voice is deep and the words spoken with what might be a West Country twang. But as the sailor pulls himself with breath-taking nimbleness aboard the top, I see his dark muscled calves and know he is an African. In the hours since we cleared Whitehaven, this is the first I have seen of him. And though he is here aboard the *Swallow* and not the *Resolve* could this be the same African lad I raced at Lammas Fair? I need no further encouragement to climb up and find out for sure.

Holding tightly to the stiff shroud cables on the underside of the platform, I lean my weight outward as far as I dare and feel over the top. A hand, warm and firm, takes hold of my fingers and guides them toward a stoutly anchored cable. And then a strong arm has hold of my elbow. Despite the frock-flap of my coat catching in the shroud-anchors I am pulled, wriggling onto the swaying top.

His face grins down at me. 'You'll be needing a different coat if you're to be a sailor.'

Then, with no thought to the dizzying drop, he lets go of the rigging and crouches down to pull my coat-flap free. I have no doubt now that he is the African from Lammas Fair, the same lad who witnessed with me the triumph of a collier eating a cock whole. The same lad, I suspect, who as a boy attended Fliss to the Assembly Rooms.

'Not much further.' He lifts his chin toward the topgallant

sail thrashing above us. 'I'll come up behind you.'

I nod. His calm assurance gives me courage to continue my climb.

On the dancing yardarm, I lean over the beam to tug at the topgallant's sail-cloth and wedge my bare shins between the ropes. A final yank from the African sailor frees the sail which, with a crack, balloons out. I catch my comrade's eye, and for a moment, as I take in the great expanse of the sea, the looming bulk of the Isle of Man and the calm, smiling face at my side, my heart fizzes with joy.

The crew call him Coffee though that cannot, surely, be his name. His proper place is, indeed, aboard the *Resolve* but he has been lent by Littlewood to Captain Power whilst the *Resolve* is in the shipwright's dock.

Once we have safely descended the foremast and I have the leisure to look at him squarely, I have a strong urge to speak to the African, if only to thank him for helping me over the foremast top. But I am too timid for such an interchange. The sailors do not seem to engage their fellows in any conversation but merely shout instructions and obscenities at each other then reply with manly laughter or even manlier indifference.

Yet, notwithstanding this lack of communication, the *Swallow* works like a just-wound clock. The bosun, whose job it is to maintain the vessel's best and safest pace, is constantly pointing men up and down the masts to pull in one sail or let another out. No matter how steady the breeze nor how slight the swell, the cables and sails require perpetual adjustment. Ropes are loosed from their capstans or cleats only to be tightened again a half hour later. All of those aboard seem to know their exact purpose in the functioning of this complex mechanism.

My own place in the crew, as the youngest aboard, is to be at the beck and call of all, whether to fetch a pail of water for the cook, or pry open a stiff knot for the bosun, or fetch a slice of bacon to Captain Power at the wheel. The voyage to carry a hold-ful of Whitehaven coal to the banks of the Liffey should take no more than a few weeks, less if the winds are favourable. And my father hopes these weeks will fill me with passion for a life at sea.

By dusk of the first day afloat, I was indeed stirred by all that I had seen and felt in that short space of time. Then, the bosun tells me, as if it is a thing of no consequence, that I'm to share a hammock with Old Barnacle, a filthy-clothed bow-legged seaman whose actual age is impossible to tell. I blink at him, too shocked to reply. The hard look in Riddle's eye stifles any argument.

And so, with the snuffing of the single candle that has lit the lower deck between dusk and the eight o'clock bells, I climb into a hanging sheet of sailcloth and try to cosy my head against frozen claw-feet of Old Barnacle. No-one appears to see anything unusual in this arrangement. Old Barnacle himself hardly seems to notice I am there and falls into snoring on the very instant that his body adopts an approximation of horizontal. But I lie stiffly awake. As the *Swallow*'s bow judders against the waves, I blink at each groan of the timbers and flinch at each shout from the Watch above.

Our hammock hovers an arm's length below the beams of the deck-head and directly above two hogsheads of tobacco. The pungent aromas rising from this cargo at least mask the peculiar stench inside the hammock that must be Old Barnacle. Even nastier odours float in from a nearby necessary-bucket which is our only privy.

Nothing on the lower deck is odourless. The cook's stores, piled around the galley stove are in varying states of staleness. Even the quantity of spare rigging that takes up much of the stowage space gives off a waft of pitch. And with the hatches and scuttles closed against the wind, there is no air to shift the reek of black dust oozing up from the weight of coal in the hold. So powerful is this smell in the black of the first night, that I begin to imagine myself not at sea at all but in the dirt-damp tunnels of a mine.

Gradually, weak light from stern-lantern spills down the

ladders to the lower deck and I start to make out the shapes around me. The crew's sail-cloth hammocks float like glow-worms in the grey air. And my last thought, as I slip, shivering into sleep, is to wonder which of these cocoons the African.

The second day of the voyage passed in a similar daze of novelty. The *Swallow* made uneventful progress in a moderate swell within sight of the Lancashire coast, but each moment was, to me, full of surprise. I marvelled at the crew who appeared to feel no discomfort from the constant cold wetness of their clothes. They hardly bothered with stockings or shoes and seemed to enjoy their dreadful rations of pickled pork and gritty pease pudding. So eager were they to guzzle these horrible victuals that the sailors rarely sat to dine and often ate with neither with plate nor spoon.

Yet I also understood, in the glory of a vessel running in full sail on a gusty winter morning, the compensations of life at sea. And the sailors, once I grew more used to their strange language and ways, had their own peculiar fascinations.

First to befriend me was the cook, a wizened Manxman of indeterminate age and no apparent name. His right leg below the knee was a broom handle and he used it to beat time as he sang again and again the same tune with different words. The tune was *The Keel Row*, but the verses would give commentary on the voyage or on those of us aboard.

On that second day, the cook could be heard tapping a beat with his wooden foot when the *Swallow*'s only passenger emerged from his cot.

Here he comes the lubber, the lubber, the lu-bber,
Here he comes the lubber, a-puking o'er the deck.

This passenger was a Mr Satterthwaite who had some business in Dublin and was prepared to tolerate the rough conditions of the *Swallow* for a passage that cost him only half a crown, though his gullet, raw from vomit, may have regretted this choice. I myself was grateful to Natty for ensuring that our many expeditions on the jolly-boat had hardened my stomach to the nauseous motion of a small ship lying low in the water.

As I wait that morning beside the galley stove with a pail for dirty swillings from the pottage pan, I realise that I have made an appearance in the cook's song.

The Raven is a seabird, a seabird, a sea-bird,
The Raven is a seabird that nests the foremast top.

As this is sung, the African happens to pass along the other side of the galley. He catches my eye as he stoops beneath the beams of the deck-head but I look away, embarrassed. Instantly, I regret my shyness. Panic rises. Will he think me haughty? Disdainful of his lowly station or the colour of his skin? My little cowardice blooms in my mind into an almighty insult. And soon my chest is weighted with the dismal conviction that he'll never look my way again.

Later, as I stand by the stove with the crew who are lining up for mugs of almost hot pottage, the cook raises his ladle in my direction.

'Any songs have ye, laddie?'

I blink and realise that the assembled company are for the first time paying me attention. The African is there too, his gaze clear and alert in my direction and I know that that if I am to have any of these seamen's respect, I must meet this test head-on.

'Some,' I reply with forced loudness.

'Let's hear one, then.'

I take a breath. My voice is not bad, but the tender songs I love to sing with Fliss must surely lay me open to ridicule. I decide on the manliest I know, the hanging ballad sung by Poll. I cough then launch into the blood-thirstiest part that tells of the convict pushing his mistress off the cliff. My voice grows lustier as the verses get more gruesome.

At this dreadful fall, in blood she did sprawl,
And had not the power on heaven to call,
And to blacken the crime, the babe which was mine,

I could perceive stirring within her some time.

Around me, the sailors' eyes widen. Old Barnacle's eye might even be moist. I press on.

In hopes the sea would wash her away,
I hastened homeward without more delay,
But was taken soon to have my sad doom,
And must perish shamefully just in my bloom.

Apart from the slurps of pottage, the company remain silent for while. Then the cook, in his queer Manx way, says. 'The good lad you be. Is there any more?'

Heartened, I nod and take a long breath.

But oh! My God, why should my saviour die,
If not to save sinners as heinous as I?
Then come cart and rope, both strangle and choke,
For in my redeemer I still trust and hope.

With this a general murmuring and nodding goes around the company.

'Glad I am to have no wife,' says Old Barnacle wiping his eye.

'And me,' says the cook then points his ladle at the African. 'What say you, lad?'

'I?' the African replies. 'I have no wife and no opinion on the matter.'

'No?' says Old Barnacle with a toothless leer. 'I thought you lot all have two wives apiece.'

He gives a wry grin. 'At least I'm not married to the *Swallow*. Like you.'

Growling, the cook thrusts his ladle like a rapier but the company all laugh. I laugh too and meet the African's handsome gaze.

Then, later that same day he comes past me as I am re-stacking the cook's stores that have become disordered by the *Swallow*'s movement. As he is filling mugs of fresh water from the barrel, I glance at him sideways and realise that though his movements have an easy manly grace, he cannot be more than a few years older than me.

He turns to me as he replaces the barrel lid. 'Is it true, your song?'

'Aye,' I say, after a jolt of surprise. 'At least it said so on the ballad sheet.'

'A sad tale.'

'It is.'

He moves off then and after he has gone, I feel my heart racing. I know that if I have the chance again, I will speak to him with more courage.

And indeed, later that same day we are both charged with scrubbing at some stubborn tar stains at the rear of the main deck. The weather is still fair but there is an icy bite to the wind. I scrub at the boards with a bristle brush and seawater until my fingers lose all feeling.

'Coffee,' I call over to him, partly to see how he will respond.

'Aye?'

'Is this good enough?' I point with my brush at the greyish stain still on the wood.

'A bit longer at it, I'd say.'

Before he turns back, I quickly pose my question. 'Is Coffee your real name?'

He frowns but doesn't seem annoyed. 'That's what I am called.'

'Though not your proper name?'

He gives a rueful half-laugh and shrugs.

'No-one could be christened *Coffee*,' I persist.

''Tis not a matter of christening.'

'What then?'

He sighs then nods. 'My name is Josiah Bone. Jossy, if you like.'

'Jossy. Not Coffee?'

'Aye.'

'I am Kit Ravenglass.'

'I know,' he says. 'The son of Mr Henry Ravenglass of Queen Street, Whitehaven.'

'Yes. That's right.'

I look at him harder then and see beneath the new manliness that is firming his strong features, there is still an outline of the boy.

'Was it you who came to our house once, as my sister's attendant, for the Assembly Rooms ball?'

'It was.' He scrubs a little harder at the boards. 'A foul night, as I recall.'

My mind is thrust back to the front door closing behind Fliss and her boy attendant, the rain lashing at their finery.

'Do you still have your turban?'

He laughs, with a deep rumbling sound that I wish would continue. 'No, no. I had forgot they made me wear that.'

'I wished I had one. I was jealous of you.'

'Jealous?'

He looks at me, eyebrows raised and suddenly I'm embarrassed. 'You looked so fine.' I blush.

He laughs as if this is the funniest riddle he has heard in a long time. Then he blinks and his face stills to a look of concern. 'And may I, if you don't object, ask how fares Miss Ravenglass?'

'You remember her?'

'That I do.'

'She is well, thank you.'

Jossy takes a breath in and out as he nods.

'Shall I convey your compliments to her?'

His eyes widen and he shakes his head quickly. 'Oh, no, no.' Then he laughs. 'But thanks for the offer.'

Still smiling, he goes back to scrubbing but my eyes linger on his form. I can't help but admire how well his fitted short jacket and flowing breeches suit his shapely limbs. Then, realising suddenly that my stare could be interpreted as over-curious, I jerk my attention back to the tar stain. But as the voyage of the *Swallow* continued, Jossy doubtless became aware that my eyes were perpetually turning his way.

the second chapter

Everything aboard the *Swallow* changed with the weather. Late on the afternoon that we passed by the mouth of the Mersey, a vicious gale blew without warning from the west. Rain came in rods, beating against the main deck, coursing down open hatchways. The *Swallow* pounded into deep troughs between waves that were near as tall as the foremast.

Even the cook declares that he must go up to the main deck and lend as much weight to the hauling as his peg-leg will allow. I peep my head into a batter of rain above the hatchway and amidst the howling storm and the angry shouting men heaving ropes, I see Captain Power at the wheel. His countenance, beneath his dripping broad-brimmed hat, is grim but steady.

And then towering over me at the hatch is Bosun Riddle, his face enraged.

'Why are you not above? Did you not hear the captain's order for all hands on deck?'

'I was coming up, sir.'

'*I was coming up, sir.*' Through the rain, Riddle mimics me in a simpering girly whine. 'Well, get yersel' up, now. In fact, get yersel' up the mainmast.'

'The mainmast?'

'Aye. Are y' deaf?' Riddle couches down and with a swipe, knocks my skull against the ladder.

'Sir, I can't go up there, not in this.'

'Why not? Are you too much of a girl?'

'Sir?'

'We've all seen yer poncey ways.'

'I don't…'

'All that prancing and simpering. You're a disgrace. Not a sailor at all. More like a bloody woman.'

Even beneath the shivery churning of my innards, I feel a quaking which goes deeper than the effect of any heaving ship. Is this what people think of me, even grown men? That I am more girl than boy? Is everyone I ever meet laughing at me behind my back? I am filled with a sudden cold resolve to prove him wrong.

Saying nothing, I bend as steadily as the roll of the hull will allow to remove my shoes and stockings and stow them inside a coil of rope. Following Jossy's advice, I leave my long coat there too. Then I haul on to the upper deck and toward the base of the mainmast as rain whips at me from all directions.

Riddle is hard on my heels. He puts his mouth to my ear. 'Get up that mast and help reef the mainsail. Don't come down until it's tied entirely away.'

I go to the mast but even on the first rung of the rope-ladder, the lurch of the ship pitches me back to the deck. Driving me on, though, is a hot flame of rage against Riddle and a determination to prove myself a man.

Despite the slipperiness, I quickly reach the mainsail yard which is thankfully below the perilous platform of the mainmast top. I must reach out and grasp the swaying yardarm and at the same time leap my feet from the mast-shrouds to the brace rope that is strung below the wooden beam. Drenched and gasping for breath, I lean out, hoping that the yard and its ropes will swing my way. But the rope flits and flies in the gale. Any lunge I might make from the greasy mast rigging towards the yard seems as good as a dive on to the deck below.

And yet, a sailor is already at work on the yard, arms hanging over the swaying beam as he pulls up the soaking sailcloth, hand over hand, bundling it against the wooden spar and tying complicated knots at the reef points.

Suddenly, the yard swings toward me and, without proper thought, I let go the greasy rigging and stretch out my arms. There is a moment when the beam seems to wriggle under my arms and my shoeless feet kick tether-less in air. But then one toe feels the rope and somehow I am standing on it with arms draped over the yard grasping at the sail. I see now why the topmen prefer to go barefoot. Had I been wearing shoes, I'd now be dead.

'Good catch.'

This is Bride, a wiry Irish lad who scuttles up beside me. I copy his movements but despite pulling as hard as I can on the sailcloth, my efforts seem to add little. I merely cling on to the canvas and take some weight of the sail as he lashes and knots.

Soon, the sail is stowed and tied, and the Irishman jabs his thumb upwards.

'Topsail next,' he shouts.

I am aghast. 'Me as well?'

Bride grins.

I'm about to shake my head to refuse but then I see a face looking down at me from the top. It is Jossy. And what I dread even more than a fall through the rigging, is that he, like Riddle, might think me weak-limbed and cowardly or, God forbid, girly. With that thought in my head and without taking full measure of the gap, I leap toward the shrouds.

Exactly what happens next is not entirely clear in my mind. My left foot reaches the ratline then slips, toe first, to the other side and wedges itself between the cables just as a gust of wind smashes the yard into me from behind. A crack rings out loud as a gunshot.

'Jesus!' I cry.

My hands find the shrouds and somehow hold on, keeping me from falling whilst my good foot gets some purchase on a ratline. But the unnatural crunch in my other foot has already told me that any movement of it would be torture.

Bride jumps like a squirrel to the ropes beside me.

'Up y' go, boy.'

'My foot,' I say, stupidly.

'What d'you say?'

But Jossy has already descended at my other side.

'Are you hurt?'

'My ankle…'

'I will help you down.'

'No!' I protest. 'I cannot move it!'

'Neither can you stay here.' Jossy puts a hand to my shoulder and squeezes it. 'I will descend first. Lean your weight on me.'

His firm hand and strong words inject me with a fortitude I could not otherwise have summoned. Somehow with Jossy beneath me, I'm able to hop down the ratlines. And though I sometimes shout out in pain and need to rest my behind on Jossy's muscled shoulder, we gradually move down the swaying mast.

Once at the deck, Jossy shoulders me upright but as I ease weight on to my bad foot, a hammer blow of agony travels up one side of my whole body.

'Aaaaaargh!'

Riddle slaps my head. 'Stand up straight, you little molly.'

Jossy doesn't flinch but stays beside me, sturdy as a capstan on the heaving deck. 'The yard swung at his leg, mister,' he says.

Riddle spits into the gale. 'Delicate as a parson's daughter.'

'It is the ankle bone. Broken I think,' Jossy persists.

Riddle shakes his head. 'Get him from my sight.'

With my arm over his shoulder, I cling tight to Jossy as he glides me through the beating rain and closing darkness. His soothing words spoken through the howl of the wind bring me comfort like a warm stove in a cold house.

Somehow, Jossy gets me down the hatch to the lower deck. Alongside the galley, he lays me amid bundles of cordage. Gently lifting my injured leg, he packs the loose rope to wedge my raised foot so that it will stay, as far as the movement of the brig will allow, in one position. As he does this, the pain is so great I scream aloud. Jossy brings me a cup of water from the barrel and holds my head as I take a sip.

'Rest you still,' he says. 'The cook will see to you presently.'

Then he leaves me alone in the pitching, creaking hull to drift in and out of sleep.

I passed the night in a fitful sweat of short sleeps broken by the agonising grind of bone against bone in my foot. During one stab of pain, I had shamefully lost control of my bladder and started to sob. But my own water added little to the already soaking state of my clothes and the dampness of the lower deck. By morning, the rain had abated and although the swell was still high, the cook announced that it was calm enough for him to take a look at my leg.

In the grey morning light, I hear, through the chattering of my teeth, the *thunk* of a bottle being uncorked. The cook stomps to my side and holds out a dark-glassed bottle.

'There's the breakfast, lad,' he says and brings the rum to my lips.

I take a gulp, then cough and splutter most of it up. But the cook persists and soon a hot glow of liquor runs through my core.

'What will you do with me?' I ask, roused by the spirit.

'Best not to ask,' he replies.

Then, with a toothless grin he breaks into song.

'The Raven got his wing broke, his wing broke, his wi-ng broke,
The Raven got his wing broke a-flying off the yards.'

Suddenly, from nowhere, strong hands are upon me and I am being man-handled from my cordage-bed. Between them, Jossy and Bride carry me, despite my cries of *aargh!* and *no!* and *not like that!* to the carpenter's bench. Here they lay me gingerly down and the cook circles a lighted candle around my bare foot. Holding my breath, I raise my head. My ankle joint has swelled to a horrible size and the skin is turning into an artist's palette of colours.

'Now then, Raven,' the cook puts a hand to my shoulder and pushes me down against the bench, 'as we say where I come from, you must be dunnal while I see what's amiss with that foot.'

'What's dunnal?' I squeak.

'Brave, like a man.'

He gives a sideways nod at Jossy and Bride and their four strong hands pin me to the bench. The cook picks up my bad foot rotates in the air.

'Waaaaaa! Waaaaa!' I scream.

'Quiet, now,' he says, 'or the bone I'll not be hearing.'

He puts his ear closer to the excruciating grinding inside my foot.

My mouth freezes in a wide, silent scream until a lump of tarry wood is wedged inside it. The cook prods and presses the swollen flesh then lowers my leg on to my folded coat.

'Well lad, there's only one thing for it.'

Teeth clamped on wood, my eyes are saucer-wide as the cook bends to the base of the bench. And then, with a toothless grin and a flourish like a swordsman pulling a rapier from his scabbard, he holds aloft a rusty, wood-handled saw.

I stare numbly at this implement until a ring of blackness seems to close in around it. The creaking of timbers and slap of waves quieten. I am suddenly hot in every part of my body. The blackness circling the saw thickens and the muffled quietness deepens. Soon all is silence, and the saw seems to be very small object at the end of a dark tunnel. I feel myself sinking backwards into a soundless blank.

And then after a long queer dream, I awake to a sharp tugging on my leg and the sound of sawing. Slowly my eyes open. Sawdust showers over the carpenter's bench and I see that I am lying on the boards of the lower deck. And above me, the cook bends over the bench, huffing as he saws. It cannot be my leg he is working on, unless it is already made of wood.

Hardly, daring to look, I raise my head. But my right foot, though bruised and horribly swollen, is still attached to me. Perhaps the worst is still to come. Another wave of dread chills through me and a silent tear slides down the side of my face and into my ear.

Then, I feel a hand reach down from behind me and wipe the tear away with a rag. I look up and Jossy is there, his brown eyes unblinking.

'My foot...' I croak.

'Be still.' He says and gently wipes my face again.

Then the cook's hammer drops to the bench and he picks up the thing he has made.

'The ready it is,' the cook says in his singular way. 'Keep yourself dunnal, lad.'

I close my eyes, unable to contemplate the amputation that is surely coming.

'Where will you cut?' I whimper.

'Cut?'

'My leg.'

The cook cackles and shakes his head. 'I got you good and proper with that saw, didn't I, lad?'

'What?'

'A joke it be, that's all.'

'Joke? What..?'

'The perfect it worked though, didn't it?' The cackling goes on.

For a moment I am silenced by the realisation of what must pass for a joke on the Isle of Man.

'What will you do to me now?' I manage.

The cook pushes his hat up and wipes his eyes with his sleeve. 'Fear ye not, lad. The worst be done. You was passed out when the bone was set so we didn't have to waste no rum on you neither.'

'It will heal?' I manage.

'Aye. Should do. The young you be, don't you? I've had a feel while you were out for any loose chippings and there don't seem to be none. If I'm wrong, bone splinters'll poison the blood and kill ye. But if you is still alive when we gets back to Whitehaven, you'll maybes have a limp, but not worse.'

This news, though not entirely reassuring, sounds so much better than the thought of a tarred stump and a peg-leg, that I cry out with joy. But then the cook holds up the wooden item he has been cutting and hammering on the bench. It is two deal planks fashioned into the shape of an L.

'This will be your boot for what's left of the voyage. But you must not stand on it. I'll give you use of my crutch to be your other leg.' He casts an eye at the ladder hatch and lowers his voice. 'Sit you down with the leg upward as much as you can, whatever the bosun might say. I'll tell him there's mice in the sail-stores and mending to be done. Is there any use from you with a needle?'

I nod vigorously.

But my relief is too hasty, for the cook is now gathering strips of rag from a cubby hole beneath the bench and what follows is perhaps most painful of all as my broken ankle is tied into a strict right angle on the L-shaped splint. I bellow and weep and beg, no longer having the strength to pretend myself a man.

Thereafter, Jossy and Bride haul me, whimpering to the bosun's smelly berth and lay me out on his cot with my plank boot raised. Jossy puts a cup of briny water to my lips and I thank him with my eyes. As he drops the curtain across the bosun's doorway, Jossy's backward glance seems to assure me that I have a friend aboard. In the familiar fold of a bed, I fall instantly to dreamless sleep.

A rude shaking wakes me. It is Riddle.

'Don't think this gives ye a ticket to laze abed,' he says, pulling at my sleeve.

The swell beneath the hull has lessened and the light through the lower deck has faded. Is it dusk already? Trying to sit up, I lift my strapped foot but it strains against the rags that bind it to the wood and the bones grate into a sickeningly unnatural angle.

'Aaaaaargh!' I yell.

Riddle curls his lip. 'Be quiet! You little jessie… get yersel' on deck.'

I try again to rise but realise that any further motion shall likely make me piss myself.

'Sir, beg pardon but I must use the pot.'

'Must ye indeed?' He whines and mockingly waggles his head. Even in my physical distress, I wonder, painfully, if this is how I sound to others. But Riddle says no more as he reaches down under the cot and uncovers a stinking pail.

Awkwardly, I twist myself around, putting my good foot to the floor and leaving the broken one aloft on the edge of the cot. Unbuttoning my breeches, I glance up at Riddle, expecting him to quit the berth whilst I relieve myself. But he is looking on with interest. My attention is pulled then to my pizzle and the correct angle needed for a tidy report into the bucket. This is not easy. My stream is powerful and the deck, although heaving less than before, continues to rise and fall, making the pail a moving target.

But though my water splashes up against the insides of the bucket, there is hardly a drip outside it. Re-buttoning, I take some pride in my neat aim and look up at Riddle for approval. But his eyes are still on my breech flap and seem reluctant to leave it.

'Do you want me out of your bed, sir?'

His gaze comes back to mine. His face is red, though with anger or something else, I can't tell. But it stirs a recollection. For inside the bush of his beard, I suddenly see a younger, clean-shaven sailor, one whose pig-tail drapes over his shoulder as he sits on an upturned barrel and embroiders a bare-breasted mermaid on to a red waistcoat.

For the first time aboard bile rises in my gullet. So it was Riddle who mocked me even when I was a child. His nasty face has infected my most secret fancies ever since. I swallow hard and will not let the sick out of my mouth.

'Stay in it or go. But I'll be back at First Watch.'

Then he turns swiftly and quits his cabin.

For the rest of that day, the cook appears now and then with a cup of water or broth. I don't try to stand. But I'm filled with unease and I know that come the Watch bells at eight, I must have quit the bosun's cot and somehow made a bed elsewhere. The thought of moving so far appals me.

When the First Watch bell sounds, I hear the usual shunting and grunting of men coming down from the main deck and others replacing them. Light seeps around the door-curtain dulls as candles are quelled. And before I fully rouse myself to move, I hear footsteps descending from above. The curtain is pulled back and someone enters.

I raise myself to sitting. 'I'll go now, sir.'

The man does not respond. In the dimness, his wiry outline seems to fill the doorway and I know it is Riddle by the bush of his beard. Still he says nothing. As I lean myself on to my elbow and wonder how I shall haul my body to the galley, a movement starts up about his person. It is a determined fumbling as if he is rooting for something in his fob pocket. Whatever the item is, he seems to be having great difficulty in removing it.

'Sir, can I..?'

But he cuts me off with a muffled 'Quiet.'

The groping in the region of Riddle's breeches continues but more intensely. I close my eyes and ease a finger into my ear to keep out the squelchy slapping sound. As long as I stay unmoving perhaps this bodily function will come to an end without my having to see anything and only half hear it.

Then suddenly, there comes a voice, at the doorway.

'Bosun, sir.'

'What?' Riddle breathes.

'You're wanted, sir.'

It is Jossy.

'What for, damn you?'

'A light has been sighted.'

'The captain…' Riddle cannot quite finish.

'Sir, the captain has asked for your opinion on whether 'tis Holyhead, or some vessel offshore.'

'A minute…'

'He is anxious for your opinion.'

Riddle's sigh becomes a groan. 'Damn your black eyes.'

But, with a final adjustment to the front fall of his breeches, he flings back the curtain and leaves. The soft glow of a storm lantern spills into the closet. Jossy's warm features are caught in its light.

'Quickly, Kit, I'll help you to another place.'

Never had I been more heartened to see anyone. And though it was an agony to move my grating bones to a nest in the sailcloth store, the pain was almost cancelled out by the joy of hearing my name on Jossy's lips and to feel the wrap of his protecting arms around me.

the third chapter

For the rest of that displeasant voyage, I hid from Riddle in my nest amongst the spare sails. The cook gave me vegetables to peel and a needle for sailcloth repairs and if Riddle came down the galley-end of the lower deck, I'd grab a spare sail that had no need of stitching and get to work. Should he come too close, the needle would serve in my defence like a tiny cutlass. But perhaps thanks to Jossy's watchful presence, Riddle stayed away.

Despite taking the longer route that passed by Liverpool and Holyhead, we made good time to Dublin in less than ten days. At the mouth of the Liffey, Jossy came below excitedly and helped get me up to the main deck to see the distant smoky pall so vast that I sensed it must be hanging above a true metropolis. My spirits soared at the thought of sailing into such a place. But before we ever got near the city, Captain Power took a side channel and moored the *Swallow* on the muddy beach at Clontarf which became my home for the next two weeks.

At every low tide, when the *Swallow* dropped to the strand, sturdy horse-carts would pull alongside the tilted hull. Coal was then whipped from the hold with ropes and pulleys and loaded, basket by basket, into the carts. Once the hold was empty of Whitehaven coal, the process was reversed and the horse carts brought rough rocks and sand that was basketed into the hold as ballast. This small piece of Ireland was to be our only cargo on the return voyage.

For much of this time at mooring, the crew took turns to don their shore-slops and head into the city. Even Jossy went.

But I was imprisoned by my injury. When the tide was low and the *Swallow* took the ground, the precarious angle of the deck made any movement of my L-shaped splint even more treacherous. So I stayed in the rope-nest. Sometimes I was the only soul aboard and so idle that I took to embroidering a spare headsail with near-invisible flowers and fruits in white thread. I wondered what the topman would think when it was one day unfurled. Later, when I asked Jossy what he had seen of Dublin, he said only crumbling wharves and herring-shacks. But I think he was being kind.

Once the hold was full of beach, the *Swallow* set sail for Whitehaven on a journey almost as miserable as the last and when we sighted the Fire-Engine chimney at Saltom Pit, I could not help letting out a *huzzah!* By then I was getting about the decks with the help of the cook's broom but could not wait for the feel of unmoving ground. Yet I had to wait a further three days at sea with the *Swallow* anchored within sight of Whitehaven harbour whilst the whole tedious process of emptying the hold with pulleys, baskets and well-muscled arms resumed, and the weight of seashore we had took from Clontarf was tipped over the stern rail.

I spent this time looking at my home from the sea and worrying about what my father would think to my failure as a sailor. I knew that he wished me to come home enthused about the voyage and eager for more maritime adventure. But I had already resolved never to put to sea again and I told myself I would do anything at all to ensure that I never did.

Finally, on a wet December morning, the *Swallow* edged into the harbour and Jossy was sent to knock on the side-passage door at Queen Street to announce our arrival. My father came aboard the *Swallow* soon after and though I was sitting on the main deck still strapped in my splint, he hardly looked my way. Instead, he went straight to the stern to engage Captain Power in a lengthy dialogue about the price of coal. Profit always came first.

When my father finally comes across the deck toward me, my chest is pounding.

'Our Kit,' he says and shakes his head.

And I must have been a sorry sight, crumpled against the deck-rail like a street-beggar with my splint and crutch. I have no doubt about his profound embarrassment at having a son such as me.

'Your leg's broke.'

His face seems to be battling with itself.

'Yes, Father.'

He sniffs. 'Worse things happen. At sea.'

'Yes, Father.'

And with that, he turns and quits the vessel.

It is left to Jossy to bring me home and after supporting my hobbling some way along the Pier, he stops and sighs.

'Why not get on me?' His look has a mix of amusement and concern. Then he kneels down beside me. 'Get on my back, if you can.'

I blink, not quite believing this offer. But then, with some discomfort, I climb on piggy-back and circle my arms around his broad shoulders.

'Right?' He says, gently hitching his forearms beneath my knees.

'Aye,' I whisper. I have never felt quite so right before.

And so we set off through the quayside streets. There are a few jeers our way and in truth I do feel shame, but only for using my friend as a means of transport. But guilt is outdone a hundred times by the pleasure I feel in our closeness. It all I can do to resist laying my head against his strong neck to breath in the salty warmth of his skin.

'Jossy...' I whisper in his ear.

'Aye?'

He is a little breathless from his load and I am shaken from my reverie by the reality of his voice. I did not mean to ask a question, only to run his name around my mouth.

'...am I too great a burden?' I manage.

'Why no, not at all.' His words sound as smooth and warm as his skin. 'And we haven't far to go.'

We are already at the Market Place and my throat tightens for despite the pain in my foot, I wish that I might stay forever on this journey, clamped tight to Jossy, and never reach Queen Street.

But then we are entering the covered carriageway beside the house and the women are all in the yard waiting for me.

'Master Kit!' shouts Poll rushing to me and I slide from Jossy's back to be gripped by the firm hands of Poll and Aunt Ravenglass. Fliss looks on, wrapped in a blanket and biting her nails.

The women fussing, lead me off without so much as a look Jossy's way. I turn my head awkwardly back to catch his eye but he has taken off his hat and is bowing to Fliss. I try to get his attention and wave goodbye, but Fliss has him engaged in some discourse or other, and I am being clucked up the steps and into the dining parlour.

There, as I'm laid on the settle in a mound of cushions and covers, remorse strikes me. Why did I not thank Jossy, when I had the chance, for his friendship and kindness? A hot fire blazes in the grate and I am overwhelmed by the colourful comfort of a stationary room. I tell myself that once I am well enough to walk to the harbour, I will seek Jossy out. But I know very well that by then he might have already departed on another voyage. Fat tears slip down my cheek.

Fliss flusters in and takes my hand. 'Does it hurt, Kit?'

'What?'

'Your leg, of course.'

'Oh,' I say, 'yes, it does.' And then, 'what were you talking about, with the sailor?'

'This and that.'

'He's the same lad that attended you at the Assembly Rooms.'

'Is he?' Fliss says, apparently with little interest. 'Now be quiet and have your soup.'

And like a babe, I let Poll feed me with spoonfuls of my

favourite split-pea soup laden with chunks of ham shank. Before the bowl is finished, I am asleep and don't wake up until the candles are alight.

Next morning, I awake in my own bed. Fliss, draped in our father's old, flowered banyan, brings a posset for me herself.

'What was it like?' She says, sitting carefully so as not to touch my foot. *Dorinda's Gift* is in her hand.

'What?'

'The voyage.'

I shrug. 'I'm not going on one again.'

'Because of your leg?'

I take a gulp of warming posset. 'Because of everything about it.'

That was a lie, of course. There was one part of being at sea that I had liked very much. Though I was not about to tell Fliss of my fondness for Jossy.

'Shall you ever walk again?'

'Why, yes!' I cry. 'They all say so.' But the question unsettles me. 'Dorinda will confirm it, I'm sure.'

Fliss takes my cup and finds a question for the 'Finger of Fortune.' I read aloud: *Will the patient recover from his illness?* My finger hovers over the stars and my stomach gives a little leap as the starry triangle is selected. *The patient will soon recover – there is NO danger.*

I put my hand over my heart and sigh. Fliss gives me a long kiss on the cheek.

'There,' she says. 'We may trust Dorinda.'

'Aye,' I reply, a little unnerved by the power we seem to have invested in this paper pamphlet.

'I must ask her something too,' says Fliss and licks her lips.

'What?'

'This, here.'

She points to the question. *Does the person love and regard me?*

'Which person?' I whisper, but I know she means Daniel Bragg.

'Sssh!' she says, smiling.

Her finger shakes a little as it hovers over the stars and her eyes are open as it falls on to the page. Dorinda's reply is stern. *DECLINE a courtship that may be your destruction.*

Fliss's hand recoils back from the almanack as if on fire. She is quiet for a moment then swallows hard.

'It only says *may*.' Her voice is awkwardly high.

'Hmmm.' Stella, long absent, rises suddenly inside me with disapproval in her voice. 'But perhaps this person is unsuited for your affections.'

Stella and I certainly agree with Dorinda in her view of Daniel Bragg. Much as I try to copy his manly demeanour, I despise him for his snide remarks and sly ways.

Stella bats her lashes at Fliss. 'Perhaps it is time for you to cast your gaze about.'

Fliss's eyes narrow. Last time I tried to capture her attention by becoming Stella, she threw me a sneering glance and said, *are you not getting too old for that nonsense?* Which shut Stella up.

But today Stella is fearless. 'Or perhaps,' she oozes as she pats Fliss's hand, 'you must simply be patient and wait for this person to prove himself through a long sea voyage.'

We both know Daniel Bragg's aim is to gain my father's favour as a son-in-law by proving himself in the Virginia trade. And plans were already afoot for a dockyard overhaul of the *Swallow*. She would have a full scraping and caulking of the hull and new cordage throughout. And the hold was to be altered for carrying people not coal. Platforms would be erected above the level of ballast and bilge and become the home for the duration of the transatlantic voyage to poor Cumberland folk who had sold their future labour for a term of years to my father.

The cost of *Swallow*'s re-fit would be recouped when the poor folk's service was sold on to Virginian farmers by way of indentures. Further profit for the voyage would proceed from the *Swallow*'s carriage of cloth, brandy and metal goods to

Virginia, and hogsheads of tobacco on the return. And on this new venture, whilst responsibility for the safe passage of the *Swallow* would lie in the hands of Captain Power, care of the profit was to be put in the charge of Daniel Bragg.

By the end of April, the *Swallow* is newly spruced as a cargo vessel for the tobacco trade and ready to leave Whitehaven for Virginia. And on an unseasonably cold afternoon, I walked almost without a limp to witness her departure from the quayside alongside the rest of the Ravenglass household.

Despite the sharp air, Fliss wears her new spring frock of shimmering pink tabby with a gauzy muslin apron and frills of lace at the sleeve. This is not the most practical attire for a chilly afternoon on Whitehaven harbour and Poll, close behind her, fusses with the squirrel-lined cloak. But Fliss insists that she will not wear it. I know, without her needing to say, that she intends for Daniel's last glimpse of home to be herself standing, radiant, at the edge of the Tongue.

The Sugar Tongue is busy with brigs and sloops moored sometimes two-abreast on both sides of the wide stone quay. The vessels' rigging criss-crosses the dull sky and seabirds dart about the ropes like pilchards around nets. Mariners roll hogshead barrels and trundle barrows around a shabbily dressed gathering, some of them carrying bundles who stand on the Tongue beside the *Swallow*.

Seeing the brig again I cannot help but look about for Jossy. I had passed the winter in a fug of coal fires and female fussing as my ankle healed and was thankful every day for the comforts of my home compared to the hard, undulating dampness of the *Swallow*. But every day I thought of Jossy. Had he gone from the *Swallow* back to Captain Littlewood? Or was he lent out to another ship-master? The winter was rough that year, and when gales blew in from the west sometimes bringing snow, my heart ached for my friend out on the sea.

But at the Tongue, I see no sign of him amongst the crew.

Ravenglass

My father is on the deck giving his final instructions to Captain Power and Daniel Bragg. The men all look serious, but Daniel's agitation is clear from his constant picking at the cuff of his new coat. Fliss, shivering, does seem to attract his gaze.

Our party stands a little way off from the ragged group that I suppose includes kin of the passengers for the voyage. An enthusiastic response was received to my father's advertisement calling for *'any persons whatever that hath a mind to go over on a Virginia voyage as a servant indentured for a term of years,'* to apply to Captain Power aboard the *Swallow*. The captain had also paid crimp-men in the inns about the town to lure likely passengers from those drinkers who had spent their last coin on a mug of ale.

Standing apart from the miserably dressed throng on deck is tall thin woman in a close-fitting grey bonnet who has made her way to the bow and stands at the rail. Facing her on the Tongue is another female, maybe a girl, whose head is covered by a similar grey bonnet. The two females stand unmoving as they face each other.

Then there is a general commotion aboard as the crew, most of whom I know well from the Dublin voyage, set about the ropes. Bride is up on the main yards and I see the cook lope up from the lower deck. With a shout of *ahoy young Raven!* he waves his hat in my direction.

'Ahoy!' I shout back and do a little leaping dance to demonstrate the success of his bone-setting skills.

He nods with satisfaction and breaks into song though the only words I can make out are *'Swallow'* and *'…for "baccy, for 'baccy, for 'ba-ccy…'*

Much as I look, Jossy is nowhere to be seen.

My father at last quits the *Swallow* and the plank is pulled in behind him but then there is a shout of *wait awhile!* I look round and my innards leap. For Jossy is hurrying along the Tongue waving a package wrapped in hessian.

'Cook!' He shouts nearing the edge. 'Will you carry a message for me?'

The cook stumps over to the rail, the top of which is level with the tongue and cranes his neck upward.

'Coffee, lad! What have you there?'

'A package, to take to Rappahannock. Will you see to it?'

'I will. Where's it to go?'

'To the house of Mr Bone. For his cow-woman. Any by the wharf at Hobbs Hole will know it. There is a note inside with directions and a sixpence for your trouble.'

Jossy throws down the package down to him in a neat lob. 'Thanks to you, cook.'

The cook raises the package by way of acknowledgement and stumps back to the hatch.

Jossy stays on the Tongue to watch the casting off. He has not yet seen me, I think, and I am shy to speak to him in the midst of my family. I fold myself beside Fliss while Jossy to her other side seems rapt in the activity on deck. Ropes are hauled in and with a shout to the rowers on the tow-boats, the *Swallow* slides steadily away from the Tongue.

Then, at the *Swallow*'s bow the tall woman passenger lifts off her drab bonnet. She stands, hatless in a cloud of flaxen hair and stares at the lone girl on the Tongue. This girl then loosens her own bonnet and lets it fall back on the strings. It is Hannah Salkeld.

She looks even scrawnier than when I last saw her laid struggling on the floor of the Bear Mouth. Today she stands stock still, her eyes not leaving those of the hatless woman on the deck. Tears stream down both of their cheeks but neither makes a sound.

Without meaning to, I slink further behind Fliss's skirts so that Hannah will not see me. These past months, I have done my best to drive the scene at the Bear Mouth from my mind. Not only does the memory fill me shame at my cowardice in failing to protect Hannah from Natty's boys, it also brings back her disquieting words about my mother.

'Godspeed!' my father calls and all the passengers, except for the tall weeping woman, look his way.

Daniel waves his final farewell though whether to Fliss or my father I cannot tell.

Then the poor folk around us surge forward waving raggy handkerchiefs and Fliss comes perilously close to the edge of the Tongue.

'Fliss!' There is alarm in my aunt's voice. 'Have a care!'

At this, Jossy, who is standing closest, raises a protective arm in front of her stomacher to shield her from the drop. I have a sudden vision of Fliss falling into the sea and Jossy plunging in after to pull her ashore. I have no doubt that he would do it.

But Fliss steps back and nods a smile of thanks to Jossy. Slowly, slowly the *Swallow* is hauled across the harbour. Bosun Riddle is at the wheel. I shudder for the many nasty weeks at sea that lie ahead for the lonely female who is Hannah Salkeld's kin. As the *Swallow* edges past the Light-House, the woman's gaze does not leave Hannah's face.

Perhaps some indentured servants return from America to England but I have never heard of any. And to pay for this voyage and her keep as a servant, the woman must have sold her labour for a term of at least four years. Anything can happen in that length of time.

As the *Swallow* leaves the harbour and the sad throng disperses from the Tongue, Fliss finally allows Poll to put the cloak around her shoulders and my father, with an unpleasantly satisfied air, leads the way back toward the town. I hang back looking around for Jossy and suddenly he is beside me.

He wears a buff-coloured sleeved waistcoat with a long-frocked front and seems quite at ease out of his sailor's short clothes. He looks older too and has clearly passed the cusp between boy and man.

He nods a greeting and smiles. 'Your foot is healed, then.' He glances at my ankle.

'Yes.'

'The cook has many talents.'

'Indeed,' I reply, 'though singing is not one of them.'

Jossy gives a laugh. 'Nor cooking.'

I laugh too.

'You are not going with the *Swallow*?' Jossy says.

I shake my head. 'Nor you?'

'My master has hired me out to work as pot-boy to the landlord of the Indian King.'

'Would you not rather be a sailor?'

He shrugs.

As we reach the back of the Tongue. I take a last look at the *Swallow*. Only her topsails are showing beyond the main pier. And between the bustle of loading and unloading on the piers, I catch a glimpse of Hannah Salkeld. She is still at the furthest end of the Tongue and doesn't seem to have moved, not even to cover her head against the chill breeze. Despite my guilt and unease, I have a sudden urge to go to her and offer comfort. And perhaps I would have done so had Jossy not been there. My selfish desire to stay by him was too strong to resist.

'Virginia seems a long distance for the *Swallow* to go,' I say, staying in step with him as we go from sand to cobbles at the edge of the harbour.

Jossy raises his brows to consider this. 'Perhaps. Though Captain Power is an excellent master and Riddle has done the Atlantic crossing many times.'

I slide him a sideways glance as we turn toward the Market Place. 'Have you ever been to Virginia?'

'Of course.' He gives a remorseful laugh. "Tis where I was raised.'

'Ah yes, I see, in Hobbs Hole.'

He looks at me surprised.

'The packet you passed to the cook…' I say quickly.

His face relaxes and he nods. 'Three yards of yellow cambric.'

My heart drops.

'For a petticoat?' I ask, trying to keep the envy from my voice at the thought he might have a sweetheart there.

He raises one side of his mouth in a smile. 'Perhaps.'

We cross the Market Place cobbles puddled with slurry. The traders are mostly gone for the day though a stout fish-girl with a basket on her head wanders about calling *Crabs! Any Crabs!*

At the corner with Roper Street, I stop.

'I'm going that way, by Tickell Lane,' I say, but do not move.

'Right.' Jossy nods.

'Perhaps I'll see you again while you're at the Indian King.'

'Aye.'

For an instant, his expression becomes boyish and I see in my mind's eye his face shining in candlelight beneath a pink silken turban.

I have a sudden sense of teetering on a brink. For I know that this is the moment when I should walk away and have no more to do with him. If I do not, I might fall, fast and free, into an abyss. But I cannot stop myself.

'I have not yet thanked you, Jossy, for all you did for me aboard the *Swallow*.'

'What did I do?'

He seems genuinely confused and for a second I am downcast that he has no sense of having given me his special attentions.

'You helped me with my leg, and…' I wonder whether to mention his help in rescuing me from Riddle's foul habits but I lack the courage, '…and on the yards.'

'Not well enough on the yards, I fear!'

'Well,' I persist. 'Your presence gave me comfort and I'm grateful to you.'

He puts one foot forward and sweeps back his arm in an elegant bow. 'Your servant, Master Kit.'

There is the faintest hint of mockery in his politeness but I return the courtesy with my best bow.

'Can I repay your kindness?'

He smiles gently and I am dazzled anew by the beauty of his features.

'There is no need.'

'Is there nothing I can do for you?'

A young sailor who passes by nods a brief greeting to Jossy and I feel a flash of senseless jealousy. But Jossy's gaze returns to me.

'Well, there is something, in fact, although I am loath to ask.'

'Please say.'

He laughs and shakes his head. 'No. Maybe it is too much.'

'Please. Anything.'

He laughs again and raises his eyebrows. 'Anything? You may regret that.'

'I won't.'

'All right then. I may be ashore in Whitehaven a good while. The *Resolve* is in the shipwrights' dock and could be there until winter. Captain Littlewood may send me to sea on another vessel but for now, I'll be ashore in a long coat at the Indian King. And what I would dearly like…'

'Yes? What?'

'Is to be better able to read.'

'And… you want me to teach you?'

'If it would not be a great trouble to you. I partly know my letters already.'

'It would be no trouble to me at all.'

Here I have to stop myself whooping with delight and throwing my hat into the air.

'Thank you, Master Kit.'

'Kit alone will do.'

He gives another of his elegant bows. Here I am glad to turn away from him so that I may hide the idiotic smile that is spreading across my face.

the fourth chapter

And so, during the summer that I was thirteen year old, I became a teacher to my new friend. It was not hard for us to meet. My father did not send me any more to school but kept me in the counting-house where I did the work that had been formerly Daniel Bragg's. I learnt to keep the ledgers in balance, account for the cargoes and bargain for ships' supplies. But, when there was not over-much to do, it was easy to slip out in the mornings and meet Jossy.

If the weather was fine, we would wander along Roper Street to King George's Church and sit in the paddock behind the churchyard. As is the way with boys, we often did not speak of much except what ships were in the harbour and who brawled with who in King Street. I would bring a book with me or else a two week-old copy of the *Newcastle Courant*. Jossy could read a good deal before we started and very soon there was not much for me to do but help him sound out unfamiliar words in the reports of naval skirmishes and horses races, and the notices of rewards for runaway apprentices and strayed dogs.

On a bird-sung morning in July I brought, for a change, *Dorinda's Gift*. Jossy had not before seen an almanack for ladies and was full of interest. Climbing over the churchyard wall, we sit with our faces facing into the sunlight. The Lowther mansion squats in the hazed distance and in the paddock before us, two hares stand on hind legs, their black-tipped ears twitching as they begin to spar. As I flick through the well-thumbed pamphlet, past the saints' days and sunrises, markets and royal birthdays.

Jossy stops me when he sees a page of riddles.

'Let me try one,' he says and reads aloud.

'These have not any skin nor flesh nor bone,
But yet have fingers and thumbs of their own.'

I know the answer because I have read this page many times.

'Do you know what it is?' I ask him.

Jossy replies without hesitation. 'Gloves.'

I bump the grass with my fist and laugh. 'How did you get it so quick?'

He smiles and shakes his head as if the answer were as glaring as the Light-House on a winter evening. I glance up and let my eyes linger upon him for as long as I can without his noticing. It has become my habit to take in one exquisite detail at a time. On this occasion it is his eyelashes which curl more perfectly than any English eyelash could.

He turns to the page headed *Monthly Charts* and frowns. Little crosses are inked at four-weekly intervals in Fliss's hand. I have a notion of what these may indicate and so I lean over and quickly turn the pages.

'Here, look, you should ask something of *Dorinda's Finger of Fortune*. Read a question out and Dorinda will supply an answer.'

Jossy's brows knit further as he considers the possibilities on the page.

'Have you chosen?' I ask.

He gives a bashful smile and reads. *'Shall I be married?'*

'All right,' I say, forcing a laugh and lean a little closer toward him. 'Close your eyes then let your finger fall upon the stars.' He doesn't seem to mind that our heads are almost touching.

'You will marry but not for MANY years,' Jossy reads and seems surprised by this answer which fills me with relief.

'Do you have a sweetheart in Virginia?' I venture.

'No!' He pulls his head back in consternation. 'What makes you think that?'

I feel myself blushing at the thought of the hessian-wrapped package now sailing on the *Swallow*. 'The three yards of yellow cambric…'

'Oh yes.' He gives a chuckle. 'For my nurse.'

'Your nurse?'

'My only kin in the world. Though I have not seen her since Mr Bone sold me to Captain Littlewood. I hope she is still living and receives my gift.'

A sour taste rises in my throat. 'He sold you?'

Jossy's eyebrows rise. 'Of course.'

I blink, dumbfounded. For until this moment, I have considered the purchase and sale of Africans only as a matter of price and profit the same as any other cargo. I once asked my father, in order to rile him, if it was not cruel to chain the Africans aboard the *Resolve* and take them from their kin. He gave me a long, chary look and said it was most certainly not, for these people were slaves in their own lands too and treated far worse there than they would be in Barbados. And, in British lands, they also had the possibility of turning to God. This was an odd thing for my father to say as he had little truck with religion himself, but I had no counter to his argument. Until now.

I look into Jossy's eyes and imagine him a little boy.

'And… your mother?' I croak.

'I never knew her. Mr Bone's cow-woman did her best to raise me after I came to the farm as an infant.'

'But where were you born?'

'I have no idea.'

'Not in Africa then?'

He shrugs.

'And what became of your mother?'

Jossy shrugs again.

I sigh and shake my head at the sad turn of our talk. 'Then we have something in common,' I say, 'for I never knew my mother neither.'

'Ah,' Jossy nods. 'Did she die when you were a babe?'

'Aye. But I know nothing more than that. Not how she died nor where is her grave.'

Jossy is quiet for a while. Then he says, 'I imagine my mother's grave to be at the bottom of the ocean.'

'Oh! How is that?'

'I have seen for myself how things work on a slaver.'

'Was she aboard a slaver?'

'I've always thought that, though I've no way of knowing.'

For a long moment Jossy frowns at the distant fell tops, luminous in their summer green. How I yearn to reach out and cover his hand with my own. Would he shake off such a girlish gesture? And how can I, whose father is part-owner of a slaver, presume to offer any sympathy?

But Jossy turns to me and smiles. 'Say, Kit,' he asks. 'Will you not try your finger with Dorinda?'

'All right,' I manage.

My eyes flit over the questions. '*Can I rely upon this person?*' I read, in a sudden surge of boldness.

Jossy's eyes narrow. 'Which person?'

'I shall not jinx the answer by saying,' I reply coyly, but then glow at Dorinda's reply. '*This person exceeds ALL others in every respect.*'

'Good answer!' Jossy laughs.

And I have to peel my dazzled gaze away from his face.

For the rest of that summer, whilst the *Resolve* was in the shipyard and Jossy heaving barrels at the Indian King, I became more familiar with the details of my father's business. So when Yorkshire pack-horse men began to deliver to Queen Street great quantities of perpetuana cloths, and grooved iron bars, as long as a man, came in from Furness, I realised that another Guinea voyage was approaching for the *Resolve*. A sort of foreboding then descended.

One day in August, when we took delivery of a load of copper bars from a Swansea sloop, and seeing an opening for argument, I asked my father what was the purpose of so much raw metalwork.

'It has become the most reliable currency for the Guinea Coast,' he replied. 'They have a constant need for raw metal that can be melted down and fashioned into tools and knives by the native blacksmiths.'

'And the Halifax worsteds? Surely it is too hot there for woollen coats?'

'Cloth too can act as money.'

I thought then of Jossy's yellow cambric for his nurse. Perhaps it was not to be made into a petticoat but traded for food.

'Father?'

'Aye, son?'

'Is it Christian to profit from the buying and selling of people?'

He stops and looks at me. We are in the strong-room which, with its thick sandstone walls, always stays cool. But father has grown hot in assisting with the carrying in of copper and so has removed his wig and coat. We have moved casks and chests and bundles to make space on the floor for the half-tarnished copper bars. My father's face has reddened. Although too round to be called handsome, his countenance has a strength and openness that encourages familiarity and trust. But now his look hardens as he readies for a fight.

'Of course it is Christian. Look at yon holier-than-thou dissenters, the Lutwidges and Milners. Are they not the richest in the African trade?'

'But how can it be right...'

His eyes narrow. 'Has someone been feeding you stories?'

This seems an odd riposte.

'Who do you mean?'

'Never mind.' My father's tone softens. 'You surely know, Christopher, that the slaves are fed and clothed by their masters. They do not starve as paupers here might. And well you know that a share of my profit from the trade goes toward relief of Whitehaven's poor.'

'But many Africans die on the passage.'

'As do some of the crew.'

'But there are mothers and children amongst the Africans…'

My father clangs a metal bar onto the pile. 'I have told you before the good reasons why this trade has grown up. Africa is awash with slaves. In fact, it is a country suffering from an excess of people because the men take so many wives. Why should not some of these excess souls go over to help work the empty lands in the Americas? Britain suffers because too many of our own working people have been tempted away to the colonies.'

The thrill of argument spurs me on. My father has never seemed more aggravating. 'And is not the *Swallow* profiting from this same movement of English people abroad to Virginia?'

'Enough, boy.' He stands straight and looks me for an unnerving minute. Then he shakes his head. 'You are too much like your mother.'

At this, I freeze, astonished at words *your mother* emerging from my father's mouth. It is the first time in my life that I have ever heard him mention her. I want to ask him what exactly has brought her likeness into his mind. Is it my dislike of the slave-trade? Or that I find him so aggravating? But only one question rises to my lips.

'Father?'

'Yes?'

'Did my mother try to kill me?'

His face is blank for a moment. Then his eyes narrow.

'Who has said this to you? Someone in our household?'

'No!'

'Or on the *Swallow*? Not that Salkeld girl…'

'No.'

I try to keep conviction in my voice though I feel it fading. 'Who then?'

'I… I, a lad I met in the street…'

My father shakes his head. He clearly knows I am lying.

'You must shut your ears to scurrilous talk about our family.'

He places a hand on my shoulder and I try not to shrink from its weight. 'Listen, Christopher. I'll not have this issue of the African trade come between us. I know there is much in it that is not pleasant. The risks are great and the trader must have a firm mind and a strong stomach.' He looks at me harder, with a deep intent. 'Taking a part in this trade is the truest test of a proper man, a man such as I want you to become.'

With this, my father turns back to counting the copper bars and a cold wave cascades down my spine. I realise that if sailing on a slaver is to be the test of my manhood, I'll never be a proper man in his eyes.

Only when my father has quitted the ware-house for the ale-house do I realise that he didn't once deny the truth of my question about my mother. I resolve to ask Fliss what she knows and not again to be fobbed off and silenced. Though when I find her later in the best parlour seeming idle and morose I fear my interrogation will only lower her spirits further.

Her low mood, I have no doubt, stems from the continuing absence of Daniel Bragg. An outward voyage to Virginia is reckoned to be six weeks and the return, with a fair wind, perhaps less. But the length of time needed for merchant trading once ashore is unpredictable. Daniel Bragg had been tasked to find Virginia planters willing to purchase the indentures of the *Swallow*'s passengers and to sell him tobacco bales in return. The *Swallow*, being a new visitor to the Rappahannock, lacked an existing local agent who could ease the to and fro of trade. And though my father's bills of exchange were drawn on reliable bankers in Liverpool and Newcastle, the planters needed to be convinced of their dependability. Much about these transactions was based on trust. And a cocksure Northern lad of not yet twenty year old did not seem, even to me, to be the best sort of person to gain their confidence.

But the *Swallow* has not yet been gone a three-month. So no one is allowing themselves to worry about the many accidents of weather, waves or poor navigation that could cause a ship never to be heard of again. No one, perhaps, except Fliss.

A gloomy romance, *Fantomina*, lies open on the padded settle beside my sister as she stares blankly at the window.

'Have you no stitching to do?' I ask opening the lid of the workbox.

'What?' She looks up. Her eyes are hooded and her fair skin has become sallow.

I flick vaguely though the trays of raw buttons and threads. 'I thought you were working a linen panel with yellow silks?'

'Hmmm. It's there.'

She points lazily to a pile of linen pieces on the carpet. Fingering through them, I pull out the partly worked length and smooth it over her lap.

The various stitches are all in same glossy saffron-coloured silk. Couched outlines are filled with satin stitch creating a pattern of interlocking leaves and floral arabesques. I tell Fliss I have never seen work so fine, though in truth, the use of a single colour makes the effect too restrained for my liking.

'What is it for, this panel?' I ask.

Fliss shrugs. 'A cushion, perhaps?'

'Oh? It looks more like the front of a waistcoat.'

She shoots me a guarded look and I know that I am right. A churn in my stomach tells me without any room for doubt that the saffron-silk waistcoat will be a homecoming gift. The thought of Daniel Bragg wearing it hardens my heart.

'Fliss?'

'Hmmm?'

'Father spoke to me earlier… of our mother.'

A spark comes into her eye. 'What of her?'

'Well, nothing. Except he said that I was too much like her.'

She snorts. 'You are not.'

'How so?'

'You are honest and true.'

Her meaning thumps into me. 'And she was not?'

'She wore a mask that was loving and kind but it concealed her true purpose.'

'What purpose, Fliss? Did she... did she try to hurt me?'

'You?' Fliss gives a harsh laugh and her hand goes to the ribband across her neck. Then she shakes her head. 'Don't ask. 'Tis better not to know.'

'Why, Fliss? It's not fair that you know about her and I don't, just because you're older.'

My sister looks at me then with a straight hard stare, her eyes aflame. 'You wish to know what she did? Well, then,' she pulls at the long-tailed bow across her neck and the silk ribbon falls away. 'This. This is what she did.'

I have seen the scar before but only fleetingly. Now it stands prominent, a red and white weal across the whole width of my sister's neck.

'On purpose?'

Fliss re-ties the bow behind her neck. 'It was hardly an accident.'

'What happened?'

She takes a long juddering breath. 'I can't speak of it. Even if I wanted to. My tongue will not move through the words.'

Her head is lowered and her eyes sorrowful again. I go to the settle and kneel beside her, resting my head on her knee. She strokes my hair and we do not say more. But I'm suddenly sensible of the shadowy presence of a tall, fair woman in plain dress who hovers, silent but ever present, at the edge of both our minds.

the fifth chapter

In spite of the many disasters that could have befell her, the *Swallow* returned from Virginia five months after her departure with a healthy crew and a profit that Daniel Bragg proclaimed a triumph though I estimated it could not be more than £80.

Masters had been found for all the surviving indentured passengers and a decent price obtained for the small outward cargo of window glass. The cash proceeds of these sales had been ploughed into tobacco, but as expected, additional purchases by bill proved hard to come by. And then, on arrival back in Whitehaven it was found that faulty cooperage had allowed water into two of the half-ton hogsheads and the valuable tobacco pressed inside was partly ruined.

Worse still, a violent storm on the outward journey had ripped apart the mainsail and several of the topgallants so bad that they could not be repaired. Captain Power would not countenance a departure without a replacement of the spare sails in the hold and sailcloth in Chesapeake had proved eye-watering dear. Near £20 was spent on spare sails and other necessaries for the *Swallow*'s return.

So the true profit was hardly more than a good coal run to Dublin. I wondered whether the unprepossessing outcome of this Atlantic voyage would persuade my father to rip out the platforms from the *Swallow* and return her hold to coal. This would certainly be less costly and risky than making her into a slaver. But it was not in my father's nature to take the easy way.

I confide all this to Jossy on a rainy morning late in October, when I meet with him in a covered place by the smiths' yards on the Steer. A copy of the *Newcastle Courant* is in my hands but this is the only pretence that our meeting is a lesson. Jossy could always read well enough and I had little to teach him. When I suggested instructing him in nautical calculation it turned out he knew the equations better than I. He knew the full workings of a Quadrant too, which was further than I had got with scholarly seamanship at Natty's Academy.

From the Steer we can see across the harbour to where the *Resolve* is moored afloat at the Countermole. Men move about the deck and the yards and I guess that they are rigging the new cordage for which my father has just paid out almost £67. By now, I know enough about my father's finances for the thought of this expense to give my chest a tug of unease. And the impending departure of the *Resolve* weighs ever heavier in my thoughts because I know that when she sets sail for Guinea, Jossy will be aboard. A glance from the vessel to my friend knits tighter the hard knot of yearning in my chest.

'Would you not rather stay in Whitehaven than go with the *Resolve*?' I ask him, unable to resist spilling out the sadness inside me.

Jossy glances at me then shrugs. I know him well enough by now to sense that if he had the freedom to do so he would answer *yes*. But he cannot, and so he is vexed with me for asking the question. The heaviness in my chest presses me onward.

'You could remain at the tavern over winter.'

'Kit.' He turns his head to look at me straight. 'You know I can't.'

'Why not?'

'Because Captain Littlewood is my master and he wants me aboard the *Resolve*.'

'But you should have a choice, shouldn't you? How long have you been in his service?'

'It is not a case of time served. I am no apprentice, as you can well see.'

He spreads his arms to indicate the colour of his skin. A tide of sad longing sweeps through me.

'But you are not his slave.'

'What am I then?'

'You cannot be a slave. You are in England.'

Jossy gives a tinny laugh.

'It's not a jest,' I say crossly. 'My father insists that liberty is the sacred right of all King George's subjects. This is the benefit of our protestant monarchy. English laws will not support slavery.'

Jossy raises his eyebrows high and puts his head to one side. 'Whatever white people call it, as 'prentice or slave I am bound to my master forever.'

'What do you mean, *white* people?'

Jossy smiles wryly. 'It is what the English are called in America and Barbados.'

'I am not white.' I chuckle and look at the colour of my hand for reassurance.

He puts his clenched fist next to mine. 'If I am black, then you are white.'

I blink as I try to take this in. 'But you could try to escape.'

'From *White*haven?' he says, with irony.

'Why, yes,' I say though my voice falters.

Jossy snorts. 'My master would put up a large reward with the justices to find me. And how many other black men d'ye reckon there are in Cumberland? How far do you think I would get?'

Tears threaten to well behind my eyes and I grasp at any line of reasoning with him. 'I have heard it said that once baptised, even Africans cannot be held as slaves. I could take you to King George's Church and instruct the parson to receive you into the faith.'

At this, Jossy reaches out to me. And with a swooping leap of my heart, I feel him lay the strength of his warm hand over my cold thin one.

'My friend,' he says with a rueful smile, 'I am more than grateful for your concern. But I must tell you that I was baptised some years ago and it has made not an ounce of difference to my situation.'

I hang my head and feel the shame of a heavy tear slip down my cheek. He pats my hand, and with a jollity that only makes me sadder, he goads me to open the *Newcastle Courant*.

'Come,' he says, 'what sort of teacher are you that will not hear me read?'

His eyes skim the page, and he reads out a report. The words, said aloud, have a power to chill the blood.

'*This day War was proclaimed against Spain. His Majesty's messengers were dispatched with the Proclamation to all the great towns of England and Scotland... We hear that two Men of War, two* ... what is this word?

'Bomb-Ketches.'

'*...two Bomb-Ketches and fireships are to sail forthwith to the West-Indies... In the King of Spain's Dominions, they work without ceasing in fitting out Privateers and sing Te Deums for the taking of English Prizes ...*'

Jossy continues reading without error. But the account of an impending naval conflict in the seas around Barbados only magnify my swell of anxiety about the coming voyage of the *Resolve*.

In the days leading up to her departure, I loiter about the Market Place and harbour hoping to see Jossy, and my stomach sinks as I meet him coming up Roper Street wearing his short sailor's jacket and carrying a sail-cloth bundle.

'Jossy!' I hail him casually as if the meeting is by chance.

He raises a hand and comes over. I suspect he can tell from my shivering that I have been waiting for him.

'Are you away to sea?' My voice is shaking.

He nods.

'I hope you will keep up your reading whilst aboard,' I manage.

'I'll try.' He nods. 'With whatever matter I may find.'

'Or with this?'

Clumsily, I pull out from under my coat a leather-bound volume that I have grabbed from Fliss's chamber and open the title page.

'*Love in Excess or the Fatal Enquiry, a Novel*,' Jossy reads. His face clouds. 'Does this belong to you?'

'My sister. But she has read it many times.'

'Does she know that you are offering it to me?'

I frown. This seems an odd and somewhat rude response. 'She will not mind. Should she miss it, I'll buy her Mrs Haywood's new work instead.'

Jossy shakes his head. 'I can't take it from you, Kit.'

'Why not?'

'Your sister might think ill of me.' His expression lightens. 'And besides, on board it would be damaged by water and salty air.'

'Oh. I see.' I push the book back under my coat.

Jossy touches his hat. 'Well. Good-bye, then, Master Kit.'

For a moment I search his eyes and try to convey the anguish threatening to overwhelm me.

My gaze drops to the wet ground. 'Good-bye.'

As he turns to go, I am so overcome with the dread of never seeing him again that I reach out and touch his shoulder but then try, at the last minute, to disguise this as a manly backslap. My hand is too uncertain, though, and the gesture seems more like an assault. For a second, Jossy looks back at me perplexed. And that expression is his last that I see.

Straight away, the shame I felt at my pathetic parting gesture caused angry tears to wash down my face. Hurrying away from the Market Place, I kept walking out of town along the Egremont road almost to the Bottle Works, weeping all the way. When eventually I got home, the *Resolve* was Africa-bound. I replaced the novel in Fliss's chamber without her noticing it had ever gone.

My sister did not seem much cheered by Daniel's return.

There was already talk of him leaving again on the next voyage of the *Swallow* so she was no doubt dreading a further separation. I imagined that this was why yellow silk arabesques were appearing more rapidly on her white linen panel.

'That is no cushion panel, is it?' I ask her as we sit by the window in the best parlour taking the best of the thin light from a January afternoon. 'Is it not a waistcoat?'

She looks up at me through her eyelashes and I know I am right. I almost ask who it is for when it hits me then that this would make very fine attire for a bridegroom, and the most likely wearer would be Daniel Bragg. Perhaps there could be a wedding even before the *Swallow* departs.

My heart skitters at this thought and I try a roundabout enquiry to find out more.

'Has Aunt Ravenglass had a reply from Mrs Sadler at Kendal?'

Fliss's needles darts into a yellow flame-stitch carnation. The thread is made suddenly golden by a flash of late winter sunlight. 'What?'

'Did our aunt not write to that lady last month about her son?'

Fliss, puts down her sewing and looks at me with amusement. 'You think this is a gift for young Mr Sadler, do you? A suitor I have not seen nor even corresponded with?'

'Our aunt has heard very good things about him.'

Fliss snorts. 'Our aunt is ever the optimist.'

'Is that not how matches are made?' I continue a little shame-faced.

'Not if they are love-matches.' Fliss sighs as she goes back to her work. 'And anyway, our aunt's approach will come to nothing.'

'Why?'

'Because the gossip about our family always precedes us.'

'What gossip?'

She sighs and looks away. Her fingers stroke the ribbon at her neck.

'From that first night at the Assembly Rooms I knew how

it would be.'

Her despondency alarms me and Stella sneaks into my voice. 'If tempted to a lowly match, you should not be hasty, dearest.'

Fliss puts her head to one side and sighs. 'I shall be nineteen this year, Kit. If I don't marry soon, father will send me husband-hunting in Chester or York. And I couldn't bear it.'

What she really means is that she could not bear to marry anyone except Daniel Bragg. The thought fills me with vexation.

'Perhaps an excursion would do you good.' Stella becomes forceful. 'And the best men are not to be found in Whitehaven.'

Fliss tuts. 'What about you?'

'I'm not a man.' Stella titters.

'You soon will be.'

'No.' Stella is determined. 'I won't!'

Though how I could become anything else, I couldn't say.

After this conversation, I should not have been surprised by the events of the following Shrove Tuesday. For that year, though it seemed an extravagance given the state of his ledger books, my father endowed the town's Shrovetide game with ten barrels of strong ale and a ball made by Moorhouse the chandler from bridle leather and horsehair.

The February Tuesday dawned crisp and blue, and not long after the first pancakes of the day had been eaten, crowds gathered in the Market Place. Our ball game is played every year between shipwrights and quarrymen and is famous in the tradition of sports without rules. The object was to 'hail' the ball and thereby get to keep it, but exactly how this 'hailing' was done remained mysterious. The hailing place for the shipwrights was the harbour wall while that for the quarrymen was the back of the last house on Swing-Pump Lane which is built into the cliff at the southern edge of the town.

And so, the game was a battle of land against sea. Sailors, fishermen and harbour-porters piled in behind the shipwrights, whilst farm-lads, shopmen and miners did their damnedest to hail the ball for the quarrymen. My father's heart lay with the sea, and although it had been years since he joined in the game himself, there was quickness in his step as he carried the new ball toward the Market Place. My own feet dragged for I hated Shrove Tuesday more than any other day of the year, and especially now that I was instructed to take part in the horrid game myself. The previous year, my broken ankle had provided an excuse that was genuine. This year, being tall for my thirteen years and in rude health, I could not escape it. Though to me there seemed no more displeasant a place than the inside of a scrum of sweaty men chasing a stuffed ball.

This ball rides proudly on my father's outstretched hand. The buff leather is painted with a red inscription of the year; *1740,* and what looks to be *R & R*. I wonder why there are two R's. Is my father honouring me with an initial? But as we reach the Market Place and my father plants himself in front of the ale barrels, I realise my mistake. Fliss stands to one side of him and Daniel Bragg the other. The smug grin across Daniel's face should alone have indicated to me what was about to happen next.

To some cheering, my father climbs up upon the trestle between his barrels that are lined up on their sides and ready to pour.

'This Shrovetide, the ball has been painted to commemorate a grand happening.'

I wince the coarseness of voice. 'Which is,' he continues with flattened Cumberland vowels, 'the betrothal of my daughter Felicity to my associate in trade, Daniel Bragg.'

As if rehearsed, Fliss and Daniel both take a step forward with a curtsy and a bow to the crowd. A cheer goes up though I imagine it is only for the prospect of toasting the happy couple with ale. My father leans down then and hands the ball to Daniel. As he does so I see my mistake. It is *B & R* that is painted on the leather. *Bragg & Ravenglass.*

Dizzy with dismay, I clasp the edge of the trestle. Daniel is not merely about to take my sister from me but also any place

I might hope for in my father's business. He is, in fact, the son that my father should have had.

Still holding the ball, Daniel unbuttons his coat and waistcoat and passes them insolently, I feel, for Poll to hold. Then in his freshly pressed white shirt and black breeches he steps toward the heave of men in the centre of the Market Place.

Pock-marked and wigless, the ball players have become a single writhe of toothless mouths and elbows. All are hard muscled and rough-skinned, and they would happily commit murder to get their hands on the ball.

Daniel beams as he takes the painted ball in both hands, turns his back to this mob and throws it blindly backwards over his head. A cry goes up from the players and the game is underway, though the ball has disappeared into the seethe of men. Daniel hurries to the bellowing scrimmage, and at the edge of it, he looks back and beckons me in.

'Hey, Kit, come on! Come here with the men.'

And I see that apart from my father, everyone around me is female.

'Aye lad, get along,' says my father, waving me onward.

Refusing to remove my coat or hat I edge reluctantly toward the tight pack of ball players. I cannot bear to touch any of their groggy shirts or stained waistcoats and so I loiter at their edge biting my nails. Then, from the dark forest of stumpy ragged-stockinged legs, the ball rolls out straight towards me.

'Grab it, quarryman!' someone shouts.

The ball is right by my feet. No-one else in that instant might pick it up more easily. Yet I cannot bring myself to touch nor even kick the nasty thing.

'Kit! The ball, Kit! Lob it to the harbour!'

It is my father, still standing on the trestle for the best view. But I am too slow. A hulking, wagon-way carter has pushed me aside and hoicked the ball toward the inland end of the Market Place. The scrimmage breaks then into a stampede of running and pushing toward Swing-Pump Lane. I can run faster than any of them but I hang back. And as I turn, I catch my father's clamp-lipped head-shake and I know, with the nasty clench of certitude in my stomach, that whatever I might do in my life, I will never be more to him than a disappointment.

The game continues until after dark and although Daniel Bragg is not the one to hail the ball at the harbour wall, he is in the thick of play until the end. His voice is loudest amongst the *huzzah's* that signal a shipwrights' victory. Fliss is in the yard to greet his return with a fresh shirt and a mug of ale. I watch them from the window of the indoor kitchen as lantern-light glints in Fliss's eyes. Something undoable has changed in her, I feel, though I can't quite decide what it is. I have no doubt that my sister's fate is now entwined entirely with that of Daniel Bragg and whatever he does will rebound directly on her.

the sixth chapter

Once the *Swallow* was hauled into the shipwrights' yard, the work dragged on through spring and into early summer. In addition to the usual refurbishments for a long voyage, the fresh sailcloth and cordage and the re-pitching of the hull, there were other more specific works required for her new purpose for, despite the mounting costs, my father was set on making her into a slaver.

During this time, Daniel Bragg re-installed himself in the counting-house. He was insufferably puffed up on the glory of his £80 profit from Virginia and his betrothal to Fliss even though my father had decreed the marriage could not take place until after Daniel's return from a Guinea voyage.

Daniel had strong views about the *Swallow*'s preparation for this voyage and my father seemed stupidly amenable to his outlandish suggestions for cargo. Daniel declared that the Africans were interested only in novelties and persuaded my father to invest in several expensive mechanical toys; a monkey that played a tiny drum and a duck that quacked and then shat itself. Daniel declared that these would find a ready market amongst the kings of the Guinea coast. I tried to reason with my father that these costly, fragile items were too great a risk, but he replied that Daniel had successfully sold window glass across the Atlantic, though even I, a thirteen year old boy, could see that selling building materials to Virginian farmers was a vastly different enterprise to persuading the tribal headmen of the Gold Coast to buy a mechanical shitting duck.

For me, the *Swallow*'s departure could not come soon enough. Once she had cleared Whitehaven for Africa, we would not see Daniel Bragg again for over a year. Perhaps, with luck, he would never return.

And so, being tasked with a message for Captain Power and eager to hasten the departure of the *Swallow*, I run all the way to the Sugar Tongue. The work on the brig is almost complete and she is greatly changed from the grimy collier on which I had tried and failed to be a mariner. The main deck, being scrubbed, painted and varnished now has the gay look of a royal barge and a small cannon has been installed at the bow with a hatch beneath the rail.

The cook hails me as I cross the plank. 'Young Raven!'

I pull at my hat-brim. 'Is the master in his cabin?'

'Aye, lad. What ye be wanting of him?'

'The answer to a question from my father.'

'Is it about water?'

I frown. 'No. At least I don't think so. My father wants to know how many bushels of horse-beans are needed as feeding for the cargo.'

The cook shakes his head. 'The water's the worry. Let me be showing you how things are set up below.' He flicks a glance over his shoulder. 'Say you not that this comes from me, mind, but they is not set up aright.'

'How so?'

'Casks, laddie, casks!'

I have no notion of what he means but follow him down the hatch.

The lower deck is also brighter and cleaner than I have ever seen it. There is a new galley stove and beside it a separate brick hearth. Upon this sits a wide copper pan which, I know, is for cooking up the horse-bean slush to feed the Africans during middle passage. The cook thumps over to the lower hatch and I follow warily as he grapples his way down a newly fixed ladder into the hold.

Previously, I had only seen coal enter and exit from this hatch, and the faint odour of coal dust still lingers. But otherwise the hold is transformed by a wooden platform built over bottom of the hull. This is covered by ironmongery. And though I have seen the orders and bills to the smiths, my heart gives a hard beat when I behold what their cruel handiwork comprises. The wooden platform is completely obscured by an array of heavy metal chains and sharp-edged shackles.

A dreadful thought comes to me.

'Is this the only platform?' I ask the cook.

'What's you on about boy?'

'We ordered chains for one hundred and fifty slaves. They can't all be accommodated on this platform.'

'Where's else would they go? Down in the bilges?'

'But how could a hundred and fifty people travel in this space?'

The cook looks blank. 'Some of they will be bairns, I reckon, so they'll take up less space. And the bigguns'll have to sit upright. Or lie one atop the other.'

I stand, looking at the platform, trying to imagine so many human beings in this cramped space. And in my mind's eye I see among them a young woman with Jossy's eyes and an infant at her breast.

'Anyways, boy, look at this.'

The cook pulls me to the edge of the platform and points to a sort of trough edged with a wooden lip and filled with gravel. Placed inside the gravel are around twenty lidded water casks.

'What?' I ask.

''Tis not enough. Even for the crew alone that is not enough in the tropics. You must tell your father to buy more casks or none of his cargo and likely few of his crew will reach Barbados.'

'It is up to Captain Power to ask not me.'

The cook clears his throat and spits. 'Power's never been south of Lisbon. Even Virginia were too hot for him. He's got no notion what it will be like.'

'And you have?'

'Oh aye. I been to the Gambia River afore. My leg's still there.'

'Oh.' A tremor goes through me as I remember him holding a saw over my broken ankle. 'Well, I'll mention it to my father.' But I am already climbing the ladder to be away from that horrible hold as fast as I may.

As I suspected he would, my father said 'no' to more casks. He had already paid a cooper's bill for near £39 and was loath to spend more. When I asked him about drinking water, my father said he had worked out the number of casks that the *Swallow* required based on provision aboard the *Resolve*. The *Swallow* was a smaller vessel and required less. Even horse-beans, of which Captain Power had requested two hundred and fifty bushels, was penny-pinched to two hundred.

To me it seemed impossible that a modest vessel like the *Swallow* could safely navigate the poorly mapped shores and colossal waves of the great ocean, let alone fill her hold to bursting with shackled Africans. Disease and starvation seemed inevitable, for the crew as well as for the human cargo.

Yet Daniel Bragg was as avid as my father for the venture to begin. My father was increasingly anxious to recoup his investment as his credit began to tighten, while Daniel Bragg no doubt believed the voyage would secure his fortune and his marriage to Fliss. Even Fliss seemed eager for the *Swallow*, with Daniel upon it, to leave. She must have realised that a sooner departure would bring a swifter return. And she did not go down to the Tongue to watch Daniel set his face to the sea as the *Swallow* glided past the Light-House out of Whitehaven harbour. Perhaps the length of the impending voyage would have made this particular farewell too painful.

After the *Swallow*'s departure, my father fell into a type of leisure that veered toward melancholy. He stayed up very late drinking either at the Indian King or closeted on his own, then rarely rose until noon. This was not like him and even at my young age, I began to suspect that things were sorely amiss with his affairs. The ledgers and account books told me something about these matters but there was much that my father kept to himself. I knew that he'd spent only a few shillings short of £500 in re-fitting, insuring and provisioning the *Swallow* for the Guinea voyage. And although his sum might be repaid tenfold if most of the intended cargo of one hundred and fifty Africans lived to be sold in Bridgetown and commanded a good price, there were very many 'ifs' in this equation.

Until the *Resolve* and the *Swallow* returned, our only income might be a few pounds a quarter from the copperas works and the other small ventures about the town in which my father had an interest. The dependable returns from the Dublin coal trade had gone and we could not continue to live as we did without borrowing. Like any merchant, my father was accustomed to using credit, but even he seemed uneasy at the mounting scale of his debts.

On the first proper cold day of September, he stops Poll from lighting the fire that is laid in the dining parlour and Fliss has to wrap herself in a blanket during our afternoon dinner. Once the table is cleared, my father, already not entirely sober, pours himself a glass of brandy. I can no longer contain a reproach.

'Are you not going to the counting-house today, Father?'

'Why?'

'It might help us all if you did.'

'Pah! Useless!' He finishes the glass and pours another.

'But there must be something you can do to produce more funds.'

'What would you suggest?'

There is a sneer in his voice and I'm determined, even at fourteen year old, to maintain our household if he will not.

'We could set up a workshop or manufactory.' I had not thought of such a thing until this moment. Instantly, it seems obvious.

'To make what?' His lip curls.

'Baskets maybe. Or sailors' chests.'

'Pah!' My father reaches for his enamel box, takes up a fingernail-ful of snuff like a gesture of disdain, then sniffs it heartily into his left nostril.

'Or snuff?' I say.

Then he lets out an uncouth '*Ah*' followed by a cough of phlegm which he spits into the unlit fire. 'Snuff?'

'Why, yes.' I try to stifle my disgust. 'We have those faulty hogsheads of Virginia tobacco from the *Swallow* which are duty paid. I know we can't get a good enough price for them, but most of the tobacco inside is usable. All it would take is some grinding and I could sell it about the town, especially by the Bear Mouth.'

The miners, as a rule, put out their pipes before going underground to avoid smoke and sparks. Snuff is their preferred pungent in the black bowels of the mine.

'A snuff mill…' My father stares at the rain-running window as he considers the idea. He turns back to me. 'The grinding cannot be done easily by hand, you know.'

'Well, I could set up a donkey mill in the stable. We'd just need millstones…'

'And a donkey.'

I expect a bang of his fist on the table to end this nonsense. But instead, my father nods.

'That's not a bad idea,' he says, 'not bad at all, son.'

It has been a very long while since he last called me 'son.'

And so, that autumn was spent setting up a snuff mill in the stables behind our yard. When he was not drunk, my father assisted with its equipping but left me to take the lead. I approached the scheme eagerly, clearing out the stable of general detritus, going to the sandstone quarry by Tom Hurd Rocks to order grinding stones and walking out to Cleator where I heard of a farmer willing to loan out his donkey over the winter.

'What are you wanting it for?' this farmer asks.

'Only for to eat up the windfalls in our orchard,' I say, feeling suddenly foolish to admit my plan. 'What is her name?'

'The donkey?'

'Aye.'

At this he shakes his head and looks at me with the same mixture of disdain, wariness and sympathy he might bestow on a lunatick. 'Watch the teeth,' is all he says as he hands me the halter rope.

I started by calling the donkey Jenny, but from that first afternoon when she made plain her reluctance to move to Whitehaven by biting me three times along the way, I spoke to her only in curses.

Getting the donkey's assistance was only one of my many difficulties with snuff-making. At first, I could not understand why no one in Whitehaven before me had come up with the idea of converting damaged tobacco stock, which otherwise went in the furnace behind the Custom House to avoid payment of duty, into premium snuff. The white-smith who owed my father a favour helped set up a small rolling mill in our stable, and Aunt Ravenglass gave me the use of her big horse-hair sieve and physick bowls on condition I cleaned them thoroughly of tobacco.

But it was very far from the easy venture I'd had in mind. The first obstacle I encountered, as with so much else in our damp county, was the weather. The successful grinding of dried tobacco leaves into powdery snuff requires the elimination of moisture. An open-doored stable on the Cumberland coast is not the best place to undertake this process at any time of year but especially not in November.

Once I had cajoled Jenny into her harness then persuaded her with stick, apple and curses to walk in the tight circle of the millstone, I saw my efforts were merely turning the tobacco to a nasty grit-filled mush. Even when I finally succeeded in drying both leaf and stones sufficiently to produce a powder, the amount that would pass easily through the fine sieve was minimal. A further grind by hand would be required. The process left me exhausted. And the sleep of our whole household was marred by the sudden thunder of Jenny's nocturnal braying.

Then, on a raw morning near Christmas, I went to the orchard and found the ass gone. This seemed like a final nail in the coffin of my career as a snuff-manufacturer.

'God in heaven!' I shout and kick at a gnarly trunk, forgetting entirely that this is the same foot that got broke upon the *Swallow*.

Hot pain shoots into my ankle. Have I injured it again? Old aches return afresh, and with them a weight of anguish in my chest. I sink down against the apple tree, overwhelmed not just by pain but by the ever-present disquiet I feel about my father's finances and his drunkenness, Fliss's attachment to Daniel Bragg and the unspoken shame that seems to shadow me everywhere. Above all, I yearn for Jossy. I have a sudden vision of my dearest friend's smooth neck as I'm carried on his back from the harbour. Sobs rise into my mouth. My head sinks into my hands. And sorrow flows out of me between wracking gulps of air.

So I do not hear the swishing of feet and skirts through the wet grass until two dainty hooves come to a stop beside me. I look up. Jenny stands meekly on a halter rope held by Hannah Salkeld.

Hannah holds out the tail of the rope. 'She belongs here, does she not?'

I wipe my cheeks. 'Aye.'

Gingerly, I pull myself up by the tree and test my bad foot on the ground. All seems well, and I take a step. But my ankle buckles. Hannah darts forward to catch my elbow.

'Are you injured?'

I stand more weight on to my foot and find that it holds. 'Not as bad as I feared. Thank you.' I take the rope. 'Where did you find her?'

'Back of Irish Street, on the Egremont road.'

'Going to Cleator I should think.'

'Why's that?'

'That's where she came from. My dislike of her seems reciprocated.'

'She was happy enough to come back here with me,' says Hannah.

'Well, thank you for returning her.'

'It's no bother.'

Hannah seems almost a grown woman now, warmly dressed in a sturdy grazet petticoat under a quilted plum bed-jacket. The charity cape is long gone. This sight of her in respectable working clothes sharpens the ever-nagging stab of guilt that has made me turn around whenever I think I spy her in the distance. But today, there is no avoiding it.

'I am sorry, you know,' I blurt.

'What for?'

'For what happened... at the Bear Mouth.'

I shrink inwardly at the memory of the baying, spittle-faced boys and of me, out of sight in my new Quilted-Petticoat with ears stopped up against Hannah's cries.

'Aye, well.' Hannah's lips tighten and she turns to go. I sense that she would have preferred my silence about her ordeals to any apology.

'Wait, Hannah.'

I take a step toward her, but my ankle buckles and I cry out. Again, Hannah catches my elbow. I find myself leaning on her as she helps me back to the tree.

'You should rest that foot.'

The donkey's head dives to tear at a mouthful of grass and the rope jerks from my hand.

Hannah picks it up. 'Should I help you with the donkey?'

'Would you? I can't get her to do anything. But she seems to like you.'

Hannah laughs. 'It's just a donkey.'

'But the trouble she has given me...'

Again, Hannah laughs.

I push back the hair from my brow and look at her straight.

'I'd be very much obliged if you'd come again to assist with her. And,' I hesitate, 'perhaps with my venture in general.'

She frowns. 'How do you mean?'

And I proceed to tell her about my tribulations with the home-made snuff mill. All the while, Hannah listens carefully and nods.

'I imagine 'tis like the preparation of salt,' she says. 'Heat is all.'

'You know about making salt?'

'Aye. I'm employed at the salt-works under Bransty cliff, though only when the weather is right. It's getting to be the time of year when those days are few. Where is your snuff-mill?'

'In yon stable.'

She laughs again and I find a strangely familiar and comforting reassurance in the sound.

'I'll pay you,' I tell her. 'As soon as I've sold some snuff.'

And so, Hannah Salkeld began to help me with the snuff-mill. Her manner with me was often curt, but with the donkey she was all gentleness and Jenny was entirely cured of her biting habit. Hannah was full of practical wisdom too. As she rightly suspected, heat was the key to success. She told me about the boiling house at the salt-works where huge rectangular pans of briny sea-water were placed above a brick furnace for the liquor to be boiled away. I persuaded Aunt Ravenglass to let me place my bowls by the fire in the back kitchen. Firstly, they were filled with raw tobacco and then half-ground leaves and then powder. Each stage of grinding was interspersed with drying and sieving.

Aunt Ravenglass wrinkled her nose at the fuggy smell and also at the sight of Hannah Salkeld leaving the yard by way of the orchard.

'Is there no-one else can assist you?' my aunt sniffs.

'Why?' I ask. 'She is a hard worker. And has tamed the donkey.'

Aunt Ravenglass sniffs again. 'As long as she doesn't come in the house.'

'Why not?' But my voice wavers with the sense of secrets coming near that I would rather stayed distant.

'Come lad, you are no dimwit. Why do you think she has the same name as her mother?'

'Hannah?'

'No, boy. Salkeld.' My aunt sighs and shakes her head. 'She is a bastard.'

'Oh.' The revelation does not shock me so much as deepen my intrigue. 'But is she not my kin?'

'Less said on that the better.' Aunt Ravenglass scrutinises her pestle for traces of tobacco. 'Just keep her out of your father's way.'

And my aunt will not say more.

But as I become easier with Hannah in the hours we spend together grinding and sieving tobacco and pandering to the donkey, I ask her about our family connection. She tells me that her mother and mine were sisters, close as could be, having been orphaned and without other siblings. Hannah's mother, Patience, and her father, a mariner, were wed in a Quaker ceremony which church folk call unlawful and not a true marriage. And it is for this reason, as well as her mother's Quaker insistence on staying a Salkeld after marriage, that the name was passed on to Hannah. Her father cannot defend her because he was lost to the sea when she was little more than a babe, but she is, she declares, legitimate in the eyes of God which is all that matters. Only unkind folk call her a bastard.

Hannah says nothing about the Ravenglass family but I am close, very close, to asking her what she meant by those words in the Bear Mouth about my mother trying to kill me. But then, as Hannah is recalling her own mother's departure to Virginia almost two years since, she becomes tearful. I too recall the unwavering last look toward her daughter from the tall woman at the bow of the *Swallow* and I can't then face more upset for either of us. My question must wait for another day.

A week or so later, we have a small sack of snuff prepared which my father tests and pronounces 'more than tolerable.' I tell Hannah that I will try to sell it to the miners. I don't mention the Bear Mouth.

'Once I have sold some, I'll bring you your share of the profit.'

She shakes her head. 'Keep your profit, if you will do me a favour instead.'

'What?'

'Tell me where my mother is.'

'Your mother? How would I know?'

'She sold herself under an indenture to Captain Power. There could be a record of it in a ledger. If you can tell me directions for whoever bought her labour, I will write to her there.'

'You have heard nothing from her?'

'How would she get the means to write? She was entirely penniless. That's why she went.'

I nod and hope Hannah is right about the reason for her mother's silence.

'What is her trade?'

'Seamstress.'

And so, next day when my father is at the Coffee House, I take a look through the ledger, journal and log-book for the *Swallow*'s Virginia voyage. These salt-spattered documents are kept in the unlocked drawer of my father's Counting-House desk. The supercargo's stained leather-bound journal begins, in Daniel Bragg's small laboured hand, on the day after the departure of the *Swallow*.

24th day of April, 1739
Friday.

Hazy weather with small rain.

The Swallow is now begun its voyage to Virginia. God preserve us and send us a prosperous safe return. Amen.

Pages pass with little to note except a gale or two and

constant complaints from the passengers about the shortness of the rations. Then in late June the *Swallow* reaches the great inland sea of Chesapeake. Captain Power moors midstream in the Rappahannock River to imprison the passengers until buyers can be found for their labour, for if any of the indentured passengers succeeded in running off, they would have had their passage to America for free.

In July, Daniel hires a horse and rides about the riverside counties to hawk his wares and sniff out tobacco barns. With Riddle's help, he has some luck.

28th day of July, 1739
Monday.
Rappahannock –

Thunder storms

The bo'sun has heard of an overseer Thomas Crowder of the Home Plantation of the estate of Robert Carter in Lancaster County who has a mind to acquire skilled craftsmen under indenture. They have a good crop in their stores. I have no doubt that trade may be made with this plantation and will proceed there forthwith.

The journal says no more about this but in the ledger I find a record of indentures swapped for tobacco from the Carter estate.

12th Aug, 1739
To: Indentures for a period of 5 years at £6 no.6.
carpenter (2) bricklayer (2) glazier (1) seamstress (1)
For: Tobacco Hogsheads no. 6

There may have been another seamstress amongst the passengers but intuition tells me that I have found Hannah's mother. I also have a sense that her labour has been sold too cheap, though in the excitement of my find I don't remember to check the value of indentures against the prevailing tobacco price and so verify Daniel Bragg's figures.

Instead, I grab a scrap of paper and sit at my father's desk with his quill and ink.

Patience Salkeld, seamstress,
Indentured to Thomas Crowder, overseer of the
Home Plantation, in the estate of Robert Carter Esq.
of Lancaster County, Virginia.

Then I blow on the words and fold the paper three times before putting it in my pocket.

the seventh chapter

It is still dark as I haul my sack of snuff to the Bear Mouth. Morning is arriving slowly through a November fog thickened by coal-smoke. Before I see the pitmen tramping toward an early shift, I hear the clacking of tallow candles tied with long wicks through their buttonholes. Then, the men appear from the dank air with flannel nightcaps wedged under their hats. The tunnelled miles of the mine are always colder than the winter above them and darker than any night.

The gang of colliers, most of them not much older than me, stop before the rock archway of the Bear Mouth to knock out their clay pipes.

'Will you try some of my snuff?' I say and offer my sack.

'How much?' grunts the biggest lad.

'A fingernail-ful for free.'

All hands then dive into the hessian sack followed by a deal of sniffing and some satisfied hacking of phlegm. Soon I am spooning the clay-brown dust at a ha'penny a scoop into kerchiefs and leather pouches. Most of the pitmen who pass by will happily pay for anything that promises some comfort for their long day of toil in waterlogged tunnels beneath the sea-bed.

The thread of miners slows, but other workers pass by on their way toward the harbour or the wagon-way. Pit-brow girls, quarrymen and porters all stop to buy a portion of snuff. I try not to look into the Bear Mouth as I wield my spoon, but the jutting wall inside keeps catching my eye. It was here that I cowered in my yellow petticoat whilst Hannah Salkeld was debased by my schoolmates. The thought of this horrid episode makes me want to swill up my own mouthful of phlegm and spit it on to the blackened ground.

Near noon, the fog clears to a reveal a wintry sparkle on the sea beyond the harbour. At the other end of the bay, beneath the rise of Bransty Cliffs, smoke is billowing from the chimney of the boiling house at the salt-works. Pennies weight my coat pockets. It is time to count my profits and give Hannah her share.

On the table in the dining parlour, I pile the ha'pennies, farthings and pennies into nine shillings and thri'pence and stand back, amazed at what I have earned. Then, after raking the coins into a kerchief, I can't suppress a proud smile as I enter the counting-house.

'Father!'

He is at his desk, the wig thrown down beside him and a knitted house-cap pulled low over his brow. His chin rests on clasped hands and a sour greasy smell surrounds him. He does not seem to hear me.

'Father! I made near ten shillings by selling snuff at the mine!'

At this, he raises an eyebrow and almost smiles. 'Did you, lad? That's grand.'

His voice conveys nothing but gloom.

'Here,' I clink the kerchief of coins onto the desktop. 'It will go toward the duty paid on the hogsheads.'

My snuff venture, as I am well aware, is still short of true profit.

My father opens the kerchief and stirs a finger through the dull coins. Two Georges, father and son, stare impassively out from the coins, their profiles almost identical under the laurel circlets of Roman emperors.

'Keep it safe, son,' my father says, pushing the money back toward me. 'And invest it well.'

'I don't need to buy more tobacco leaf, there's plenty left.'

'Anyway, keep the money.'

'I thought to help our household's expenses.'

My father turns to me and puts a hand on my shoulder. He takes in a long breath. And then, as I look on horrified, his breath splutters out into a sob.

'Father!'

I am stunned. My father's eyes are tight shut and his fist pushed up against his nose. I have never seen him weep before. Indeed, I had no notion that such a thing was possible.

The hand on my shoulder pats, as if I am the one in distress. Then, my father shakes his head and give a shuddering sigh.

'Do you know what day this is, Kit?'

'It is Tuesday. The twenty-second of November, Father.'

'Do you not recall why the date is special?'

I blink. My mind is fugged by my father's tears. Is it something to do with the King's birthday? But that was some weeks ago, though my father did not mark the occasion with his usual liberality at the Indian King. I can only shake my head.

'This should be my benefaction day for poor girls of the town.'

I remember then. 'Oh. Aye. The capes.'

'But the interest on my initial benefaction was again insufficient to buy enough broadcloth this year. And when the parson asked me for an additional sum, I had to refuse him. So there will be no new red capes about the town this winter.'

He pushes the side of his fist against his nose and turns his face away from me. His back heaves. I reach out my hand and it hovers above the dull stuff of his coat. But I am too unused to touching him to begin now.

Instead, I try to speak brightly. 'Once the *Resolve* and the *Swallow* return you may endow the charity twice over.'

But my father's head is already shaking. 'I swore...' he speaks very quietly through labouring breaths, 'I swore that I would mark this day every year.'

Until now, the day on which pauper girls received their red capes adorned with a black velvet R for Ravenglass seemed simply to mark the start of winter.

'Why this day?'

'As part of my assuagement.' My father rubs his sleeve across his nose and his brow.

I frown, not understanding.

'On your mother's birthday.'

My heart slows. *Your mother.* What can he mean by 'assuagement'?

'Did she bid you look after the poor?'

My father turns to me then with watery reddened eyes. 'Would that it was so simple.'

'Why, Father? Will you not tell me?'

But he shakes his head and covers his eyes with his hand.

A cold beat of dread passes through me and I'm seized by a compulsion to flee. Hastily gathering the coins into my kerchief, I don't look back at my father as I quit the counting-house down the ladder and leave by the door to the yard.

I keep walking, through the covered carriageway and into the street. I have walked the full straight length of Church Street before I realise where I am going. Then it is not far from the corner of the old churchyard to Bransty cliffs.

Below the crumbling cliffs, the brick boiling-house gives off a throb of briny heat. Beyond it lie the salterns where sea water is trapped at high tide then pushed gradually through evaporation pools toward the boiling-house. A woman in plum-coloured jacket with petticoat hitched up above her knees is wading up and down the nearest pool and pushing a wooden skimmer across the thickening sea-water.

I wait by the edge of the pool until Hannah sees me. The afternoon has grown sharp and bright with the bite of winter. Not far off, waves crash into shingle. Above, seabirds scream.

Finally, Hannah turns and comes toward me. The dense water hardly ripples around her bare legs.

'Did you sell any?'

Her words, as always, are abrupt but her smile is gentle.

'Aye. Near ten shilling-worth.'

Her eyebrows raise and she nods approvingly.

'I have your share here,' I say, 'if you don't mind it in farthings.'

She frowns. 'Did you not find out what I asked you?'

'Aye. I have that as well.' I reach beneath the coins to the felted corner of my coat pocket and pull up the folded paper. 'Though I can't promise that the directions will lead to your mother.'

Hannah lays down the skimmer then steps out of the water. Her feet are the same colour as her bed-jacket. I have handed her the note before stopping to consider whether she can read, but she opens it without a word. As she bends her head to the words, the wind drags a clump of fair hair from the knitted cap tied under her chin. Her eyes, though more violet than blue, have a shape and keenness that give her a look of Fliss.

'*Home Plantation*,' she reads. 'It sounds... grandiose.'

I shrug. 'There is no-one I may ask any more about it until the *Swallow* returns.'

Hannah re-folds the paper and slips it inside the slit of her petticoat. 'Thank you.'

I nod and tighten my muffler against the wind. 'Please, take these farthings for your labour.'

She shakes her head. 'I seek no more from you. I said the directions for my mother were all I wanted and I keep to my word.'

Hannah's refusal of the coins brings a tightening to my throat. 'But...' I struggle for words. 'But I want to pay you.'

'I am paid.'

'Please...' I turn away to hide the welling of my tears. 'It will help me make amends...'

'For what?' Hannah's eyes narrow.

'For the Bear Mouth.'

She is silent. I can't help filling the silence with words she would probably prefer not to hear.

'And... and you said then that I owed you for my father's sins.'

'Did I?'

'I saw how he beat you.'

'At the church, you mean?'

I nod and heave a sigh of shame.

The redness blanches from Hannah's cheeks. 'It wasn't the beating that caused me to hate your father. Though it did not help.'

'What else has he done?'

She stares at me cool and unblinking. 'If you do not know, I shouldn't be the one to tell you.'

'No one will tell me. Hannah, please.'

Hannah's sigh is swallowed by surf rolling stones on to the strand but her gaze does not waver from mine. 'After my father died, my mother became penniless. She had no-one to call on. Even the Friends would not help her because of what your mother had done. So she asked your father for help but he would have naught to do with us.'

My brow, my whole face wrinkles with confusion. 'Why? What had my mother done?'

She blinks and turns her head to the pewter-grey sea.

'Hannah. Please tell me what you know of this.'

'It is not my place...'

'Please, Hannah, please.' Again, my eyes are brimming.

She takes a long breath and looks at me straight. 'Do you really wish to know?'

'I do.'

She nods and then speaks without emotion. 'When you were a babe not long walking, your mother took a knife and with it she killed your brother. She tried to kill you and your sister too but was stopped in time. Then she was taken to the House of Correction. But before there could be any trial, she tore up her petticoat and used it to hang herself in her cell.'

For a moment I am numb. The words make no sense.

'She... She did what?'

'She killed your brother and herself. And grievous wounded Fliss. You are the lucky one.'

'I... lucky?'

The numbness inside me turns cold. How can this be true? My mother killed her own child. Tried to kill all her children. It is senseless. Unthinkable. Yet the story is too astounding, and too ghastly, to be made up. The coldness in me freezes to an ice-hard lump at my core.

Hannah continues to look at me in her blunt, steady way. I am shivering now. My mouth opens as if to reply. Perhaps I mean to ask how it can be that I've known nothing of all this till now. But no sound comes out. And any words I might utter would only dissolve into the bitter, salt-laden wind.

the eighth chapter

I never doubted the truth of Hannah's declaration. Yet returning home from the saltern, I found our household going about its usual domestic business as if nothing had changed. But to me, the whole world had tilted away from its natural axis.

I find Fliss in the best parlour once again at work on the yellow and white waistcoat. Though more than a year has passed since she began it, she has continually found ways to embellish the decoration by adding fancy pocket flaps in perforated white-work, or an appliqué of scallops in silver-gilt.

Now, she is adorning the one of the twenty wooden buttons with a passementerie of silver-wire threads. She glances up at me from the work.

'Kit.' She frowns. 'Does something ail you?'

My cheeks are indeed hot and damp, though not from any ailment.

I shrug. 'Maybe.'

'What? A chill? You should not have stood so long by the mine.'

'It's not that.'

'What then?'

She looks up at me again, the half-worked button in one hand, a length of metal thread in her other.

Here is my chance. But the words seem ridiculous. *I just heard that our mother killed our brother with a knife then tried to kill us too.* How can that make any sense in a warm, well-cushioned parlour where the mantel clock ticks and my sister decorates buttons with silver threads? Yet in my core I know it to be true. Hearing the tale from Fliss's lips will not change it, nor wipe out all the years that I have been kept in ignorance while the whole town talks about me behind their hands.

'Kit, what is it?'

Fliss's eyes are anxious and her fingers toy with the ribband at her neck. The velvet dips as she touches it and a red corner of her scar peeks out. I shut my eyes to it. But all I then see is a tall fair woman holding a sharpened knife over a little girl.

'Kit?' Fliss is peering at me.

'Umm?'

'Are you sickening for something?'

I shake my head. What I most need is an answer, but one that only Verity Salkeld can provide. Not what she did but why. My resolve to speak of our mother's crimes suddenly shatters.

'I'm just tired after rising early,' I say, standing up. 'I'll sleep for a while.'

So I go then to my room. But not for sleep.

Before unbuttoning my breeches, I push the box-chest in front of the bedchamber door. Then despite the chilly air, I take off all of my clothes and the harsh winter light bludgeons my white limbs. Standing naked and close to the window, I carefully check each part of me for any scar that might have been caused by a knife. I pull my skin taut and crane my neck to the reflecting glass. But there is nothing.

This knowledge brings not relief but a strange sadness. It is as if, by leaving me with no mark, my mother must have loved me less than my brother and sister. My back, of course, I cannot see. So, I reassure myself that until there is someone I can entrust with the task of looking, I will not be sure what blemishes might lie there.

Then, still naked, I kneel down beside my bed and reach beneath it. Rolled tight in the corner is the yellow Quilted-Petticoat that I won at Lammas Fair. Since that day, I have worn it only occasionally and in secret but its presence below me as I sleep is a source of both excitement and comfort. As I unroll the petticoat, its sulphurous gleam brings a smile to my lips. I caress the skirt's cool smoothness with both palms. And then I put it on.

The petticoat is now a little shorter than it should be but with a swift twirl of my bare feet it flares out to a perfect bell. I try out a variety of positions to enjoy the long expanse of silkiness against my bare legs. I find myself aping the way that Fliss might sit or stand or walk or lie. The heavy swish of the cloth and the airiness beneath it fills me with joy. The simple act of donning a skirt changes me entirely. I am suddenly dainty, graceful, perfected. And for the rest of that awful afternoon, my head is too full of these pleasant feelings to allow any darker thoughts an entry.

As I grew closer to turning fifteen year old, the conviction grew in me that I would never become a man, or at least not a man like any other male person that I knew. Since the days of my childish play-acting as Stella, my hankering for petticoats, powder and patches, had not abated. I had learned to hide my love for womanly things from Fliss and the others in the house so well that sometimes I even convinced myself that this passion had evaporated from me like sea-water from salt. But in the weeks that followed Hannah's revelation, I could find solace only by giving in to my desires.

So when Fliss is elsewhere, I go to her closet and take items that I know she has not worn lately; an old linen pinner with holy-point lappets, a knitted jacket, a pair of open slippers with braided heels, the hardly worn saffron stomacher from her mantua-gown. I try various combinations of these garments, and various poses to show them to best effect, wishing only that I might see a better reflection of myself than the skirted ghost in my attic window-glass. Sometimes, I catch a glimpse of this reflected me and gasp at my womanliness. My resemblance to the female both delights and appals me. If I can look so perfectly feminine, perhaps this is my true self. Perhaps the boy is but a carapace around the girl inside me.

I wondered more than once what Jossy would make of my girlish self. Would he admire the delicate grace of my limbs once they were clothed in skirts and lace? Or would he be horrified at my queerness? Perhaps he would merely laugh out loud at a lad prancing about in his sister's clothes. I was glad though, that I would never know the answer to these questions. My female finery, like my mother's crimes, must always be kept to myself.

As the wet winter that year dragged into a damp spring I lost the heart for further snuff-making. And when donkey returned to Cleator for her summer duties I knew that my days as a tobacco miller were at an end.

My father's finances improved briefly through the sale of his interest in the copperas works, but with each summer day his hopes for the return of a ship were raised, only to be quashed by each sinking of a blood-orange sun behind the edge of the sea.

By midsummer 1741, the *Resolve* had been at sea for more than eighteen months and the *Swallow* for more than a year. And although neither time would be accounted too long for a voyage to the Guinea Coast and the West Indies, it was at least possible that one or the other of the vessels might now return. Fliss seemed determined not to think about any eventuality and instead to busy her mind with embroidery though she had already covered both the yellow and white waistcoat panels with threads and was now adding spangles.

Then in August, news came to us from the harbour that likely sails had been sighted in the offing. And, by the time I reached the harbour, I saw that it was true. The *Resolve* was returned.

This news brought instant commotion to our house like a street-dog kicked awake. All inside fell to yelping and running this way and that in preparation for offloading and for the entertainment of Captain Littlewood. My own heart clamoured with a mix of fear and joy at the thought of seeing Jossy. Yet so many crewmen never returned from a slaving voyage. What were the chances that he would still be aboard?

I watch the vessel approach the Tongue hardly daring to breathe. Yet the first thing that I see upon the deck of the *Resolve* is the outline of a blue jacket on a square back that I know to be his. Waving furiously, I let out a joyful cry of his name.

But as Jossy turns, he seems to look past me as if searching the harbour's quays for something or someone else. He has grown and aged during the voyage. There is no doubt now that he is a man. Then I see Captain Littlewood. Straight away I know from his countenance that the voyage has failed. I glance at my father next to me. His eyes already have a hollow look. The hope of profit is gone. The only question now is, how great is the loss?

After returning from his ship-board conference with Captain Littlewood, my father took to his chamber. For a day and a night nothing was heard from him save calls for another bottle of rum. So the full disaster of the voyage remained obscured from the women of the house and from me.

the ninth chapter

The day after the return of the *Resolve* dawns strangely sultry as if the ship has brought with her the climate of the tropics. Eager to speak with Jossy, I loiter on the Steer from early morning and eventually I am rewarded by the sight of him hauling a bundle of frayed rope along the harbourside.

As I go up to him, his new-found manliness brings a hesitancy to my step but he nods and greets me warmly.

'Master Kit.'

'Good day Jossy. Where are you going?'

'To the shipwright, to see if he will buy this for oakum.' He throws a look at the rope on his shoulder.

'May I walk with you?'

There is a slight shrug of his shoulder which I take to be a *yes*.

We pick a path along the Steer between piles of wood and barrels awaiting loading. But the traffic is sparse. The tide is out, and the few vessels tied up at the Sugar Tongue and the Countermole have dropped to their sides on the muddy strand.

'I'm glad to see you back safe.' I venture.

'Aye.'

'Though the voyage was not a success.'

Jossy makes a noise that might be a cough or a snort. 'No.'

'My father is too disappointed to speak of it.'

Jossy looks at me straight for the first time and raises an eyebrow. But all he says is, 'Here we are. I must find the shipwright.'

I nod and watch him go into the yard and hail the foreman before dropping the rope bundle from his shoulder. I wait for him to return.

'Still here?' he says.

Embarrassment surges. 'I… I wish to ask you about the voyage. There seems no-one else who will tell me.'

Jossy gives me a straight hard look. I hope that my excuse will convince him, as there is truth in it, though mainly I wish to return to my friend's side for as long as he will allow. His assent is no more than a twitch of his chin.

'Shall we go to the shore?' I suggest. 'The tide is out far enough to walk round to the rocks.'

We follow the Steer until the sandy track turns into shingly beach. Jagged cliffs, blasted by every high tide, rise above us. Once we turn past the headland, the harbour and town are hidden and Jossy and I are entirely alone on the narrow strip of land between sandstone crags and the milky expanse of the sea. Only the black outlines of Tom Hurd Rocks interrupt the horizon.

Picking up a flat smooth pebble and crouching down, I skim it across the flat water near the shore.

'Five,' I say, counting the stone's bounces.

Then Jossy makes a throw.

'Seven,' he says and smiles at last.

I look at him sidelong. His new manliness makes him even more handsome.

'So the voyage didn't go well?'

He picks up another pebble and flings it with excessive force against a small wave where instantly, it sinks. 'Death followed the *Resolve* like a westerly wind.'

'There was contagion aboard?'

He shrugs. 'The usual fevers and flux.'

'And many Africans succumbed?'

'More than half of all those that boarded. On what they were fed and allowed to drink, they had no chance.'

'Yet, if even half were sold at a decent price, there should have been some profit.'

'Profit!' Jossy picks up another stone so that I can't see his expression. Six, seven, eight touches of the flat sea. Perhaps more. He gives a scornful laugh. 'The ledger will not show what went on.'

'How do you mean?'

'Littlewood and Riddle profited well enough.'

'How? Have they swindled us?'

'Well, the R iron wasn't heated until we reached Barbados.'

'The R iron? I don't follow.'

He gives the slightest shake of his head then turns to face the horizon. 'Each person who is purchased is given a mark from a hot iron to show who owns them. This should be done as soon as they come aboard the vessel. An R for *Resolve* or L for *Littlewood*. But on this voyage all were left unbranded except for the eight Africans in the captain's portion. And, when one of these died, Littlewood simply branded another from the hold with his L.'

'So he protected his own interests by adding to our losses?'

Jossy's look at me, no longer hidden, is a glare. 'His only interest is in protecting profit. And it seems he's not alone.'

Stomach sinking, I realise how my words have sounded, and I can't bear that he thinks me no better than the odious captain. As Jossy stoops to pick up a pebble, I imagine for the first time what an orange-hot branding iron would do to human flesh and, with a jolt, wonder if he has one of these marks somewhere on his body.

The pebble skips across the water. I lose count of the times it touches the shallow sea before it finally slips under the surface. A drench of shame washes through me.

I stand up. 'I'll tell my father about Littlewood's cruelty and thieving.'

Jossy shrugs with one shoulder. 'My word will provide no proof.'

'What about others aboard?'

'They have all received enough of Littlewood's personal

profit to stay quiet.'

'But not you?'

'Why should he waste anything on me?' Jossy kicks into the shingle and reaches down to pick out a perfectly smooth oval of grey shale. He caresses it with his middle finger, but lets it drop back into the stones. Then he turns and walks away.

It was to be another whole year before the outcome of the *Swallow*'s voyage became known. And during that year, the absent vessel cast a dull shadow over all in the Ravenglass household.

Fliss continued her work on the wedding waistcoat by adding foil roundels and couched scallops to the spangles. Once the pockets were edged with silver frogging and free-hanging tassels, the effect slipped from ornate to excess.

By spring, even Fliss realised that there was no more work that could be reasonably done to the waistcoat and she set it aside. But nothing else would interest her. In frequent bouts of restless energy, she took to wrapping herself in an old cloak and going out of the house alone. Sometimes she was gone for hours.

Aunt Ravenglass berated her more than once for this dangerous habit. Did Fliss not realise what ruffians inhabited every part of this town and the surrounding countryside? What was she doing anyway, out for so long? Fliss did not seem to care and remonstrated, passionate and wild-eyed. Was she not free to take the air or would her aunt have her always indoors? At least, Aunt Ravenglass implored, take Poll with you or Kit. But Fliss just rolled her eyes.

Once, on a blustering early morn in May, when I heard her moving about in her chamber and guessed that she was preparing to go out, I decided to follow her. Staying unnoticed, I watch her cross the wakening marketplace and go up the steep path along the wagon-way toward Saltom. Her squirrel-lined hood marks her out from the pit-girls in blanket shawls and short drugget petticoats. But she keeps pace with them as they climb, stepping aside to watch the horseless coal-wagons thunder down the slope on ridged iron wheels that hug the wooden rails. The pit-girls laugh and shout obscenities at the stony-faced waggoners who grip tight to the rod that acts as a brake on two ton of coal hurtling toward the sea. Fliss of course, is quiet.

At the top, she departs from the path and hikes across the tussocky grass on the cliff-top. I cannot keep close for fear of her seeing me and wonder if she will descend toward the cliff's rocky grottoes below. If she does, I will cast off secrecy and go to pull her away for the caves are renowned for the dangers of loose boulders and mischievous fairies. But Fliss stays near the cliff-edge. The wind is still high and I fear that she is too close to the drop, but presently, she stops, pulls down her hood and looks out to sea.

I lose any sense of how long I sit, behind a lip of stone and grass, watching my sister. Her gaze drifts to the chimney of the Fire-Engine at Saltom pit and then out toward the Isle of Man. The isle lies hazy on the horizon like a lurking crocodile. Though I have no doubt it is not reptiles my sister looks for but the sails of the *Swallow*.

If my father could have summoned the energy, he would no doubt have joined Fliss in her cliff-top vigil. But the absence of the vessel upon which his whole fortune now depended had sapped him of the will to do anything save lift a glass to his lips. His five sixteenths of interest in the *Resolve* had now been sold off at less than a good price owing to the uncertainties that the naval war had brought to merchant shipping. Indeed, selling the shares for so little had been a madness which had not gone unnoticed. My father's creditworthiness amongst his erstwhile backers and bankers soon evaporated.

Once two whole years had passed since the departure of Daniel Bragg and the *Swallow*, the prospect loomed larger by the day, though it could not be spoke aloud, that they might never return.

Our divorce from the *Resolve* meant that I knew little of Jossy's whereabouts and had seen him only for a few brief moments upon the harbour. Whilst the *Resolve* was in dock, he had spent the winter on loan to various Dublin-bound colliers. The new shareholders of the *Resolve* were reluctant to send their vessel on another Guinea voyage on account of the dangers presented by the war. There was even a rumour that they had discussed re-fitting the vessel, under a letter of marque, as a twenty-gun frigate to sail in the King's service as a privateer. My heart missed a beat for the dangers Jossy would face on board such a warship. But the *Resolve* remained moored in the bay and Jossy, I imagined, had found a place at his master's bidding elsewhere.

And then, as I sit on the wind-whipped cliff-top spying on my sister, I see Jossy coming towards me. He is walking from the direction of Saltom and he is dressed as a miner, his worsted stockings streaked with coal-dusted mud and his hat caked with candle-wax.

'Jossy!' I stand and wave, no longer caring if my sister sees me.

He seems startled, but stops while I run over to him.

'You are a miner!' I say, panting.

'For now, aye. Littlewood has hired me out to the pit.'

'Oh. How is it?'

He shrugs. 'Cold and damp. And hard labour. Being under the sea is not much different to being on top of it.' At last, he smiles. 'What of you? Any more voyages?'

I shake my head. 'Our fortunes now depend on the *Swallow* alone. But she has been gone more than a two-year. Are you going to town?'

For a second, he hesitates and looks searchingly toward the sea. Then he nods. Before we start to walk downhill, I glance back at Fliss who stands like a statue on the headland.

'Have you heard anything of the *Swallow*?' Jossy asks.

'There was a report of her at Bridgetown last year. But that seems too long ago for all to be well. My father is putting the delay down to the war. If too many of the crew have been pressed, she might be laid up still at Barbados.'

Jossy turns to me with a quizzical look. 'I heard a rumour of her at St Kitts.'

The suggestion is so unexpected that I am confused, especially with what sounds like my name on his lips.

'St Kitts?'

'The slave price in Barbados was low,' Jossy goes on, 'and they had heard it was higher at St Kitts. But it was on the voyage there that Captain Power died.'

'Captain Power is dead?'

He shrugs. ''Twas only a rumour.'

I shake my head and feel it thud with the heaviness of impending disaster. 'The cook told me that the vessel was not well-supplied with water casks… but that could not have caused Captain Power to die, could it?'

Jossy shrugs.

'But without him, who would then act as master?'

'Riddle, I expect.'

We share a glance then and there is no doubt that our thoughts are aligned on the displeasant prospect of the Bosun Riddle being in sole command of the crew.

'Do you know when this was, Jossy? My father should be told.'

He hesitates. 'A while back. But there many things said on the harbourside that turn out not to be the case.'

'The *Swallow* has been gone so long, though. We are starting to fear she'll not return.'

He puts his head to one side then looks back toward the headland. Coal-dirt smears his forehead and cheeks. 'Two years is not an unlikely length for such a voyage, not in a time of war.'

Perhaps he is right. And anyway, what would be gained by conveying this alarming rumour to my father?

I glance at him sideways as we walk. We are more or less of a height now and he is as dark as I am fair, but I cannot help think that there is a pleasing symmetry in this, as if we were made to be seen side by side. For a moment I have a vision, so strong that it is more premonition than fancy, of us walking arm in arm, he in my coat and I wearing my Quilted-Petticoat. I make myself step a little away from Jossy to avoid any temptation to reach out to him and slip my arm through his.

'Are you to make a further voyage with the *Resolve*?' I ask, pushing my voice deeper and more manly.

Jossy shakes his head. 'She is moored up for this year. They are hoping for safer crossings next.'

'Back to the Guinea coast?'

A shadow crosses Jossy's face. 'I reckon.'

'So you'll have to go back there too?'

Jossy turns to me then and looks me directly in the eye. But he makes no sign of assent or denial. The silence between us is unnerving and I flounder for something to say.

'Have you found much reading matter of late? I could teach you some writing, if you like, whilst you remain a landsman.'

Jossy's stare does not waver. 'I don't think that would be wise.'

'Why not?'

'A friendship between us could be taken wrong.'

My heart drops but I attempt a laugh. 'Can it? How so?'

But his only reply is another long, unblinking look. And of course I understand perfectly what he means. As if to prove it, a hot blush rise to my cheeks. My embarrassment is laced with anger too, at the unworthiness of his suspicions as much as at their truth. I have not felt such humiliation since my school mates used to call me Kitty.

Jossy touches his wax-dripped hat. 'Good day to you Master Kit.'

Without reply, I march away from him back up the cliff to look for my sister. But she is no longer there.

I saw Jossy again several times that summer when he was working shifts at Saltom pit and sleeping in an outhouse on the Steer. But following his rebuff, I made it my business to avoid him for each sighting brought with it a damp cloud of melancholy. I was not alone in my gloom. The general malaise of shipping in the harbour on account of the war and the vexingly wet summer weather cast a pall of gloom across the town.

The mood in our household grew ever darker. I knew that my father had already drawn a loan against the insured loss of the *Swallow*, so his expectation of the likely outcome of the voyage was clear. By August he had sold the Turkey carpet from the best parlour and, despite Aunt Ravenglass's strident objections, a rarely used China tea service and a full set of spare bedding also went to Mr Shaw's sale-room.

Fliss continued her solitary outings and I had no doubt that these took her to the cliff. But I did not again follow her. The futility of her southward vigil across the sea was too miserable to behold.

One showery September morning as she descended the attic stairs, I saw with a jolt how pallid her complexion had become. Gone was the fresh fair skin that was the chief source of her beauty. Grey pallor and angry red blemishes had taken its place. The emptiness in her eyes tore at my heart.

'Don't go out, Fliss, at least not yet.'

She turns and looks at me without fully seeing. A shrug is her only reply.

'Shall we look at *Dorinda's Gift* together? It has been such a long time.'

There is risk in the pursuit, I know. An unhappy intimation from the *Finger of Fortune* might only compound Fliss's melancholy. But the chance that the game will lighten the intercourse between us seems worth the risk.

Fliss, though, throws me a flash of anger. 'There is no point to it.'

'Except diversion,' I persist, 'which we all crave.' I go to her and take her arm. 'Come and sit a while, at least until the rain has passed.'

She lets herself be brought to the best parlour and perches uneasily on the settle. The room seems forlorn without the Turkey carpet though I never noticed it at all when it was there.

I bring out *Dorinda's Gift* from the pile of half-worked fabric. Although apparently complete, the wedding waistcoat still languishes at the bottom of the pile wrapped in thin muslin.

'Have you asked aught of the 'Finger' this week?'

There is a twitch of Fliss's shoulder which suggests that she has and the replies were not favourable.

'Let us do it together. It always works best with two of us.'

A spark of life enters her gaze as she recognises a chance to set aside Dorinda's previously unhappy auguries and procure better ones.

My smile wavers. 'Which will you choose?'

'*Will the stranger return from abroad?*' She looks up imploring. 'I have asked this before but maybe I did not do it right. Will you check where my finger lands?'

I nod and watch for her finger landing fully over one single V-shaped constellation. Together, silently, we read the answer. *The stranger's RETURN will bring misfortunes.*

My stomach gives a tug of apprehension. But when I glance at Fliss, a strange calmness has spread across her face. As if she has seen the future and knows that she cannot escape it.

And Dorinda, as usual, was right, for it was not more than a week or two later when the *Swallow*, after a voyage of near two years and five months, sailed at last into Whitehaven harbour.

the tenth chapter

Misfortune was too a small word for the chaos and despair that followed the return of the *Swallow*. The vessel arrived back, just as Jossy had predicted, under the command of Bosun Riddle following the sudden death overboard of Captain Power. Her hold was filled with little beyond ballast. Fine white Caribbee sand buried the wooden platforms where Africans had lain wretchedly shackled to their neighbours, one atop another. More than half of them had died. That, at least, was the account recorded in the ledgers carried ashore by a gaunt and grim-faced Daniel Bragg.

Fliss seemed delirious at the appearance of her betrothed although catapulted from anxious melancholy into a type of mania. I found her in the best parlour staring at the wedding waistcoat and banging repeatedly at her forehead with the heel of her hand.

Perhaps she was berating herself for spending so long on this fancy garment while neglecting to make Daniel a practical suit of clothes. After so long at sea in extremes of heat and damp, the clothes he had took with him were little more than salt-bleached rags. These had been supplemented only by a very faded superfine coat that I suspected had belonged to Captain Power.

At the foot of the ladder in the strong-room, I tried to listen as my father in the counting-house above went over the records of the voyage with Daniel Bragg. It was not at all clear how a voyage of such duration had incurred such great losses. But I could not make clear sense of the snippets I overheard.

At one point, Daniel gave an account of a looting raid by a Spanish privateer. Then it became clear that the episode had taken place not on the *Swallow* but a different vessel entirely.

My father seemed to lack the heart to hold Daniel to any account and attributed the voyage's losses to contagion amongst the Africans, the requisition of stores by the Navy and storm-damage. The debt now outstripped the value of the vessel herself and the *Swallow* was already put up for public sale. But I knew that Daniel Bragg was to blame and a fire raged in me to expose the robbery he had done to our profit.

So, when my father has gone to the Indian King, and Fliss and Daniel are engaged in high-pitched whispers in the dining-parlour, I creep to counting-house. Knowing where the key is kept, I unlock the drawer that holds the *Swallow*'s records.

First I turn to the streaked leather-bound journal written exclusively in Daniel's hand. This record begins with the southward voyage in mid-summer 1740 when men o'war, English and Spanish, are sighted but not closely encountered, and though the winds are sluggish, the *Swallow* meets few difficulties.

In July they reach the mouth of the Gambia River but are persuaded by local rumour to continue along the coast for more abundant supplies of captives taken in a recent war between Africans. In August, the first trading posts of the Gold Coast are sighted, and Captain Power and Daniel Bragg, both novices in this enterprise, begin their trading with the African caboceers. But lacking any knowledge of African languages and customs, this is no simple matter.

27th August,
Saturday.
Dickey's Cove-
Gold Coast.

Squally heat

Two canoes came up with several girl slaves and elephants' teeth but tho' we showed them all our commodities (inc. brass duck) we could not prevail upon them to trade with us.

Despite a terrifying tornado that leaves the top foresails in shreds, they remain moored in this place for more than two weeks. There are some small successes but a general sense of failure.

19th September,
Monday.
Dickey's Cove -
Gold Coast.

A thick horizon

This morning we brought on board a man slave bought for 3 ells of broadcloth and two knives. An Englishman, Mr Crossley, came aboard from the castle and told us that we should never sell all our goods if we rated them so dear. But I fear further discount would ruin our profit.

Eventually, after sailing on to other trading points, they find the price of iron bars considerably risen due to a general clamour for metalwork amongst the warring Africans. Gunpowder increases in price too. And so, despite the *Swallow* spending much more time and expense on the Gold Coast than anyone had anticipated, by the turn of the year, her hold is filled with one hundred and forty six men, women and children and she is ready to embark on her Atlantic crossing.

Not long into this Middle Passage, Daniel abandons his usual buoyancy and complains of the dwindling, rancid rations and the shortage of drinking water. What water is left in the casks *'exceeding stinks.'* Then, as hurricanes still howl in the western seas, rain arrives but with it weather so bad that it tests every soul on board. After the stifling heat of Guinea, he is surprised by the biting cold of the Atlantic winds. Even in his coat and muffler, Cumberland–raised Daniel is cold. But the Africans in the hold, who have known only heat, are near naked. Daniel wonders if this why that they begin, steadily, to die. Though the blame, he says, also lies with the captives themselves.

17th March
Friday.

Fresh gale and great swell

We now have 34 slaves dead and many queasy. Most appear to be in the grip of a fixed melancholy with the belief, I am told, that if they die, they will return to their homeland. Many refuse to eat. Using my authority over our cargo, I instructed the Cook (who acts as our surgeon) to apply the speculum oris to the mouths of several and force into them horse-bean mush and lard.

Still Africans die. When they sight Barbados in March 1741 only seventy two are left alive in the hold. According to the journal, seventy four of their fellows have been thrown into the sea, along with five of the crew who also succumbed to fever and flux. I lower my head into my hand at the imagination of so much human misery on so small a vessel.

But then, Daniel's journal comes to an abrupt end. The

master's log, recording directional courses, knots and winds, is kept with great assiduousness until Captain Power's apparent death, in a storm, not long after clearing Barbados. But if I read his log aright, the course being plotted in his last entries is more north easterly than it should be for a homeward passage. There is no mention at all of St Kitts.

The ledger adds little more to the *Swallow*'s story. There is a note of the Bills of Exchange, one for the sum of four hundred guineas another for three hundred and twenty five, drawn on two Bristol merchants. These were received as payment for the Africans (as far as I can ascertain, thirty one of them) who were sold by auction in Bridgetown. Later in the ledger there is a scribbled note that the larger of the Bristol bills has been spent on repair to the foremast but no detail of when or where this work took place nor exactly how much it cost. What happened to the other bill is not clear, though I suspect that Daniel Bragg knows full well.

Before laying my suspicions before my father, I decide to question Daniel myself. I know this must be approached with cunning, especially given his strange dark mood. As I am counting the quires of paper still left in the Spanish leather box on my father's desk, I see Daniel staring without blinking at the wall. His blind staring goes on for more than a minute and I decide the time has come to interrogate.

'Daniel?'

'Aye.' He does not look round.

'Did you ever see the branding iron in use?' I try to adopt an air of boyishly macabre fascination.

Daniel jerks from his reverie. 'What?'

'The branding iron, did you ever see it being used on human flesh?'

'Aye. What of it?'

''Tis a fearful thing to have letters burnt into your skin. I am curious as to how it is done.'

He shrugs. 'If the iron is hot enough and it is done quick even the infants do not squeal for long.'

My natural repugnance breaks through. 'It is done to children?'

'Of course. Are they not our property too?'

I try to recover my pose of school-boy ghoulishness. 'Was there a noxious smell of burning flesh?'

He yawns. 'There are many foul smells on the Careenage.'

I take a quick breath. 'Is that in St Kitts?'

Daniel is suddenly still.

'Why do you mention the place?'

'I heard that the *Swallow* put in there.'

'How? How did you hear that?'

'A rumour, that's all.'

With a sudden clatter, Daniel stands up. His chair slaps back onto the bare floor and he does not stop to pick it up before he strides over to the desk. He stands over me very close and a sour manly smell oozes down. I wonder if he has had a bath since coming on shore. 'A rumour put about by who?'

Despite his muscled height and seething anger, Daniel no longer frightens me. Perhaps because I sense that I am in the right. For today I am the hunter and he is my quarry.

'The sailors gossip like old women.' I say with a laugh in my voice. 'Maybe they connected 'Kitts' with 'Ravenglass' for some reason that escapes me.' I laugh again.

'Hmmm,' Daniel stands back. He does not smile at my jest.

'Although I see from Captain Power's notes a suggestion of a north-north-easterly course that might support such a rumour.'

Daniel snorts. 'He was gone before we even sighted Dominica.'

'Gone?'

His eyes narrow. 'In the hurricane.'

'So the *Swallow* was making for St Kitts by way of Dominica?'

He lowers his face so close that the ends of our noses are almost touching. 'I have told your father everything about this voyage. And I most certainly will not say any more about it to you, *lad*.'

A disparaging irony infuses his last word. But I remain undeterred. 'Have you told my father about St Kitts?'

I see his big hand beside me clench into a fist but it does not otherwise move.

'You have no notion, do you, of what a voyage on a slaver is like?'

His breath is rotten in my face.

'No. Tell me.'

He snorts. 'Where would we start on such tale without causing offence to your refined sensibilities?'

I shrug. 'Perhaps with what happened to the thirty five Africans unaccounted for in the ledger.'

Here, roughly, he takes hold of me by the upper arms. 'Listen, lad. The things that happen on a slaving voyage could not be imagined by a coddled milord such as you.'

Now, at last, my heart knocks against my chest, not with fear but rage.

'Tempting, wasn't it, for you and Riddle to pocket a Bill of Exchange to the value of three hundred and twenty five guineas? Especially once Captain Power was safe in his watery grave.'

Fiercely, Daniel lets go my arms and pushes me into my father's chair. 'I have explained everything to Mr Ravenglass,' he says. 'And I will say nothing more to you. You are ridiculous.'

'Excellent. Then you will have no fear when I communicate my own conclusions to my father.'

Daniel is still for a second and then he stands straight and folds his arms. 'Which would leave your sister a perpetually embarrassed spinster. She has no hope except me.'

By then, my blood was too hot to consider the strange implications of his words. They seemed no more than arrogant slurs that sent rage boiling through me. So I had no hesitation in going to my father and setting out how I imagined he had been swindled by the man he had trusted with both his fortune and his daughter. But my father merely put a hand across his mouth and shook his head.

Ravenglass

The last I see of my sister's betrothed is from our back landing window when I spot him with Fliss out in the orchard. They are too far away to be overheard, but I see Fliss, dishevelled, pick up her skirts above the fallen leaves and start to run ahead of Daniel out of the trees. Her face is red and tear-streaked. Daniel's head is bowed and he does not call after her nor try to catch her up. Fliss leaves the yard by the covered carriageway and doesn't return until evening. And next morning, with the first frost of autumn, Daniel Bragg is gone.

I overhear my father telling Aunt Ravenglass that he neither knows nor cares where the blackguard has gone but my heart quickens as I imagine how Fliss will react. A wave of guilt chills through me as I think of my own part in this drama.

That winter, our household's hopes were all pinned on a sale of the *Swallow* but, stripped of sails and tied up at the edge of the strand, she was a sorry-looking vessel. My father could not afford even to place a reserve on her price, and so, in the New Year of 1743, she went under Mr Shaw's auction-hammer for a mere hundred and fifty guineas.

Not long after the sale, I spy her pulled up on to the shipwright's yard for the replacement of her foremast and several other major works commissioned by the new owners. And sitting beside the *Swallow*'s hull, like a mother minding an overlarge babe, is the cook.

'Young Raven!'

He beckons me over and I wave to him as I cross the shipyard. Despite an icy wind, the air is infused with the tang of tar and fresh-sawn wood. A pile of old rope and a sack of oakum lie at each side of the one-legged sailor.

He nods and winks. 'Still dancing a jig?'

I laugh and make a flourishing leap that ends in a bow with my mended ankle foremost.

The cook nods. 'Just as well I didn't put that foot to the saw.'

'Were you going to?' I ask, shocked. But another wink is his only reply.

'I thought you'd have found another ship by now,' I say, glancing up.

The black and barnacled underside of the *Swallow* rises above us like the carcass of a whale.

He shakes his head. 'The staying I'll be with the old bird. They is aiming to put her back to a collier for the Dublin trade.'

'With Riddle as master?'

The cook laughs loud and long as if what I have said is in fact the funniest riddle he has ever heard.

'Nay, lad. I'd not be with her if he was.'

Vexation rises up in me, itching like a nettle-rash at the way my father has lost his fortune.

'Tell me Cook, did the *Swallow* put in at St Kitts on her last voyage?'

The cook picks up a stub of rope and pulls at it with black-nailed fingers.

'Was said I'd get a guinea to keep quiet about it.' He looks up at me with a canny smile. 'But I never saw any such coin.'

'Were some Africans sold there? After Riddle had taken over as master?'

The cook takes up a long-stemmed clay pipe from the ground and sucks hard. 'That I canna say. Though the sorry creatures we unloaded on to that forsaken isle did not, thanking Christ, return to the *Swallow*.'

I shake my head. 'And Captain Power? How exactly did meet his maker?'

The cook's face darkens. 'Do ye not know?'

'Overboard in a gale, it was said.'

'That's true enough.'

'Did you see him go over?'

He takes a long draw on the pipe and puffs out tobacco smoke from the corner of his mouth. 'Only Riddle and Bragg saw that.'

My heart drops in my chest. 'When did it happen?'

'Afore Dominica. Whilst the three of them was arguing.'

'Did they disagree often?'

He shrugs. 'They never stopped their arganey the whole voyage.'

I take a long breath. I have now no doubt that together, Bosun Riddle and Daniel Bragg have embezzled all profit from the human cargo sold in Barbados and then added to it with an entirely unrecorded sale in St Kitts. They have also quite possibly murdered Captain Power.

The cook leans back and starts up his old tune.

'The Raven and the Swallow, the Swallow the Swall-ow,
The Raven and the Swallow were never meant to part.'

I sigh and pat the cook's sleeve. 'Do you know where Riddle and Bragg are now, cook?'

He takes up his pipe and puffs tobacco smoke into his cheek. 'Riddle left here sharpish. Word is he joined as mate on *HMS Wasp*, a twenty one gun sloop out of Ellenborough. He be on his way back Carib waters by now, I fancy. Under 'em soon with any luck.'

'And Daniel Bragg? Did you hear where he went?'

The cook clears his throat and spits. 'Heard he paid passage on a coal brig.'

'Bound for Dublin?'

'No. Bristol.'

My knees weaken. 'Bristol? Are you sure?'

Cook nods and I find myself walking around and around in a tight circle so that I don't fall down.

'Are you aright, lad?'

'Aye,' I say, though I am not. For I have now not the slightest doubt that Daniel Bragg had with him on that coal brig, secreted somewhere about his person, a Bill of Exchange drawn on Mr Jefferies of Broad Street, Bristol and made out for a sum of three hundred and twenty five guineas, payable to the bearer in silver or gold.

The cook starts up his well-worn tune afresh.
'The Raven cracks a riddle, a riddle, a ri-ddle,
The Raven cracks a riddle but shall not stoop to brag.'

As I hastily bid him farewell, the curious verse lodges in my ear and refuses to leave.

I decide not to speak to Fliss about the circumstances of Daniel Bragg's departure hoping that if nothing is said about him, she might, before long, allow her affections to fix upon a more worthy subject. I had no inkling of the growing reason why this could now never happen.

That winter, Fliss no longer walked the cliff-tops but stayed cocooned in her chamber becoming yet more pale and ill-looking. She rarely dressed herself properly, often wearing an old knitted smock over her petticoat. From some angles she seemed emaciated, from others swollen. I started to imagine that she was being devoured by a tumour growing inside her. Some days, I was so thoroughly convinced that Fliss was dying that I ate as little as she.

During the freezing months of that year, Fliss rarely joined us in the dining parlour of an evening, insisting, even when Aunt Ravenglass complained about the waste of good candle wax, that she could be warm only in her bed. But when the first signs of spring appeared, I told myself that Fliss was getting better and one April evening so mild that a window was open, she came down from her chamber and stayed with us in the best parlour to sew.

'Good.' My Aunt Ravenglass declared as Fliss sat down with a needle. 'You can fashion yourself something more becoming than that shabby old smock.'

Fliss goes to the pile of mending and half-sewn linen on the floor beside the workbox. She bends awkwardly and pulls out the embroidered waistcoat wrapped in muslin. I glance at Poll. She, like me is holding her breath as Fliss unwraps the waistcoat and holds it to the fading light at the window with a quizzical eye.

'I used to think this beautiful,' Fliss says, her head to one side. 'But now it is ruined. I have ruined it.'

'No!' Poll and I say together, though Fliss is right. Heavy gilt frogging overshadows the waistcoat's delicate silken arabesques. I cannot help but see the waistcoat as an emblem of her romance with Daniel Bragg, though the garment now looks too wide and short in the body to fit him.

Poll casts me a nervous glance. We are both wary of what Fliss will do next. It is easy to imagine her unpicking all her fine work or even perhaps, shredding the thing violently to pieces.

Instead she surprises us all with a half-smile as she brings the waistcoat over to me.

'Perhaps you should have it, Kit.'

'Me?' I look up from the little fan-stitch hearts I am stitching in raspberry-coloured wool.

'Aye.' Fliss holds up the garish waistcoat, spangles flashing. 'You have the skill to re-fashion it to your own taste.'

'Of course,' I say, struggling to keep my smile steady.

'Put it on, then, and I will pin it to fit.'

There is no longer a mirror in the best parlour but Poll and Aunt Ravenglass sit with needles suspended and I can see approval reflected in their faces. Perhaps the waistcoat's peculiar extravagance suits me.

'It is a little wide and the arm holes too big,' Fliss says. 'But you can take it apart and re-cut the back panel.'

'Will you not help me?' I ask, unease growing.

'You will manage perfectly well on your own.'

My fingers stroke the exotic landscape of precious threads that now weighs across my body. I can't think of this love token as mine. 'Are you sure you want me to have it?'

'Aye,' she nods. 'It will look very well on you.'

The ghost of a smile stays on her face but tears lurk behind.

I want to hope that this gifting of the waistcoat to me is a symbol of my sister's renunciation of Daniel Bragg. But there is something unnatural in her calmness. A meek acceptance of misfortune is as foreign to Fliss's nature as to my own. Passion runs as strong in her. And I feel, with a shiver, as if her true self has been scooped out and taken away by Daniel Bragg.

'Thank you,' I say and kiss her on the mouth. Her lips are cold and thin. 'Fliss...'

'What?'

For the first time in many weeks I catch her gaze and hold it. But there is a sheen of emptiness across her eyes. Anything I could say will sound meaningless.

'Thank you with all my heart,' I manage.

She nods and goes to close the window. A black thunder cloud has darkened the room and cooled the breeze. As Fliss leaves the best parlour, she turns and blows me a kiss. Then she goes up to her room.

the eleventh chapter

It was that same night when my father burst into my bedchamber, his shirt drenched and filthy, to waken me by shouting in my face that Fliss was gone.

'What do you mean, gone?'

I raise my hand to shield the glare of a single candle flame. My father's face is dark behind it.

'She's not here. Her bed is empty.'

He slumps down to sit on my counterpane.

'Have you looked through the house?'

He nods but I cannot see his face. His shirt is so sodden and smeared with mud it clings to his back.

'And been outside?'

He turns to me, silent for a moment. 'I found the yard door unbolted.'

'Why would she have gone out?'

He opens his hands in seeming despair. 'Why would she be anywhere save her bed?'

I raise myself up to sitting. 'What o'clock is it?'

'Past four.'

'Has she gone to Poll's bed? She would always do that as a child.'

He shakes his head. Only later do I think it odd that he did not go to check.

I run my hand through my hair and rub my face. Vexation at being woken mixes with fear. 'How did you find she was gone?'

My father pauses. 'I thought I heard a commotion from her chamber, as if something heavy had fallen. But when I went in it was empty.'

'Was that not a thunder-clap?'

His head shakes. 'We must look for her on the cliff-top.'

'The cliff-top?'

A cold quaking starts in my chest. Could Fliss, in some fit of lunacy have returned in the dark to her old haunt along Saltom cliff-top? Surely not. But now my father has planted this fear in my mind, I will not rest.

Jumping from the bed, I unlatch the shutter at the window. The moon is a clipped white fingernail in the blackness.

I turn back to my father. 'We'll need torches.'

He nods grimly.

And so, with hastily donned stockings, breeches and a coat over my nightshirt, I follow my father up the cliff path with an unlit torch in my hand. Light from his link flares over the stony path between the twin rails of the wagon-way. The earlier storm has passed leaving the dark air damp and still. We do not meet a soul. Even the harbour, always a ceaseless cauldron of mumbles and creaks, seems quiet. The Light-House throws a dim glow behind tilted masts as their vessels have been dropped on to the inner strand by the outgoing tide. At the outer pier, yellowish lights from lanterns on the *HMS Prince of Orange*, a lately docked sixty gun man o'war, prick the blackness of water and sky. An unseen seabird flies too close to me. Its piping cry raises a cold shiver on my neck.

When we reach the top of the climb, my father's torch has burnt low and he holds the spluttering stub to the tip of my new link. As we wait for the flame to catch, his face shines with sweat and tears in the fiery glow. I lift my new-lit torch high and look as far as I am able across the undulating grassy headland. Hidden waves crash over rolling shingle. Between the waves comes the heart-beat thump of the Fire-Engine at Saltom pit and I fancy I can see above the pale lip of land a furl of grey smoke from the engine house chimney.

'Shall we call for her?' My voice trembles.

'Call?' My father, terrifyingly, is also shaking.

'Her name.'

'Aye. Go on, son. Call for her.'

I look all around the empty dark.

'Fliss… Fliss!'

I cough. My shouting is so weak, I feel suddenly sick.

My father grabs my coat sleeve. 'Come towards the sea. Watch your step.'

'Fliss! Fliss! Fliss!' I shout as we stumble across the tussocky grass.

'Stop that now, son,' my father says quietly and I am glad to. I do not like even the thought of Fliss being out here alone.

The grind of waves comes closer and I sense we must be near the place that Fliss was wont to stand in her long vigil for the *Swallow*.

'How did she seem last evening?' my father asks.

'As she has been…' I shrug. Then I shake my head. 'No… I mean…' I decide there is no reason to tell him of Fliss's queer moods. 'She gave me the fancy-worked waistcoat she has been making so long. And it seemed as if a weight had lifted from her.'

My father does not reply and when I look at him, I see through the greyness that his eyes are closed.

'Put out the link now,' he says. 'We'll soon see the light.'

I push the torch into a hunk of wet grass and twist it until the flame is gone. Then we stand with our backs to the sea and search the eastern sky for the hidden outline of mountains. The air is lightening. Slowly, the cliff-top takes on the ashy outlines of dawn. Other birds add their screeches to the piping of the sea-waders.

In the dead light, my father's face looks worse than I have ever seen it.

'We should go to the edge now,' he says.

And almost before we reach the drop, my body seems to realise what my eyes are about to see. I am trembling so hard I can scarce walk.

At the edge, I peer down through the dimmest of grey lights, past the craggy ledges to the speckled strip of shingle with the heave and drag of low waves. At the harbour end of the cove stands the black outline of the new Quarrymen's Pier. Beside it just below the tide-line, something big and pale is lying in the water. With each flop of grey surf, the thing is tugged into a semblance of life. The light is still thick enough for me to hope that the object may be a roll of old sailcloth or a dead sheep.

'Father…'

He does not look my way, nor make any move at all.

'Father, is it..?

'There is enough light now,' he says flatly. 'I'll go down first.'

The cliff is not as steep as it looks from above being hummocked with clumps of rocky red soil and coarse grass. As we descend, my breath is shallow and my mind empty. Stones skitter from my feet on to my father's back and head but he doesn't seem to notice.

When we arrive, panting, on the shingle I try not to look toward the thing in the shallows. Rinsed clear by the storm, the sky slices across the pewter sea.

'Come, Christopher,' my father says. 'You must help me.'

And so we go over to the pale thing in the shallows. My first look upon it stops my heart and numbs all feeling. For the thing is a woman, face down in the water and nudged by the tide against one of the rocky ledges that step out to Tom Hurd Rocks. Without any thought at all, I find myself humming. It is a familiar tune. The words to it roll unbidden about my head.

'With the whip in my hand, she not able to stand
Ran backwards and fell from the rock to the Strand,

The white soles of her bare feet and her legs are scratched and bruised. Her shift has rucked up above her knees and only the weight of her sodden knitted smock is keeping her privates covered.

'At this dreadful fall, in blood she did sprawl,
And had not the power on Heaven to call…'

My father splashes out to her and kneels down in the limp

waves. He puts his hands on the body then he looks up at me. I am frozen between yearning to know and longing to stay ignorant.

'No,' I say, but already he has turned the body.

Her eyes are open and her mouth is blue. The uncovered scar on her neck is so raw it seems to have become opened and bled. I can't even wonder if a fall from the cliff might have produced blood in this way. My mind is too numbed with shock. For this is unquestionably Fliss. But she is gone. She is gone. She is gone.

'Help me, my son,' my father says and I go closer. I lay my hands on her and find that I do not mind, for the cold thing I am touching seems so little like my sister.

We each hold a shoulder and as gently as we may, we pull the body free from the sea-water and on to the shingle bank.

'No,' I say again but without conviction. The eyes are empty of the spark that made this fleshly thing into Fliss. I slump down beside her and thrust my own hands into the shingle, relishing the pain.

'Which makes my heart ache, and ready to break,
I pray, my dear saviour, some pity now take.'

My father puts a hand to my shoulder and grips it tight. 'We must take her to the coroner. Go to the harbour and find a man to help. I've not the strength left in me …'

I start to cry.

'Go,' he nods at me and keeps on nodding. 'I'll stay here with her.'

Tears stream my face as I trudge through shingle and up toward the harbour. The ballad will not go away.

'In hope that the sea would wash her away,
I hastened homewards without more delay.'

But the rest of my mind is frozen. For how can any of this be true? How can I not yet have awakened from this most horrible of dreams? Time starts to move in jerks. I am already unable to piece the past hour back together in my mind. Nothing seems real. Even the harbour, with the glow of a new day through spider-webs of mast-rigging, looks like a painting in oils.

I wonder who I might call upon for help. Any I ask would be glad to assist, either out of respect to my father, or curiosity about a dead girl. But what will I say to them? The words *my sister is dead* simply will not form in my mouth. Then I see the arches beneath the loading gallery on the Steer and realise who I must ask.

When the coal tubs reach the bottom of the wagon-way, their coal is tipped into a great holding pen above the Steer before being sent thundering down wooden hurries to the harbour-side. Some of the arches beneath this pen are used as workshops by smiths and coopers. One of the arches is, I know, where Jossy sleeps.

I go to the place and find the entrance covered by planks of wood and a flap of sailcloth. I have not seen him since our unhappy meeting on the cliff path the previous year and there is no telling whether he is still here.

'Jossy!'

Perhaps he has moved on. And even if he is here, he may not be willing to go with me.

'Jossy!' I hammer on a plank with my fist. 'If you are there... Please! Please.'

The sailcloth moves back and he is suddenly before me, his shirt open and his feet bare.

'Kit!' He steps forward, his face aghast, and takes a firm hold of the top of my arm. At that moment his touch is the single thing around me that seems real. 'What is it?'

Then I start to sob and can't stop.

Jossy's grip on me tightens. 'Kit! Tell me.'

'My sister,' I gulp.

Snot and tears bathe my face.

'Felicity?' Jossy's eyes widen. 'What? What has happened?' My upper arms are in his vice-like grip. No one has ever touched me in such a way before.

'She fell... below the cliff.'

Even as I say it, I puzzle how a fall from such an uneven cliff can have been the thing that killed her.

'Fell? No! How can that be?'

I shake my head.

'How is she? And the...' He seems to stop himself from saying more.

'She...' Words snare in my throat and I cannot say more.

'I'm coming,' Jossy says, forcing feet into battered shoes and grabbing his sailor's jacket. 'Should I fetch the surgeon from the *Prince of Orange?*'

Mutely, I shake my head and tears flow afresh.

'Why not? I'm sure he'd come ashore.'

My head shakes again. 'No, no.'

And then I meet Jossy's fierce gaze. As he takes in my meaning, he gives a long shuddering sigh and a veil falls across his eyes like a curtain across a door.

'Will you help?' I ask.

But he is already walking and I find myself hurrying to keep pace with him as I retrace my way back toward the sea. Only the side of his face is visible to me but his cheek glistens wet.

As we round the headland, my mind persuades me that I am mistaken. For how can Fliss be gone? And when my father comes into view, I see that he has laid his coat across her. Perhaps her breath has returned and he is keeping her warm. Perhaps I should run to the *Prince of Orange* and yell for the surgeon to attend her.

But then I see that my father is kneeling beside Fliss in an attitude of prayer. I miss my step and stumble against the stones. I have never seen my father offer up any prayer outside his public devotions at King George's Church and the sight of him in his shirt, ashen-faced and dishevelled yet rapt in supplication to God, brings a surge of bile to my throat. It is as if he has lost his mind.

When he hears the crunch of stones beneath our feet, he stands. He comes up to Jossy and lays a hand on his breast.

'Is that you, Littlewood's boy?'

'Yes, sir.'

My father nods and almost smiles. 'Good. You are strong. Can you carry her unaided?'

'I can, sir.' Jossy's face is blank.

'Will you carry her gently?'

Jossy does not answer but stoops to lift Fliss up in his arms like a bridegroom. For a second, I think his lips touch her matted hair, though this is only because of the lolling of her lifeless head. Her bare legs are wrapped in my father's coat for modesty's sake and though Jossy lifts the dead weight of her easily, the queerly heavy listing of her limbs is the most horrible sight I ever saw.

Fliss's face is hidden as her head falls against Jossy's shoulder and even now I wonder if she could be alive. I take my father's arm and we cling together as we walk behind Jossy to the Steer.

Many are about now, sailors, carters, street-sellers. As we approach, all move aside and turn to stare. Some of the men, even on the ship decks, remove their hats.

When we reach the Tongue, Jossy stops.

'To Queen Street?' he asks though his voice is queer.

'No lad,' my father croaks. 'To the Custom House. There will have to be an inquest for a sudden death.'

We skirt the strand and follow the growing reek of tobacco smoke. In the courtyard behind the Custom House, the Customs men have set a fire to burn up tobacco bales too damaged to be worth the payment of duty. They have done it early to avoid nuisance to the inn from the noxious fumes. As we pass under the archway into the Custom House yard, I'm hit by the stench of burning tobacco and a roaring pulse of heat from the bonfire's yellow flames. It feels as if we are entering into the very mouth of hell.

the twelfth chapter

Toward the end of that same morning, in the Landing Waiters' office that backs on to the Custom House yard, men in wigs and best coats stand up, one by one, to swear the juryman's oath. While my father stands rigid, watching, my own legs refuse to bear any weight and I slump down to the floor with my back against the wall.

The office is fresh-painted and bare. It is the largest room on the ground floor of the Custom House and the Customs men are well used to it being taken over by the coroner for an immediate inquest when some drunken sailor is scooped too late from the harbour. But today, on the trestle set up in the coolness by the window, a female body is laid out under the sailcloth sheet.

I cannot bear to look at Fliss's bloated, shrouded form. How can this motionless thing be my sister? And yet it is. My father does not seem to see the body. Nor does he notice me slump down to sit on the floor. He seems consumed by the passing of the bible from hand to hand as each of the jurors swear their oath. Early this morning as soon as he was told of the sudden death, the coroner, Mr Shaw, put out word of the inquest and within a few hours, a jury of sixteen townsmen men has assembled to pronounce upon the nature of my sister's death.

I recognise some of them. Mr Moorhouse, the chandler, Mr Pratt, the peruke-shop owner. But none are inclined to meet my eye. Mr Shaw is the auctioneer from Scotch Street and well-used to directing a room full of men. Once the oaths are sworn, he addresses the company describing the jurors' solemn duty to inquire on behalf of King George into how, when, where and in what manner Felicity Ravenglass came to her death. Witnesses will be summoned to assist with the inquiries and a verdict, which must be agreed by all sixteen jurors, cannot be pronounced until each of them in turn has viewed the corpse.

Here, there is a small interlude as a maid comes in the back yard entrance from The George Inn next door with a bottle of rum and a basket full of thimble glasses. As she hands around the half-filled glasses, Mr Shaw in his blue velvet sale-day coat nods for glasses to be offered to the two Land Waiters who have remained in their office and also to the witnesses, that is, my father, Jossy and I.

This is the only time I can ever recall that my father has refused strong drink and I too cannot bear the thought of such a taste in my mouth. But when I glance at Jossy beside me, he has already thrown back the rum into his throat.

Mr Shaw begins by asking who shall be named the First Finder.

My father steps forward to the middle of the room. 'I, sir.'

Mr Shaw nods. 'Very good, Mr Ravenglass. My commiserations. Now, if you would take hold of the Good Book, swear your oath and then tell these here assembled good and lawful men of Whitehaven the circumstances of your sad discovery.'

As my father takes the bible and swears the oath, I see in a way that others in the room will not, that he is quite unlike his true self. He is wigless and wearing the sea-stained coat that had covered Fliss's body, but his stance is of a Lord Mayor addressing his aldermen. His voice booms out, but an octave lower and less rooted in Cumberland than usual. This proud act is intended to convey my father's confidence in his words. But even in my stupor of shock and grief, I wonder if it could instead create an impression of pretence.

'I awoke at around three of the clock this morning, there being some great noise,' my father begins. 'I thought I must see that all was well, but finding my daughter's bed empty, I searched about the house for her and then in the stable-yard. Finding no trace of her, I awakened my son and together we went to the cliff above the harbour. And at first light, looking down, I saw... her.'

Only at the end of his speech does he falter. Mr Shaw gestures for the maid a glass of rum to be brought but again my father refuses.

'Why did you go looking upon the cliff?' the coroner asks, after a polite moment to allow my father composure.

'It was her habit to go up there. My son thought she may have walked there in her sleep.'

My heart drops like a pendulum in my chest. I said no such thing. The cliff-top was my father's idea. Why should he not say so?

The jurymen exchange glances.

'And what was the attitude of the body?'

'Lying face down in the water and trapped against a rocky ledge,' my father says.

'Covered by water?'

'Aye.'

'How deep did you wade out to her?'

'Almost to my waist.'

Again my stomach twists for this was not at all how we found her in the shingle-rolled shallows. Our stockings were wetted only to our knees.

'And so,' the coroner continues, 'it was your assumption that your daughter had died by drowning?'

'It was.'

'And when you approached the corpse, did this assumption change?'

'It did not.'

'Thank you, Mr Ravenglass.'

The coroner turns to talk to the jurors who stand in a huddle, their backs to the cold fireplace as if it is lit. Whispers pass between them.

Then Mr Shaw turns again to my father. 'Was it apparent to you how your daughter might have entered the water?'

From where I sit on the floor at the back of the room, I cannot quite see the whole of my father's face but even without the rum, it has flushed red.

'I imagined she must have fell from the Quarrymen's Bulwark.'

My father's voice is loud still has a pretence of confidence but I have to stop myself shaking my head. Fliss was nowhere near the bulwark, and the outward tide could not have pulled her from there to the place we found her. If she fell it must have been from the cliff, though the more I think on it, the more unlikely this seems.

'Did she walk forth from your house clothed only as we see her now?'

My father hesitates, but for no more than a second. 'Her stockings and shoes were took by the sea, I suppose.'

'But surely she could not have wandered to this fearful place on a moonless night and still remain asleep. Why would she go there?'

'I do not know, sir.' My father hangs his head.

But Mr Shaw nods as if the answer seems good enough, and turns back to the jurors. Their conference goes on some while and at one point I see the coroner turn to look at me with an eyebrow raised. It has not occurred to me that I might also be called to give evidence. The ceiling above me starts to spin. What will I say if they ask where the body lay? I cannot contradict my father, but I will perjure myself unless I do.

Mr Shaw nods to my father. 'That is all. And we shall spare your son the ordeal of questioning on the assumption that his answers will reflect your own.'

My heart skitters before it slows.

'Instead,' Mr Shaw goes on, 'we summon the African who carried the corpse hither. Come, boy.'

The coroner beckons Jossy forward with an extravagant

gesticulation as if he will not otherwise understand.

Jossy goes to the centre of the room and takes the place my father has just quitted. I look up, shame-faced. It is my doing that Jossy must stand here under the cold gaze of so many Whitehaven worthies. If I had not asked him for help, he would have now been at work in the mine.

'Tell us your name, boy.'

'Josiah Bone.'

'And your occupation?'

'Able seaman. And lately, a hewer at Saltom pit.'

The coroner nods. 'Will you swear an oath on our holy bible?'

'Yes, sir, I will.'

'You are baptised into the English church?'

'I am.'

'Good.' He hands Jossy the dense volume bound in worn black leather. 'And shall I read you the oath?'

'I can read it myself, sir.' Jossy holds up the card. '*I do swear this oath by Almighty God…*'

His reading voice is quiet but firm and unhesitating. A stab of pride brings a fat tear to my eye.

The coroner takes back the book and Jossy stands like a naval rating with feet apart and hands clasped behind his back.

'Tell us, Mr Bone, how you came to be carrying the corpse.'

'I was asked to, by Master Ravenglass,' he glances back at me.

'Why did he come to you?'

'We sailed together aboard the *Swallow* and are used to doing favours for one another.'

For a second, like the wheeling of a bat on a summer night, I glimpse a smirk cross the jurors' faces. But it is gone so swiftly I can't be sure it was ever there.

'What did the young master say?' Mr Shaw continues.

'That he needed help… for his sister.'

'What sort of help?'

'Because she had taken a fall and…'

Here Jossy's gaze slips toward the trestle in the window and he falters. For a second his eyes close and he seems to sway as if dizzy.

'Take your time, boy.' Mr Shaw nods an encouragement. 'Indeed. So you went with him around the headland?'

'Yes, sir.'

'And when you first saw the corpse, where was it?'

Jossy takes a breath. 'On the strand.'

'And as you came close to the corpse, what was your assumption about how she had met her end?'

'I can't say, sir.'

There is an intake of breath about the room.

'Come now,' Mr Shaw says sharply. 'You must have had some thought about it. That she had fell, perhaps, as Master Ravenglass had told you?'

Jossy shakes his head. 'She was too unmarked for a fall to have killed her.'

'Perhaps she hit her head on a rock? There is a mark on her forehead.'

'The graze is slight, I think.'

'So she must have died by drowning, as her father has suggested?'

'At first I thought that, but then I saw that it could not be the case.' Jossy speaks quietly and does not take his eyes from the coroner.

'But her clothes were wet through were they not?'

'Yes, sir.'

'Although there had been rain which also might have caused the soaking.' Mr Shaw passes his gaze along the bench of jurors who nod in assent.

'No. It was sea-water.'

'You sound very sure.'

'If there is one thing in which I am expert, sir, it is sea-water.'

A laugh goes around the room but it is quickly suppressed. I glance at my father. He still stands rod-straight but a cloud has crossed his face, and it seems made of despair more than anger.

Mr Shaw continues. 'So drowning must have seemed most likely?'

'Not to me, sir.'

'Why not?'

'I have seen many fresh-drowned men and there is always a deal of froth about their faces. There was nothing like that on hers.'

'Mr Bone, think carefully about this. You have ruled out falling and drowning as likely causes of death. Was there anything else about the state of the body that might have indicated to you the true cause?'

Jossy is still for a moment. Then he hangs his head as if overcome.

'You must answer, boy.'

'I... I couldn't say.'

'You mean there was nothing else to see?'

'That is so, sir.'

Mr Shaw frowns. 'And how did her neck appear to you?'

'Sir...' for the first time, Jossy throws a look at my father. 'I don't know, sir.'

Around the room eyebrows rise, but Mr Shaw glances at the jurymen and then nods. 'Thank you, Mr Bone.'

Jossy gives a slight bow. 'May I go now, sir, to Saltom? I'm needed at the pit.'

'Certainly.'

At the door, Jossy casts me a glance at me though his eyes are bloodshot and blank. As he leaves, acrid smoke clouds into the room from the embers of Virginia tobacco still smouldering in the yard.

'Well, gentlemen jurors,' says Mr Shaw. 'We have now reached the most onerous part of our duties, our solemn and awful requirement to view the body.'

Amongst the jurors, there is a murmur of assent mixed with dismay and, horridly, excitement.

My head drops to my knees, arms wrapping my head to stop up my ears. Out of one squinting eye, I see the coroner move across the room toward the window and put his hand on the sheet across the trestle. My eye snaps shut but even so I fear I will puke. How Fliss would hate their prying eyes upon her, and there is not even a ribband around her neck! I try to conjure up a picture of Fliss at her happiest, in one of our home-made theatricals, she in my clothes and I in hers.

'Mr Ravenglass!'

It is the coroner's voice, and so sharp that I cannot help looking up. The sailcloth sheet, thank Jesus, has been returned to its former place.

'Step forward again, Mr Ravenglass. You are still under oath.'

My father does as he is asked.

'I and the jurors have further questions for you, having viewed your daughter's body.' There is a murmuring amongst the jurymen and Mr Shaw coughs before he begins. 'Firstly, I must ask about the marks around her neck.'

'It is an old scar, from childhood,' my father replies quickly.

'But the wound is raw with signs of fresh blood.'

'The skin must have re-opened during her fall into the sea.'

'You think so? Even though there are no other signs of injury, apart from some scratches on her legs?'

My father is silent. I turn my head to observe him more squarely, and I have no doubt that he is holding back some truth, though what it could be and why he should do so, I cannot imagine. A queasy swirl of dread fills my gut.

'And I must enquire about the last time that you spoke to your daughter. When was that, and what was her state of mind?'

My father shifts his stance. 'I spoke to her yesterday. She was as she always is... was.'

'How was that?'

'Quiet... biddable...'

My blood stirs an inner voice that shouts *No! No!* For these things were the very opposite of Fliss.

Even Mr Shaw raises an eyebrow. 'And no parting letter nor papers from the lady have been found?'

'No. None.'

I wonder what sort of papers he has in mind, though perhaps I would rather not know.

'Because we imagine that her disposition must have been somewhat changed by the nature of her condition.'

'No!' My father snaps. 'It was not.'

Mr Shaw stares at my father for several silent seconds. I look from one to the other, baffled by what this condition might be.

Then the coroner says, 'Very well,' and turns back to the jurors.

Beside me, with hardly a sound except for the crackle of dying flames, the door opens and a plainly dressed woman slips in from the yard. From my place on the floor I cannot see her face as she crosses the room but her grazet petticoat almost brushes against my father's coat as she speaks quietly to the coroner. Mr Shaw gives her some reply and even before she has turned around I know it is Hannah Salkeld. My pulse quickens.

'A witness has come forward,' Mr Shaw says nodding at Hannah. 'Please step before us and prepare to swear your oath.'

Hannah's voice is high but clear. 'I will take no oath, sir, for I always speak truth.'

There is a murmur about the room with the whisper of *dissenter*.

'Then if you wish to give your testimony,' Mr Shaw says without much surprise, 'you must make an affirmation.' He goes to the table where papers are spread and takes a hand-written a card from inside the bible, but Hannah is already speaking.

'I Hannah Salkeld do declare in the presence of Almighty God the witness of the truth of what I say.'

Eyebrows are raised amongst the jurymen but Mr Shaw nods and stands before Hannah.

'Now then mistress, tell us all clearly why you have come hither.'

I can see only the back of Hannah's head. A wide-brimmed

felt hat is pulled low over her linen cap and tied under her chin. Her words, addressed to the coroner and the jurors, don't falter.

'I heard the call put about the town for witnesses,' Hannah says, 'and so it is my duty as a Christian citizen to tell you what I saw last night.'

'It is,' Mr Shaw nods. 'Go ahead, mistress.'

'Last night, as I returned to my lodgings from the salterns, I came close to a man carrying a heavy load across the Steer toward the headland. I now feel sure that this was Henry Ravenglass carrying the body of his daughter.'

A gasp goes about the room and my heart knocks against my chest. Next to me, I sense my father flinch but I can't bear to look at him. All his hostility to Hannah will have been justified in his mind by the falsehood she has just spoken, for falsehood it surely must be.

'Order!' Mr Shaw raps the table with the stoppered rum bottle as if it is an auctioneer's gavel. 'Order! Gentlemen!' He clears his throat then turns back to Hannah. 'Now, that is a grave claim, mistress. You must elaborate. What time was this exactly and what made you arrive at your conclusion?'

'Sometime after midnight.'

'Why so late?'

'Yesterday was our first salt-boiling of the year and we stayed late to tend the furnace until the flames were all extinguished. The pans may be damaged beyond repair if they are left to burn dry. It was an hour or so beyond midnight when the fires were fully out.'

'And where exactly did you see the person you thought to be Mr Ravenglass? There was very little moon last night as I recall.'

'My lodging is near the Market Place, and it is my habit when it's dark to return there along the strand. The harbour is always lit by the Light-House and also last night by the lanterns on the war-ship. I was about to turn inland to the Market Place when I saw a figure crossing the Steer. He was struggling with the heavy load across his shoulder.'

'A load that might have been a body?'

'Yes.'

'And what makes you think that this person was Henry Ravenglass?' Mr Shaw glances over at my father.

Hannah shrugs. 'The frame and demeanour of the man. I am very well acquainted with his appearance.'

'Did you see his face?'

'Not directly.'

Mr Shaw raises an eyebrow. 'You are his kin, are you not?'

'Not by blood. He was married to my mother's sister.'

'And do you have some grievance against the man?'

Hannah's stance stiffens. 'Why should that have any bearing on what I saw?'

'So, you do?'

'I saw him last night carrying a body toward Tom Hurd Rocks. That is my testimony.'

'Well, mistress.' Mr Shaw puts on his spectacles and looks down at the papers on the table as he speaks. 'That will be all. We cannot take your testimony into account as it has no definite relevance to this case. You may leave this hearing.'

Hannah does not move. 'I know what I saw. And it is not by chance, I say, that there have been several foul deaths in the Ravenglass family...'

Mr Shaw's eyes flash. 'Leave, madam. Now.'

Hannah turns on her heel, grazet petticoat flaring, and strides toward the door. Just before she exits, she gives me a glare and bangs the door shut. For some moments, all I hear is my own heart beating. I know that Hannah would never lie. But in this, surely, she must be mistaken.

Mr Shaw then announces that he will retire with the jurymen to the Searchers' Office on the other side of the covered carriageway to confer on the verdict. Having gathered up his papers, he leads the jurymen away.

My father and I are left waiting in the back corner of the

office while the Customs and Excise men move toward the fireplace. They whisper between themselves and cast us occasional glances, but they seem reluctant to return to their tall desks. For that would require coming closer to the front window, and to Fliss.

'Come lad.' My father pulls me up by the arm and guides me to sit on to the jurors' bench. Then he sinks down beside me.

'At least they did not require you to speak,' he says and gives a shuddering sigh.

I open my mouth to reply but close it again. Nothing I might say seems to have any point or importance. My hand is shaking and I thrust it beneath my leg. No matter what words are used, my mind still will not take in the meaning of Fliss's life being at an end.

Then my father leans down to me and lowers his voice to a murmur. 'Whatever the verdict may say, Christopher, be assured that everything I have ever done was intended for the good of your sister.'

I look up at him, blinking. 'What do you mean, Father?'

He only takes a long breath and closes his eyes. Hannah cannot be right. She cannot. But perhaps some jurymen will believe her.

'What will happen, Father, if they think her… think her death is not an accident?'

His voice is very quiet. 'If killed by her own hand, there will be no funeral nor headstone. Perhaps not even a church burial.' My father shakes his head. 'So that is not a verdict I could ever accept.'

'Or killed by another?'

'If they have a suspicion of murder, the coroner will direct that the suspected person be apprehended and taken to the House of Correction to await trial.'

My gaze latches on to my father's. 'But what if they think…'

He raises his forefinger and taps his lips. 'Say no more, son, and fear not. At least, not until we have heard the verdict.'

The future dives away from me like an abyss. For the next

minutes, or perhaps hours, I stay there on the bench, head against the wall and eyes closed. All that runs through my mind are a few repeated lines from that dreadful hanging ballad.

'Filthy and foul is my poor sinful soul,
Terror and horror in my conscience do roll.'

The song so fills my head that I don't at first notice the return of the jurymen.

But then, my father is pulling us both to our feet. He pushes me with him toward the centre of the office. Though the tobacco bonfire in the yard is almost out, its pungent odour fills the room. A small, variously dressed crowd has gathered at the front window of the office, all wanting to be first to hear the verdict. Their faces stare in through the glass, eager and ghoulish, at the swollen outline of Fliss's corpse.

'The jurymen are all agreed,' says Mr Shaw, 'that on this Tuesday the thirtieth of April in this year 1743, Felicity Ravenglass, being disordered in her mind and great with child, did, through misfortune alone and not otherwise, fall from the new bulwark above Whitehaven harbour in the place called Tom Hurd Rocks and there died of suffocation by water.'

A spasm wracks my father's body before he speaks. 'What? An accident, you say?'

The coroner gives a single solemn nod. And then, all pretence gone, my father drops, sobbing, to the floor.

the thirteenth chapter

It was said that my Aunt Ravenglass's wailing could be heard as far away as Roper Street. No-one could believe how hard she took the news of Fliss's death. My aunt had been little more than a child herself when she'd stepped into the maternal void left by my mother. She must have come to think of me and Fliss as her own, perhaps even more so once the likelihood of marriage retreated.

My aunt's grief so incapacitated her that it was left to Poll, on the day of the inquest, to have tickets sent about the town inviting citizens of quality to follow my sister's corpse on the morrow. That the morrow happened to be May Day added both to the pomp and the piteousness of her funeral.

By the time Fliss was carried home from the Custom House on the coffin-maker's hand-cart, Aunt Ravenglass had roused herself from the dining-parlour floor and dressed all in black. Poll was hardly less distraught and the two women, both weeping, together took charge of the rites.

The dining parlour had been made ready with the furniture cleared save for a line of chairs to support the coffin, and a waxed sheet laid on the ground with bowls of water for the washing of the corpse. Mr Moorhouse, the chandler, sent a gift of white superfine cloth which was probably worth more than the two shillings he'd received in juror's fee. Perhaps the gift of a shroud assuaged the shame he felt for having viewed Fliss in her helpless, pregnant nakedness.

I stayed in the dining parlour all night with the coffin alongside

Aunt Ravenglass and Poll. I could not abide the thought of climbing the attic stairs and passing through Fliss's empty chamber to my own. Nor could I bear the thought of sleeping. For each time I awoke, I would have to re-acquaint myself anew with the fact of her death. It would be as if she had died all over again.

The first mourners arrive at noon in black hoods and hatbands. But most can't disguise the cheery glow on their faces from their Maying. They are shown from front door to dining parlour where Fliss's body is wrapped in white superfine and laid inside her deep coffin. Just her face, as pale as the wool around it, is left open. The waxy skin and a silver shilling weighting each eyelid give her head the look of a manikin in the peruke-shop. Only the graze on her forehead makes her human.

Ever-green leaves and white-budded blackthorn fill the lower part of the coffin disguising the mound of her stomach. In the first damp light of May morning, Poll had gone out with the revellers to collect greenery and blossom from the paddocks and hedgerows around the Flatt. Sprigs of hawthorn and yew have been woven by Poll into a maiden's crants, a garlanded crown that will accompany the coffin and stay ever after in the church.

As I stare at this flower-covered cage resting on the floor below Fliss's feet, it strikes me as a sad twin of the Fell Faery's gay headdress that was garlanded with blossom and tankards. Fliss, if she were here, would have been the one to laugh with me at the thought of my young self parading in such an object. There is no one else on earth that knows me so completely as she, nor loves me so well. How can it be that she is not here? Surely her real self will, at any moment, flounce in laughing and shoo away all this frippery of grief.

'I'm sorry for your loss.'

I look up, blinking. It is Mrs Cleasby, the mantua-maker, swathed in bombazine with a raven-feather shine. I clench my teeth and nod. Speech is impossible.

'I had no idea Miss Felicity was… ill.'

Mrs Cleasby is clearly inviting conversation but a nod will be all she gets from me.

I'm sure she knows full well the circumstances of the death. The coroner's stark verdict left no-one in any doubt that my sister was with child, and it must have launched a storm of gossip through the harbour and the streets.

'Such a beautiful young lady. And so much to live for...' Mrs Cleasby holds a black-feathered fan to her face in a show of grief.

'A glass, madam?' Though her face is tear-marked and reddened, Poll comes forward with a tray of burnt Madeira wine in tall glasses. 'And biscake?' She has also baked small, hard funeral cakes in the shape of coffins.

'Very apt,' Mrs Cleasby says taking two.

'Mr Ravenglass is receiving visitors in the closet across the passage,' says Poll to the room in general. 'Where a fire is lit.'

By the window, Mr and Mrs Shaw, well used to funerals, nod and make sad, soothing noises. As Mrs Cleasby glides towards the door, she glances at the dark square on the faded green wainscot where a painting in oils of the *Resolve* used to hang. The painting has already been through Mr Shaw's sale room. He and everyone here, I imagine bitterly, must already know well the growing layers of shame that are enveloping the name of Ravenglass.

Poll leans her head to mine. 'You should go to your father too, pet.'

I shake my head. Since the inquest, a knot of unease in my stomach has hardened with each thought of my father. He did not tell the full truth to the coroner. Yet I can't bring myself to contemplate what it would mean if Hannah Salkeld's accusation was correct.

'Go on. Go to him, lad.'

Poll takes firm hold of my elbow and pushes me forward but again I shake my head. I can't bear to be near my father.

Mrs Cleasby has reached the doorway, but then she steps suddenly back, her fan flying to her face.

'Ugh!' she says, only half under her breath.

There is a commotion in the passage and Aunt Ravenglass enters the room her face covered by a black gauze veil. Before her, she carries a small pewter bowl. Her face beneath the veil is deathly white.

'The sin-eater is here,' she whispers to the room.

Mrs Cleasby sinks back towards the window and is joined there by the Shaws. An arch look passes between them.

Mr Gwilym's smell, more animal than human, enters the dining parlour before the man himself. He is perhaps not much older than my father, though a toothless mouth and a stooped gait give him the look of an ancient. Every item of clothing on his body, even stockings, shirt and stock is greasy black.

Without a nod to any of the company, he goes eagerly to the coffin and stands beside it as Aunt Ravenglass places the pewter bowl on Fliss's chest and surrounds it with coffin-shaped biscakes. Then she hands Gwilym a glass of burnt wine and a biscake which he takes as a signal to go to work.

A mumbling starts up between his gaunt cheeks which may be a prayer but his voice is too low and garbled to tell. He touches his biscake to the shroud then dips it into his wine and then into the sparkle of Whitehaven salt lying in the pewter bowl. Then he thrusts it into his mouth and gobbles down the whole wet, reddened mess.

'Repent ye!'

His words are suddenly clear. And the sound of them, in his deep Welsh voice, runs a finger of dread along my spine. I step away from the cold grate and closer to the coffin as Gwilym repeats the ritual with another biscake.

'Repent ye!'

The same words. Louder this time, and I have no doubt it is the same accent, nay, the exact same voice, that came out of the magpie as it spoke to Fliss from our dinner table during that long-ago meal with Captain Littlewood. My whole body starts to shake. And at the other side of the coffin, as the sin-eater dips, gobbles and incants, my aunt stands frozen. I know that she too has recognised the magpie in the man.

At last, Gwilym slurps the dregs of his salty wine. He makes a small bow to the coffin and without looking up, puts an open hand over my sister's face. Aunt Ravenglass drops a sixpence into it. And then the sin-eater shuffles away leaving the linger of his meaty scent.

My aunt in watered black tabby and Poll in plain black stuff, together go to the foot of the coffin and raise up the crants-crown from the floor. Then they place it across the coffin over Fliss's belly.

There is a gasp.

'But that is for a maiden!' Mrs Cleasby says, her face aghast.

Aunt Ravenglass turns to her. 'Indeed, madam.'

'But... but she was no virgin.'

My aunt stands firmer and taller. Her voice is croaking but clear. 'Whatever sins were there have been removed by Mr Gwilym. She will be buried as the innocent that she was.'

Mrs Cleasby's face is red but she says nothing.

I follow my aunt into the passage and catch up with her by the square balusters of the staircase.

I touch her arm. 'Aunt, what do you know about... about Fliss's child?'

She looks at me for a long hard moment. 'It matters not now, does it?'

'But it was Daniel Bragg's doing...'

'Say no more about it. Not ever.'

She shakes her head as if exasperated and I see in this gesture how little I mean to her, how little any of us mean to her next to Fliss.

Going back down the passage, I realise that perhaps the coffin is already sealed and being lifted away by white-gloved carpenter's men. I have seen my sister's face for the last time.

The shaking throughout my whole body will not stop, yet still I cannot make myself fully believe what is happening. At the door, a glare of spring sunlight flings black spots into my eyes. They float across my vision threatening to join up and push me into fainting oblivion. But slowly, my sight clears. The coffin, now covered with a black velvet pall, has been now laid on a wheeled bier and crowned by the maiden-crants of May greenery.

My father, in his longest wig and black brocade coat, is already on the street and pointing his ebony cane to direct the carpenter's men in their white hatbands. By our front gate, pauper girls huddle. Despite the growing warmth of the sun, all are wearing their red winter capes emblazoned with a black R for Ravenglass. The promise of a sixpence each has coaxed twenty wearers of the now fading cloaks to join the procession. The girls stand two abreast, ten at the front of the bier and ten behind. On the command from my father, the caped girls begin to walk and to sing.

> *'Thy precious time misspent, redeem,*
> *Each present day thy last esteem.*
> *Improve thy talent with due care,*
> *For the great day thyself prepare.'*

The song rises, thinly at first and then with more vigour, filling the narrow street with girlish voices and Cumberland vowels. Behind the pauper girls, walk my father and I and then my Aunt Ravenglass, veiled from head to toe in black gauze. Poll and the servants are followed at the rear by a growing tail of mourners. Having somehow raised the means, my father has spared no expense. Perhaps sympathy for the loss of his daughter has produced new sources of credit.

We take a circuitous route to King George's Church via Irish Street, and the Market Place before proceeding down the full length of Roper Street. The streets are well peopled with tipsy, bilious revellers enjoying a spectacle that will spin out the festivities of May Morning into the afternoon. Most are sober enough to remove their hats and their grins as the cortege passes by.

On the Market Place, some officers and ratings of the man o'war, the *Prince of Orange* have set up a recruiting table outside the Anchor Inn. As the funeral bier and its escort of singing pauper girls reaches them, the Navy men stand to attention and place their hats against their breasts. Their commander, in a powdered wig and a coat with gold buttons, bows to my father. And to my surprise, my father nods back and raises his cane. Even in my dazed stupor I register the familiar look that passes between them. And then, to my consternation, the naval officer seems to incline his head toward me. There is a look of deep intent in his eyes and a smile hiding at the edges of his mouth. Hastily I look away. My heart starts to race. There is some meaning in this salutation but I have no wish to contemplate what it might be.

An endless, expensive peal of bells along Roper Street draws us toward the squat tower and plinthed portico of King George's Church. Amongst the faces on the corner Roper Street, I glimpse Hannah Salkeld with a black hood over her white cap and an expression that seems to reflect the grief broiling inside me. I look quickly away. I can't unhear her accusation against my father, but neither can I confront it.

Then at the back of the throng around the churchyard gates, I think I glimpse Jossy. But I dare not search him out. A look from him will have me blubbing like a girl.

During the graveside words I keep myself upright and conscious, though this is not easy. The scene seems to recede as if viewed through the wrong end of a spyglass. I see my father shuddering with sobs, his whole body quaking yet noiseless as Fliss's coffin lowers into the chasm in the ground. Yet I feel myself a distant observer. Nothing about what my eyes are seeing seems real. And in the grip of this unearthly calm, the presence alongside us of my unknown brother's lichened headstone serves only to heighten the fantastical quality of this terrible day.

That night, exhausted as I was, I could neither weep nor sleep. Instead my mind fell into an agitation which came always back to the same question. What happened to Fliss? It should have been no great surprise to me that Daniel Bragg had got her with child, but why did she conceal this fact for so long, even from me? I suspect Aunt Ravenglass knew the truth but did she tell my father? There is no knowing what his reaction would have been. Outrage, wrath, despair or compassion are all possible. It strikes me how barely I know the man I have both despised and loved all my life.

And what if I hadn't told my father of Daniel's malpractice? Would Daniel Bragg and Fliss now be married and joyfully awaiting a child? Guilt, like a stinging gnat, buzzes around my head. I find myself lighting a candle and going into Fliss's closet.

Her clothes are all there in chests and drawers, folded and wrapped and smelling of her. I finger my way through them; her lawn nightshifts and caps, the washed cloths for her courses, the petticoats of flannel, tammy and chince. Placing the candlestick on a chest, I bring out the grander pieces; the wide pannier cage and silver-trimmed stomacher, the sky-blue mantua-gown. Now that she is not here, I have leisure to enjoy the soft feel and intricate work of these garments without worrying that Fliss will catch me. Indeed, there is nothing now to stop me putting them on.

Without another thought, I disrobe myself of my own nightshirt and, from naked, begin to re-dress myself just as Fliss would have done. First, red wool stockings gartered with ribbands above the knee. Then comes a short linen shift and over it the faded red wool stays, boned with whalebone and edged with pink silk. Lacing them behind my back is awkward but I manage to pull them tight. The panniers are next, the cage positioned firmly around my waist its wideness giving shape to a heavy cambric petticoat, and then the gown of sky-blue satinett. A deal of pins are needed to fix on the stomacher stiff with its metallic trimming. Each one brings me closer to Fliss. The actions of this dressing are her actions, the feel and weight of each garment are exactly as she would have felt them.

And as soon as Fliss's clothes are on me, I feel instantly at home with myself. I pull back my hair and fix her best lace pinner to my head, bringing the long lappets over each shoulder. Lastly, I tie a black velvet ribbon around my neck and adjust it to the place where Fliss's scar would be.

Then I go to the pier-glass on the wall. Fliss looks out of the dim light and stares straight at me.

'Poor, Kit,' she says in her lovely clear voice. 'Poor boy.'

I do not know how long I stand there, watching Fliss weep. Time seems to have ceased. Until, with a sudden convulsion in the darkness, there is a clatter of the door and my father bursts in.

He is dressed in his old flowered banyan, a candlestick in his hand and his nightcap awry.

'Sweet Jesus,' he breathes and his eyebrows rise into a look of horror.

I can do nothing but stand before him in my feminine finery.

'Kit?' He seems unsure. 'What are you doing?'

I stand stock still. Surely the answer to that question is plain.

He shakes his head. 'How has it come to this? I did my best, for you both. But I see that in every respect I have failed.'

'How did you fail Fliss, Father?' I whisper and hear my sister's voice in my own.

His head shakes. 'Don't, Kit.'

My father's reddened, tear-lined cheeks and hunched, diminished bulk bring me no emotion except distaste, and a growing conviction that Hannah was right.

'The coroner's verdict was wrong, wasn't it?' I say. 'Her death was no accident.'

And in hearing these words from my own mouth, I suddenly see their truth.

'Do not ask me, son.'

'How did she die, Father?'

'It is best that you do not know.'

'But you do? How do you know?'

My father shows no flash of anger at this but only shakes his head. Then, he makes a great sigh.

'Christopher, I was not going to tell you until a day or two had passed after the funeral. But I see, in this...' he looks up and down the mantua-gown, '...this spectacle, the rightness of the action I have taken for you.'

'Action?'

'Yes, Christopher. It will be for your benefit.'

But the sour dropping of my heart tells me the exact opposite.

'What will?'

'That I have joined you to the sea service.'

My hand goes to my breast and my finger traces the edge of the silver ruffles on the stiffened stomacher. I feel the delicacy of the silver threads, the smoothness of the Florentine silk, the solidness of whalebone beneath. But under it all, my insides are liquid with panic.

'Captain Phillips of the *Prince of Orange* was delighted to pay a bounty on your behalf,' my father continues briskly. 'He kindly accepted my word for the extent of your existing nautical education and will take you on as his servant with a view to your becoming a midshipman within a year if all is well.'

'No!' My voice shocks me with its angry vigour.

My father raises a hand to silence me. 'This is your best chance, Christopher. The Navy gives a ladder that may be scaled to any height you choose. Admirals have started from less.'

'No, Father. No.'

My anger is turning to alarm. I am trapped like a rabbit in a snare. Pain lies at every turn.

He takes a long breath and shakes his head as he exhales. 'You know you can no longer rely on me for your path in life. All my wealth is gone, and more. This is your only chance to escape my debts.'

'But…'

'Enough.' My father waves both hands decisively apart. 'It is already done. I have taken King George's bounty for your service and so you now have no choice. You must, this minute, take off that grotesque garb and ready yourself, sir, to join a man o' war.'

He strides from the room, the door slamming behind him and I sink to the floor in an air-filled mound of whalebone and satinett. The sea service! How can I bear it? My voyage aboard the *Swallow* more than four year before had been bad enough, but I could not begin to contemplate embarking upon a lifetime in the King's Navy where the usual ship-board privations would be combined with discipline even fiercer than on a merchant vessel, even besides the terror of combat at sea.

A sob chokes out of me as the awful reality of my future seeps in. I'd rather join Fliss in death than join the Navy. Yet I don't want to die. Tears splash on to satinett as I stand up and begin to turn a tight circle, again and again, in the chamber and in my thoughts.

I lurch, stricken, from grief to panic and back to grief. One minute I am consumed by fantasies of Fliss's last breaths. Did she really suffocate on sea-water? Or did human hands play a part in her end? Perhaps the man Hannah saw on the Steer was some ruffian who choked her to death and dumped her body into the sea.

Then, in my next vision, I see myself clinging to the highest yards of the *Prince of Orange* too fearful to descend as a devilish bosun below on the main deck brandishes his lash. But if I escape my duty to the King by fleeing, I can see no fate that doesn't end with me freezing in a ditch beside some distant turnpike, or swinging from a gallows-noose.

the fourteenth chapter

The recruiting officers and impress men of *HMS Prince of Orange* were doing good trade at the sign of the Anchor and word was that the ship would soon be fully manned. I was now legally obliged to join her and voyage by way of Plymouth to the West Indies where I would serve for at least five years in the defence of British shipping from the Spaniards.

I vowed that I would never set foot upon the *Prince of Orange*, though how I could avoid this fate by running away, when well-armed marines from the ship were patrolling the town and guarding the highways, was beyond me. My mind spiralled between the fanciful possibilities of escape and an ever-deepening sorrow for my dead sister. In my few lucid moments, I began to believe that unless something inside me changed completely, I would go irreversibly mad.

On the third day after the funeral, my father sends me with a pair of pearl earrings and some books to Snell's the pawnbroker's. The weather is exceptionally fine for early May and fresh stucco gleams on the walls of new houses along the way. But I think only of the pearls in my pocket which I know belonged to Fliss. And there is at least one of Fliss's books in the bundle under my arm. Anger brews inside me at the thought of my father's callousness in giving away Fliss's things for money.

Then, a roaring commotion jolts my attention back to the street. Marching toward me is a gang of hard-bitten sailors escorted by four red-coated marines. Between them, they propel a prisoner along King Street with curses and blows. The captive's hands are bound and blood drips from his battered face.

'Get on with you, you madge-faced meater!' cries a bald-headed sailor wielding a tarred club.

The prisoner, kicked from behind, stumbles to stay upright. He is wearing the long clothes of a landsman but the disguise is a poor one, for his rolling walk alone gives him away as a sailor. I wonder how far this deserter had got before being captured by the press men from the *Prince of Orange*.

I am not yet a deserter, but a fit of cold shiveriness seizes me as they pass. How could I ever elude the cunning reach and brute strength of the Navy's enforcers? I hurry away from the impress-gang and around the next corner into Duke Street but find myself still shivery at Mr Snell's door. My fist trembles as I raise it. But before I can knock, a hatch slides open revealing two dark eyes. Then swiftly the hatch closes. Keys clank and the whole door pulls back to reveal a brown-skinned woman in a fine green gown and matching house-cap. The woman ushers me in.

For a moment, still quaking, I can do no more than stare at the pleasing sheen of her dress. She seems too finely attired to be a servant. And then, when I turn my attention toward the voices in the room, I see Jossy.

Once more a sailor, he wears white petticoat breeches and a short blue jacket. The only sign of his having been a hewer in the mine is the rim of wax around his cocked hat. He is talking to Mr Snell, the pawnbroker, a thin-faced man in a kid-sleeved waistcoat. Their heads bend over a pair of dirty breeches on the counter between them. My stomach gives a leap but I wait, gathering myself, until their price is agreed and the shilling is in Jossy's pocket. Then I speak.

'Good day to you, Mr Bone.'

Jossy turns in surprise and gives a slight bow. 'Mr Ravenglass.'

His eyes seem reddened with tiredness, but they throw me a look of concern. The horrors of the past week are no doubt etched on my own features.

'Are you going with the *Resolve* again?' I ask, trying to keep emotion from my voice.

'Aye.' He sounds hoarse.

'She is to set sail soon?'

He nods. 'Within days.'

My heart thumps against my ribs. 'Where are you bound?'

'Why, the Guinea Coast.'

'And Barbados?'

'Jamaica, this time.'

The woman in green shoots us a guarded look and my heart-thump quickens. I have a sudden sense of the world tilting, and in a queer way, opening up. As if I am at the summit of the highest fell with downward paths all around me and each one leading to an entirely different place.

'It is a very fine day, Mr Bone.' I say, suddenly choosing one of those paths. 'Would you join me for a turn up to Brackenthwaite and a last look at our town?'

Jossy's eyes are wary but he nods.

Mr Snell looks at me over his spectacles. 'You have goods for me, sir?'

'Excuse me.' I make a slight bow. 'I'll return with them later.'

Outside, Jossy and I cross the road into Senhouse Street without speaking though I sense he is holding back. The silence seems awkward.

'Who was that finely dressed woman at Snell's?' I ask, by way of conversation.

'His new wife,' Jossy replies, but in such a very downcast tone that I say no more.

Then, once we are beyond the chapel, he turns to me.

'I am sorry, Kit…' he looks over his shoulder. No one is around. 'I'm sorry for what I said at the inquest.'

I frown. 'There is nothing…'

'There is.' His voice is sharp. 'What I said… about drowning…'

I shake my head but he goes on.

'It did not gratify me to contradict your father but I felt I must speak the truth as I saw it for … for your sister's sake.'

I take a quick breath and my throat tightens. 'I know it was the truth.' I swallow hard. 'Though what you said made no difference to the verdict.'

'No.' Jossy looks at the ground. 'And perhaps that was for the best.'

I almost ask what he means but I'm already close to tears.

We press on past the last houses of the town and step from paved road to open lane. Jossy's gait seems to lighten as we leave the track and start to climb tussocky pasture toward the windmill.

Breathing harder as the hillside steepens, I slide Jossy a sideways glance. 'Are you eager to return to sea?'

'Lord, no.' He snorts and shakes his head.

My stomach gives a flutter 'Do you not care for an Atlantic voyage?'

'It is not the crossing I dislike, but the nature of the vessel.'

'A slaver, you mean?'

'Aye, a slaver.'

Jossy stops, hands on his waist and for a moment we both look over the glossy slate roofs of the town.

'I vowed after the last Guinea voyage that I would never do it again.'

'But you are forced into it?'

'Littlewood has told Mr Spedding the colliery steward that I can work there no longer. And so, as you see,' he opens his arms to indicate his working clothes, 'I am a sailor again.'

'Do you have no say in it?'

Jossy gives me a sideways look that makes me feel the stupidity of my question then he sets off again. The hill is sharp and I gulp air as I try to keep pace with him. But Jossy's breaths hardly quicken, his muscles hardened by the ceaseless exercise of labour in the mine.

'Then our situations are the same,' I say, breathless.

Eyebrows raised, he shakes his head.

'They are, in a way,' I persist. 'My father has taken a King's bounty for me from the *Prince of Orange*. So I am now in bondage to the Navy.'

'And you don't wish to be?'

'I will myself jump off Saltom cliff before I join that ship.'

'Nay!' Jossy claps a hand to my shoulder and squeezes hard. 'Don't ever say such a thing.' The fierce look in his eye startles me. I feel a sob rise.

'But it's true. I can't do it!'

My voice cracks and his hand on me becomes gentler.

'Then can you not persuade your father to return the bounty?'

'I know he will not for he wants me at sea. And he wants the money.'

'So what shall you do?'

I look my friend in the eye and hold my breath as I speak. 'I've a mind to flee.'

Jossy blinks. Then he nods three times with deep intent. Without saying more, we turn and press on up the sunlit grassy slope. The windmill's canvas sails are limp against their ladder-frames. Only a few white clouds spot the blue of the sky. New grass brightens the fell-tops.

Just below the mill, I sink on to the ground and Jossy sits down beside me. Whitehaven spreads out before us, a grid of paved roads and handsome three-storey houses that is pinned like a gaudy brooch into the fold of green hills. From this height, the town seems made of baby-houses and the harbour a pond of toy ships. Every setting for the dramas of my childhood is visible; the house of Nathaniel Bravery where I was so cruelly chastised, the House of Correction where, I'm sure, my disgraced mother spent her last days, and in the distance, the squat tower of King George's church where my brother and now my sister lie in their coffins beneath the damp earth.

'Was this the book you offered me once?'

Jossy's finger is on the small pile of bound volumes at my side.

'*Love in Excess*? Aye, it is.'

'It was your sister's?'

I nod.

'What is it about?'

'The story of two ladies both in love with the same handsome nobleman.'

Jossy frowns but does not look up from the book. On a whim I pick it up and hold it out to him.

'Here, take it now, please.'

'No, it wouldn't be right.'

'Please. I know Fliss would rather you have it than Mr Snell.'

At this Jossy seems to wince. But he puts his fingers on the tooled-leather cover. I imagine he has never owned a book before. Perhaps he has not even read one.

'I will not accept it as a gift, but I would happily borrow it from you, if you are agreeable.'

'Keep it for as long as you wish.'

'Thank you,' Jossy nods. 'But I will return it to you, I promise.'

I smile sadly. 'It doesn't matter when. Perhaps the tale will keep your thoughts away from the business of the voyage.'

He shakes his head. 'It would have to be a dramatic tale indeed to do that.'

I turn to my friend. 'Is it so bad, a Guinea voyage?'

'Yes, it is.'

'How so?'

'Ah…' Jossy closes his eyes for a second. 'The true horror is hard to put into words.'

'Tell me.'

'One grim detail might suffice, if you have the stomach to hear it.'

'I want to hear, yes.'

For a moment he closes his eyes. 'As you know, on the middle passage, food can be in short supply, but we must try our best to keep the people in the hold alive and so preserve the ship's profit. But die they do. So value must be extracted from their corpses. And Captain Littlewood does this by means of fishing.'

'Fishing?'

'Aye. Sharks always follow a laden slave ship. The creatures seem to know which vessels carry people in their holds. The shark is not a palatable fish, seamen will not abide its flesh, but the captive Africans have no choice. If we can catch and cook a shark we can feed that to them and keep their rations, such as they are, for the crew. Bait of course is key to fishing and what better bait than human meat?'

'You mean, hooks are baited with..?

'A leg, or an arm. Yes. And it was my job to cut up the bait.'

'Sweet Jesus…' I feel my stomach turn and look out toward the glisten of the sea.

'The worst though was when it was a child who had died. I was told to string them to the fishing line in one piece.'

'Oh…' I take a gulp of air and fix my eyes on the distant glitter of the harbour. I can just make out the full-rigged silhouette of the *Resolve* at the bulwark. Does my father know all this? How can he continue in the trade if he does?

'Jossy,' I turn to him and cannot stop my hand resting on his sleeve. 'You must not go back to Littlewood.'

His head shakes. 'Escape from here is too difficult. All around here know me well.'

'Then we'll go far from here.'

'We?'

'Aye. You and me together. What do you say?'

Jossy sighs. 'My presence would only add to your danger.'

'Or mine to yours! My bounty has been taken and so as soon as I leave Whitehaven I will be a deserter. The impress men will be on my tail.'

'But I'd be too easily discovered. So we would be doubly at

risk together.'

'Except,' I say, in a sudden rush of ideas, 'that together we can assume a special disguise.'

'How?'

Jossy's dark eyes, so serious with intent, bewitch me. If he were willing, I would strike out with him this minute on the road to Carlisle.

'By changing our dress. If the change is convincing enough, we'll have at least a chance of evading our pursuers.'

'Really?' Jossy looks intrigued but sceptical.

'Why, yes,' I say.

And at that moment I almost believe it myself.

the fifteenth chapter

The hardest of my undisclosed partings was from Poll, especially as she continued to prepare special comforts to help me in my grief. In the back kitchen, she warms caudle and says her rhubarb dumplings will revive my appetite. I sit by her at the table and watch her tears drip into suet dough.

'Don't cry, Poll. You will make me start up again.'

'Cry, lad, if you like. There's no shame in it.' Poll presses her apron to her face but looks over it with a fierce eye. 'I knew no good would come of her wanderings.'

'Do you think,' my voice cracks, 'that the verdict was right? That it was an accident?'

Poll sighs. 'The child inside her was not put there by an accident.'

I clench my fist against the table-top. 'That rogue Daniel Bragg is surely to blame.'

Poll's zealous eye gives the tiniest twitch.

'What do you think happened to her, Poll?'

Poll casts me a distraught look. 'Don't think on it, pet. 'Tis best just to remember her at her happiest. I learnt that with your mother.' She wipes her eye with a floury hand. 'At least mother and daughter are together again.'

I glance up and bite my cheek. 'You think my mother is in heaven?'

'Why, yes,' Poll says with passion. 'If not her then none should enter those pearl gates. Your mother was a true child of God.'

'Even though her actions were so wicked?'

Poll puts her head to one side. Her voice is quiet, almost a whisper. 'She could not help herself at the end, but I believe her heart was always full of Godliness and love.'

'Then why..?'

But I am too choked to say more, and jolt up, scraping the chair legs, suddenly desperate to leave this house of secrets and ghosts. And, to my later deepest regret, I quit the room without a backward glance at Poll.

Alone in Fliss's closet, I put my face against the cool satinett of the mantua-gown and breathe in the scent of my sister's disappointments. Was death her intention? The sight of her body tugged and prodded by the icy sea comes back to me. Her lips blue, her eyes dull, her sodden woollen smock clamped to the swollen belly as we turned her over. How stupid I was to assume this swelling came from an ingestion of sea-water! And how could I have not seen, all winter long, that a child was growing inside her?

Perhaps the coroner's phrase 'disordered in the mind' was as good as saying Fliss died by her own hand. And yet, Hannah Salkeld saw a man carrying a body. Perhaps Fliss did not choose to die. The thought lightens me for a second. But would I prefer my sister to have been foully murdered? I strike my brow with my fist. A howl brews in my throat and I stuff my mouth with sky-blue satinett.

Only the thought of Jossy waiting lifts me from the floor. I can't let him down. The day is passing and I must make ready. The list of items I need is growing but chief among them is any remaining part of my bounty from the *Prince of Orange*. I suspect that my father has received thirty shillings or more from Captain Phillips though much of this may have already been spent on the funeral or on the payment of my father's sundry debts. If any remains, I have an idea how to locate it.

At first there is no reply when I knock at my father's chamber. But then there is a sound between a groan and a shout. I go in. Brocade hangings at the window and around the bed are pulled tight against the sun. Stale tobacco smoke and brandy-fumes fug the room.

Blinking, I go to the bed. My father is between the sheets but still wearing the shirt and waistcoat from his funeral best. He has not shaved for days.

'Kit,' he says, opening one eye.

'Father.'

'What is it?' The eye closes.

'I am making ready to take my leave.'

'Eh?'

'To join the *Prince of Orange*.'

'Oh. Aye.'

'I could do with a sea-chest and Mr Moorhouse has a good one for three shillings. I have asked, but he will not allow us credit.'

'Sea-chest,' my father sighs. 'I thought you'd take mine.'

'It has been in the stable for years. John uses it to store the apples.'

'Does he?'

'Aye. And it is too big. And heavy.'

'Three shillings…'

'I thought you might allow it, from my bounty.'

'Son, I wish…'

'I'll pay you back.'

My father sighs, his eyes still closed, and fumbles beneath the sheets. As one eye again opens, his hand comes out, clutching a tiny key.

'Bring it me back directly. You may take ten shillings if you find enough there. For your ship-board purse.'

'Thank you, Father.'

In the counting-house, his desk-top is in disarray. Ledger books, the recent entries almost illegible, are strewn open across it. The lid is left off his inkpot and unsharpened quills are scattered as if a screaming goose has been held up and plucked over the desk.

I know that his coin box is in the locked top drawer though I have never, till now, been allowed to open it myself. Inside, the coins are unsorted and I cannot judge the value of the contents without counting them in piles. There is no gold. The guineas and half guineas must have gone long ago. But the silver adds up to eighteen shillings.

I count out ten shillings in sixpences and shillings. It does not look like much so I grab a handful of uncounted coppers that may add up to another shilling or two. And then, in a hot surge of panic about the journey ahead, I scoop every coin on the desk into my coat pocket. It is only fair, I tell myself. The bounty is mine to steal.

As I go to replace the box, something at the back of the drawer shines and, with a stomach-tug, I pull it out further. It is a package wrapped in finest black silk and tied with a black silk ribband. Heart drumming, I pull the ribband loose and the contents spill onto the desk. Three skeins of fair hair are tied in more black silk. In one of the ribbands, the hair is short and wispy like a baby's. The other two hold longer silky tresses. One is a shade darker than the other but their fine texture is the same. I stroke each lock with the back of a finger, and then touch the end of the pig-tail on my own shoulder. I have no doubt that these locks of hair are the only parts of my brother, sister and mother that remain above ground.

Also inside the package is a sheet of browning paper folded and sealed with an unbroken clot of grey wax. Turning it over, my hand is shaking. Inked on the front is a single faded word. *Husband*.

My heart quickens. The hand is my mother's I have no doubt, and the unread letter is as hideous to me as her ghost. Without letting my shaking hands touch the parchment, I tie it back with the locks of hair into black silk and return the package to the drawer.

As I replace the little key beside my father in his chamber, his stubbled cheeks snore on and his rum-soaked breath turns my stomach. I am all he has left in the world and yet he has sold me to the Navy. So I will feel no guilt about taking his money and leaving without a word.

The sea-chest from Mr Moorhouse was two shillings not three but it has a good lock and sturdy rope handles. Aunt Ravenglass nods approvingly as I bring it in to the house in the late afternoon.

'That looks serviceable,' she says. 'I will paint your initials on it before you go to the ship.'

Her face is pale and drawn, and though her voice has more of its usual vigour, the loss of Fliss seems to have altered her in some indefinable way. I cannot imagine how she will continue to live here with only my father and the servants.

'Thank you, Aunt.'

'Good boy,' she says and lays a hand on my shoulder. I can't remember her ever before giving me a gesture of spontaneous fondness, though it was fitting that she should do so then for it was the last time I ever saw her.

That night, my window remains open so I may better hear the striking of the clock at King George's Church. As I wait, the house below me quietens. So the midnight chimes come as a jolt. At once, I make for the stairs. My descent is painstaking for fear that my loaded sea-chest will bang against the balusters. But trepidation gives me strength, and even with a further bundle tied to my back I am able to carry the wooden box gently.

On the landing, I stop for a second to let my eyes become accustomed to the deep darkness of the middle of the house. I hear, for a last time, the shuddering sleep of Aunt Ravenglass and the rumble of my father's snores. Then, I go down. To avoid waking Poll in the indoor kitchen, I must grapple noiselessly with the lock and bolts on the front door. But I know how to ease them back softly. I have practiced. The door whispers to a close behind me and then I am out in the street.

The few swaying figures I meet going through the sleeping town take no notice of a boy with ribbands on his shoes and a sea-chest in his arms. Perhaps they think me a sailor discharged from a voyage and heading home, which is of course the opposite of my position. The greatest danger for me lies on Bransty Row at the foot of the steep road that is the only northerly way in and out of the town. Here, red-coated marines from the *Prince of Orange*, have ignited a brazier and a few of them sit beside it waiting to check passing traffic for deserters. Deserters like me.

But I cross the road far enough from them to avoid their notice. The salt-works is dark as I skirt its tall chimney and reflecting pools. I find myself staring in the hope of seeing a woman in a felt bonnet. Regret prickles at the thought of seeing Hannah Salkeld no more.

The sea-chest weighs heavier on my arms and for a moment I have to stop and rest. There are things inside the box that I did not really need to bring. The waistcoat that Fliss made for a bridegroom, her copy of *Fantomina* that never went to the pawnbroker. But everything inside it, the earrings and book, the shifts and garters and pins, even *Dorinda's Gift*, all have a value that I can use. As does the box itself.

I look around to make sure that no-one is watching and I'm suddenly dizzy. Darkness blurs sea and strand to the same grey emptiness. Only the thought of Jossy waiting, gives me courage to go onwards.

Picking up the box, I skirt the rocky strand and head into the scrubland of marram and gorse that thickens toward the foot of the sandstone cliffs. There are many caves in these cliffs, and in one of them, a dot of candlelight is shining. This dot is my beacon.

I hear a muffled call.

'Kit!'

And then, Jossy is beside me.

'My friend!' he says and claps his hand to my arm.

When he unburdens me of the sea-chest, it is all I can do not to fall into his arms and weep. Soon, once I've rid myself of all pretence of manliness, I'll be able to weep whenever I choose.

'Come,' says Jossy, leading me into the cave. 'Let's move toward the back. I've seen no one but we must take care.'

The cave is dank and dripping. A foul smell of decay comes from the furthest rocky depths and I take care where I put my feet.

Jossy says. 'Are you ready to undress?'

I nod and, by the light of his candle, unlock my sea-chest and untie my bundle.

Together we take off our clothes. Jossy lays his blue sailor's jacket, his neckerchief and petticoat breeches inside the sailcloth hammock that is spread open on a rock. I glimpse Fliss's book amongst his things.

Then he pulls his checked linen shirt over his head and I bite my lip as he stands before me in his nakedness. No Grecian statue could have more perfection. A surge deeper than desire goes through me and I know that this must be love.

Then, as he turns to lay the shirt with his other things, I see the scar on his left shoulder. It is a black indent in his brown skin, a shape, stretched and misshapen, but in the shadowy relief of the candlelight, there is no doubt that it is in the form of an R.

I turn away to take off my own shirt and hide the conflict of feeling that must be reflected on my face. Is that R for *Resolve*, which may as well be for *Ravenglass*? With a deep breath and an effort to appear untroubled, I turn back to him and hand him the clothes I have just taken off.

'They may be too small,' I say.

But when Jossy is dressed as me he fills my coat, waistcoat and breeches more elegantly than I ever could.

'Can I help you?' he asks as I begin to struggle with laces and strings.

'Aye,' I say and present my back to him.

I don't really need help tying the petticoat, pocket and stays but I yearn to feel his hands on the fastenings, and perhaps, by chance, on my skin.

I have chosen Fliss's blue riding habit as my travelling outfit, the one with silver buttons that she wore when she first spied Daniel Bragg. My hair is no good as a woman's, but I have brought with me a selection of caps to use until it grows. The blue paragon skirt is a little too short and my shoes, with so much walking ahead must be my own. But they are well disguised by ribbands in bows.

Soon, we are ready in our new personifications. Fliss's riding-coat fits well enough and I know that I can adopt a convincingly feminine walk. Then I notice my hands. Several nails are rudely broken and the skin around my knuckles is still scratched and red from grappling with shingle by Tom Hurd Rocks. They look nothing like the hands of a lady. And I have nothing to cover them with.

'Gloves…' I shake my head in bitter frustration. 'I've forgot to bring my sister's gloves.'

Holding my hands out in front of me for us both to consider, I am struck by the lunacy of my scheme. To pass myself off as a lady, to live as a female for who knows how long…

Wildly, my eyes search his. 'Is this madness, Jossy?'

He takes both my hands in his and squeezes them. 'You look fine in this garb, Kit, very fine indeed. Have faith in yourself.' A smile, like the sun through a thunder cloud, then blooms across his face. 'Do you remember that collier we once watched at Lammas Fair?'

I frown and then nod slowly. 'The one who ate a live cock?'

'Aye. Think on him. For no matter how crazy an endeavour may seem, if you truly believe it can be done, anything is possible.'

'Yes,' I nod. 'Yes.'

And, magically heartened by Jossy's strength and by the curious memory of a pitman eating cock-feathers and claws, I find myself laughing. Jossy keeps hold of my hands as he begins to laugh too. It may come from a sort of mania, but our mirth fills the cave like music. I know then that even if our quest for freedom fails, we will have given it our all.

'Are you hungry?' I ask, still holding Jossy's hands. 'I have rhubarb dumplings.'

'Save them,' he replies, stepping back and loosening his grip. His smile becomes serious. 'What am I to call you now?'

I pause, not having before thought of this before, though the question is obvious. Our names will be in runaway advertisements, so we must have new ones.

'When there is anyone around, I suppose you should call me madam or ma'am,' I feel myself blush, 'as a servant would.'

'And when we are alone?'

In the cave-candlelight his eyes shine over me as they take in my sister's skirt and riding-jacket. In them, I am neither Kit nor Fliss but a better version of us both.

'Stella,' I say, without a thought.

The name has come to me unbidden, but instantly I recognise the person I shall be.

'And I?' Jossy says, his gaze not leaving my face.

'Isaac,' I say quickly. 'That is, if you don't mind my choosing.'

'Why Isaac?'

'It was the name of my brother.'

A queer look comes to his face and his eyes seem to shine with tears.

He nods. 'Your brother. Aye.'

For a long moment, Jossy's eyes search my face. Perhaps he is looking for any remnants of maleness in my countenance. Perhaps he is wondering what sort of person Stella will be.

Then he says, 'Well, Stella, we must make haste to travel as far as we can before sunrise. Are you ready?'

'Yes.'

So, dressed as Stella and Isaac, we each take hold of a rope handle to share the burden of the sea-chest, and together in the scant moonlight, we hurry northward along a pale rocky track between the dark cliffs and the dull sea.

the third part

—

as Stella

the first chapter

On the third night of our journey we were beyond Cockermouth but still many miles from Carlisle. Having studied my father's book of maps, I had decided that the lesser of the two ways to our county town would be safest, though his route was never less than hilly and brought us close to Cumberland's most dreadful terrain. So Jossy and I, in our guises of a lady and her servant, covered a deal of ground but few miles.

Late on that third day, in a drizzling dusk, we had passed around the head of a vast lake and been forced to soak ourselves by fording several small rivers and streams.

Even in May, the wayside makes a bone-cold bed and my sleep, at the wooded edge of a shaley beach, was flimsy and filled with feverish dreams. But when the greying light of the new day wakes me, I find a nightmare made real. Jossy has gone.

I rise, shaking, and look around. Fatigue and fear ache through me.

'Jossy!' I hiss.

I cannot call his name too loud. There is no telling who may be on the lookout for us.

'Isaac!' I try, a little louder.

Only distant crows reply.

I button my jacket and start to pick my way through the thicket. Perhaps Jossy has gone to the lake to drink or wash. Perhaps he has gone looking for bread in a nearby cottage, though an iciness in my stomach tells me that he would have woke me first.

The dawn light is ashy but clear. And as I approach the water's edge, I see with awful sharpness the terrifying sight before me. On the road to this place there have been several horrible peaks with cataracts foaming from craggy summits. But none of those had the dreadful glowering bulk of the mountainous beast before me. Vast purple slopes rising into the clouds are mirrored in the lake, so that water and sky are both obliterated by a gloomy colossus that must be Skidda Hill.

A sudden tear stripes my cheek. How have I lived my whole life so close to this dismal monster yet remained insensible of its presence? Everyone around me must have known what those inconsequential bumps on Whitehaven's eastern horizon signified. Only I had no notion of their true character.

While Skidda fills my eyes and my thoughts, I don't at first notice the dark object on the surface of the lake. But when I see what it is, I start to run.

'Jossy!'

Without thought I undress. Riding-coat and petticoat drop to the clinking shale, then shoes, stockings and stays. Wearing only Fliss's shift, I wade into the shallows. The smack of cold water has me gasping up for air but I go on deeper and colder, seeing only the back of my friend's head.

'Jossy!'

Cold water slaps the air from my lungs. Dread places an icy vice around my heart. Wading is painful and slow, but soon brown lake-water laps at my chest. Still he doesn't turn. The water is surely past his chin.

'Please, Jossy.' There is desperation in my plea.

Then, he turns and my heart twists. His face is drenched, his eyes red. Despair seems to have him in its grip.

'Come back, Jossy. Please.' Now I am weeping too. 'Please!'

'Kit.' His voice is so thin and uncertain. 'I can't... .'

I will not let him finish. 'It matters not to me which way you go from here, whether back to safety or out under the depths of the lake. As long as you take me with you.'

At this Jossy is silent, his chin quivering. Then he lets out a wail, as much of anger as sorrow. I push closer through the weight of the lake and reach to touch him. Mud-scented water laps at my lips. The barren mountain looms above the lake's abyss. Another few steps toward it would indeed resolve so many of our pressing fears and with them a deal of grief and pain. Breath wheezes from my chest, but I grasp Jossy's arm.

'Which is it to be, Jossy? Life or death?'

He blinks as if he does not know the answer.

'But I will not be without you, Jossy. That I swear.'

His lips tremble as he tries to speak. 'You must go on.'

I squeeze harder on his flesh. 'Not on my own.'

He shudders. His voice is a whisper. 'Your sister would want you to live.'

I meet Jossy's gaze without blinking. 'She would. So come with me.'

And without another word between us, my hand finds his and clasps it. Joined together, we wade back to the shallows.

The burdens of being a runaway are clearly weighing on Jossy more heavily than I had imagined. Perhaps he sees no good prospect of escape for himself, and he may be right. When I told him of my plan to go to Carlisle and find lodgings and labour by the day, his eyebrows rose up though he said nothing. He must be despairing of my thin plan yet unable to think of a better one.

In the shallows near the lake's edge, we search for footholds on the slimy stones and haul ourselves to the shore. As we reach dry ground I let go of Jossy's hand and both of us sink, panting on to smooth shingle.

Jossy wears only his shirt. His head drops onto his raised knees. I slide a look at his bare legs, and the patterns of small scars, like embroidery stitches, that cover them. Jossy takes a shuddering breath and goes to speak. I am expecting him to say that my plan is not sound, and we must travel farther than Carlisle. I'm ready to assent to anything he asks.

But instead he says, 'Some in Whitehaven think Felicity was killed by her father.'

I hang my head. 'I suppose it is the talk of the town.'

'Aye.'

'What do you think, Jossy?'

'I heard tell of Hannah Salkeld's testimony. So maybe…'

'No.' I shake my head. 'I can't believe it of my father. But I know Daniel Bragg brought about her ruin.'

'Daniel Bragg?' Jossy gives me a sharp sideways look. 'Because you think him the father of Felicity's child?'

'Aye. And I swear that if I ever see him again, I will kill him.'

This is the first time I have voiced my intentions towards Daniel Bragg, even to myself. But once the words are spoken, the design becomes fixed in my mind.

Jossy sighs. 'The wound across your sister's neck… I saw how inflamed it was compared to before…'

His words tail off. How had he seen the scar before, when Fliss was always at pains to keep it covered? Then I remember he must have been in the Assembly Rooms, all those years ago, when her neck-ribband slipped.

My damp fingers start to trace mirrored figures of eight on the stones. 'The cause of that injury was a thing my family always hid from me.'

'You mean, your mother's crime?'

I glance up. It seems that Whitehaven gossip about Verity Salkeld has reached even Jossy.

'Jossy…' my voice is shaking now. 'Have you ever heard tell of a mother killing her own children?'

He nods. 'In slave quarters, yes. It is not unheard of.'

'Why would they do that?'

'It can be a form of protection from future torments. A sign of love, even.' He stares at the fearful summit of Skidda Hill.

Could my mother have feared something so greatly that she had rather kill her children than have them live in its thrall? Could she have feared my father in that way? But for all his faults I can't see how he could have cast such a monstrous shadow.

Jossy squints as if in pain as he turns his face to mine. 'May I ask you Kit, what was the last thing your sister said to you before she died?'

I think back to the best parlour and that last blown kiss. Repeatedly, I pick up the same smooth round stone and then drop it. 'She gave me a waistcoat she had been making, I think for Daniel Bragg, and said she wished me to have it.'

'Ah,' Jossy nods sadly. 'Was it embroidered with yellow threads?'

'Why, yes. How do you know?'

'And did she say anything that made you think she was disordered in her mind as the coroner said?'

I shrug and wonder why he has not answered my question. 'She was not herself. And though I know now why that was, I saw no hint of her condition at the time. Does that make me stupid?'

Jossy shakes his head. 'No, not at all. She likely disguised it well.'

I frown. 'Did you see the yellow-threaded waistcoat somewhere?'

'I came to your house once with a message from Littlewood and she had it with her in the parlour while I waited for your father.'

A flash of senseless jealousy sears through me. How did Jossy make a visit to the house without me knowing? And talk to Fliss without her telling me?

'I have the waistcoat in my sea-chest,' I say, determined to regain his full attention, 'if you'd like to see it again.'

'You do? Yes, I would like that very much.'

He pulls me to my feet and even once we are side by side in our dripping white linen, he does not let go of my hand. It is, perhaps, a brotherly grasp to support us both as we go barefoot over the stony beach and collect my scattered clothes. Yet I feel within it, small tender squeezes that could convey more.

At last, he releases me so that I may carry my skirts and stays as we go toward the thicket. I slip on my shoes but his feet are untroubled by shingle and flotsam as we return to the place where we slept.

The waistcoat is at the bottom of the sea-chest. I spread it over the closed lid and its arabesques of yellow silk and glistening sliver spangles bring a glow to the leaf-shadowed glade.

'May I touch it?' Jossy asks.

'Put it on if you like.'

He raises a wary eyebrow at me but then reaches down for the waistcoat. As he slips it on over his wet shirt, I notice how perfectly the garment fits him, as if it has been made to his measurements, and how wonderfully the ornate decoration becomes him. The fancy sequins, that I had thought tawdry, seem magnificent against his dark skin.

'That looks so well on you. 'Tis a shame you can't wear it whilst acting the servant.'

Jossy shakes his head and sighs very deeply. 'A shame indeed.'

His face glistens with lake water and I cannot quite read the look in his eyes. My innards give a little twist and I bend to my bundle for the spare shift. The linen is clean and dry but I suddenly feel reluctant to put it on. Can I really keep up this pretence to be Stella for the whole of our time on the road? Overwhelmed by the thought of what we have taken on with this flight, I peel off my wet linen and for a second stand before Jossy in my naked maleness.

'I… I don't have to stay in disguise, you know. I could become myself again.'

He gives me a long queer look and the fierceness of his gaze embarrasses me. 'No,' he says with sorrow in his voice. 'Stay in your sister's clothes.'

Even a few days on the road had altered manners between us entirely. In one sense, we had become equals in our status as runaways and distrustful of every person except each other. Yet I also sensed a growing change in how he treated me. Even on a lonely track across empty heathland when there was no need to play the servant he insisted on carrying the sea-chest himself. Once, he picked me up without asking and carried me across a beck 'to save my skirts.' I, to my shame, did not object for I yearned more than anything to feel his arms tight about me. More than once, I wondered if he had somehow forgot that I was as male as he.

Later that day, when the road to Carlisle was downhill and empty, we fell into easy conversation about ships and the sea. Once, when the terrors of the lake seemed all forgotten, we enjoyed a moment of high spirits, jostling each other and laughing as if still mates upon the *Swallow*. Jossy, at that instant, had never seemed more beautiful. But as we walked across the bridge into the town, I sensed, growing inside me, a feminine dependence upon him.

Being walled and surmounted by spires, Carlisle rose from its crag above the river like a grand ancient citadel. But once inside those red stone walls, houses crumbled into hovels, and filth swilled down the twisting alleys. In the main thoroughfare past the largest church, I had to lift my skirts above a torrent of blood from a bullock lately slaughtered. Compared to Whitehaven with its wide modern streets Carlisle, though our county seat, seemed miserable as a village.

Jossy and I attract many glances, and some downright leers, as we make for the Market Place. I walk a little in front of him as befits a lady with her servant and he alone carries both bundles and chest. The quantity of cabbage stalks and squashed leeks as well as drunkards laid out on the cobbles mean that it must be market day. I remember to avert my eyes from a carter going to piss against a stall as he unloads his barrow. His spray catches the edge of the cloth where mutton pies are laid out for sale.

'Isaac,' I turn to Jossy and adopt the voice of Stella at her haughtiest. 'We shall dine at an inn. Pray enquire for the best one hereabouts.'

I reach through the slit in my skirt into the pocket which is still heavy with coin scooped from my father's desk. Jossy takes the penny with a dubious look. But he goes to a rag-woman in a straw bonnet and half-clean apron who stands beside a display of shoes, single as well as pairs, laid out on a sheet. And the coin is exchanged for directions to the sign of the King's Head.

As we make our way toward the alleyway, Jossy stays close to me and lowers his voice.

'Is this the best use of your money?'

A be-wigged ostler passes close enough to hear us and Stella speaks up. 'Indeed it is. We must a have good meal inside us before travelling onward.'

But as we take a side-street overshaded with gables it is the demonic hunger of the seventeen year old boy that claws at my belly.

'Very well,' Jossy says, coolly. 'Give me a handful of your pennies. The landlord and pot boy will want sweeteners.'

I drop the coins into his hand and dip my head to follow him through the smoke-stained doorway. A king in a pointed crown creaks on the sign above us.

Inside, the air is soused in beer and stale water. Without a word, Jossy deposits his burdens near the doorway and goes for the landlord. The tavern is a smoky labyrinth of uneven floors and ill-painted passages. A log smoulders in the fireplace. A bleary tradesman in a leather apron raises his tankard to me with a grin.

'This way, madam.' The landlord appears. He is unshaven but his wig is tidy and his hands clean. I follow him into the beery labyrinth as Jossy pulls the sea-chest away from the door.

'Isaac?'

'I'll stay here with the bags, ma'am,' Jossy nods and encourages me forward with his eyes.

The thri'penny tip has secured me a private dining space which is, I suppose, suitable for a lady travelling alone.

I'm led into a wattle booth with a small round table and a bristling wicker-seated chair. There is a chamber pot in the corner and above it a glass-less internal window that would, were I to use the pot, leave no-one in the main parlour in any doubt of my business. Through this opening, I can, just, see the entrance door, though not Jossy who is out of sight with the luggage.

'We have chops or eels,' says the landlord.

'Chops.'

'Fried, broiled, soused or stewed?'

'Fried.'

'Ale or wine?'

Here I hesitate. For though wine would be more fitting to Stella's station, it will be twice the price.

'Is your ale fresh-brewed?' Stella inquires with a voice even more imperious than usual and less tinged with Irish-ness.

'Yesterday, madam.'

'Very well. A quart of it. And a pewter cup, if you please. The same for my servant.'

The landlord gives a bow that is almost free of mockery.

When he leaves, I find myself shaking. This is the first time that Stella has spoken to a stranger. On the road, Jossy had been the one to buy eggs or bread from farms along the way. But my fear of being found out is cancelled by my stomach's craving for hot food. Until the plate arrives with a pair of greasy mutton chops on a steaming pillow of pudding, I can think of nothing else. The landlord brings a separate jar of treacle and in my hunger, I smother almost all of it across the meat as well as the pudding. My first gulp of ale is fresh and flowery as a hedgerow.

And so, I don't notice, at first, the party that comes in by the side door. There are at least six of them, their leader in a powdered wig, the others in knotted neckerchiefs and gaudy hats. They have the air of men looking for a fight. Though what they are really seeking is sailors.

'Look lads, a Blackamoor!'

This bark, in a rough London voice, jerks me up from my pudding like a slap. Jossy's reply is too low to hear and through the wattle-edged window, I can see only the short-jacketed backs of the sailors. Other voices join the conversation. I guess the most civil of them to be the wigged officer. My appetite has vanished.

'That's no bother for us,' I hear the officer reply to whatever Jossy has said. 'You lot are born to the waves. Would you not rather be roaming the oceans under sail? And we take no account of any man's complexion when sharing out prizes.'

Again Jossy's answer is muffled. But I have a horrible sense that he has sent the commander of the impress men my way.

Hastily, I wipe my face on the tablecloth and put on my hat making sure that the cocked point is low over my eyes. It is only just in place when the powdered wig appears at my booth window above a sallow, dark-browed face.

'My compliments, madam.' The officer gives as much of a bow as the tight passage will allow. 'Lieutenant Peel of His Majesty's frigate *Wasp*.'

'How do you do?' Stella is remarkably composed. Perhaps she thinks it unlikely that Lieutenant Peel is seeking deserters from the *Prince of Orange*. But my insides flit about. The name *Wasp* feels ominous, though I can't think why.

'I see you have a blackie, ma'am,' the Lieutenant smiles, 'who I believe would be an excellent addition to our crew. Could you be tempted to part with him for a King's bounty?'

'Oh no,' Stella says haughtily and then titters. 'He is no sailor!'

'No matter. I would take a black, land-boy though he is, above many an English tar.' The Lieutenant's mates have gathered behind him at the window and they break into over-loud laughter at his slight jest.

'Well, I cannot spare him whilst on my travels.'

'And once you reach your destination?'

'I should have to let my husband decide. For the right compensation, he may be persuaded to let the boy go into sea service. But I could not possibly take such a decision on my own.' My ungloved, ringless hands are, thank the Lord, already folded on my lap below the tablecloth.

'Of course. I understand.' The lieutenant tilts his head graciously. 'And what is your husband's name, madam?'

'Mr William Fletcher, of Cheapside.'

'London?'

'Indeed.'

'Madam,' he looks offended, 'you are far from home to be alone, if I may say.'

'I have my servant.'

'Only one?'

'I have been staying at my father's house in Dublin.'

'Dublin? Then to London via Carlisle?'

'I have also visited my cousins. In Whitehaven.'

'Ah, I see.'

Stella tilts her head with a coquettish smile. 'I did not, I think, notice the *Wasp* in the harbour there.'

'No. Quite right. We are anchored at Ellenborough.'

'Ah.' Stella nods, sagely.

But my insides leap with the sudden recollection of the cook's words. Hadn't Riddle been last heard of as a mate aboard *HMS Wasp* out of Ellenborough? Perhaps the black-hearted bosun is here, now, with the impress gang. Perhaps he has already recognised Jossy…

'Well, ma'am, you'll have a wait and a half for the London coach. There is not another until Saturday, I believe.'

'Yes. I know.' Stella picks up her tankard. 'Your health, sir.' She takes a rudely long swig of ale. 'And good day to you.'

The lieutenant touches his hat and each sailor, as he passes the opening, makes a leering mockery of bidding me farewell. I have the sense that every man in the inn, except Jossy, is sniggering at me.

With a shaking hand I pour myself more ale from the jug and take another long drink. But my heart is punching so hard against my stays that I cannot abide another mouthful to eat, even though some treacly pudding is left on the plate. Will the *Wasp* men press Jossy anyway, no matter what I have said? They would be within their rights to do so if they think him a sailor. And then I should be alone.

My heart quickens yet more as the gang circulate around the inn-goers. I hear their banter and offer of bounty, prizes and fair rations aboard the *Wasp*. But none of the drinkers seem tempted today and not having the look of seafarers, none can be forced.

Before the press-men exit, the Lieutenant throws a final word Jossy's way.

'Captain Wainwright of the *Wasp* would be glad to have you aboard, boy. He is an exceptional master and he would see you treated fairly at all times. You would have a proud and happy life with us serving the King across the oceans of the world.'

When I hear these words I am struck by sudden terror. Perhaps Jossy will go with him. Why should he not? The offer sounds a great deal better than trudging northern roads with a boy in female clothing. When the seamen leave by the door, I strain my neck to see each coat and check that Jossy isn't amongst them. But in a drench of relief, they all leave without him. I go to the wall-opening and peer round. But although I can see almost to the place where he sat, he is not there. A needle of fear goes through me.

It is not seemly for a lady, even whilst travelling, to walk through a tavern and I have been provided with a small handbell to ring for the landlord's attention. But the sharp tinkle brings no answer. I go to the wattle-window and ring again, looking all the time toward the spot where Jossy should be.

I can stand it no longer and exit the booth into the uneven passage. But as soon as I see the empty space on the flagged-floor, I know that my sea-chest and bundle have gone. As has Jossy. All that seems left of him beside the doorway, is a trencher smeared with meat grease and treacle. Inside Stella's tough carapace, my heart shrivels.

But Stella remains sturdy, twirling about and addressing all within a considerable earshot. 'My man!' she shrills. 'Where is my man?'

The bleary drinker by the fireplace points toward the back room where barrels are raised on their sides and covered by cloths.

Stella catches sight of the landlord and strides forward. 'Tell me, if you please, where is my servant?'

The landlord flicks a stinking cloth on to his shoulder. 'If you're done, that'll be three shillings and eight-pence.'

'What? We only had chops.'

'And ale.'

'But I did not drink it all.'

'That is the cost.'

As I reach into my pocket and lay coins on the counter, the landlord looks not at the sixpences and pennies, but at my fingers. Then he peers, eyes narrowed at my face.

Hastily, my hands fall to my sides. 'Now, where is my servant?'

The landlord's eyes then drop to the coins and he sees that near five shillings has landed on his board.

'Out the back. He is afeared that the *Wasp* men will be at the front to deliver their sting.'

Stella, bravely, rolls her eyes and conceals the shiver of relief inside me. 'Pray, then, lead me to him.'

Beside a locked door, Jossy sits slumped on the sea-chest and stares blanky at some fixed point on the stone flags. He doesn't stir at my approach.

The landlord unbolts quietly and nods toward Jossy. 'Which way are you heading?'

Quickly, I answer. 'Point us, if you would, to the London road.'

My idea that Carlisle might become a home of sorts for Jossy and I has long evaporated.

The landlord then embarks on complicated instructions for an approach to this destination from the back of the inn and without traversing the market place. This route requires us to navigate a maze of smelly alleys that clamour with ragged children. Each time Stella claps her hands to disperse them, or lifts her skirts over a squelch of detritus, I glance back at Jossy but his darkly troubled eyes stare blankly at the ground.

the second chapter

In the strengthening late afternoon sun, I sit on the sea-chest and use *Dorinda's Gift* to fan myself. Beside me, Jossy leans against a milestone. *Carlisle 4 miles*, it says and then *London 295 miles*.

'Can she still tell us our fortune?' Jossy asks, glancing at the almanack.

Stella fans a little quicker as a shepherd and his dogs go by. 'We have no time for that, Isaac.'

But the truth is that I am scared to ask. The *Finger of Fortune*'s answers can be severe, and the chances of a lucky prediction in our current situation seem slim.

'A carter will come soon and take us south,' Stella pronounces though I have not seen any carts at all since leaving the city.

No lady would travel this mud-churned road on foot, but wheels are a rare luxury. Even horseback we cannot afford.

Jossy gives a snort. 'How much coin do you have left?'

'Plenty for now.'

Stella remains in my voice even though we are now alone. She seems piqued by the directness of Jossy's question.

'Enough to get even one person to London?' He persists.

'We don't need to go as far as London.'

'How far, then?'

For a second Stella departs. 'Just well away from the *Prince of Orange*.'

He shakes his head. 'The impress men are everywhere these days.'

A sudden thought brings a tug to my stomach. 'Did you know that Riddle is with the *Wasp*?'

Jossy shrugs. 'That's the rumour.'

'Without him aboard, would you have gone with them?'

He sighs but says nothing. My stomach tugs again.

'I suppose if you were bound to a man o' war you could escape Littlewood once and for all.'

'Ellenborough is too close to Whitehaven,' Jossy says with a shrug.

'Or otherwise you would have left me for the *Wasp*?'

But Jossy doesn't answer. His attention has turned south where, a little way off, there is a commotion on the road.

Two horses, being led in-hand, are rearing up and screeching as their attendant struggles to keep a grip on the ropes. Between the horses stands a piebald donkey that is obstinately resisting the groom's efforts to continue their journey north. One of the horses, a chestnut stallion, wears a hood that drapes his whole head and neck leaving only muzzle and eyes uncovered. This hood gives him the sinister look of an equine executioner. And, indeed, as the stallion shrieks a high-pitched neigh and again rears up, his hoof seems to collide with the groom's head. The man's long-peaked hat flies off and he flops to the ground.

Stella shouts out but Jossy reaches him first. The groom might already be dead except that he still holds fast to the rope attached to the chestnut stallion. I go first, by habit, to the donkey and the familiarity there is in handling the beast brings a stab of longing for home. I'd never have imagined pining for the snuff-mill and cantankerous Jenny, though I realise that I mostly miss those days I spent working with Hannah.

By the time I've grasped hold of the grey mare, the groom is sitting up and reaching across the ground for his hat.

'No bother, no bother,' he says in a countrified southern voice.

He wears a short-frocked coat of green Exeter serge that has the look of livery with brass buttons and gold-braided cuffs. There is a trickle of blood on his forehead.

'Can you stand?' Jossy asks and I chide myself for envying the groom as Jossy lifts him up with both hands under his armpits.

'Oh aye, sir,' the groom replies, though he sways on his feet.

I step forward to steady his elbow. 'We must stay with you a while until you are quite well.' Stella's voice will brook no dispute.

'No bother, Mi'lady, no bother,' the groom says again.

'We'll walk with you a little if you like. How far are you going?' Stella says, graciously.

'To the Town Moor,' the groom replies, peering at me through narrowed eyes.

'Is that close by?'

'Newcastle-upon-Tyne.'

'Great God!' Stella laughs. 'Then not close at all.'

The groom puts his whole hand across his eyes as if he can no longer see. 'Only a few more days.'

Jossy and I exchange a look.

'Can you perhaps rest a while before continuing?' Jossy says. 'Or ride one of your mounts?'

'Oh no.' The groom shakes his head though his eyes are still closed. 'The Mister won't permit it. Not in the least. Lameness is too great a risk.'

'Or the donkey?' I say, almost forgetting to be Stella. 'If the beast will carry you and our things, then my servant Isaac and I can lead your horses.'

The groom looks uncertain and winces into the light. 'I am to turn near here, for Weatheral,' he says looking about for the road and speaking, it seems, to himself.

'Then mount up,' Stella instructs, 'for we are going that way too.'

Jossy shoots me a narrowed look but he helps the groom on to the donkey between the panniers it already carries. The sea-chest balances in front of the groom and the bundles strap on behind. I lead the grey mare who seems the more docile and Jossy takes the hooded stallion. Soon both are walking calmly at each side of the donkey along the lane that leads north and east.

The groom complains loudly of a headache though this does

not stop him talking. His name is Dickie Archer, he says, and he is a stable-lad-jockey to Mr Hardman of Allerton Hall who has made a great fortune in the West India trade out of Liverpool docks and is spending a good part of that fortune on horseflesh. Dickie's expensive charges are Flycatcher, the stallion, upon whom wagers of near two hundred pound have already been laid for the Whitsun races at Newcastle, and Squint, the mare, who is yet to prove her full worth but for whom her owner has even higher hopes.

Both beasts are swaddled, despite the mild weather, in fine casimere rugs belted with the girths of tiny saddles. Flycatcher is especially high-strung and must wear a hood at all times to ease his violent itch toward flying insects. It was a bee, Dickie says, that caused him to rear up. But many other irritants along the way will make him similarly riled. Were it not for the presence of the donkey, who is his especial companion, the horse would not suffer to be taken anywhere to race.

'Should you not have another lad with you to assist on the road?' Stella asks, a little outraged at Mr Hardman's parsimony in the transport of his valuable beasts.

'Oh, no,' Dickie says, seeming offended. 'I can manage the 'osses on my own.'

I give him a sideways glance but he notices no irony in the recent predicament from which we have just rescued him. His face has a tight weather-beaten look, the skin stretched across the bone, which makes his age impossible to guess. He is clearly not a deep thinker. But I imagine this quality makes him honest with Mr Hardman's property and fearless in the saddle.

The evening is long and we walk several miles listening to Dickie's chatter. Jossy shoots several looks my way which seem to question our direction of travel but Dickie's arrival feels to me like a portent for our journey. And why should east not be as good a course to follow as southward? Before long, Dickie announces that there is dampness in the air and stabling must be found for his charges forthwith. They are warm-blooded, he explains, and any chill could impair the strength of their muscles. So a dry barn must be found before dusk approaches.

Lambs bleat and frolic in the hedged meadows alongside a shallow river but buildings of any sort are few. Dickie snorts at a farmstead with sheds for outbuildings as being too lowly for the famous Flycatcher to tolerate. His master seems to have trusted Dickie with a generous purse for the journey though its contents must be spent primarily on the comfort of Flycatcher and Squint.

By the time we reach the place where the river must be forded, Dickie is much recovered. Keeping a hand on the sea-chest to steady it, he dismounts the donkey in one agile jump.

Then he turns to me with a small bow. 'Will you ride, Mi'lady? Though you should sit astride through the splash for safety's sake.'

Stella inclines her head graciously and Dickie drops down on all fours beside the donkey making himself into a human mounting-block. Jossy and I exchange a wide-eyed look, but I lift up my skirts and I try not to step too heavily on his back. Sitting awkwardly between the panniers, I hoist a leg over the donkey's neck keeping my dirty-stockinged calves covered with petticoats.

Dickie takes Flycatcher's rope in one hand and leads the donkey with the other. Squint seems skittish as she is passed into Jossy's care. He pats a portion of bare flank at the top of her foreleg and strokes her smooth muscled neck as he makes gentle shushing sounds into her ears. It's a surprise even to myself that I can feel jealousy for a horse. Then Jossy clucks the racehorse forward into the swift-flowing shallows.

The donkey seems overburdened and uncertain as it clops into the stony stream. Yet even as I cling to the panniers, I can't help but notice the special beauty of the scene before me. Squint's prancing hooves throw up rainbows of spray from the tree-shaded river. Wood-pigeons coo overhead. And as Jossy throws a backward glance my way and our eyes meet, he smiles. The expression is brief but filled with sudden joy. I tell myself to preserve this memory. For that picture of Jossy smiling back at me as he leads a dancing racehorse through the sunset-dappled stream may serve as a salve for my mind in any gloomy times to come.

In the hamlet across the ford, Dickie finds a farmyard with brick-built stabling which he pronounces acceptable for Flycatcher.

He hands the horse's rope to Jossy. 'If you'd hold him a moment, good sir, whilst I enquire within. And then you may be on your way.'

Jossy flicks an anxious look at me but Stella comes to our rescue.

'It is rather late,' she says, yawning, 'to seek our own lodging. Could you ask if we may also stay with you?'

'Oh, but I sleep next to the 'osses.'

'We shouldn't mind that for one night. Or indeed for more than one night, until we reach Newcastle.'

'You wish to travel with me and the 'osses?' Dickie blinks. 'To the Town Moor?'

'If you would not mind. Transport is so hard to come by in these parts. And the donkey seems to tolerate me aboard. I will pay you, of course, for the ride. And Isaac can lead Squint.'

Dickie looks up then, assaying me with a long and penetrating gaze. I wonder if he is perhaps not quite so dull as he seems.

'As you wish, Mi'lady. But I have ample funds. There'll be no charge.'

Flycatcher snorts and stamps as Dickie scurries off into the farmyard and Jossy tightens his hold on the rope.

He turns to me, frowning. 'Is this wise?'

'What? Travelling with Dickie, do you mean? I can't be seen walking the whole way to Newcastle.'

'I thought inland parts were your aim. Newcastle is a port.'

'But on a different sea. Surely, we'll be out of reach of our pursuers there.'

Jossy's eyes narrow. Then he shrugs. 'As you like.'

Vexation rises in me. 'If you wish for us to turn back south, let's do so now.'

'There's no direction that's safe.'

Stella huffs. 'Well, it's too late to decide now. We'll stay here for tonight.'

Jossy's face falls into a blank. 'Take care what you say to this jockey. There's something most doubtful about him.'

But it turned out that Dickie was an easy travelling companion, apart from his excessive fondness for drink. That first night he was generous in sharing with us the sustenance he'd bought from the farmer which consisted wholly of beer. And in the fug of first light, though a disagreement on the direction of our journeying remained, neither Jossy nor I had the stomach to do anything other than tail in Dickie's wake.

The following nights were the same. After long sore days on the donkey's back, I drank whatever Dickie offered before falling into sleep on a bed of straw. The days trudged us through a landscape of desolate moors and stony crags. As he led Flycatcher, Dickie kept Stella amused with tales told in his odd breathy twang of the many races he had ridden and, if he was to be believed, mostly won.

The stallion was generally placid if kept alongside his donkey. But Squint, the grey mare, was increasingly fractious. She skittered at every bird-squawk and passing traveller and once bit Flycatcher on the arse, though her teeth made little impression through his high-quality blankets. I wondered if she didn't care for Jossy leading her, but Dickie said she was likely coming into season and must be kept well apart from Flycatcher who was not her intended mate. It would be impossible to keep the stallion off her once she started lifting her docked tail and winking her thing in his direction. So Jossy was bade walk her a little way behind us. I could not imagine how Dickie would have managed all this on his own.

The barns we stayed at on the first few nights were mean

places though stone-built. When the ale ran out, Dickie pulled a flask from the donkey panniers containing best Barbados rum which, he said, was a gift from Mr Hardman to celebrate their win at Chester. Jossy said he did not care for any so Dickie and I almost finished the flask between us.

Next day I found myself having to rest my head on the donkey's coarse-cropped mane as we walked but Dickie showed no ill-effects at all. He had risen early so that we would make it that day to a place called Heddon. And it was here that we slept in the first of our lodgings that might be called an inn. Dickie seemed familiar with the place and led the horses straight into a well-kept courtyard with horse-stalls and a farrier's shop.

Then he handed Flycatcher's rope to Jossy. 'There'll be stabling in the byre.' He nodded to a stone-built barn that formed one side of the courtyard. 'I must go and pay my respects to Haddocks.' And without further explanation he disappeared.

After settling the horses, Jossy procures ale and two slices of pie from the inn and confirm that we might sleep in the hayloft above the horses.

I sit on the loft floor, holding my hands out to him as he climbs the ladder, greedy for the pie.

'Did you see Dickie in there?' I ask between mouthfuls of jellified pork and tough pastry.

'Aye,' Jossy pours out a mug of ale. 'He is with a circle of keen drinkers. There for the night, I'd wager.'

'He says we'll reach the race-course tomorrow.'

'Yes.' Jossy gives me a long look without blinking. 'Then what?'

Stella has no hesitation. 'We shall see the races,' she says.

'And all the company at the races shall see us.'

I frown. What does he mean? I blink down at my soiled skirts and the forlorn feathers on my hat as it lies on the straw. 'Is this dress ...' The barn door is wide open to dust-specked evening air. I drop my voice to a whisper. 'Do you fear we might be recognised?'

'I don't know.' Jossy sighs. 'But I am wondering, when we part from Dickie at the races, whether we should become ourselves again.'

'No!'

Even as I exclaim I am not sure why Jossy's suggestion should throw me into such a passionate objection. Two lads, even one an African, would draw little attention amongst a race-going throng. And, in truth, every practical thing about our progress would be easier without me being Stella.

But I cannot bear to part myself from Fliss's clothes, nor, if I am honest, from the sense of myself as Stella. For Stella is superior in every way to Kit, more beautiful, more worldly, more bold. She is a woman that any man might admire. Even Jossy.

'I will improve myself tonight,' I say. 'I will brush my skirt and hat. Wash my stockings and handkerchief. I will make myself more fit to be a lady.'

Jossy puts his head to one side and scrutinizes my face. And then he reaches out and with the back of his finger, touches the curve of my cheek. I cannot help but close my eyes at the feel of his fingers on my skin.

'Should you use my blade?' he asks.

For a second, still consumed by the imprint of his skin against mine, I cannot think what he means.

'For your chin stubble,' he says. 'I'll fix it if you like.'

And then, understanding that he means to shave me, I nod.

We go to a corner of the hayloft where a slate is missing from the roof and a shaft of evening sun falls through. I remove my stays and sit on a hay-bale in my petticoat and shift. Jossy, better equipped than I, has brought a sharp blade and a soap-ball in his hammock bundle. My beard is sparse and light. I have hardly had any cause to shave before and my occasional visits to Mr Askew the barber and hair-dresser, had been more to feel the luxuriance of his lotions and pomade than for the removal of any manly stubble.

Jossy's hands are hardened by labour but his fingers are assured and gentle. I feel no nervousness at his razor travelling over my neck and close my eyes as I submit to his whispered commands, *head back*, *over a little*, *a little more*. My breathing becomes shallow. Heat grows beneath my petticoat. And inside my closed eyes, I pray that this shave may never end.

But soon, he steps away.

'You can open your eyes now,' he says with a laugh as he dips my handkerchief in a horse bucket then hands it to me.

As I wipe my neck with it, I cast about for a way to make him touch me again.

'Would you do something for me, Jossy?' I ask and begin to shiver.

Jossy turns his head warily. 'What?'

'Will you look at the skin of my back?'

'Your skin?'

'Aye,' I say, bending forward and lifting up the linen shift until it hangs around my neck. 'Tell me if there you see any scars.'

'Have you been whipped?'

I shake my head. 'It's knife-marks that I think might be there.'

Jossy edges closer. I bend my head forward as he examines me.

'Feel for the marks with your hands,' I whisper.

There is a pause and then Jossy places a finger on my spine and runs it up toward each shoulder blade. For a few moments he is silent and I hold my breath, praying for him to place his whole warm palm against my skin.

But his hand pulls away. 'Nothing. I think it is the clearest back I ever saw.'

My desire is suddenly shot through with jealous doubt. How many other naked backs has he seen?

'How would you come by knife cuts to your back?'

'The same way Fliss did to her neck.'

'Oh. Yes. I see.'

Lowering my shift, I turn to face him. I can't bear for him to move away. And as I look at his sad profile in the dust-mote dusk of the loft, I'm overcome by a yearning so hot I know I can't contain it.

Heart thumping, I reach out to Jossy and rest my hand gently on his. He turns back to look at me. His hand doesn't move. And so, breathing hard, I take firmer hold and raise his hand to my face. Jossy's eyelids do not blink. His hand is limp in mine.

Hardly daring to breathe, I move his fingertips across the new softness of my cheek.

'Does this feel soft enough to you?' I breathe.

A teardrop slips easily over my smooth skin.

For a moment, Jossy's hand stays limp inside mine and he stares into my eyes, though so blankly that I can't discern what emotion lies behind them.

'Kit...'

He says my name gruffly, but with that one word reveals his conflict of temptation mixed with reluctance. I bring his fingers to my lips.

'Please, Jossy, say nothing. Think of nothing. Just stay there and be still.'

And in that soft quietness of the summer barn, with the echoing call of doves and the flitting of half-seen bats, I kiss his fingers and his hand, and then, our gaze locked together I press my lips to his mouth.

His lips are dry and, for a second, quite still. And then Jossy starts to move. He grabs my shoulders in a firm grip and returns my kiss with a warm open mouth. I cradle his cheeks in my hands.

'Jossy...' I murmur. 'Jossy.'

But swiftly, so swiftly that I hardly realise it is happening, one of his hands has moved beneath my petticoats and is caressing my thigh. In a firm, practised movement he turns me around and flips the flounced petticoat up on to my back.

Then, bending me forward so that I must lean my hands on the bale, he presses himself against my buttocks and I feel how ready he is, behind me, to do more. He reaches around me. There is one delicious, delirious brush of his fingers against the place of mine that is straining for their caress. And that one touch almost completes the dream I have rehearsed for so long. I cry out in joy. But, with a sudden jolt and a limpid rush of cool air, Jossy pulls away.

'Jossy?' I pant, and look over my shoulder, another tear welling. 'Please Jossy. Don't stop.'

His back is turned to me but his head is bent and his shoulders hunched. He shakes his head and says nothing. And, without a word he climbs down the ladder into the stalls where the animals are tied and then out of the barn, while I collapse on the straw and sob.

He was gone so long that night I didn't see him again until the light turned grey. I awake dry-mouthed and heavy-headed, though this time from crying not drink. Jossy lies on the straw at the far end of the loft wrapped in his hammock so that I can't see his face. Then I recall what passed between us, and my heart gives a leap of terror followed by a flutter of regret that things did not go further. I cannot conceive of how he will be towards me when he awakes and I have to fight the urge to wake him and find out.

It can't be much after five o'clock but in the byre below the hayloft, Dickie whistles as he ministers to the horses. On my way outside to squat behind the byre, I bid him good day.

'It is a good day, it is,' he says with a chuckle. ''Tis a race day.'

And there seems a special urgency in his grooming rituals this morning. Both horses are stripped of their woollen layers to reveal the hard glistening flanks that Dickie rubs with handfuls of straw and then a dry cloth before trussing the creatures up again in their cocoons of blankets and hood.

On my return from behind the barn, Dickie is holding a bucket to Flycatcher's snout. From the smell of it, the morning oats are well soused with beer. The horse munches greedily.

'We'll be off directly, Mi'lady,' Dickie says, 'as long you can wake your man. He took in a deal of brandy last night,' a grin creases the weatherbeat face and he winks. 'Almost as much as me.'

'Even though you're racing today?' I am so surprised by his admission that I almost forget to be Stella.

'That's right Mi'lady. The drink is a requirement.' I must look dumbfounded and he goes on. 'Because later, you see, I shall be weighed.'

'Weighed?'

'Squint is a four year old so she must not carry more than nine stone including the tack. The brandy, see, if you'll excuse my saying so, it flushes me out and so it affords me an extra thirty ounces, or maybe even more.'

'Oh. Very handy,' Stella almost titters. 'And you have no ill effects of drink for the race?'

'I is used to it.' Dickie grins. 'Unlike your man. Out of practice since his sea-faring days, I reckon.'

Stella gives Dickie a conspiratorial smile but my gut twists. What else has Jossy let slip about himself in his drunkenness? And about me?

'I shall make myself ready Mi'lady.' From the donkey pannier, Dickie pulls a short jacket of stout loretto silk in dazzling emerald green. 'Then we'll be off.'

He seems to have no doubt that I shall be going to the races, as if Newcastle's Town Moor had been Mistress Stella's intended destination all along.

But at the top of the hayloft ladder, I stop and look at Jossy's sleeping form. If I don't wake him, I could depart with Dickie alone. All embarrassment would then be saved and I could perhaps make my own way in the world without being a hindrance to my friend. Or perhaps, I should let Dickie depart without us. Then Jossy and I could again be alone. Closing my eyes, I bite my lip with confusion. And, for the first time on our journey of near three weeks, I am so uncertain of the best way forward that my urge to consult Dorinda cannot be resisted.

Moving quietly so that Jossy slumbers on, I unlock the sea-chest and find the battered almanack amongst Fliss's things. There is only one question to put to the 'Finger.' *Will my friend be true in his dealings?* I close my eyes tight over the stars. But there is no doubt about the constellation selected nor the clarity of Dorinda's answer. *Your PRETENDED friend hates you secretly.*

A vile taste rises in my mouth and with a gasp I swallow it down. Surely this is wrong. Dorinda, for once, must be mistaken. I glance at Jossy's hammock curled in the hayloft like a great maggot that is now beginning to writhe. Then beneath me, through a gap in the boards, my eye is distracted by a liquid flash of emerald silk. Dickie, who thinks himself hidden in the byre, is taking off his shirt. I peer closer. And it is clear, even through this narrow gap, that beneath Dickie's shirt is not skin, but a tight buff-leather binding, almost like stays.

Jossy moans and stretches his arms from the sail-cloth cocoon and I feel a surge of despair at my constant failure to understand the human heart. I should know better than anyone that what appears on the surface of everyday life is not always to be trusted.

the third chapter

When we near the Town Moor, Dickie hurries deep into a hawthorn thicket, unbuttoning his breeches as he goes. The moans that then pour out of the bush seem to indicate his brandy-induced evacuation has been a success.

The road has become busier with horse traffic and more wheeled vehicles than we have seen on the whole of our journey thus far. Jossy has come forward to hold both horses, though the donkey, with me upon it, remains firmly between them. It is my first moment of privacy with him since last night.

I lean toward him and try to smile though I fear it's a grimace. 'You don't mind us going to the race field before the town?' I speak quietly but my voice wavers between Stella's and my own.

He doesn't look at me. 'It makes no odds.'

But then Dickie bristles out of the hedgerow straightening his breeches beneath the frock of his coat, and I sit up straight.

'Not far now, Mi'lady.' Dickie pulls at the velvet peak of his best cap as his eyes flit about.

We are on a main road, though the surface is still rough and rutted, along the edge of a wide valley above the river. But soon, Dickie turns us uphill to follow the growing flow of traffic. Flycatcher seems to sense what lies ahead and grows restive, prancing and neighing as he tries to break into a trot. Dickie's stern words to the stallion have little effect so he pulls the whip from the donkey-luggage. The mere sight of this implement which looks like a brother to Natty's black pudding, is enough to pacify the horse for a while. Then a high-wheeled carriage with matching bay horses and flamboyantly liveried coachmen hurtles past us, and Flycatcher starts up his whinnying and snorting once again.

But it is not long before the road levels out and there, filling our sight is the vast green of a treeless common. At the far side, the grassland is staked out with white posts topped by yellow flags. This, I imagine to be the race-course. In the other direction, the field is covered with huts, tents and carriages in a gathering more sizeable than I have ever seen at a fair or sport-day in Whitehaven. This gay scene lifts my spirits. I feel as impatient as Flycatcher to join the festivities and forget my heartaches for a brief while.

'We must watch you race!' Stella cries to Dickie amid the chatter of race-goers as we near the tents that Dickie calls the 'Rubbing Houses.' The clanking, nickering and screeching of horses fills the air.

''Tis just the heats first, but yes, certainly, Mi'lady if you please. Keep a little off from the finish so you don't get trampled, and leave your chest with the donkey. It won't come to no harm.'

The donkey was installed in one corner of a Rubbing House peopled by stable-lads and grooms who all clapped Dickie on the back and greeted him with affectionate obscenities. So, with my coin inside my pocket, Jossy and I left Dickie to his weighing-scales while we set off to find a pie.

We don't have far to look. In fact, I have never seen so many roving pie-sellers in one place. And I have rarely been so hungry.

'Not here!' Jossy hisses as I pay a lad then tear open the oozing pastry with my teeth. 'A lady would not eat that here.'

'No-one is paying us any attention,' I reply through a mouthful of cold goose.

'And a lady would not eat with her hands.' He looks at me with a disdain that stings like nettles in June.

'I wouldn't neither if I had gloves,' I mutter and swallow down the last of the pie.

Then I shoot him a sideways look but Jossy has turned away from me. A merry reel has just struck up on pipe and drum within a nearby tented booth. The sound of it runs a cold churn through my goose-filled innards but too late, we turn the corner and almost walk into the flags and drums of a ship's recruiters.

'Come, lad, here's a taste of Naval ale for you.' A white-wigged midshipman holds a pewter tankard toward Jossy.

And before I can hurry him on, Jossy has taken the cup and is gulping down beer.

As he drinks, the brass-buttoned midshipman puts a hand on Jossy's shoulder. 'Tastes just right, doesn't it, lad? You'll have a gallon of the same each and every day when you join our crew. And if you are also thirsty for opportunity, you'll find it on His Majesty's Ship the *Happy Endeavour*, a seventy-four gun ship-of-the-line. One of the Navy's finest.'

Jossy hands back the cup. The midshipman laughs then raises it to me. Both of his front teeth are silver. 'Your servant is certainly thirsty ma'am.'

'He is employed by both myself and my husband,' Stella declares, though with wavering conviction.

'Servants are easy to come by, sailors less so.' The midshipman tips his hat in my direction then he turns back to Jossy. 'What say you lad, to the King's bounty and a life aboard the *Happy Endeavour*?'

At this, the midshipman flicks me a glance and for an almost invisible instant, his tongue bulges into his cheek and his eyes roll. The effect is so lewd that I wonder if I have imagined it. And Jossy must also have noticed but he doesn't seem inclined to move away.

'Who is her commander?' Jossy asks carefully.

The midshipman's face lights up. 'Captain Jennings. There's no finer ship-master in the sea service. You have heard of him I'll warrant, for you look like a lad who knows the sea.' He leans toward Jossy and his voice takes on a graver, more intimate tone. 'And my friendly advice to you lad, is that you'll do far better to join the *Happy Endeavour* of your own volition than wait to be lifted forcibly by some gang of an inferior vessel.'

Jossy seems for a second to hesitate.

'Isaac, come-hither!' Stella commands.

But when Jossy does as he is bidden, my own voice threads though Stella's desperate mumble of words. 'You're not… you wouldn't, would you, join a ship?'

Jossy makes no answer and my chest feels too tight to say more.

'Would you, Jossy?' I whisper.

'Right now, I can't say what I would and wouldn't do.'

The flatness in his words makes me want to weep.

'Isaac. Look here.' Stella strengthens and comes briskly to my rescue. She is pointing now at a nearby trinket-seller with wares laid out on the grass. 'I can find some new gloves from this pedlar's pack.'

Jossy stands behind me as I bend to examine the gloves and enquire prices of the pedlar who is ragged apart from his coal-black shoes with polished brass buckles. I pick up some of his wares. My hands are not over-large but most ladies' gloves, I know, will be too small. The deerskin pair is the finest on display but will clearly not fit me. I try instead some in calfskin but reject them as too mannish. Those in knitted silk are a little stained and perhaps have been stolen from some tradesman's wife, but they fit me well enough and make my hands seem as dainty as they likely ever will be. The knitted gloves are cheaper too, at only half a crown.

'There.' My confidence in Stella lifts as she splays a newly gloved hand in front of us as we walk toward the race-course. With my fingers encased in dense silk thread the last masculine part of me is hidden from public gaze.

Gaily-jacketed jockeys bounce on their gleaming mounts through the churn of spectators. Gentry, townsfolk and commoners, all in their finest coats and hats crowd the roped-off portion of the course that forms the start and finish lines.

Jossy casts an eye at my glove. 'Very fine,' he says but his voice seems sullen. 'How much money is left?'

'Enough,' I say, vexation growing.

'Enough for a bed?'

I twitch him a sideways glance, wondering if his words might be an invitation of sorts. But Jossy's stare at me is blank.

'I couldn't go bare-handed any longer,' I whisper in my own voice, Stella having suddenly deserted me. 'My hands could give me away.'

Jossy snorts and shakes his head. 'A pair of gloves will not make you into your sister.'

'What?' my heart stops in my chest. 'What has Fliss to do with..?'

But the words die, for Jossy's face has contorted into bitterness and grief. And I understand suddenly that Fliss has been there, unseen, in every conversation that Jossy and I ever had. Perhaps his only reason for befriending me was to be closer to her.

'You were in love with my sister?' I ask, lamely.

Jossy wipes his cheek with the back of his hand and says nothing. His tears are answer enough.

'And is that why you have stayed with me? To remind you of her?'

Again the blank look descends across his eyes. Sudden bitterness rises in me. Jossy has worn my clothes and eaten the food I've bought him yet he has duped me, for he has been all the time scouring me for the ghost of my sister.

We have somehow come closer to the starting ropes. Carriages are crowded around it, some with gentlemen standing on their roofs. Foot-spectators fill the spaces between and all shout for the horses who carry their wagers, *Ticklefeather! Buttocks!* And yes, *Squint!*

I turn my back on Jossy to punish him for the crime of loving Fliss from afar. A couple of apprentices with flowered neckcloths and burring Northumberland voices squeeze between us. I find myself pushed up by them against an elegantly-spoked carriage wheel as tall as my head.

'Can wor have a sniff of yer quiff, pet?' says one of the 'prentices.

'Or a sip of yer money-honey,' says the other collapsing into guffaws.

For a moment I can't avoid their leering faces and beery breath. Yet while repulsed by their lewdness, I feel a small satisfaction that at least they, unlike Jossy, think of me as a woman.

Then the horses, two bays, a black, Squint the grey and a chestnut come into clear view, jostling as they line up between two starting ropes laid out across the course. The crowd surges towards them. I catch a glimpse of an emerald back and for a second see Dickie's taut face beneath his peaked cap. He casts a scowl at the Duke of Perth's black filly to his left who tries to nip at Squint's flank.

'Hurrah for Squint!' Stella yells in her excitement and I do my best not to look around for Jossy.

And then, with a forward lurch of the crowd, the front rope is dropped and they are off.

In the heat of the communal pursuit for a view, I cannot stop myself running with the throng. Jossy must be close behind. I find a raise in the ground near the finish post and catch a fine sight of the six young horses galloping across the Town Moor. Squint is easy to spot, being the only grey. She is not at the front, but Dickie in his emerald jacket has a quiet, upright ease in the saddle that marks him out. The other jockeys flap and whip at their mounts, but Dickie, employing a looser rein, eases Squint through the turns and she noses ahead. Only on the home straight does he use the whip. But, as hooves and reins and flying horse-slather hurtle towards the screaming crowd, Squint has a clear lead. Will Dickie slow her to avoid the spectators who have seeped across the course? A glance at his face tells me he will not. And a prentice boy falls on to the turf just inches away from Squint's hammering, oiled hooves. Then, to a cheering and throwing up of hats, the finish flag is waved and Squint is through to the final of the Freemen's Plate worth Fifty Pounds.

'Huzzah, huzzah!'

Overcome by admiration for Dickie's courage and skill, I become a part of the shifting beer-soused crowd, who reach out with cries of *gan on bonny lass!* for a touch of Squint's steaming flesh. So great is the press of farm-lads and herring-girls around me that I cannot get myself close enough for a touch. But I catch Dickie's eye and though his expression remains stern, he gives me a most definite wink.

The crowd surrounds Squint and Dickie as they edge toward the rubbing tents, but I pull myself free of their press and stand, panting to look around for Jossy. He is not there. And like a bad omen, the tooting of a naval pipe and drum flitters through the crowd. But I know he would never leave without his sailcloth bundle. So I hurry back to the tent where the donkey stands beside our things to await Jossy there.

The throng following the horses is so dense I struggle to make progress. Foreboding tightens my chest. Wandering sellers push past me crying out their wares and groups of men block the way as they pass money between them in wagers won and lost. I half wonder whether to find a blackleg who will take all the remaining coin in my pocket in a bet on Squint to win the Freemen's Plate. This thought makes me put a hand through the slit in my skirt to remind myself exactly how much is left. But as my hand pats around the gathered camlet beneath my riding-skirt, there is nothing. Not even the quilted pocket itself. In the crush of race-watching, the strings must have snapped, of more likely were cut by a thief. But however it came about, the whole pocket with all of my money is gone.

'Oh!'

I cry out and twirl around. But I see, instantly and very clearly that there is nothing to be done.

At that moment a lad comes toward me with the familiar

rolling walk of the seafarer. He wears his manliness as easily as his ribband-bedecked jacket and he smiles at me with moist, lazy lips. Then he stares a little harder and nods. His smile becomes a lewd, knowing grin. The sailor opens his mouth to speak to me and I hurry away. I have no wish to hear whatever obscenities he might offer.

I walk fast, head down, and away from the crowd trying not to think of anything at all. Only when I see again the glove pedlar do I stop and catch my breath. Nearby, the *Happy Endeavour*'s musicians have struck up a loud marching tune and from the recruiters' booth, a small procession is setting out behind the drummer-boy and pipers. The midshipman who gave Jossy ale is at the rear and between them is a small line of today's recruits. They are a sorry-looking band of long-coated landsmen and wiry farm-boys. But in their midst is one proper sailor in a short blue jacket and petticoat breeches with a sailcloth hammock slung across one shoulder. This recruit stands out, not just for his nautical looks but also for the handsome strength of his frame and the darkness of his skin. For there, marching toward the quayside, toward the *Happy Endeavour* and the Spanish war, is Jossy.

Should I run after him, or cry out? But my reason tells me it is too late. The bounty is already accepted, the course of Jossy's life in the King's sea service aboard a man o' war is already set.

Shock impales me and as pipe and drum fade, I can barely walk. I have lost my money and Jossy too. Then panic whips me into movement. All that stands between me and a life of beggary is my sea-chest.

The hubbub of the race-crowd around the grooms' Rubbing Houses sucks me into a quicksand of humanity that I must push and strive to get through, all the time eaten by fear that my belongings will be gone and I'll have not a thing of my own but the female clothes in which I stand.

When I reach the tent which I feel sure is the one Dickie

showed us, I look over the heads of the crowd gathered at the entrance but can see no sign of Flycatcher or Squint. I tell myself that I shall visit every tent and if I still cannot find my things, Stella shall go to the Finish Post and throw herself under the hooves of whichever horse wins the Freemen's Plate.

Then, as the crowd seethes forward, I reach the rope across the tent's entrance and see a young groom, no more than a boy, in laced green livery snoozing on straw. Behind him, the pied donkey turns to me and puts back its ears, perhaps fearing that I am about to mount up. This is certainly Flycatcher's stablemate. But there is no sign of my sea-chest.

Stella, God bless her, remains steely.

'Young man,' she commands. 'Young man, wake up!'

The groom yawns. 'What?'

'Is Dickie Archer here?'

'No, he has gone to see Mr Hardman.'

'But he has some of my belongings.'

'A chest, is it?' the lad says. 'Mistress Stella?' Then he touches his hat and lifts the rope allowing me into the tent.

The groom pushes at the donkey's rump to get to the back of the tent where a black mare swaddled in blankets stands asleep. He bends down by the hitching post and clears a mound of straw to reveal my sea-chest. The sight almost makes me drop to a blubbering heap. Thankfully Stella is made of sterner stuff than I.

'There's some loose clothes an'all,' the lad says.

'Loose?'

'Men's things.'

With a leap of hope I wonder if Jossy has thought better of his enlistment and come back.

'Did my man bring them?'

'The darkie, aye. He got changed into sailor's slops.'

Then the groom hands me my own brown frock coat and rolled breeches containing my old waistcoat as well as my shirt, stockings and hat. My throat tightens at the thought of Jossy having no desire to keep any thing of mine.

I make my way past the donkey and slump down onto the sea-chest. 'I'll wait here for Dickie.'

The lad shrugs. 'He has another heat to run.'

But my eyes are already closed in a bid to disguise weeping. My mind is in turmoil. Jossy has decided to leave me for good and it is my fault. For if I hadn't kissed him, he would still be here. If only I had guessed his devotion to Fliss I could have made a better imitation of her ways and lured him closer to me. But this thought brings a fresh spurt of grief. Am I really so callous that I would use my dead sister to ensnare Jossy into my base urges? Is it not time, I wonder, to leave my woman's guise behind? Perhaps the return of my coat and breeches is a sign. But how can I be alone, without even Stella for strength? And the thought of becoming a lad again sickens me.

Yet however much I may need cash, I cannot think either of selling my boy-clothes. For that too would feel like a type of death. I have told myself that Stella is a clever disguise that will keep me safe from the impress men, but of course she is more to me than that. I shiver at the thought of the day, which may not be close but will certainly come, when I must choose once and for all between petticoats and breeches.

For now though, I rouse myself from tears and try to be thankful that at least I kept the key to my sea-chest safe on a thread around my neck and not in my now-lost pocket. And as I press my breeches that still hold a scent of Jossy, into the base of the box, I realise that everything inside it has some value, no matter how little. I am not entirely destitute, though my store, even if I stop travelling, cannot last long.

Having stood up, I realise that a distasteful event is pressing and cannot be much longer put off so I must find the nearest necessary place for ladies. I ask the lad and he looks up from the pile of newspapers which he is tearing into squares, perhaps for some elaborate ministering to the horses, and points me to a space between the Rubbing Houses where some urchins, for a farthing, will keep others away until my deposit is complete. My stomach churns for I have not even a farthing in coin to give them, and a strip of lace from my under-petticoat will have to serve instead.

'Would you be wanting some of this, ma'am?' asks the groom holding up the torn-off back page of the *Newcastle Courant*.

My womanly blushes are entirely genuine, but I thank him and take the paper with me.

It is two weeks old and as I turn over the torn page to the advertisements, my stomach tells me with a flutter what I am about to see. And there, amid the notices offering rewards for strayed horses, lost cloaks and stolen sheep, is one for a runaway.

On Friday the 3rd instant

Run away from Capt. Littlewood of Whitehaven

Josiah (or Jossy or Coffee) Bone, a Negro, about twenty years old. He is of short stature though strong. Full set of teeth. Last seen wearing a sailor's blue jacket. Whoever secures him and gives notice at the sign of the Indian King in Roper Street, Whitehaven shall have a Guinea reward.

My heart batters so hard on my ribs that all urgency to visit the necessary-place departs. Emotions swirl through me, shock that news of Jossy's escape has already travelled across the country, fear at who might be seeking that Guinea reward. And, of course, outrage that anyone would describe Jossy as 'short.'

Did Jossy know, I wonder, how determinedly Captain Littlewood would seek to get him back? Perhaps Jossy had always known that Naval service would be his only true escape.

Suddenly, my urgent need can no longer be put off and I find the corner for my business. When finished, I take care to wipe my arse on the exact part of the page that shows Captain Littlewood's name. Then I stamp the newspaper into the mud, again and again, until I am shaking. One thing now is clear. For all the distance I have travelled, Newcastle is not far enough from Whitehaven.

Some way off, gunshot and a great whooping of the crowd indicates that the final race is over. Faint cries of *Squint! Squint! Squint!* tell me that Dickie has won. I hurry back to the tent where the victorious pair are pressed all around by whooping and huzzahing. Dickie almost seems to smile. But Squint must have her rubbing and swaddling without delay and as soon as he pulls the horse to a panting halt, Dickie dismounts in one athletic bound. I blink as he does so, not quite convinced by what my eyes have seen. For, all down the back of his buck-skin breeches from waist vent to crotch, is an oozing line of dark blood.

Following in Squint's wake through the crowd, the lad lets me into the rubbing tent. Dickie hitches the mare to the post and gets to work with circular handfuls of straw on her steaming rump.

'Dickie!' I exclaim, 'you won!'

'Aye, Mi'lady, I did that, I did that.'

'But you are hurt?'

'What?'

'The blood…' I glance down at his breeches.

But Dickie, unsurprised, merely reaches for his frock coat and puts it on to cover the stain.

I frown. The flowering blood, the glimpsed binding about his chest, the strangeness of his ways… And then, with a hollow beat of my heart, I am struck by the unshakable conviction that Dickie Archer is a woman.

I stand slack-mouthed and blinking, confounded by the curiousness of this truth and its cold irony. Stella is suddenly absent. Dickie casts me a wincing glance then turns his face toward Squint. He half-whistles a made-up tune as he runs his hand along her glistening flanks.

Others must surely have guessed Dickie's secret, but I can't be certain. His masculinity seems entirely natural. Though short and spry, he walks with the square, stiff-legged gait that I'd tried so hard to copy from Daniel Bragg during my years at the Nautical Academy. And Dickie's voice, though breathy and hollow, has a rhythm and vocabulary that make him sound just like a man. He is more a man, in his way, than I will ever be.

I see in that instant what I must do.

'Dickie,' I cry, abandoning Stella. 'Please help me! You're the only one who can.'

He turns his face to me with a look of perfect understanding.

It seemed uncouth to embarrass Dickie further by spelling out my exact predicament which I was certain he already knew. And I had no doubt he could be trusted to keep my secret. So I confided in him merely that I was a runaway and that my pursuers were closing in. I wept bitterly over the theft of my pocket and the departure of my companion Jossy leaving me friendless and at a loss what to do. Dickie patted my hand with many reassurances and calls to *dry your eyes, Mi'lady*, and told me that he would help me on to a safe course.

And so I found myself, early the next morning, trailing my riding-skirt hem through the thick dew that coated the Town Moor. One side of the race-course field was edged by the Great North Road and it was here, in race week, that the London coach would make a stop.

Dickie follows me, carrying my sea-chest and my frock-coat bundle more nimbly than even Jossy had done. Despite my strong sense of revelation about his true sex, I could not stop myself thinking of Dickie as a man.

'How many days is the journey to London?'

'Oh no, Mi'lady.' Dickie's step does not falter. "Tis coming from London, not going there.'

'Oh.' This throws me. 'Where is it going, then?'

'Why, Edinburgh, Mi'lady.'

'Edinburgh?' My stomach twists at the alien word in my mouth. 'But I thought I would be going to the capital.'

'It is the capital, Mi'lady. Of Scotland, anyways. The fare to London is three pounds, you see, and I was given only a guinea from the plate by Mr Hardman. But that will cover your way to Edinburgh.'

'Is the coach fare a whole guinea?'

'Well, it's a pound, but I have taken the liberty of using the extra shilling as your tip for the coachmen.'

'Dickie, that is too much, I...'

'Think nothing of it Mi'lady. I have the prospect of more. Flycatcher's race is yet to come.'

'I will pay you back,' I promise, 'as soon as I may.'

But I knew I never would.

We didn't wait long for the coach and four to appear. The horses were lathered by their climb up from the town but still fighting against the stop.

'Whoa there! Softly, boys!' Dickie calls to the team as the coachman applies the brake.

I wait with Dickie, as my chest and bundle are strapped to the roof. Dickie, it seems, is well-versed and connected, and has already sent my fare, that includes lodging and luggage, to the landlord of the *Bull and Post-Boy* whence the coach came.

'Thank you, Dickie,' I say, as the steps are lowered. 'I shall always remember your kindness.'

'No bother, Mi'lady, no bother. It's for all of us to live as we must.'

For a second before I mount the steps, he lets his eyes meet mine. A look of such perfect understanding passes between us that I feel a sudden surge of hope. If Dickie can do all he does in the clothes that he wears, there must be hope of success for me in mine.

the fourth chapter

The rain set in at Berwick and did not stop for three more days on the road. Throughout this miserable journey of bone-shaking days followed by awkward nights sharing inn-beds with a brewer's wife, only Stella kept my head high. And while the passengers' suspicious looks sharpened a sensibility of my friendlessness, the nasty confines of the coach made me think solitude would be preferable to company such as this.

There was little to see through the muddied carriage window but I could tell when we neared the great city from a reek of coal-smoke that wormed into the coach and a buzz of noise like an approaching swarm.

Soon, the horses are labouring up a steep paved road and skittering down the other side, with the coachman hollering and grappling with the brake. Inside, wedged up against the brewer's wife, I grip the cracked seat and see, through the rain, a high stone wall topped by a battlement.

Then, with a neighing screech, the coach comes to a halt and a cry goes up.

'Pleasants! Cow-gate Port! Pleasants!'

The place sounds welcoming and countrified though we are clearly within the city.

'Yes!' I call out as the door opens, and then, summoning Stella, 'unstrap my chest!'

So, moments later, I find myself standing on a half-made pavement beneath towering grey-stoned tenements. Belching smoke shrouds distant chimneys. Rain beats against the walls.

I have no notion of where to go or what to do and not a single coin in my possession. Barefoot boys who have been lurking beside the archway that spans the lowest street run over and hawk words at me. I can't understand a single thing they say.

This must be the punishment for all my errors and failures; my contempt for my father, my failure to save my sister, my selfishness in love. For I have now descended into an abyss of despair and degradation from which there is no escape. With that terrible thought, grief rises up and lodges, choking, in my throat like a mouthful of half-chewed bread I cannot swallow down.

The ragged boys crowd around as if about to strip me of my hat and riding habit and leave me naked in the street. But soon I realise that their rough utterings and touches are meant to be soothing. After many calls of *where d'ye stay?* and *d'ye ken?* I told them, tearfully, of my dire need for cash. I was then led to a pawnbroker where, with a heavy breath, I exchanged Fliss's pearl earrings for enough to tip the boys and have them install me in half-clean lodgings. I told myself I would retrieve my sister's jewellery sometime soon, but I knew in my heart this was a fiction as far-fetched as *Fantomina*.

The Cawdies, as the boys called themselves, appeared to be wretches of the lowest kind but they turned out to be my saviours. Sleeping in rags on the stairways, they know every person of note in Edinburgh and, being well respected about the coffee-houses, are entrusted with valuable errands.

In the weeks that followed, the boys escorted me respectfully around the city's ancient labyrinth of steep, muck-soaked alleyways. They proved admirable guides, imparting many interesting facts for no more than the cost of a crust. At first I was overwhelmed. Never had I even imagined that so many human beings might live together in such filthy proximity. It struck me that the narrow, ascending hill on to which the whole city squeezed itself was probably no wider than the valley that accommodated Whitehaven's spacious grid of streets, yet

Edinburgh was home to near ten times the population. All these inhabitants, from gentry to lowliest commoner, were squashed, one above the other into soaring stone buildings, eight, ten or even twelve storeys high that they call Lands. On the widest streets, the sight of these magnificently tall edifices, augmented by the city's towering natural crags, caught my breath away.

Mostly however, my breath was stopped up by the unearthly stink that emanated from the tight alleyways or wyndes that criss-cross the city. It was accepted by all the inhabitants that, come the striking each night of the ten o'clock chimes, windows would open and any manner of detritus accumulated indoors during the day would be thrown out. There seemed a general faith that rain would imminently arrive and wash the excrement and rubbish down the steep wyndes to someone else's door. Used though I was to Whitehaven's nastiness piling up in Pow Beck, each step I took up the wyndes filled my nostrils with a new stink. The rankness of Edinburgh's passageways could make me stop and retch.

The inhabitants though, took little notice of their town's dirtiness. I was left staring when some lady, prettily encased in pale silk and lace, would skip up a high staircase, oblivious to the muck. Soon, I too paid less regard to the city's nastiness than to the liveliness of its civilization. Music floated down from high windows and every tavern doorway released a fiddle-jig or ballad. From coffee-houses, recitations of poets spilled into the streets.

In my tiny lodging room, knowing that the value of my possessions would in time run out, I lived as frugally as I could. But beyond selling the last of my clothes, and then the sea-chest itself, I had no idea how I would live. I even considered putting on my breeches and asking the Constable of the Cawdies whether I might become one of their number myself.

By August, my coin and the contents of my sea-chest and bundle were sorely depleted. The time was coming that I should need to make difficult decisions. A choice would soon have to be made between selling Fliss's warm flannel under-petticoat or my old breeches that Jossy had worn. I did not know how I would choose. My female garb was serving me very well and the Cawdies, I knew, would likely be less chivalrous to Kit Ravenglass than they were to the person I now called Mrs Stella Bride. And one day, when a roaring Naval press gang approached, Stella covered her face with her kerchief and I felt no more than a twitch of apprehension. Had I been exposed to them in my boy-clothes, the guilt and terror on my face would likely have given me away. But safe in Fliss's riding habit, they passed me by.

The last unpawned item of Fliss's possessions that I could not wear was *Fantomina*. Being a leather-bound volume showing little scuff, I hoped it could bring me enough to live off for weeks. When the Cawdies related where best to sell it, I did not quite catch the name but I understood that the place was at the very top of the city beside the cathedral church. From my lodging on Cowgate, this was a stout hike up Fishmarket Wynde and the day they took me there, the air contained the first proper warmth I had felt in the city.

Since leaving Whitehaven, I'd worn little except the blue riding habit. But with so much wear, the blue was a ghost of the colour it used to be and the wool too heavy for a climb in the heat. So I laid out on my pallet bed all of the garments from the sea-chest.

There is the sulphur-hued Quilted-Petticoat I won at Lammas Fair and the embroidered wedding waistcoat that my sister made for Daniel Bragg. I run my fingers over the intricate yellow and gold stitching on which she spent so many hours. The feel of the threads brings back to me the sight of the needle in her hand and her expression, amused yet tender, as she looks up me. And it brings back the sight of Jossy, putting the flamboyant waistcoat over his wet shirt beside the lake under Skidda Hill.

A tear slips down my cheek and on to the spangled stitches.

As I wipe it away, I can't help but notice how well the waistcoat sits beside the sulphur petticoat. And when I try them on together, pulling the cuffs of my masculine shirt up to the elbows, they make a pleasingly feminine costume.

The waistcoat must be adapted of course, being too wide for me. But with the lower buttons left open, it splays out to give a fashionable effect of width across the hips. The Quilted-Petticoat has been little worn and still shines although it is now too short. I tie it low on my waist but my ankles are on full display and seem distinctly unwomanly. The petticoat must be lengthened and made respectable with, if I can find one, an ivory-coloured hem-band to compliment the petticoat's existing stripe.

Once I've donned the new costume, Stella tempts me to finish it off with the cocked and feathered hat but I fear this will push the look too far to the masculine. Instead, I tie Fliss's demurest lace cap so that it covers all my hair. Thus attired, with *Fantomina* in my newly-made pocket and a bevy of ragged Cawdies as my escorts, I set off up the wynde.

I am becoming used to the cat calls and lewdness that are thrown at women of any station when walking without a male companion. The Cawdies, when I am with them, do their best to keep nuisance at arm's length and most of the insults shouted my way are so embellished with Scotchness that I cannot, mercifully, make them out. But, on my way up Fishmarket Wynde, despite the Cawdie lads at my side, I am wrong-footed by a man's approach. He is so well dressed in a deep-cuffed coat of red felted wool that I stop for a second on the steps, panting a little, to listen to his request.

'Say, Missy,' he says with a slight bow, 'can ye direct me to Cock Alley?'

I frown and look to the Cawdies who might know this place but they are shaking their heads.

Then the gentleman smiles. 'Ah, no. I see I am mistaken, *Mister-ess*,' he gives the word a sarcastic extra syllable. 'It's the

Windward Passage I must seek from you.'

I stand stupefied, wondering what he means, but the Cawdies come to my rescue with a shout of *away with ye* to the man. The Cawdie lad without any top teeth gently takes my hand to lead me higher on the staircase. But I cannot help looking back at the man in the red coat who tips his hat with a lascivious licking of his lips. And I have a horrible presentiment that once all my money is gone, I might have no choice but to seek him out again.

The book-seller's premises provides a fragrant haven from the streets. It is housed in the Luckenbooths, a vast and curious building that rears up from the buttresses of the cathedral church and occupies almost the whole width of the city's main thoroughfare. At one end of this block, with lofty turreted walls and barred windows, stands Edinburgh's main gaol, the Tolbooth. At the other end, past the shops of respectable mercers and drapers on one side of the block and the stalls of trinket and toy-sellers on the other, is a tall square tenement graced with rows of large modern windows that houses Mr Ramsay's Wig Shop and Circulating Library.

Even Stella is dumbstruck by the interior. Serious gentlemen browse the maze of stacked bookshelves and overflowing newspaper tables, as well as the clusters of perukes that are displayed upon disquietingly life-like wax heads. As I enter the rooms, a group of fancily dressed young ladies look up from their periodicals. Then they whisper behind their hands, their eyes all on me.

Fearing to speak, I hand over *Fantomina* to the Cawdie chief. His negotiations with an aged man in a house-cap who I take to be Mr Ramsay, are furious in tone though I can make out little of what is said. The result exceeds all my expectations and of the seven shillings and sixpence obtained, I give the full sixpence to the Cawdies who look at the coin as if it is a diamond of the Indies before they run off, whooping. And then I, in my flushness, decide to go shopping.

On the more respectable side of the Luckenbooths the shops

open on to the street beneath overhanging awnings. Twisting staircases provide the only way into the workrooms and lodgings above. I pass by several enticing draperies which exude luxury and expense, but when I reach the millinery shop it seems a more likely place to find a new hem-band for my Quilted-Petticoat.

The shop is a cavern of delights. Fans, gorgeously coloured and outlandishly large, muffs and tippets in sable and fox, rolls of black lace and white spotted muslin, gloves, caps, hoops, stays, ribbands, fringes and gauze cover the counters and shelves. My mouth falls open as my eyes roam, trying to commit each delicious detail to memory.

'Can I help ye, mistress?'

One of the shop-women comes around from her counter. In her scarlet fringes and gold lace, she had seemed a part of the merchandise. But now that my eyes are upon her, I can't pull them away.

'Was it something... particular ye're after?'

'Well, yes madam, if you please.' Stella tries her politest voice which has a hint of Irish condescension. 'I'm seeking to add a length of ivory-coloured stuff to this Quilted-Petticoat.'

'Let me take a look at ye,' the shop-lady says.

She is older than the girls beside her, perhaps old enough to be their mother, and she seems in her extravagant panniers to be as wide as she is short. A cloud of yellow hair floats beneath her starched gauze bonnet and her right eye is covered entirely by a green velvet patch.

She takes a long look at the hem of my petticoat and I squirm at the state of my worn out men's shoes and boyish ankles. Her eyes rise slowly to my face, and then back to my waistcoat.

'That's a fine piece of work ye have on there.'

'My waistcoat?'

'Aye.'

'Thank you, madam.'

'Is it your own work?'

'Yes,' I lie.

'Did ye make the frogging yerself?'

'I did.'

'Can ye make tassels and fringes as well?'

'Madam, I…'

'Please excuse me, mistress,' the shopkeeper makes a slight bow. 'I think I have just the stuff ye're after upstairs in our work-parlour. Would ye care to come up with me and inspect it?' Her single eye is a penetrating shade of china-blue.

It seems a little strange that the milliner would not call one of her girls to fetch the cloth down to me, but I see no reason not to go with her and so I indicate my assent with a gracious incline of my head.

'Good.' The shopkeeper turns to the girls at the far counter. Both are puffed up in a confection of lace ruffled caps and muslin neckerchiefs. 'Lucy, Jane, tend the shop for me, and one of ye run up and get me should Missus Jenner come in.'

The girls, both seeming younger than I, exchange a perplexed look and then nod.

I follow the milliner out of the shop and up a twisting staircase on the exterior of the building. Although the striking scarlet, black and gold of her dress make her appearance very different to mine, she too wears a man's shirt and waistcoat pulled tight over a quilted petticoat.

Outside, the constricted street is full of animal smells and traffic noise but the milliner's work-parlour is remarkably quiet and pleasant. Seeming to forget about the ivory silk, she indicates a cushioned chair at a round tea-table.

'I wonder,' she says, 'if ye have the leisure, whether ye might take a glass of something with me?'

I hesitate and must look surprised by this invitation.

'My apologies if ye think me forward,' she says, 'but I have not come so far in trade without speaking what is on my mind.'

'Not at all,' I say, realising that there is nothing I would like more at this moment than a comfy seat and a drink.

The milliner pours two glasses of Madeira wine and sits down with me at the tea-table. She tells me her name is Mrs Mary McMenemy and she has owned what she considers to be the finest millinery shop in Edinburgh for almost ten years. It is an excellent trade, she tells me, though one which requires constant labour and a sharp eye for talent. The reputation of the milliner, Mrs McMenemy declares, is dependent entirely upon the skill of her girls. Materials and some ready-made items are bought in but they are finished and embellished in her own work-parlour. And the special style and needle-working skills of her girl-apprentices is what sets her shop above the others. This ensures her a healthy profit.

'Very interesting, Mrs McMenemy,' I say. 'I shall be happy to patronise your establishment whenever I may.'

'I wonder though, Mistress Bride, whether ye might wish to do more than that.'

'How do you mean?'

'I could not help noticing, by yer shoes, that you might be in need of rather more than a strip of ivory silk for your hem.'

'Well, I...' Stella is flustered and considering an indignant exit.

'Please, mistress,' Mrs McMenemy puts a hand on my Quilted-Petticoat and pats my knee. The gesture is unexpectedly comforting. 'Do not be offended. I speak plainly because I have a strong intuition that we may provide each other with mutual benefits. The millinery trade offers fine opportunities for anyone with a head for business and an eye for fashion. I suspect that ye're just such a person.'

Her one eye is unwavering.

'Mrs McMenemy, I freely admit that I presently find myself in straitened circumstances due to a death in the family, but I can assure you...'

'No need for aw that,' her voice loses its polished edge. 'I can offer ye bed and board, fancy apparel and a thorough education in the skills of the trade in return for hard work whenever it is required and quiet discretion. And on this occasion I'll waive any apprentice fee. What d'ye say?'

'I… I…'

'Ye like to wield the needle, do ye not?'

'I do.'

'Well, then. Think on it at least, and let me know.'

As I nod, I begin to realise where my fate might lie.

'Would ye mind though, to let me see your hands.'

'Oh.' My stomach tumbles. 'Without gloves?'

'Aye.'

Peeling off the knitted gloves finger by finger, I know that my less than feminine hands will be my downfall. The canny milliner will surely see what I really am and withdraw her offer before it has properly been made. And as Mrs McMenemy takes my hands in hers and turns them over and then back again, I hang my head.

'Not married then?' she asks.

'My late husband was a mariner, he…'

She raises a hand to silence me. 'Aye. Ye don't need to go into it. For I think ye'll fit well wi' us here. Very well, in fact.'

'Really?' I look up, amazed.

Surely she now knows me for exactly what I am. But her keen gaze does not falter.

'Aye, really. I've enough milksop hands and simpering lassies in the shop already. There's a growing fashion, I'm sure ye know, for embroidered decorations and button coverings in metal threads, gold and silver filés and the like. I need hands tough enough to work those threads yet also delicate for the tiniest stitches. I think the hands I see before me are exactly that.'

I look up into the single blue eye and know with a thump of my heart that she is right.

the fifth chapter

And so, less than a two-month after my miserable arrival in the city, I became comfortably installed as a girl-apprentice in the Edinburgh millinery shop of Mrs Mary McMenemy.

I worried, of course, whether I could keep my true sex secret whilst living so closely with females. But I reasoned that I would be in the millinery shop only long enough to gain a grounding in the apparel trade. This would allow me to find a more secure situation elsewhere, though whether wearing skirts or breeches I couldn't say.

Missus Mac, as the girls called her, expressed no interest at all in my life before I came to Scotland, except for what stitches I could embroider. The first task she set me was to make roundels of embroidered fruits and flowers entirely in metal threads. These decorations were so troublesome to make they often drew blood but my pain was worthwhile. When sewn onto an old plain gown the roundels brought an instant flourish of high fashion.

Missus Mac frequently declared that the days of unadorned satins and demure lace trimmings were dead and done with. The future lay in ornament and display and the more extravagant, the better. I found myself clapping my hands with delight at each new extravagance she brought into the shop, ever-wider fans and more-feathery bonnets, fringes opulently tasselled and spangled, jewelled carnival masks.

Lucy and Jane would smile politely at these things but they both leaned toward more restrained trimmings. Jane

Mathewson, the more buxom though austere of the two, was the daughter of a Presbyterian minister from Kelso. Lucy Mair, the younger and more gigglisome, had a mother in Leith who was the widow of a sea-captain and had paid an apprentice fee (of thirty whole pounds Lucy confided) for Lucy to learn the milliner's trade. This was in case she should one day also be left with no husband though I could not imagine that pretty, good-hearted Lucy would ever be on her own for long.

Lucy became my closest confidante for she too knew the ways of seamen, and we would often tell each other stories we'd heard from seafarers. I told her of my Dublin voyage, though not that when upon it, I had worn breeches and climbed to the highest top-gallant yards. Lucy was nevertheless wide-eyed with interest having only stood on the deck of a vessel when it was moored in Leith harbour. Jane, who nearby was threading white ribbands through a child's christening gown, yawned.

Jane sometimes looked at me askance, when I let my laugh drop too low, or more worryingly, when I had not recently pumiced my beard. We three prentice girls shared a lodging room two floors above the work parlour and did so very cosily. Despite the confined space of our beds, the girls were demurely brought up to cover themselves as they undressed and I soon perfected the same shift-changing jig that protected our modesty and concealed my true self. Sometimes, the girls complained of their monthly flowers but I saw little of the associated detritus and simply added my own complaints about the trials of female life to theirs.

I did not, thankfully, seem to grow any taller as the months went by although my beard became more troubling. Lucy caught me once, when I thought I was alone in the upper chambers, with a red chin and the pumice stone in my hand. I confessed to her, tearfully, that I suffered as many females do from a surfeit of hair in embarrassing places. She comforted me most gently and promised to tell no one else. She even bought for me a present of a ready-made sugaring paste designed for just such a purpose.

And so, I became engrossed in my new world of the millinery shop. I did not need to leave the Luckenbooths often for the city's delights went by our door. I especially loved to lean out of an upper window when the cathedral's musical bells chimed toward the end of each morning. These were nothing like the dour mathematical ringing of English church bells, but instead played a proper tune as clear as a harpsichord. The tunes varied every day, sometimes having a religious sound, but more usually filling the air with Irish dances or Italian overtures. Below me, as I listened, I might see a juggler or a puppet show, or watch the spell-binding procession of humanity, from barefoot Highlanders wearing nought but a shirt and a length of tartan blanket, to full-wigged lawyers hurrying to the courts.

Mary McMenemy herself occupied a large part of my imagination. Although tiny and round, she filled any space she entered with her eye-catching apparel and surprising turns of phrase. Always rising after her apprentices, she would greet us in the work-parlour with a call of *good morrow ma bitches*, and start the day with a drink of whisky gruel. Lucy told me that Missus Mac had lost her eye in the mis-firing of a pistol but this accident had not dented her love for firearms of which she owned a considerable number. Jane said that Missus Mac had a lover who was a judge in the Parliament Close. But though our mistress often returned to the shop very late, we were never sure where she had been.

During my first year as an apprentice, I felt myself growing both in skill with the needle and in my knowledge of trade. I became adept at hard, intricate work, metal-trimmed passementerie buttons and spangles stamped from foil. Once Missus Mac was satisfied with my embroidery skills, she entrusted me with one of her most valuable commissions, a red silk stomacher to be decorated entirely with silver filé thread into a Tree of Life design. At the top of the triangular garment, the red ground was almost entirely covered by swags of silver foliage. Some of the thread was applied directly in satin stitch and the rest couched down with discreet linen threads.

I found, as I concentrated all my artistry and skill on this masterpiece, that each stitch brought a further measure of peace to the past turmoils in my head. The wrenching pain of losing Fliss, and then Jossy and my absence from home, was calmed, stitch by stitch, through the weeks of intricate work on the stomacher.

When finished, the stomacher was weighted with almost two pounds of pure silver and I felt a similar weight in woe had lifted from my shoulders. Mary McMenemy had a tear in her eye as she stroked the finished work. Then with a cry of *come ye here, ma best wee bitch*, she kissed me full on the mouth.

Jane and Lucy, as they witnessed this peculiar congratulation, looked a little envious of my place in Missus Mac's estimation, though they were no doubt relieved to avoid her kiss. The girls were polite enough to be complimentary about the stomacher, though much narrower looks came my way from Martha Robson, the millinery shop's newest girl-apprentice.

She had come to the Luckenbooths almost a year after my own arrival. Being from a family of Berwick butchers enriched by their cattle farms, Mrs McMenemy had not spared the hefty fee for her apprenticing. Martha told us that she was an orphan who had lived mainly with her grandparents but she gave out very little else about her circumstances. At eighteen she was almost my age which was somewhat old to begin an apprenticeship and though her needlework was tolerable, she seemed to think it far superior to mine. And for this reason, or perhaps some other, she became evermore resentful of any privilege or praise that Mrs McMenemy might bestow upon me.

And indeed, many privileges had come my way. The mistress had grown to trust me not just with the finest embroidering but also with her account books and correspondence. Perhaps as a result of my early education in trade, I had a ready ability to source at the best price the draperies and fancy goods that stocked the shop and store-rooms. Unlike the other girls, I didn't spend much time serving customers in the shop but I imagined that this was because I could be much more usefully employed in the work-parlour either with my needle or with an ink-pot and quill.

My certainty on this matter was badly shaken on a thundery Sunday in May, just after my nineteenth birthday. At the sound of the Cathedral's musical chimes, Mrs McMenemy rolled out of her chamber like a floral orb from an Oriental garden. Swathed in illegally imported Indian chince and a wide-brimmed straw hat covered in silk roses, she would have seemed almost girlish if not for her velvet eye-patch and the two brass-mounted horse-pistols thrust under a leather belt around her waist.

'Well, ma bitches, I'm away to ma shooting,' she says, 'and I want nae young men in here whilst I'm away.' With this, she smiles and seems to give a wink in my direction.

The girls pass each other sidelong looks amidst blushes and murmurs of *aye, no worries, Missus Mac.*

Then, we go to the window and watch as she descends the twisting staircase to the street before being handed by a liveried footman into a high-wheeled carriage with matching black horses and blinds pulled down.

As the carriage pulls away, Jane huffs with annoyance.

'As if we would bring men in here! There is already enough talk of this being a bordel.'

'Is there?' I say going back to the work-table and picking up a golden shell half-finished in needlepoint lace. 'Why would that be?'

'Och, the Missus has no morals, as well ye know.'

I wondered what Mrs McMenemy has said to Jane to so annoy her.

'I fear those things are said of all millinery shops,' says Lucy buttering the heel of a loaf. "Tis just because we're a female trade.'

Martha lays aside the lawn stock she is edging. 'That might not be the sole reason.' She turns to look directly at me.

'Why?' Jane frowns. 'What else is there?'

Martha shrugs. 'Well, you know.' Pushing her work away she pulls a small leather-bound book from the pocket inside her skirt and begins to flick through it. Her grandmother has paid her subscription to Mr Ramsay's Circulating Library and she loves to flaunt in front of us each new volume she has rented.

Jane shakes her head indignantly. 'Well, my father would never have paid a penny toward my time-serving had he heard any lewd remarks about apprentice-girls.'

'What say you, Stella?' Martha smiles with a look of playful amusement but I see the venom in her eyes. 'Have you seen any young men about the place?'

Lucy, chewing her lump of buttered bread, looks from Martha to me and then to Jane with a look of pure confusion.

'What? Has somebody brought their beau in here?' she says through her mouthful.

'Well, certainly not me,' says Jane. 'James would never stoop to risking my reputation in such a manner.'

My eyes widen. I had no idea that Jane has a beau. 'James' is a secret that must have been already shared with the others though not with me. I wonder where on earth she has hooked and netted him.

Jane turns to me. 'Stella?'

For a moment I have no idea what she is asking. Then, I realise. 'Oh no, I have no beau,' I titter and cover my mouth with my hand.

'No. Indeed not,' says Martha with the air of a barrister resting their case. Then, ostentatiously raising up her little book, she flicks through the pages and smiles. 'Though I have found, curiously enough, this funny ditty about a person like you.'

'Like me?' My voice wavers down into a horrifying croak.

'What do you mean?'

'Why, another Stella.' With her finger between the pages, Martha holds out the book.

'I'm not much of a one for poetry,' I say without taking it.

'Oh, do read it out, Martha,' Lucy says.

'Very well.'

Already, Martha's look of satisfaction sets my heart thudding with apprehension. Her voice is a knotty mix of Scotland and Northumberland threaded through with smuggery as she reads.

'Say Stella, was Prometheus blind
And forming you mistook your kind?
No, 'twas for you alone he stole
A fire that forms a manly soul,
Then, to complete it in every way
He moulded it with female clay.'

Martha closes the book and puts it back into her pocket. Then she turns to me, smiling slyly, and her gaze seems to pierce my skirts in an examination of the truth that lay beneath.

We didn't wait long to meet Jane's secret beau for only a week or two later Missus Mac declared that we were all allowed an outing to the Bonfires. The tenth of June seemed early for a midsummer fire but I assumed this must be the Scotch tradition.

As we girls assembled in our finery before leaving the Luckenbooths, Missus Mac presented each of us with a little spray of white hedge roses and I pinned mine to my new gown of maroon and cream striped calico. Mrs McMenemy was generous with her apprentices' wardrobes saying that we were walking advertisements for her wares. For many months, Fliss's clothes had lain with the embroidered waistcoat and Quilted-Petticoat unworn in my sea-chest. My boy's coat and breeches were there too. I told myself frequently that I should sell these last items in case of embarrassment if the girls saw them. An innocent story of how they'd come into my possession was hard to think up. But for some reason, I could not bear to let my masculine garments go.

As we trot down the High Street, we four girls link arms and gaily bat away the nasty slurs and gestures of the shop-lads. In the soft evening air, the towering stone buildings of the city's grandest thoroughfare have never looked more imposing. I doubt any street in the world could be more magnificent.

Once we've passed the Tron Kirk, Jane unpins her spray of Scotch roses and flings them into the road.

'Oh!' I cry. 'Don't you want them?'

'I do not,' she says. 'Nasty Jacobite nonsense.'

'D'ye not care for White Rose Day?' Lucy asks, aghast.

'I'm celebrating the summer, not the Stuarts,' Jane snaps.

Martha gives her a sideways smirk. 'And meeting your beau?'

Jane tries to cover a grin in reply.

'What is White Rose Day?' I ask and look around the bonneted and sashed throng, most of whom wear open white roses on their hats or at their breasts.

'D'ye not know? It's the birthday of the pretended Stuart usurper in Rome,' Jane says sourly. 'Surely ye have noticed our mistress is a monstrous Jacobite?'

'No,' I confess, shocked.

'Neither has my father,' says Jane ruefully, 'or I should not still be apprenticed to her.'

It strikes me then that all the people around us wearing white roses must think King George to be the usurper while his very distant cousin in Rome, James Stuart, son of the erstwhile King James the Second, is the true monarch of the British Isles. And this James Stuart, half-brother to dead Queen Anne, would indeed be King James the Third were it not for his Papist religion.

Lucy, I notice, wears her white rose with pride and I decide to do likewise. Any cause so hated by my father should have my sympathy. And from that moment I began to think of myself as a Jacobite.

Soon, we have passed through the Nether Bow Port and out of the city walls onto the lower leafy slope of Canongate. A tingle goes through me at the fine sight of Holyrood Abbey's pointed grey turrets below the plunging rock of Salesburgh Crags. As we turn toward the fields below those cliffs, Jane lurches forward and breaks free from our linked arms. And ahead of us, a tall thin youth in a blue harriteen coat raises his hand.

In one blink of my eye, I understand both that this youth is Jane's beau and that I have met him before. In fact, I know him pretty well. Better probably than Jane. For 'James' is in fact Jim Whillans, better known to the boys of Nathaniel Bravery's Nautical Academy as The Pope.

I use the minute that it takes him to bow to Lucy and Martha to collect my face. But my innards are tumbling in dread.

'And this,' says Jane, as Jim turns to me, 'is Stella.'

As his head rises from its incline I see the inevitable flash of recognition across his features followed by disquieted confusion.

But Stella is ready.

'How do you do, sir?' she purrs, turning up the Dublin in her vowels.

Jim's only reply is a stare and another frown.

'Come on, James,' Jane says, taking his arm. 'They'll be alight afore we get there.'

And so, with the happy couple leading the way, I link arms between Lucy and Martha to study how my former classmate has grown and prepare myself for an inevitable interrogation.

As the months have gone by, everything to do with Whitehaven has faded in my mind. My poor dead sister and my suspicions about my father's part in her death, the crimes of my mother, my friendship with Hannah Salkeld, my love for Jossy, and yes, even my true sex, have dulled to memories.

Several times, I had decided to send word to my kin that I was safe. Once, I even sharpened a quill with the intention of writing to Hannah Salkeld at the salt-works. I yearned for her calm truthful words to give me news of my home. But would I wish to hear that news if it was bad? And what if my letter fell into the hands of the Navy? So the letter stayed unwritten. The daily challenges and delights of the millinery shop as well as the diversions and dramas of the shop-folk and the city around me left little time for homesickness or grief. And I felt myself more confident and comfortable as Stella than I ever did as Kit.

But confronted by a human reminder of my old life, a clamp seems to tighten about my chest. Stella may not survive this encounter. And if I am unmasked and must once more put on my breeches, is it too late to learn to be a man?

Wood-piled bonfires are dotted around the rough sloping fields at the foot of the crags beyond the Abbey grounds and a gay crowd is already assembled around them. Short-legged black cattle are being led on rope halters frilled with flowers while bagpipers and fiddlers compete to fill the air with tunes. Farm lads and lasses, merry with drink, spin each other towards fountains of orange sparks that spurt up when fresh wood is thrown to the flames.

We draw closer to the blaze. Martha hands round a silver flask of whisky and when the fiery sun sinks behind the far-off Castle crag, Jim buys a quart of gin from a passing pot-boy. In a summer twilight that keeps darkness at bay all night, Jim is laughing his old lewd laugh. And despite Jane's thundery looks, he seems determined to dance with each apprentice-girl in turn.

Lucy, of course, is his first pick. Jim wheels her around and around the fire and then out into the darkness where we can only hear her shrieking laughs. Martha is next, and when my turn comes I know it will be fruitless to refuse. Stella must keep her wits about her for anything Jim Whillans might throw our way.

But as he takes my hand, then bows, red-faced and panting, I cannot help recalling him, piss-pipe in hand, to aim his energetic stream over the side of the jolly-boat. So I must compose my face before he leads us into a slightly drunken country jig. Nonetheless, his opening remark throws me.

'I thought you were dead.'

'What?'

'You're Miss Ravenglass of Whitehaven, aren't you? Christopher's sister.'

My heart thumps so hard I cough and am almost too winded to speak.

'No, sir,' I manage.

'No, indeed, you are not dead, as I can well see!' Jim goes on growing excited. 'Though I heard there was an inquest and everything. And some questions about murder.'

The word slaps me into silence.

'Well, I am delighted that you're alive,' Jim smiles, 'and in such fine and comely health and without any... encumbrances.'

'Mr Whillans,' I shout, though I don't think that Jane has ever told us his surname. 'I have not the slightest notion what you are talking about. My name is Mistress Stella Bride and I've no brother of any description.'

'You are not Miss Stella Ravenglass?'

'No, I am not,' and I have to bite my tongue not to tell him that her name was Felicity not Stella.

'Well, the likeness is very strong. Do you have any family connections in Whitehaven?'

'Certainly not, nor any connection with the place at all, except for burning their coal in our grate when I was a child.'

'Oh.'

'Oh, indeed.'

Stella's tone sobers him and he hands me back to my sitting place by the fire with a serious bow.

The green branches on the fire soon burn down to glowing embers and then the real business of the evening begins. The fiddler quickens his bow and the company of lads and lasses, faces flushed in the firelight, begin to clap in time to his jig. Some of the lads, all of them in fact, are starting to take off their coats and hats, then waistcoats and shirts, until there is a huddle of bare-chested youths at one side of the dying bonfire. As Jim also strips himself to the waist, Jane eyes his nakedness with a hungry fascination she disguises as hilarity. And then he takes his turn with the other youths to run laughing and yelping through the red embers of the bonfire to the beat of a bagpiper's reel.

As I watch the lads circle through the hot cinders, competing to be cock of the fire-walk, I wonder if there is some way to quiz Jim Whillans without revealing anything of who I am. It is now more than two years since I last saw Whitehaven and I should dearly love any news of my family. Jim is employed by a Ships' Broker in Leith in a very good position, Jane tells me, which will afford him independent means within a few years. I imagine this trade has brought Jim into contact with Whitehaven gossip about Fliss's suspicious death and, no doubt, the scandal of her pregnant state. I wonder what place my father holds in this gossip.

'Come, Stella, 'tis the lassies' turn!'

Lucy has taken my hands and is trying to pull me to my feet and toward the fire.

'Oh no,' I say, 'not in my new gown. Missus Mac wouldn't approve.'

'Aye, come on,' Lucy persists with her tugging. "Twill bring good luck in finding us husbands.'

Martha gives a sly laugh. 'Perhaps that's not what Stella's after.'

By way of contradiction, I lift my petticoats to my knees and run giggling with the other girls through the greying embers of the fire. Jim stands at the far side, reaching out his hands to help Jane, Lucy and Martha over the warm ash, delivering a kiss of congratulation to each female fire-walker. But not to me.

Between the heat of the fire and Jim's sceptical gaze, I feel myself becoming ungainly and boyish. Suddenly my stays are unpleasantly tight. Stella feels too brittle a carapace to contain Kit inside her.

The girls are too full of gin and their own high spirits to

notice any change in me. But as we watch the garlanded cattle being pulled, bellowing, across the hot cinders, Jim shoots me dubious glances. What will Jim say to Jane about me? He will not keep his suspicions silent, that is certain.

I must avoid him at all costs from now on. No more outings if he is to be part of the company. And if he ever comes to the shop, I'll depart away to the work-parlour the instant he arrives.

But I did no such thing the following September when I found myself the alone in the millinery shop one quiet afternoon. Nibbling on a sugar-lump, I contemplate the closed boxes on the shelves which contain an array of painted fans. Missus Mac refuses to put them on display for fear they'll gather dust and spoil. But if this were my shop, I should have them out on clear view. What interest is there to a customer in a brown pasteboard box compared to a gorgeously adorned fan? It strikes me then how very much I should like to be the proprietor of this shop, or indeed of any millinery. I know myself to be expertly qualified for such a calling. And suddenly I yearn to run an emporium of fashion, to stock and decorate it to my own taste and to bend the taste of others to mine through the retailing of my wares.

At that moment, the door bursts open and Jim Whillans hurtles in.

'Raise the alarm!' he cries, red-faced and panting with a look of terror in his eye.

I place the sugar-lump under the counter and stare at him blankly.

'They have been sighted just without the city!' Jim rants on, wild-eyed. 'I must get Jane and all the girls to safety.'

At this, I almost retort how little regard he had for Hannah Salkeld's safety as he waited damp-faced and eager for his turn with her at the Bear Mouth. I have a strong urge to punch him on his freckled nose.

But Stella remains calm and as Irish in her speech as I can muster.

'Who, pray, has been sighted?' she asks. 'And what is the danger?'

'An army of Highland clans, well-armed and bloodthirsty!' Jim raves.

'To attack the city?' Stella scoffs. 'Why would they do that?'

'Because they come with their Princely leader. He is wearing Highland dress and riding a white horse.'

Stella sighs, affecting boredom. 'And who, exactly, is that?'

'Charles Edward Stuart, of course,' Jim proclaims with dread. 'Him they are calling the Young Pretender.'

the sixth chapter

This news of an approaching army was not a complete surprise. For several weeks, the *Caledonian Mercury* had been reporting the progress of the Young Pretender ever southward from the Highlands where he had landed from a French ship. The army's reported size grew as it marched, as did the newspaper's estimation of its leader. From being reported as 'the Usurper's son,' Charles Edward Stuart soon became 'the Young Pretender' then 'the Young Chevalier,' and finally when the Scottish capital was within his sights the newspaper dubbed him 'Prince Regent.'

Mrs McMenemy's main concern at the prospect of a marauding Highland horde was to get the shop as well-stocked as it could be with tartan plaids.

'Gairdner and Taylor are advertising a great choice of tartans, as well as Scots bonnets and stockings. We must not let them out-Scotch us!' she cried and asked me to write immediately to a weavers' factor in Bannockburn.

And so we began, as the Highland army and the Young Pretender came nearer, to fill the shop's shelves and drawers with Jacobite fripperies. Missus Mac set Martha and Lucy, who were the best artists amongst us, to painting the plain underside of fans with white roses and crowns, whilst I was set to embroidering the same on handkerchiefs.

Jane, who had made clear her dislike of all things Jacobite, was kept at work in the shop. She told us that James had volunteered for the Town Guard who would defend the city against the Jacobite army. But the Guard's volunteers received no help from the regular King's troops whose red coats were seen nowhere except on the Castle's impregnable ramparts at the top of the town. Each day Jane looked a little paler.

Our habit during any break from the upstairs work-table was to go to the window from where we had a clear view of the street but were far enough above any shouted lewdness's to pretend we did not hear them. Part of Gairdner and Taylor's drapery on the other side of the Land-Market was also visible from the window and I was fascinated by their exuberant window display of tartan plaids in black and yellow, blue and red, and violet and green. But though these cloths were eye-catching, I was unsure why the wearing of them might be taken as an indication of Jacobite allegiance.

My father had always maintained that the Jacobites wished to drag Britain into the darkness of absolute monarchy. As evidence of this, he cited the Royal African Company, James the Second's monopoly which had for many years kept independent English merchants away from the Guinea coast and out of the lucrative trade in people. This opinion of my father's made me increasingly amenable to the Jacobite cause. And whilst I had previously thought that a Jacobite must also be a Roman Catholic like James the Second, I'd noticed few Papists in Edinburgh. From what I'd seen of Edinburgh's dour places of worship, the Scottish religion was the very opposite of Papist. So I was curious how the Catholic king's grandson who now threatened the city, had found so much support within it.

Early on a September Tuesday when Lucy and I are the first down to the work-parlour and sharing a dish of buttermilk as we gaze across the street, I ask her about Gairdner and Taylor's display.

'Why is tartan used as the Jacobites' badge?'

'The Stuart Pretenders are Scotch, aren't they?'

'But they are mainly Papists. And there don't seem many of those in Scotland.'

Lucy shrugs. 'It's no got much to do wi' religion.'

'No?' I say, surprised. 'What is it about then?'

'Well,' she thinks for a minute and leans her elbow on the window sill, her chin on her hand. 'It's a sorry thing that we Scots no longer have our own monarch.'

'But your Scottish kings, the Stuarts, took our English throne.'

'And then were thrown off it.'

'They could have had it back were it not for their Popery.'

Lucy looks uncomfortable. 'Well, all I know is that the Stuarts are Scots. And I'd dearly love to lay my eyes on the Chevalier Prince. They say he is exceeding handsome.'

'Will you wear a tartan sash if he comes past the window?'

'I shall wear tartan stockings, shoes and shift if it makes him look my way,' Lucy laughs and I join in, leaning my forehead against hers. 'What sort o' man do ye like the look of best?' Lucy whispers in my ear, the colour rising in her cheeks.

'Why... I don't know,' I say, though instantly into my mind comes a vision of Jossy as he emerged, dripping, from the cold waters beneath Skidda Hill. 'What about you?'

'I'll tell ye what sort I definitely dinnae like,' Lucy giggles behind her hand, 'that one down there.' And she casts a sidelong look toward the horseshit-strewn street.

He is a be-draggled barefoot fellow standing gormless on the cobbles in a stained grey shirt and over it, the long length of plaid cloth that serves Highlanders as a toga-like wrap as well as a blanket or even a tent. The plaid is so dirty as to be almost black. The fellow looks my age but is so short that his pike, which seems to be a kitchen knife fixed to a broom-handle, towers above him.

He sees us looking and puts his hand to one side of his mouth to call something up. I can make no sense of it.

'What is he saying?'

Lucy shrugs and then laughs out loud as, with a clatter, the Highlander drops his home-made pike. He bends over to pick it up and the loose plaid rides right up, pulling his too-short shirt above his buttocks.

'Oh! Ecclefechen!' Lucy titters.

'What's the joke?' Martha comes up behind us and tries to peer through the narrow pane.

'It's that Highlander,' Lucy can hardly speak for laughing. 'When he bent over... I saw his whiddle-pipe and whirlygigs.'

'Lucy!' Martha tries to sound worldly but I can tell that she is keen to see them too.

'Well, I have nae...' Lucy hiccups a laugh, 'I have nae seen any before.' She collapses then into hilarity.

Martha steps back, annoyed to have missed out on the Highlander's spectacle. She turns to me. 'And have you seen any before, *Stella*?' She pronounces my name with the whining emphasis of a sceptic.

I shrug.

'Well, have ye?' Lucy asks, innocently.

I cannot bring myself to lie, yet nor can I possibly tell the truth. My blush will have to do as a reply.

'Go on, Stella, tell us,' Martha flexes her claws. 'Whose man-parts have you seen? You have seen some *very* close to home, I reckon.'

At this, Lucy's laughing is overtaken by her puzzlement at what Martha might mean. Thankfully, there is a distraction outside as the Highlander is joined by others.

'Oh look at the state of them,' I say, pointing.

Some of the Highland warriors wear hole-punched shoes and limp-feathered bonnets, but each has his own dirty plaid around him and is carrying a heavy unsheathed sword.

Then my heart begins to race as I realise what this might mean for us. If these Highlanders are from the Pretender's army, have they now entered the city's walls? And where will they next turn their murderous gaze?

'I must rouse Missus Mac,' I say, leaving the window. 'The rebels are here. We must barricade the shop!'

But on hearing of the rebel army's success, Mrs McMenemy's

first thought is not to protect her property, but rather to get out the unsold fans and have Lucy embellish them some more. For now, in addition to white roses and oak leaves, she may add a portrait of 'Prince Charlie.' Next, she instructs me to start cutting lengths of white silk to make, in the greatest speed and quantity, cockades for the Jacobites' hats.

We soon find out that no blood was shed when the Pretender's army entered the city during the night for it was let in through the Nether Bow Port by mistake. Now hundreds of the Highlanders, in their dirty shirts and plaids, are roaming the city although most look more over-awed than murderous. The talk is that Prince Charles (for even Jane is too wary to call him 'Pretender' any longer) has been seen making his processional entrance to the Abbey and Palace of Holyrood. Lucy begs Missus Mac that we be allowed to go and watch.

I too would have dearly liked to take a good look at this famous Prince who had until now spent his life in the glittering royal courts of Italy and France. Mrs McMenemy herself seemed torn, but she said she owed it to Lucy's mother to keep her safe and so we must stay indoors, though we might watch from the windows and hope that the Prince would go by. Almost at that moment, the wisdom of her caution was proved when, very close, three cannon shots fired in quick succession. The blasts were so thunderous that Lucy and I both screamed and clung on to each other. It seemed that King George's garrison, now besieged behind the Castle's impregnable walls, was sending their own lethal welcome of cannonballs right down the long straight mile of the High Street into the path of the Pretender Prince.

Even Missus Mac looked pale as we cowered indoors for the rest of the day awaiting bloody street fighting between the Jacobite ruffians and the Town Guard to break out around the Luckenbooths. But all stayed quiet.

Then in the morning of the next day, the gathering of crowds outside makes it very clear that something momentous is about to happen. Even the musical church chimes are muffled by the hubbub. As Lucy puts on her best lawn neckerchief and cap, she whispers to me that she is certain the Chevalier Prince will appear outside our window at any moment. She is not quite brave enough though, to wear a white cockade.

Then, Missus Mac, with horse-pistols stowed under her cloak goes out into the crowd, swearing that she will fight off any looters and ruffians who might attack the Luckenbooths. Not long after, she is back, now flushed and beaming, saying that the Mercat Cross has been covered with an Oriental carpet and a deal of silverware brought up from the Abbey. A drummer and a trumpeter are standing by. Despite the possible dangers, she then flings open the windows and we crowd around awaiting a fanfare or proclamation from the nearby market place.

Townsfolk fill the narrow street below and every window is crammed with expectant faces. When the drum roll and trumpet fanfare finally come, the buzz of the crowd falls silent. Missus Mac leans herself as far out of the window as her stoutness will allow and listens for the words of the crier at the Mercat Cross, though it's the murmurings from the crowd below that bring us the news.

'They've proclaimed a new king...' the words drift up to us from the street. *'King James the eighth of Scotland and third of England... and the bonny Prince Charles as his eldest son is to be Regent of Britain... Long live King James... Long live the Scottish King... Hurrah for Prince Charles the Prince Regent!'*

And with that, a great cheer goes up. Hats are thrown into the air. Clapping and huzzahs echo from all the buildings. White handkerchiefs are waved by women from every window. Indeed, it is the women and girls who seem to shout loudest and it is they who wave white linen most ardently.

Missus Mac is beside herself with glee as she leans out of the work-parlour window shouting 'God save King James' and 'God bless Scotland,' and then pulls her pistols from her belt. Her two shots, punch into the sky, leaving the window frame shivering and my ears buzzing. But soon after, the sound of clapping and huzzah-ing echoes even louder. My only disappointment in witnessing this dramatic pageant was that the Prince Regent himself did not make an appearance.

Once the new King was proclaimed, Mrs McMenemy dropped all pretence of being anything but an ardent Jacobite. White cockades and tartan sashes took prime place on the shop's counters and a steady stream of ladies arrived to purchase them. Anything with a picture of the Prince flew off the shelf and soon Lucy was painting his brown eyes and slightly weak chin on spectacle-cases, snuff boxes and brooches as well as fans.

As word spread of the shop's loyalty to the new King and his handsome young Regent, Missus Mac was called to the homes of several high-born Jacobite ladies to show them her wares and to help them re-fresh their mantua-gowns for the entertainments now taking place nightly at the Abbey in the presence of the Bonnie Prince. There was no time for creation of entirely new apparel for each event, so the skill of the milliner was essential to the fashioning of a new costume from an old gown by the use of lace trimmings, appliqué embroidered flowers and coloured-gauze kerchiefs, as well as hairpieces, rouge, patches, best-quality ceruse and on one occasion, a full set of false teeth.

It always seemed to be Martha who was chosen to accompany Mrs McMenemy on these private visits to the grandest apartments in the city, and Martha came back preening with all the fanciness she had seen inside these habitations. I tried to tell myself that Missus Mac was merely keeping Martha's grandmother sweet by giving her granddaughter access to the grande-dames of Edinburgh. But deep down, I worried that there was a more personal reason that I, in particular, was kept so much in the work-parlour and away from the customers. There was little, as I knew well, that escaped Mrs McMenemy's shrewd eye.

Then, about a month after the Young Pretender's triumphal

arrival in the city, the mistress told us that she had been summoned to attend at the Abbey and Palace itself. It was to be that very evening and I knew that Martha would inevitably be the one to accompany her. But as the late afternoon faded and I began to light the tallow candles at the table, Missus Mac told me, to my knee-weakening joy, that she needed an extra pair of strong hands and I had better put on my cloak and come with them. At this, Jane makes a sour face whilst Lucy can't conceal her tears.

Martha and the mistress had packed two bulky bundles of wares which take a deal of man-handling into the carriage that carries us the full length of the Mile to the Abbey.

On our heady journey down the hill, I thank Mrs McMenemy with great passion for allowing me along.

'Aye, well, Stella,' she replies. 'There's a special do on tonight, and it's your particular artistry we'll be needing, as well as your muscles for heaving our wares.'

At this, Martha Robson flicks me an unpleasant smile. I am too proud, as well as faintly uneasy, to enquire what sort of 'do' this is to be. But my uneasiness dissolves at the sight of the Abbey, with flares lighting the entrance-way and candles burning in every tall window between the pointed stone towers.

When the coach door opens, Missus Mac is suddenly flustered and she tells me to pick up both of the sheet-wrapped bundles from the coach and carry them together. So cumbersome are they that I have no chance to look around until we are through a colonnaded vestibule and at the foot of a sumptuous staircase. I crane my neck, gawping. A chandelier, ablaze with beeswax candles, illuminates a ceiling moulded into trumpeting angels and cornucopia of flowers and fruit. Naked figures, larger than in life, are woven into fading tapestries that cover the walls. As we ascend the wide stairs, strains of music and bursts of laughter from above grow louder.

Mrs McMenemy is ahead of us with a serious gentleman she calls Mr Gib. He leads us through dimly lit corridors and connecting ante-chambers until, from an open doorway, a flare of light and noise makes all our heads turn. I let out an amazed 'Oh!' at the sudden glimpse into a long, illuminated gallery that glitters with people of fashion in silks of every hue. Even Martha leans toward me and giggles with delight.

Then, Mr Gib opens the door to a wood-panelled ante-chamber, well-lit but furnished only by a table and chair at each end, and between them a full-length pier-glass on a stand. At one of the tables sits a lady, her dark hair pulled back from her face, and at the other a bald gentleman. Both of their faces are deathly white and both are wearing flowered silk banyans. They rise as we enter. The gentleman is uncommonly tall.

Martha and I stand a little back as Mrs McMenemy is introduced to them by Mr Gib. There is much frowning and nodding as they all engage in conversation. Then Mrs McMenemy turns to us.

'Martha, you shall help Mrs Douglas,' she indicates the dark-haired lady. 'And Stella will attend to Signor Scalzi.'

Here, for the first time, I meet the tall gentleman's gaze. There is the flicker of a smile before he indicates for me to join him at his table. He is far from young and his bald head seems too small for his body. His face has a flushed, womanish plumpness.

'You have the hair and the costume?' he asks, his voice heavy with foreignness.

I shoot a look at Missus Mac.

'Aye, it's all in there,' she indicates the bundle in my arms. 'I shall be here to help you both if there's anything amiss.'

Laying the bundle on the floor, I realise from its weight and size that there is very much more for Signor Scalzi to put on than a coat and breeches. And inside is a vast and sumptuous mantua-gown of heavy silk brocaded with yellow and white flowers, as well as a paduasoy petticoat, a full-powdered wig in a gauze bag and Mrs McMenemy's second-best pair of stays.

I look up at the foreign gentleman. 'You are to wear these, sir?'

'Indeed, at least while I am Ginerva, the King of Scotland's daughter. But then, for Act Two, you will transform me into her lover, Prince Ariodante. And be quick about it. Very good?'

Unable to look away from his peculiar stooping tallness, I blink and then nod understanding now that the 'do' must be an operatic entertainment and that for some of it Signor Scalzi is to sing the part of a woman.

Taking off the banyan, he stands in a shapeless shift with arms outstretched waiting for me to bring the stays. They fit remarkably well though he instructs me not to lace them too tight. I suggest lacing tighter at the waist and loose enough at the top to introduce a little padding at the breast, which is exactly how I lace myself into Fliss's stays each morning. With the paduasoy petticoat tied, Signor Scalzi goes to the pier-glass and pronounces the effect *bellissima!*

The mantua-gown is copiously trained though shorter than it should be for Signor Scalzi's great height. Missus Mac instructs me to loop the skirt up at each side to compensate for the lack of panniers but leave the cloth loose enough for the gown to hang almost to the floor with only the good side of the brocade on show. This exercise in drapery is more complex than any I have done before. Signor Scalzi stands, a little impatient as I kneel at his feet, fishing inside his skirts for the hidden buttons and ribband-ties that allow me to arrange the lengths of brocade into an elegantly puffed 'tail' over each of the Signor's hips.

A few pins are also required to keep the cloth showing its good side. But when I stand back and view the finished costume, with the Signor's head now clouded in a white-powdered wig and his cheeks rouged and patched, I feel a surge of pride.

'Don't ye forget these,' says Mrs McMenemy as she brings a sash of black and red tartan to lay across Signor Scalzi's shoulder and she finishes the costume of an antiquate Scottish Princess with a white Jacobite cockade at his breast.

With Martha's help, Mrs Douglas is already dressed in a black satin frocked coat, waistcoat and breeches with heeled leather riding boots and a gold-laced cocked hat. The heavy scent in the air tells me that the black moustache across the lady's top lip has been drawn with a clove charred over a candle-flame.

Then, Mr Gib beckons frantically from the door of the ante-chamber. And with a nod to each other, the performers commence their stately procession into the long gallery. Martha sidles up to me with a lascivious grin.

'Did you get a look at it?'

'At what?' I have no idea what she means.

'At that... that creature's private parts.'

'What?'

She gives an incredulous snort. 'I should ha' thought that you of all folk would know.'

'No, Martha, I don't,' Stella retorts. 'Pray enlighten me.'

'Well, you know, he's one o'them Italians who's had his cullions cut off.'

'What?' I say again, so incredulous that Stella deserts me. 'Why, in God's name would anyone do that?'

'To sing better, you ninny.'

Then, from the open door to the gallery, Missus Mac calls us over with a hiss of *ma bitches! come ye here!* and whispers that we may go in but only if we stand with our backs to the wainscot and make not the slightest sound or fidget. And so, the three of us slip into the royal presence.

No one notices us. Amidst the brilliance of the candlelight and the pomp of the decoration, all faces in the long gallery are turned toward Signor Scalzi. Standing on my toes, I see his yellow brocade gown pass between the feathered, satined and jewelled courtiers toward a small orchestra in the centre of the room.

My eyes sweep around the company of whitened, black-patched faces, looking for the Prince, but though the walls are covered by the likenesses of his long-dead ancestors, I can see no sign of Charles Edward Stuart.

Then applause sweeps around the gallery. After a pregnant silence there is a quiet exchange of words followed by a peal of laughter and I sense, from the reverence of this humorous response, that the witticism must have come from the Prince. Peering around the heads in front of me, I glimpse a golden throne beneath a crimson-velvet canopy. And on it, though his face is turned away from us, sits the Prince Regent.

Without warning, the harpsichord bursts into an overture, rising through the soaring strains of flute and violins before being cut down by the sombre viol. Skin on the back of my neck prickles as Signor Scalzi starts to sing. Never before or since have I heard such a sound from a human voice. Notes in the purest, highest soprano are fired around the room with the depth and power of male lungs. I have not the first idea what the words of his Italian song are about but its musical loveliness tugs at my heart. A sudden sadness sweeps through me leaving my cheeks wet, though I cannot say if the tears are for myself or for poor Signor Scalzi, trapped in a strange halfway state between the sexes for the sake of his art.

Soon Mrs Douglas, as the jilted Duke Polinesso, joins the duet in the deepest of female singing voices. But her voice seems thin and weak against Signor Scalzi's magnificent, resonating song.

All too soon, the glorious music is ended by calls of *brava, brava* and a burst of applause. The singers turn toward the crimson canopy, though it is Princess Ginerva who gives the bow to Prince, and Duke Polinesso the curtsy. Then they return at a stately pace to the ante-chamber.

'Oh, Signor Scalzi!' I say as I unhook and unlace the yellow brocade gown and wipe my cheeks. 'You were astonishing.'

'Of course, I was!' he smiles with amused satisfaction. 'And now, if you please, my own apparel.'

He reaches out for the pile of clothes below the table. I help him off with the stays and on with a matching suit of green velvet stamped all over in a chequerboard of tiny black hearts, a motif he must deem fitting for Ginerva's lover, Ariodante.

Just as the signor is stepping awkwardly into his breeches, I sense that someone, or several people are at the opening door of the ante-chamber. All heads turn. My own mouth falls open. For standing in the doorway is a slight man in elaborate apparel who I know to be Charles Edward Stuart, now proclaimed Prince of Wales and Regent of the British Isles, though to most he is still the Young Pretender.

His face, with a sloping chin beneath a small mouth and large brown-grey eyes, is strangely recognisable from the little portraits that Lucy has been painting onto fans. A white-powdered wig tails almost to his waist in the Continental style.

But it is his attire that dumbfounds me. The pink figured-silk coat is cut slim at the waist then extravagantly flared at the sides as if held out by panniers. His breeches are of the same gorgeous pink and richly embroidered with delicate silver flowers. And then the shoes… the shoes! Two-inch high heels are painted red to match their oversized enamel buckles. The shoe-leather seems, in the candlelight, to be pure silver. For the first time that I can remember, I want more than anything to take off my woman's garb and put on a suit of male clothes just like this one.

It is Signor Scalzi who first comes out of the trance induced by our royal visitor and bends into a low bow. The rest of us follow with curtsies. When I rise up, Mr Gib is whispering in Mrs McMenemy's ear. She looks from me to the Prince and back again. Then she beckons me forward.

'His Royal Highness has requested a small favour and I think you should perform it for him.'

I blink, then nod, too overwhelmed to speak.

Martha shoots me a look like a rapier.

'A button, from his breeks has come off,' says Mrs McMenemy says under her breath. 'There's a needle and thread in my basket.'

The Prince seems not at all embarrassed to stand in the middle of the room and open his front breech-flap. Perhaps we seamstresses and singers are too lowly to worry him or perhaps he has been trained to regard his royal person as public property.

But my fingers shake as I thread the needle, not just because I might prick the royal belly, but also because I might stab my own finger and stain the softest, whitest cotton of his shirt with my blood. As I kneel at his feet with my needle, his whole person gives off a scent of lavender and bergamot.

Then, taking up the offending button, I place my hands on the Prince's breeches and begin to sew. The button has the same fine silver purl as the embroidered leaf coronets on his cuffs. Never have I touched such fine embellishments. The coat is lined in the same ivory silk as the Prince's waistcoat, with coloured leaves and silken berries twisting around buttonholes and edges. The work has, like the Prince himself, an exotic delicacy that is decidedly foreign.

As I push the needle into the waistband of the breeches, I cannot quite get purchase on the end and I sense the Prince flinch. Have I sewed too close to his skin and pricked him with the needle-point? My heart skips. I have no option but to speak.

'Sir… your highness… might I, I mean could you open another button, so that the needle has more room?'

My voice is a feeble croak. Just when I need her most, Stella has deserted me.

But the Prince does not seem to have heard. I wonder, hotly, whether to speak again. But then he puts a hand to his crotch and unfastens a further button so that I can pull back the flap.

'Thank you, sire… sir, I mean sire.'

Then for the first time, the Prince glances down and looks me in the eye.

'You are not Scotch?' His own accent has a lilt to it that is clearly not English.

'No, sir.'

'Where are you from?'

'Cumberland,' I say, all pretence of a Dublin accent abandoned.

'Ah, yes. Cumberland,' the Prince says with emphasis, as if the name has some profound meaning.

Taking my mouth as close to his breeches as I dare, I snap the thread with my teeth.

'There, majesty, it is done.'

Without another word or glance, the Prince buttons himself up and strides back to the gallery, Mr Gib in his wake.

And only as I stand up do I see Martha's face fixed in my direction and wearing a smile triumphant with spite.

the seventh chapter

Martha Robson did not wait long to take full advantage of all she had heard on our royal outing to the Abbey.

'Why don't you sing for us?' She teases me one cold afternoon at the work-table. 'I bet we could get some notes out of you as good as the sissy Signor's!'

Stella tries to remain haughty. 'Why, pray, would you think that?'

'Oh, no reason,' Martha giggles to Jane, becoming bolder, 'except that you sometimes have his look of a...' Martha's laughter overcomes her for a moment and Jane joins in, '...of a stomping great horse-godmother!'

Stella fumes. 'You are just jealous at my having had a direct intercourse with the Prince.' But my insides are a-flitter.

'And did you not, *Stella*,' says Martha, 'in that very intercourse, lie to the noble lord?' With an inflection of her head and a nasty smile Martha infuses the name with scorn.

'Indeed not,' Stella retorts. My fingers quiver on the needle.

'Then why did you tell him you come from Cumberland?'

'Aye,' Jane pipes up. 'Ye even swore to my James that ye're a Dubliner.'

Panic flushes through me.

'I... you...' Rarely is Stella lost for words. 'You must have heard wrong.'

'Oh no,' Martha smiles. 'I heard the prince repeat the name of that place you said, Cumberland. I heard it very distinctly.'

'Which is curious,' Jane slips in, 'because James told me he noticed an uncanny resemblance between you, Stella, and a boy at his school in Cumberland.'

I almost retort that if Jane knew what her beau had done to a poor girl in the dirty entrance to a mine, she would have naught to do with the scoundrel. But instead, Stella shakes her head, exasperated.

'You girls are too, too unkind!' she says.

Then abruptly, she rises, and with a sob in her throat, stomps to the other end of the work-parlour. But as I sit down there with my work, my heart is jumping about and my hands shudder too hard to sew.

From the start, I knew that my days in the millinery were numbered. Living so close in a tight circle of females, it could only be a question of time before my true state was revealed. It seemed, in fact, a miracle that my stay had already lasted for two whole years.

I should have known, once Jim Whillans appeared, that he would bring about Stella's demise. But I had been remarkably content at the Luckenbooths where the work of the shop and the diversions of the passing city had kept remote all thoughts of my past trials and sorrows. I couldn't bear to think about leaving. The thought of being thrust again friendless into the world froze me to the core.

From the back of the work-parlour, I spy Lucy rise and come toward me. Her face is contorted into a mix of concern and suspicion.

'Don't fret ye, Stella,' she says quietly as she comes to sit beside me. 'They're nasty to ye because they're jealous.'

I shake my head. 'They just hate me.'

'No, no. They think ye Missus Mac's pet and they covet yer talent with a needle.'

With a snort I shake my head again but Lucy takes my hands in hers. As she does so, I see her cast down a dubious glance at my hands and her grip turns limp. I glance down too. The contrast between my large knuckles hardened by so much metal work and Lucy's tiny white fingers is stark.

Lucy looks up and tries to smile, but there is a wary look in her eye. 'What?' Stella asks in apparent outrage. 'Not you as well?'

Lucy's expression is a turmoil of conflicted emotions that include reassurance and sympathy but also, it is perfectly plain, suspicion.

My heart is pumping with alarm but Stella, who knows exactly what is called for, bursts into a wail of noisy tears.

With a shield of fingers across my face, I run from the work-parlour, glimpsing as I go Lucy's open mouth as well as a satisfied sideways smirk that passes from Martha to Jane. With a hefty stomp up the stairs, I make for the withdrawing-closet and fling myself inside. I need some moments alone to consider how best to parry this possibly mortal strike against Stella.

Leaning against the closet door, I wipe my face with my apron. The tears are only half-fake. A hardening weight in my belly suggests little good is coming my way. I should perhaps keep up my pretence and complain to Missus Mac about Martha and Jane's viciousness. Or I could throw myself on her mercy and confess all.

Mary McMenemy would, I imagine, be little surprised by anything I had to say. I suspected she had always known what I was, but her own social peculiarities gave her a type of tolerance. And her overriding principle was profit. She had seen that I had a talent she could exploit.

Being now in the withdrawing-closet, I suddenly have a strong urge to use the room for its intended purpose. The closet is tight-confined and I have to gather in my skirts as I bend to pull out the pot. But the shelf is bare. We all use the same commodious earthenware pot and then tip the contents to a covered pail. Even when the pail is emptied at night, the pot remains on the shelf. I have never seen it depart the closet. But now that it is not there, my pressing need to go increases.

The pail is nastily full and I can't bring myself to squat over it. Lifting my petticoats high around my waist, I take hold of my flesh-pipe and aim at the centre of the turgid liquid. But even so, a dirty brown back-spray spatters my best shift.

'Oh, no!' I shout out loud.

Then, with a cry of *Please dinnae upset yerself, Stella!* the door of the closet bangs open.

Lucy's face is, for a moment, blank. Then, both of her hands fly up to cover her open mouth. Tears well, and, in a twirl of lilac dimity, she slams the door. Heels clatter down the wooden stairs.

As I cover the pail, my chest is heaving. From below, there is the sound of Lucy sobbing between murmured questions from Martha and Jane. I can't expect Lucy to keep quiet about what she just saw and my feet are leaden as I descend again to the work-parlour.

As Lucy weeps into her apron, Martha strokes her back then casts up a triumphant eye. Lucy though, will not look at me.

'Keep that... that thing away from me!' she cries.

I stand stupefied at the bottom of the staircase, unable to decide whether to be Stella or myself.

A fresh wail then bursts from Lucy's apron. 'When I think of all the things I have said to... to Stella, in private,' she moans, 'that I would never ever, ever have said if I had known...'

'Known what?' Martha asks quite roughly. She wants the thing to be said aloud, though not by her.

'That Stella...' Lucy breaks off in another flurry of sobbing.

'Stella what?' Jane places an usually tender arm around Lucy's shoulders.

'Stella,' Lucy hiccups, 'is a lad!'

Martha can't contain her satisfaction as she marches over to me, fists clenched. 'Is this true? Are ye male?'

I can only blink.

'Aye,' Jane pipes up from the work-table. 'James is certain that the creature's name is not Stella, but Kitty or Kit.' We all turn to stare at her. 'Either that or the likeness to his school-friend Christopher Ravenglass of Whitehaven is remarkable.'

He was never my friend, I want to yell, but as I open my mouth all that comes out is a yelp of despair.

The general yowling soon brings Mrs McMenemy up from the shop.

'Jesus McChrist! What's amiss wi' ma bitches?'

It is Martha, of course, who tells her, though Missus Mac frowns at us all in equal measure. Then she shoos the girls down to the shop, sits me at the work-table and pours us each a glass of Madeira wine.

'Well,' she says, 'ye've made a good fist o' being a lassie. Praise where it's due. But the time has come for ye to spill yer beans.'

And so, at last, I tell her about my flight from the impress men of the *Prince of Orange* and my need to disguise myself in my dead sister's clothes.

'The *Prince of Orange*?' she says. 'Well, they'll no have ye, not if I can help it. Not over my dead Jacobite body.' She takes a swig of wine and pats my hand. 'But ye cannot stay here any longer.'

I nod and a tear drips off my chin.

'I'll help you as best I may,' she goes on, 'but first ye must answer which way ye want to be from now on. Is it to be lad or lass? Ye can pass as both. The choice is yours.'

Suddenly wretched, I put my face into my hands and my chest heaves with soundless sobs. The truth is, I do not know. Continued pretence as Stella requires an energy which I'm not sure I can sustain. Though neither can I face being a man. I wouldn't know where to start. The pretence involved in both seems, at this moment, horribly equal.

Missus Mac stands and pats a hand on my hunched shoulder. 'Fret ye not, ma best wee bitch. Let me enquire somewhat before ye make yer choice.'

If ever I had needed Dorinda's advice it was now. At the bottom of the sea-chest, the pamphlet is yellowed but intact from little use. For my past two years at the Luckenbooths, everything has been decided for me. And although robbed of many freedoms, my apprenticeship has unburdened me of the need to make difficult choices. I realise that I have not yearned at all for liberty.

When I ask the *Finger of Fortune* whom I should trust, Dorinda is unequivocal. *A WOMAN shall save you from misfortunes*, Dorinda says. And there is no doubt in my mind about this lady's identity. So, when Mrs McMenemy returns late in the evening, I am waiting up for her with my answer.

'I am Stella,' I whisper into Missus Mac's tippet-lined hood.

She nods. 'As I thought. And are ye fit for travelling?'

'By sea?' I ask, suddenly feeling myself cowardly.

'Och no, overland, I should say.'

'Where to?'

'All shall be revealed.' She pats my hand. 'You must bide here a while longer. But best sleep downstairs.'

And for the next few nights that is what I did, whilst keeping my distance from the other apprentices during the day. Lucy seemed set for tears whenever she looked at me. Then, at dusk on the Thursday, Mrs McMenemy bids me dress myself in my sturdiest clothes and make haste to pack my chest with only the things I cannot do without. She has found a position for me through Mr Gib, she says. I know the name of the gentleman but can't place it. My stomach twists with excitement mixed into foreboding.

Once I am in the old riding habit now faded to blue-grey, Missus Mac calls the girls to the work parlour.

'Now then ma bitches,' she says, having told Martha, Jane and Lucy to stand in a line before me. 'Stella is away to join the cause of our noble King James by serving with the household of the Prince Regent.'

I watch three pretty mouths fall open before me.

'So I want you's all to wish Stella joy and luck by presenting her with a gift. First, Jane, with the sash.' The mistress gives Jane a green and red tartan sash which she plonks over my head.

'And a parting kiss of goodwill,' says Missus Mac.

With a scowl, Jane almost touches her cheek to mine.

'Now, Martha, here is the cockade for her hat.' Martha fixes it on to Fliss's old feathered tricorn without meeting my eye. Her 'kiss' is swift and distant as a ghost's.

'And Lucy, the maud, if you please.'

Lucy, eyes lowered and cheeks reddened, presents me with a folded blanket of black and white check. It is sizeable by the look of it and woven of softest lambswool. Perhaps it is even newly made and must have cost near ten shillings.

'No, Mrs McMenemy,' I say, looking at my mentor and saviour, 'it is too much.'

'Take it, why don't ye?' she replies. ''Tis for the Prince's cause as much as your comfort.'

Lucy holds out the maud to me in one hand, still looking at the floor. She will come no nearer. As I step forward to take the blanket, I long to whisper some words of remorse and affection. But the weight of my deceit compresses my chest like over-laced stays. And to my great regret, I remain silent.

Once I have the blanket in my hands, Mrs McMenemy comes over.

'God go with ye, and with the dear Prince,' she presses her cheek to mine. 'And this'll go wi' ye also, from me.' She steps back and holds up a delicate, short-pointed dagger with a bone handle then slips it inside a snug leather sheath. 'Keep this by ye at all times. Tis small enough to hide in yer stays.' Missus Mac presses the sheathed dirk into my hand and plants a loud wet kiss full on my lips. 'Keep ye safe, ma best wee bitch.'

I turn to the girl-apprentices, companions who I have lived with for two years, sharing everything between us and hardly out of each other's sight. I know I should tell them that I am full of shame for so offending them with my pretence at womanhood. But the truth is that, beyond upsetting Lucy, I have no regret. For my life at the Luckenbooths never felt like a deceit. Stella Bride is as much me as Kit Ravenglass.

So, I say nothing except farewell. The Cawdies are called

to carry my sea-chest to the Abbey and fend off the jeers of men standing outside taverns. And it seems fitting that the boys who helped find me a haven in this towering city are also there to see me safely down the long sloping street toward the Pretender's army and away from Edinburgh for good.

Late that same night I find myself atop a baggage cart watching the Prince Regent lead his army away from the Abbey and Palace of Holyrood in a blaze of torches and cheering. *Huzzah*, I shout, *huzzah, huzzah,* my spirits soaring higher with each passing row of blue-coated horsemen and drum-beating swordsmen. I feel myself a full part of the glorious army setting forth to conquer England for King James and I try not to dwell on the inescapable fact that this march with the Jacobite rebels will brand me forever as a traitor to King George, though being a runaway from his Navy, I was one already. Foreboding needles through me more sharply when I see the leers of the marching Highlanders as they pass by. Stella's skirts will protect me from taking up arms and marching beside them, but being a woman may lay me open to other grave dangers.

Mr Gib had instructed me to be on hand to care for the Prince's wardrobe which was piled into a quantity of chests along with his personal plate and household effects on the largest wagon. My duties were to be laundry and seamstressing for the officers in general as well as for their commander in chief. But on those first days of vigorous travel, it seemed that even the Prince gave no thought to the state of his clothes and there was little for me to do but keep up with the army.

Once Edinburgh's lights and crowds were left behind, the roads became so bad that no human cargo was permitted to ride on the baggage cart. So the rest of the way into England, I walked. And though the speed of our march kept me warm enough by day, each raw night laid on dank ground deepened the cold dread in my chest.

the eighth chapter

They were a strange band of fellows, those Jacobite rebels. Most eye-catching amongst them were the Highlanders in their plaid throws and blue bonnets who spoke their own peculiar tongue and seemed entirely untroubled by the weather no matter how bitter the wind nor lashing the rain. These troops were outnumbered by men of more ordinary appearance although some, whether Irish, French or from further afield also spoke in foreign tongues. As battle-hardened men marched past me, I was glad of the bone-handled dirk in my pocket, though I knew it would likely give little protection against muscled arms so well-used to hard labour and fighting.

The progress of the Prince's baggage, of which I was meant to be a part, varied greatly in its speed depending on the road. Where the surface was paved, the heavy-fetlocked cart-horses kept pace with the fastest foot-soldiers and I skipped to keep up. Later, as the carters laboured at the wagon's wheels stuck deep in liquid ruts I would shiver and watch the battalions stride past us.

Men shouted and often jeered at me as they went by but after two years as a woman I was used to this treatment, indeed, I expected it. I had come to welcome insolent abuse from passing lads as their natural response to an unaccompanied female and it seemed proof that my guise as Stella was sound. The guarded, suspicious looks that I sometimes received made me much more uneasy.

One company of men, or rather youths, greeted me with particular gaiety as the fluctuating progress of royal baggage led me back and forth through the relentless file of marching troops. Hey Stella, they'd shout, having enquired of my name. Shall we come over and warm ye up? They seemed like harmless farm boys of my own age or younger so I always replied with some friendly quip. You're keeping yourselves plenty hot as it is, aren't you? or such like.

In those first days, the talk in the ranks was that we were heading to clash with the army of The German Usurper as they called King George. A force was known to be assembling at Newcastle under Field Marshal Wade and there was great eagerness to engage it given the triumph some weeks earlier when Prince Charles' army, although outnumbered and out-gunned, had obliterated the government's redcoats at Prestonpans.

For two days we marched on rutted roads beside low empty hills where all was wet, grey and brown. Then the ranks split. And though I only ever saw the Prince from a distance, it was clear that he and a detachment of cavalry and foot-soldiers had taken a leftward fork in the road, whilst the carts and cannons and the main body of men, continued on what I guessed to be our south-westerly path. The departure of the Prince unnerved me, and that night as we struck camp, I made sure to join a fireside where English was spoken and I would find out what rumour there was about the campaign.

The first fire I came upon was circled by the cheeky farm-boys who knew my name.

'Stella!' they call, seeing me. 'Will ye come an' have a dram wi' us?'

They laugh as they rub their hands and stamp against the raw weather. I pull the maud blanket a little tighter around my shoulders and take a long breath. Then I go to sit on a shot-box beneath their awning of tent canvas and beside the limp greenwood fire.

'Here ye are,' says one handing me a tin cup with a measure of foul drink in it that he calls aqua vitae. I knock it back and can't help a grimace which makes them all howl with delight.

'Do ye not feel warmer wi' it in your belly though, Stella?'
And they were right, I did.

They were lowland villagers attached to the Edinburgh Regiment and though all had camped with the rebel army outside the walls, only one of them had ever been inside the city. When I told them that I had been living at the Luckenbooths I might as well have said the Palace of Versailles.

They treated me with the teasing deference as befitting a woman a little older than themselves though filthy banter always hovered at the edges of our conversation. They called themselves The Bachelors' Boys, and so out of practice was I with manly talk that it was not until later I realised that this meant 'Bastards.' Each had his own nickname in the pack. There was Lard, Mulligrub, Whelk and Smiter Donnie Leach, the only one who had viewed Edinburgh's rock close up, kept his own name and seemed to be, as Will Fletcher was with Natty's boys, their leader.

'And why, pray, do they call you Whelk?' I ask the biggest of the bunch using Stella's most condescending tones.

His fattish face creases to a wicked smile. 'Shall I show ye?' he offers, and standing up, begins to unbutton his breeches.

'Nae, nae!' the others cry, laughing and pulling him down.

Donnie Leach puts his two fingers shaped like a gun to Whelk's head. 'Mistress Stella is a lady of the Prince's household. Ye'll have me tae answer tae if ye offend her.' But this was said with a mock bow and lecherous kiss blown in my direction.

Stella asks the boys, who hardly seem like Papists, why they have joined this fight for a Catholic King and there are mumblings about justice being done for the rightful Monarchs of Scotland, though I suspect that the excitement of joining a rebel army and the leaving behind of dreary cottages may have had more to do with their sedition than politics or religion.

Then, lowering her voice, Stella says, 'Do any of you know why the Prince has lately departed the ranks?'

'Och, aye,' says Donnie, smiling.

The others look blank.

'Why?' I persist.

'Will ye gi me a kiss if I tell ye?'

'Most certainly,' Stella says, 'not.'

'Aye, well, then I'll keep it to mysel',' Donnie says smugly.

'But I ken naught about that either.' Whelk says, perplexed. 'Will ye no tell me, Donnie?'

'And in exchange for that information,' Stella throws a smirk at Donnie, 'Whelk will gladly allow you a kiss.'

The faces around the dull fireside erupt into laughter. Donnie licks his lips and winks, first at Whelk then at me. But the persuasions of the gang presently coax Donnie into spouting his theory.

'The Prince wants Wade to think we's are squaring up for battle by heading into England from the east. But his jaunt in that direction is only a ruse to pull Wade northward. And we's'll already have gone into England at speed.'

'Into Cumberland?' I say, with Stella weakening.

'Aye,' Donnie nods. 'By the west. Into Cumberland.'

And it turned out, whether it was through intelligence or guesswork, that Donnie Leach was right.

A hard frost speeded our marching and I forgave the cold for saving me from the clarts. Ice-stiff ruts crunched under cart-wheels but kept them rolling. And on the eighth day of the march, I stepped into an icy Scottish river and waded out of the stream on to English mud.

My skirts were not fully dry again for weeks. Each night, despite laying my petticoats beside a dying fire, I put them on wetter than I had taken them off. The constant damp of my clothes and ever colder weather saps me of strength. Stella, I fear, is slipping too. The more out of sorts I am and the more bedraggled my appearance, the harder it becomes to hear her voice.

Once, I found myself at the end of the day beside a group of women, so-called 'wives' of the foot-soldiers, as well as officers' servants. They bade me join them in their tent to sleep, but once inside, they looked at me askance in the firelight and said little. I kept away from other women after that.

It was hard to gauge whether my appearance as a woman was convincing. I was dressing in every scrap of clothing I owned to ward off the cold. Even Dorinda's Gift was layered inside my stays for warmth, though the pages soon became sodden. The old Quilted-Petticoat fattened the riding-skirt and I even wore the embroidered wedding waistcoat over the riding-jacket. My boy's coat, though too tight to fasten, at least warmed my arms and the tartan sash kept it tied about my middle. The maud blanket that was shawled over my head all day and wrapped about my body at night had become as begrimed and smelly as a Highlander's plaid.

I began to wonder why I had been hired for the march at all as I was called on very little for mending or laundry duties and the Prince was still absent. Then, on a Sunday swathed in fog, the Pretender Prince re-joined his baggage, and me with it, outside the walls of Carlisle.

All of us in the ranks, whether foot-soldiers or followers, hoped that the Prince's return might bring some respite from our journeying. But on the morning after reaching Carlisle's walls, the order is given to break the camp that we had only just made and march eastward through the fog. A general moan of dismay goes up. The cold is now embedded so deep in my bones that my feet no longer hurt.

So the rebel army sets off late in the day to give battle to Field Marshal Wade's troops who are marching toward us from Newcastle. There is not far to walk before we make another camp, but the crossing of a fast shallow river puts paid to my previous efforts to dry out. Something about the curve of this riverbank seems familiar though the air is too dense with white fog to make much out.

As the baggage cart joins the camp a few fields from the crossing, I catch sight of the Bachelors' Boys chopping wood they have dragged along with them from the wintry trees by the river. My first thought is to avoid them, but too late Donnie Leach looks up from his axe and beckons me over. I take a breath and tell myself that the boys' jokes, or at least their aqua vitae, might cheer me.

'You again,' Donnie says with a wry look that might be either amused or contemptuous. I can't quite decide which.

'Good day to you, Mr Leach,' I say unsure where to pitch my voice.

'Ye're looking rough.'

'Well!' The insult has roused Stella from her stupor. 'The English air has certainly turned you into an insolent rogue.'

Donnie throws his small axe up in the air and catches it without looking. The gesture is threatening but Stella does not flinch.

Then Donnie laughs. 'Will ye keep us company tonight, then, Stella?'

'Only if you watch your tongue.'

Donnie gives a mock-bow in reply and then gestures to the chopped branches. Without waiting for further instructions, I start to lay them into a fire.

Dusk is setting in but we are camped early enough to eat in the light and the boys seem grateful for my help in fetching our rations from further up the line. An armed detachment has done well in 'taxing' the local householders and there is a joint of ham as well as bread and pease pudding to share out around our camp-fire. The aqua vita is gone, though, replaced by thin cold beer.

When their bellies are fuller, the boys at last start to laugh.

'Did ye hear of the stupid English bitch the Prince lodged with two nights ago?' says Donnie.

'At Stonehouse?' asks Lard.

'Aye,' Donnie says. 'Hid her child under a bed and when it was found, begged the Prince not to let his Highlanders eat it.'

The lads burst out guffawing though I can raise no more than a scant smile.

'I heard worse than that,' Whelk pipes up, loudly. ''Twas in the paper last month that an English woman became so afeared of Highlanders eating her bairns that she made two of them lie down with their heads on pillows and slit their throats.' The boys all laugh. 'After, she went downstairs and cut her belly open until the bowels spilled out. Then she slashed her own throat.'

Their laughter turns into howls of delight punctuated with gleeful cries of *silly English bitch!*

'And... and, hear this,' Whelk is almost crying with mirth, 'she lived not in Carlisle, nor Cumberland nor even Lancashire, but all the way down at London!'

The Bachelors' Boys still think the capital as distant as the moon.

As their laughing turns into back-slapping brays, I turn away and try to stop my breath racing into anguish. Was my own mother as afeared of some imagined threat as the woman who cut into her children's throats and her own stomach?

'I shall go for water before it gets too dark,' I say and grab a leather pail.

Snowflakes float through the remnants of fog as I make for the river and I'm shaking though not on account of the cold. Could it be that my mother's crimes sprang not out of evil or lunacy but from a fierce urge to protect? It can be a form of protection. Of love, even. As I look at the whitening curve of the river and the naked black trees on the far bank, I hear Jossy saying those very words. How wise he was, and how I wish I could still walk beside him. Amongst the wet snowflakes a tear slides down my face.

'Stella!'

The voice is behind me and coming closer on heavy feet. I turn. Whelk is red-faced and running. He takes the empty pail from my hand without asking.

'Let me help ye, Stella.'

I shrug and flick him a forlorn glance.

His head goes to one side. 'Are ye sad, Stella? What's amiss?'

'That dreadful story…' My voice crumples and cracks.

'The wife wi' the bowels?'

I nod. 'Perhaps she felt she had good reason to do what she did.'

'Naaa,' Whelk says and spits on to the frozen grass. 'She was just a stupid, mad bitch.'

There is an edge of cruelty in his voice that I have not heard before.

I reach for the pail in his hand. 'I can manage that myself.'

'Nay!' He swings it out of my reach.

We are almost at the stony edge of the water and the crossing place. Stragglers from the long tail of the army are wading packhorses into the flow. Whelk looks at them and narrows his eyes.

'Mebbes we should fetch some for firewood while we're here.'

'Cross the water again?' I sigh and look down at my still damp skirts.

'I can gi' ye a piggy back.' He winks.

I smile and wipe my face. He's big enough to carry me easily. And though Stella would never contemplate submitting to such an unseemly mode of transport, I dislike the idea of sodden petticoats as much as I yearn for the heat of a good fire.

'I'll take the pail,' I say and tie my maud blanket securely around my middle. Then, holding on to Whelk's shoulder with one hand and the pail in the other, I ease myself on to his back.

He catches my legs under my petticoat and hoicks me up so that my feet are above the rush of the river. Even at the fording place, the stones are slippery underfoot and I lean my body close against Whelk's back so that he does not lose his balance. The pail bangs against his arm as he heaves across the stones. His body is solid and strong though, and I have no fear of him falling into the shallow stream. I let my own body mould to his as we cross. Closing my eyes for a moment, I imagine that I am once again supported on Jossy's warm back as he carries me home from the harbour.

When we reach pale shingle, Whelk lets me down.

'Nice an' dry?' he asks.

'Yes, thank you,' I say.

'We'll have tae go further from the road. All the good sticks near it've been taken.'

'All right,' I reply, though the snow is coming down thicker now and covering the dead leaves beneath the bare trees. I pull my maud blanket tight around my shoulders and head.

'There's one,' I say, pointing at a good sized branch a little higher up the wooded bank.

Whelk looks back toward the road then shakes his head. 'Let's keep going.'

'Why?'

'Not much further.' He puts a hand to my back and leaves it there as we walk. I want to pull myself away but that would seem too impolite.

Again he looks back at the road and then nods. 'Up there.'

I can't see any branches hereabouts but thinking that Whelk must have seen a log he needs my help with, I set off uphill into the undergrowth. He is close behind and puts a hand to my waist whenever I falter.

'Is it round here?' I ask eyes scanning the lumpy black and white ground.

'Aye.' Whelk is suddenly right up behind me, his mouth against my ear. 'This'll do.'

And then with hard strong hands, he grabs both of my arms.

'What are you..? The pail falls to the ground as I struggle. 'Let go of me!'

He doesn't answer and he doesn't let go. He pulls my maud from its knot and casts it to the ground. The full weight of his body is against mine and I can't stop myself falling on to the soft cold ground.

'Let me...' I try to say but he turns me over and pushes my face into earth. The skin of my cheek tears on thorns. 'Don't!' I cry. All trace of Stella is extinguished.

'Dinna fidget,' Whelk grunts. His knees are pressed into the backs of mine and one hand is forcing my head into the soil. With his free hand, he rucks up my petticoats then fumbles at himself.

I feel the shiver of cold air on my legs, bare above my stockings. Snow spots cold on to the backs of my thighs. And then his whole body suffocates mine. A hand gouges between my buttocks and his hardness begins pressing into me. The pain is heavy yet piercing. My mouth widens on to worm-drilled dirt. My scream is swallowed by earth.

He is tight packed inside me now and there is nothing I can do to stop him. His single hand clamps onto my hair pulling my head back and forth as he rides me. Then with a spasm and a growl, he collapses on top of me and I know he is done.

For minutes, or more, he lies there. I do not move, not a finger nor an eyelid. I have no wish to breathe. When he rises up, his weight is replaced on me by a swirl of iced air. Still I do not move.

'Ye can get up now,' he says giving a gentle kick to my foot.'

I stay still.

'Did ye no like it?' There is a vaguely wounded tone to his question.

I will not give him the comfort of any response no matter how slight.

'Well, whether ye did or no, I'd be grateful if ye could testify to the boys that ma little whelk were up to the job. They didnae believe I could do it. I did though, did I not?'

I do not move.

'Stella?'

He grabs my arm and rocks me, but I keep myself rigid and my face in the soil.

'Well, suit yersel'.'

I hear him buttoning and rustling through the dry leaves about me.

'I've done ye a favour, in fact. Donnie has a wager on whether ye're a lad or a lass and he told me to find out. And I'm happy to testify that ye are indeed a lady.'

My heart gives a hollow thump. This declaration seems a greater insult to me than anything else he has done. He has not enough interest in me to even notice the most important feature of my anatomy.

'Do ye want another ride?' He tries a half-bawdy laugh and kicks me again. 'Stella!' Another, harder kick this time. But still I will not move. 'Ah well, go tae hell then. But bring the water back with ye. I'll leave ye the pail.'

I hear him stomping about the snow-covered undergrowth and then wood thuds against wood. I do not move a single muscle until his footsteps are long gone.

Then, slowly I turn over, and painfully, I sit up. And as I do so, I feel the dirk rigid in my pocket. So abased have I been that I forgot all about the weapon. Could I catch him now and take my revenge with a slash across the throat? Yet he is stronger than me and more used to fighting. Perhaps he would only turn the weapon, horribly, on me. My impotence is complete. Tears rage down my cheeks.

The light is fading now and the snow thickening. Beyond the rush of water, bonfires flicker. But through the dark web of branches, I can still make out the crossing place with the curve of the riverbank and a distant outline of village roofs beyond. And then I realise where I am.

Winter, in stripping the trees, has given the place a disguise. But closing my eyes, I can conjure again its summer garb, the green flicker of leaves above the river, the cooing of wood-pigeons in the branches and Jossy's lovely face smiling back at me as he leads a prancing grey racehorse through the sun-dappled splash.

I stand up then and turn my back on the crossing-place.

Darkness has thickened over the snowy ground but I walk without caring where my feet land. Scraps of throaty laughter blow up past me and I pull the maud blanket tight about my ears. As soon as there is silence, I turn my back on the Pretender's rebel army and take the whitening road in the opposite direction.

Somewhere on that road to Carlisle, I lie down on a snowdrift, soft as feathers. My limbs turn from cold to numb. Goose-down flakes fall from the sky on to my closed eyelids. And as I lapse into icy sleep, I hope my eyes will see nothing ever again.

the fourth part

—

resolved

the first chapter

Stella never returned from that snowy wayside near Carlisle. And there we might both have met our end had not foreign voices seeped into the snow-muffled air. Strange calls of *marav* and *beohast* made my eyelids slip open but the flutter of snowflakes soon closed them. I had not the strength to raise even a finger in protest as male hands knocked the cold white quilt from my stomach and lifted me, limp and blind as a newborn, into a rocking wooden cradle.

How long I slept through the whiff of whisky and gunpowder I can't say. But when I awoke an angel was beside me. The creature, neither male nor female, floated on thin golden wings above a red-robed saint on a green hill while naked martyrs and feathered black devils pressed from all sides. But the angel's sexless face shone serene.

My eyes travel slowly across this painted panel but the saint's journey makes no more sense to me than my own. I turn, painfully, on to my side. Only a layer of old straw separates my body from the stone flags and there are many tender places on my skin where I have lain too long in one place. High above, a lattice of stone vaults and dim arches signals that I've been brought into a grand church. All around me, men are groaning. A man laid under a plaid black with dirt props himself on an elbow so that his throat might better hack at its phlegm. Thin light from the aisle's high windows could indicate either dawn or dusk.

I close my eyes. But darkness brings a dead-weight of dread. For a second, I can't recollect the source of my horror. Then, every muscle in me flinches as I remember the press of a body heavy on my back and the forcing of my face into dead, snow-crusted leaves. A hot tear slides between my eyelids and drips into my hair.

'Are ye with us?'

It's a woman's voice, soft as a cradle-song. Her cool hand touches mine. 'I thought ye a gone 'un when they brought ye. Here…' She holds up a wooden cup and helps me raise my head for a sip of beer. 'What d'they call ye?'

Her face seems young though it is lined and beaten brown by hard weather. The eyes are clear and blue as a June morning.

'Me?' I take another drink.

The woman smiles and pats my hand. 'Can ye speak yer name?'

What is my name? I know I am not Stella anymore. After what has been done to me, how could I ever again summon her haughtiness to my bearing or her certainty to my voice? Yet neither have I the vigour to become Kit. A void has taken the place where they both used to reside. And the sex of the body that carries this void now seems unimportant.

'Jane.' I croak. It is the first name that comes to my head.

'What d'ye say? Ewan, is it?'

'No. Jane. Jane Mathewson.' I have no qualms about branding that Jane a rebel.

'Oh,' the woman says and shrugs. 'Fair enough.'

'How long have I been here? And where is this?'

'Carlisle. The big kirk. Some o' Strathallan's men brought ye in with a high fever not long after we broke the siege. They didnae know who ye were but seeing your sash, they reckoned ye one o' ours. But now I hear ye… Where d'ye belong?'

'With the Prince Regent's household,' I reply though I know this is not what she means. 'I serve as a seamstress and laundress under Mr Gib.'

'Oh aye? Well, they're all lang gone.'

'Gone? Where to?'

With a sour look, she shrugs. 'South.'

'And all the army with them?'

She nods. 'All except the garrison at the castle.'

'A garrison?' With a hollow heartbeat, my hand goes to my pocket. The dirk is still there. 'With any of the Edinburgh Regiment?'

The woman frowns then shakes her head. 'Not that I know of. All I've seen over there are the Duke o' Perth's men.'

'Oh!' The word is a sob of relief mixed with bitterness at being robbed of my revenge.

'There, lamb, there. I'll get a cup of broth. Ye must rest a while yet. But I reckon ye'll be right enough afore lang.'

Her name is Peg Strachan. She was a townswoman in Aberdeen, she says, the wife of a cordwainer who being unable to find much work had heeded the Duke of Perth's call for volunteers to join the Stuart Prince's cause. Peg, whose only babe had died the year before, followed her Tam, as she called her husband, to war. And with the cruellest of luck, Tam was one of that small handful of Jacobite rebels to die from King George's bullets at the battle of Prestonpans.

In a state of shock and grief and not knowing what else to do, Peg stayed with the army, doing the cooking and nursing and whatever other womanly tasks arose in exchange for bread and beer. The troops had treated her well she said, though I wondered what rough manners she'd been used to in Aberdeen if she thought their soldierly conduct polite.

The Highland army's savage reputation had done its work and Carlisle, though a city well-fortified with castle and high stone walls, had surrendered to the Pretended Prince without the rebels wasting a single boxful of shot. This success injected such confidence into the Jacobite leaders that within a day they decided to march onward and conquer more English towns. A garrison of only a hundred Scottish troops was left behind in Carlisle to hold the city for Prince Charles.

This garrison kept itself to the tight confines of the castle's inner keep except for the sickly troops who lived on the floor of the nearby cathedral church. Then, instructions came from the Prince's commander who had reached Penrith, to move the sickest into Carlisle castle and send all the walking wounded south, with haste, to join the tail of the marching army. Every man was needed. Rumour was that the Prince Regent would not slow his pace until he had reached London and ousted King George from his throne.

By the time the invalids came to be moved out, I had recovered from my fever and Peg was keeping me by her to help with servicing of the garrison. As Peg and I sweep up the straw in the cathedral church, I take off my boy's coat that I have been wearing since Edinburgh and reveal Fliss's fading riding-jacket and the embroidered yellow waistcoat, now stained and torn.

'That's fancy claes for sweepin',' says Peg with a laugh, eyeing the waistcoat.

I look down. 'Half way to a rag now.'

My voice has lost all trace of Stella and I no longer make any attempt to sound womanly. Perhaps I sound like a lad. And though I've made a bid at shaving with the blade of my dirk, I may look like a lad too. I have no way of knowing. But Peg treats me as a girl and the troops at the castle take their lead from her.

'Did ye work the threads yersel'?' she asks.

'My sister did most of it.'

'She's handy wi' a needle, then.'

'She was, aye.'

'Oh.' She nods and sweeps a little harder. 'I'm sorry for yer loss.'

My throat tightens.

Peg puts her head to one side. ''Tis always worse, the grief, when ye're not well in yersel'.'

I nod and bite my bottom lip.

'I have a needle and threads,' Peg goes on, nodding toward the waistcoat, 'should ye wish to try some mending. Ye could gi' it a sponging too.'

'Aye. Thank you, Peg.'

I look down at the waistcoat and I'm glad my old breeches lie in the lost sea-chest on a distant baggage cart. It means I have no temptation to put them on.

The rush of sweeping brushes echoes around the stone emptiness of the church. When the floor of the nave is cleared, we each gather up an armful of the bedding straw and carry it out to the churchyard. The spoil heap beside the ruin of an old wall steams in the cold morning air.

Peg throws straw to the pile and wipes her hands on her apron. She turns to me and pulls a comical grimace. I smile but hesitate before turning back toward the church door. In the few weeks I have known her, Peg has become as good a friend as any I ever had. I don't quite know how this happened, but I do know that I can't afford to lose her goodwill. I will not risk seeing the same look of reproach in Peg Strachan's eyes that I saw in Lucy Mair's.

'Peg?'

'Aye?'

I take a long breath. 'My name is not Jane you know.'

'Aye, I ken all that.' She gives a snort. 'I nursed ye when ye were poorly, did I not?'

A blush springs to my cheeks. 'Then you know..?'

'Aye, right enough.'

'But you have not told the Colonel?'

'Och no! Stay as ye are, ma pet.' Peg looks around and lowers her voice. 'There'll be danger at every turn for us, I reckon. But just now, ye're safer in skirts.'

'I'm not afraid to take up arms for the Prince.'

She shakes her head. 'Nae good would come of it.'

My stomach lurches. 'You think the Prince's venture will fail?'

Peg shrugs. 'Who can say?' She leans on her broom handle. 'Those poor bonnie lads, polishing their swords and muskets…' her head shakes again. 'They'll get nae mercy.' Peg leans in closer and I see the marks of old illnesses on her skin and smell her well-worn clothes. 'But I think even an English hangman wouldnae cut out the heart and bowels of a woman. So yer skirts might yet save ye from the gibbet.'

Her words punch hard for I'm a traitor to King George twice over. First I was a deserter from his Navy and then a rebel against his rule. And petticoats, once my source of secret delight and then a public disguise, may soon become my only protection against a traitor's gruesome death.

I take up Peg's suggestion and find of a triangle of weak sunshine in the castle courtyard to set about repairing the wedding waistcoat. As my needle flashes in and out of yellow leaves and arabesques, I try to picture Fliss's delicate profile, with mouth pulled down in concentration as she fashioned these same stitches. The scene is there in my mind, the parlour's panelling and Turkey carpet, the folds of Fliss's skirt, but her face is a blur. I close my eyes, overcome for a second by a longing to see my sister, just once more, even if only for a second. But the harder I try to conjure Fliss's face, the more she looks like Hannah Salkeld.

I put my needle aside, no longer having the stomach for this work. The faded waistcoat points up the ever-widening chasm of time that separates me not only from Fliss but also from Jossy. The waistcoat will never look as perfect as it did on him in a lakeside thicket under Skidda Hill.

I stay beside Peg as December gets colder, both of us sleeping almost inside the wide fireplace that serves as the garrison's kitchen in the castle's outer gatehouse. Most of our days are spent in this ancient stone room, narrow but immensely high, making what meals we can for a hundred soldiers out of the supplies they distrain from the town.

On each short walk I make from the castle to the market place, I sense the townsfolks' looks growing frostier. On his triumphal entry to Carlisle, few cheers greeted the Young

Pretender. In the garrison, we have no illusions that the people here regard us as conquerors from a foreign land.

The troops in the castle pass the time cleaning their weapons and gazing from the sandstone battlements for a fast horse bringing dispatches from the south. At first, the communications bring good news. The Prince Regent marched quickly through Lancashire picking up recruits to the Jacobite cause all along the way. In Manchester, a whole regiment of near three hundred townsmen was formed. They marched under blue and white colours bearing the words *Liberty* and *Property*, though I was beginning to wonder how the pretended King James, safe and warm in his Roman palace, could offer any succour to a hard-pressed Manchester journeyman.

Then, in the second week of December, rumours spread through the garrison like fever. The Prince Regent and his army had reached Derby, but following a disagreement with the Prince, his commanders refused to march any closer to London. Indeed, the whole army began a hasty retreat. A much larger government army, well-equipped and led by King George's son, the Duke of Cumberland, was following them northward in hard pursuit.

We knew any reliable news was several days old so perhaps the Prince Regent was already in Lancashire, or even already caught by King George's red-coated battalions. All hearts in the Carlisle garrison faltered at this thought. For if the Prince Regent failed to return, each of us knew that we should be branded rebel traitors to King George and hunted down mercilessly until captured or killed.

On the day we heard of the retreat, Peg called attention to the state of my shoes. They had been given me by Missus Mac soon after my arrival in the millinery shop and though large enough for my ungainly feet they were decidedly lady-like, with small curved heels and tooled buckles. But the winter march with its mud, snow and shallow rivers had left them in a sorry state. I'd done my best to patch the soles and nail up the cracked heels and they served me well enough in my short walks from Carlisle's castle to its market place but were good for little more.

'Have ye thought what we'll do,' Peg asks, as we stand in the gatehouse kitchen chopping turnips for a cauldron broth, 'when the garrison leaves the castle?'

I give a shrug. It's been enough, since my fever, to think of staying warm, fed and unmolested through each day. 'Have you?'

Peg sighs. 'Whatever happens, there'll be walking aplenty.' She points her knife toward my feet. 'So ye'd be wise to get yersel' new shoes.'

I see that she is right. Unless I'm to die in Carlisle, I'm unlikely to quit it by any mode of transport other than my own feet.

'How shall I pay for them?'

'Don't be waiting on coin from the purser. Our recompense as ye know, is neepy broth. But there's rag-men on the market place. One of them might take your old shoes with any other claes ye can spare in exchange for new brogs.'

Snow-laden clouds hang heavy across the business of the next Wednesday market. Faces are pinched and dour, and the market people whisper behind their hands as I pass through the pitches and stalls. I try not to notice. Snidery is directed at all Jacobite women from the castle, but I touch my face to check if it's still smooth.

Several rag-men have goods laid out, but the rag-wife has the best footwear.

'Let me try those,' I say, pointing.

The black leather is creased and the buckle tarnished but the shoes have small heels with little wear. I can't tell whether they have belonged to a man or a woman but my feet, inside them, feel instantly secure.

From under the brim of her felt bonnet, the rag-wife slides me a wary look. She curls a lip at my Edinburgh shoes when I offer them up in exchange.

'The buckles on them are all that's worth saving,' she sniffs.

'I have something else to offer.' My hand twitches on the rolled yellow waistcoat at my side.

'What?'

But as I look at the rag-wife's face, I have a sudden sense of Jossy, standing beside her and holding out a coin. A shiver goes up the nape of my neck. And my hand tightens on the waistcoat.

I fling off the good shoes and return them to her. 'Keep them for me.'

Before I can hear her retort, I stride off the square toward the narrow streets behind the Town Hall and I'm filled with a sense of re-treading my steps with Jossy two summers before. The broken cobbles make me stumble and I clutch the wedding waistcoat a little tighter.

Finding an alley-nook behind an inn, I unfasten the strings and take off my Quilted-Petticoat. I'll rue the loss of this warm layer but the bright sulphurous colour has faded to brown and the shape is distorted by being worn so long beneath the riding-skirt.

Stepping out of the alcove to fold the petticoat, I see the sign of the King's Head, the inn where I ate a solitary meal as Jossy fended off impress men from the *Wasp*. I give a sigh for all that has happened since that far-off day. But I'm glad Jossy is not here. I wouldn't want him, nor Fliss, nor any I knew before to see me now, when I'm neither Kit nor Stella but some half-hearted raggedness between the two.

'Here,' I say, holding out the Quilted-Petticoat to the rag wife. 'Take this and my old shoes for the new ones.'

She sniffs. 'And what else?'

'I have naught else. Is that not enough?'

Her eyes rove across my maud blanket and ill-fitting boy's coat, and across Fliss's riding habit.

'You've some fine buttons on that jacket there,' the rag-wife says.

I take a quick breath but know what I must do.

And so, a few minutes later, I'm handing over old shoes and

Fliss's faded riding-jacket as well as the Quilted-Petticoat in exchange for new shoes. It seems too hard a bargain and my anger rises as the rag-wife lays out the riding-jacket and fingers the silver buttons that Fliss's hands knew so well.

'I should have more than just shoes for all that.'

'Aye well. Times is hard.' The rag-wife casts me a wary look. 'But you can have this n'all.'

And she throws me a sprigged flannel handkerchief frayed along one side.

I give the handkerchief to Peg who protests but I insist and arrange it around her neck. I tell her about the Quilted-Petticoat and the riding-jacket but she says I was right to exchange them for the shoes. Cold legs and arms, she says, are better on a march than bleeding feet.

Not long after, Peg and I were tasked with binding many raw heels and rotten toes when, in the week before Christmas, the Prince Regent and his army returned to Carlisle. They rushed into the town through the English Gate and soon the castle courtyard was stuffed to the ramparts with exhausted men. Many were lame after the fast march from Derby, two hundred miles away, where they had been only two weeks before. Along the way, they had even won a small battle against red-coated troops at Clifton Moor.

I keep my dirk hilt handy to the slit in my riding-skirt as I dole out thin pottage to weary men. They look up at me with empty staring eyes, even the sauciest of them too weak for lewdness. But if I see my riverside attacker or any of the Bachelors' Boys, no matter how lamentable his condition, I will slice his throat open sooner than pour soup down it.

I saw none that I recognised that first night, and the following day to general surprise and rejoicing amongst the Highlanders, the order came to continue the army's march toward Scotland. No-one was sure where the order had come from. Prince Charles, it was said, had been in a black mood since Derby and had to be cajoled by his officers not just into giving commands but speaking at all.

An English garrison was to be left behind to hold Carlisle for King James, but the possibility that these few hundred men of the Manchester Regiment could hold the city against the might of King George's army was, to anyone of sound mind, laughable. And though I was glad that the Bachelors' Boys, if they were still alive, would be amongst the departing Scots, I watch leaden with dread as the last rebel troops hurry out of the Scotch Gate on to the road north.

Peg and I now cooked and mended for Lancashire men. They seemed less acquainted with military ways and looked grey as ghosts at the prospect of the siege that we all knew was coming. And within a day of the Prince Regent's Scottish soldiers leaving Carlisle, the first of the Duke of Cumberland's men were sighted to the south-west, just out of firing range from the town's walls. By Christmas, it was rumoured that the Loyalist militiamen of the Liverpool Blues had swelled the ranks of the Duke's army.

Carlisle's townsfolk had got better at hiding their victuals and that Christmas Day of 1745 all we had to give out to the Manchester Regiment was cabbage flavoured water and weak beer. Christmas morning dawned wet and biting cold and wrapping my maud blanket over my head, I went along the town walls above the Sallyport pouring cupfuls of beer for shivering, flat-eyed men.

A narrow stone-sided alley leads from the ramparts above the Sallyport back into the town. Nearing the end of it, my heart drops a dead beat and a familiar voice stops me where I stand. I almost drop my flagon.

'Where did you get it? Who from, I say?'

The voice is deeper than it was but I know who is speaking. The reply comes mumbled and fearful from a woman, or perhaps a girl. I edge closer.

'Tell me, you little drab! It is not yours. Where did you get it?'
My heart lurches. I have made no mistake. It is him.

Quietly I edge along the stone wall to the place where the alley opens out into a street and an archway leading to the cathedral church. Pushed up against this archway is a coster-girl, her square basket dropped to the cobbles, her face red and tear-streaked.

'From the market,' she is saying, 'paid for, fair and square.'

'It is stolen goods,' her aggressor shouts as he pulls on the silver buttons at the girl's breast. I see now the item in dispute. She is wearing Fliss's faded blue riding-coat.

I don't think that either of them has noticed me and I pull the maud over my face to hurry past them into the main street. But as I go by, I glance back at the soldier who is still pushing the frightened girl against the wall. Tied around his coat sleeve are the blue and white ribbands of the Manchester Regiment. And though he is older, bulkier and better-dressed than when I last saw him, I have no doubt at all that the enraged face beneath the rebel's blue bonnet is that of Daniel Bragg.

the second chapter

That night and the day or two after, the heavy stone of grief returned to my chest and I could think of little but my sister. I had done my best, until then, not to imagine too exactly how a child had arrived in Fliss's belly but knowing of her ardent love for Daniel Bragg, I'd assumed she must have succumbed to his advances.

Now, having seen his roughness with the girl in the riding-jacket, and knowing for myself how foully men might behave, I began to wonder if Daniel Bragg had forced himself on Fliss. My innards churned at the thought of her going through even a small measure of the shame, remorse and disgust I had felt since the filthy attack upon me at the riverside crossing-place. A shard of old guilt twisted in me too for all that Hannah Salkeld had endured at the Bear Mouth. And I shed hot tears for Fliss and Hannah as well as for myself.

Rain fell cold and hard every day that Christmastime. Despite the meagreness of rations we shared with a few hundred men of the Manchester Regiment, I became unable to eat. Fearing my fever was returning, Peg found from somewhere a half-bottle of claret and a cinnamon stick which she heated together and made me drink in one go. The wine did not improve my appetite but only sharpened my hunger for revenge against Daniel Bragg. Why should he live and prosper when Fliss was in her grave?

But now I had a miraculous opportunity to pay him back using cover of my female garb and the great battle that was surely coming. Once the opposing armies began to fight, I would have freedom to stalk my foe and finish him with my dirk. The exact cause of wounds inflicted upon the body would never be investigated or explained amid the plentiful bloodied corpses bearing colours of the Manchester Regiment that the battle would inevitably produce.

In the days after Christmas, I sought out Daniel Bragg and kept him at a distance but in my sights. He was easy enough to spot on the Town Walls above the Sallyport for he seemed to be in charge of this area and the lads around him called him 'Captain.'

I struggled to think of Daniel as anything other than a lad himself, but I could see how forthright and manly he had become. Even from a distance it was clear that his clothes, though spattered from travel, were of the best quality. He wore a long dark watch-coat of tight-fulled wool with a wide collar that was sometimes buttoned up against the wind or left open to protect his shoulders from the rain. His wide cocked hat, though now bedraggled, was gold-laced. I had chosen my boyhood template for manliness well. The other men treated him with deference. But Daniel Bragg's imposing appearance did not daunt me. My purpose was set. All that I needed to launch my attack on him was to hear the first blasts of a greater battle.

Yet in those torpid days after Christmas, there was little the garrison could do save watch from the ramparts the massing of the Duke of Cumberland's forces in distant grey fields. Occasionally, a musket shot would fire, or a cannonball land short of the Town Walls throwing up a fountain of mud. These incursions would initiate a great clamour amongst our ranks and a readying for battle. But then, tense quietness would return. When the wind stilled, we sometimes heard shouting or the squealing of horses from our enemy's lines. More disturbingly, we often heard laughter.

Each day, as I watched Daniel Bragg from afar and imagined in ever greater detail the coming fray, the tension inside me tightened. I came to wonder whether I should stop waiting for the wider battle and commence my own private attack.

Then, in the late afternoon, four days after Christmas, a loud rumour whipped around the whole garrison that Government troops had been seen, through a spyglass, building an earth battery. Soon, emplaced upon this battery, were six fearsome cannon. The rumour went on, with suspicious detail, that the new cannon were eighteen pounders from the seafront defences at Whitehaven and had been dragged hither in all haste by the town's Loyal citizens.

On hearing this I felt an odd glow of encouragement for it seemed that my old home was sending me assistance in my mission against Daniel Bragg. Sure enough, next morning, I was wakened by artillery fire, which, though distant, had a new depth of intent. The time had come. And though it was still dark in the castle gatehouse, I dressed myself as a murderer.

After buttoning the wedding waistcoat over my stays, I tied my too-small boy's coat tight with the tartan sash around my middle and secured the hilt of my unsheathed dirk inside the slit of my riding-skirt. Then I set off to the Tithe Barn where troops manning the Sallyport slept between watches.

I carried a heavy flagon but had no intention of doling cupfuls of watered beer to shivering men. Instead, after loitering at the rear of the barn, I slipped into St Cuthbert's graveyard. This served as the main latrine for the West Walls garrison, and I guessed that with the first salvos of the Whitehaven cannons, every man of the Manchester Regiment would be shitting himself. With luck, I would catch Daniel Bragg at this same business.

It didn't take long. The cannons' first shots failed to reach the town but as the morning light hardens, their aim improves. Iron balls begin to fall from the sky. A sudden crash of brick and tile comes horribly close, perhaps it is even the Tithe Barn roof. And nearby, bowels quickly loosen.

Crouching fearfully beside a tomb, I watch the procession of grey-faced squatters hurrying from ramparts to graveyard, and soon spot Daniel Bragg. He chooses a headstone, lays down his long-bored pistol and flips up the skirts of his watch-coat before dipping down behind it. Then, with much farting and sighing, Daniel goes about his squitty work. I creep closer, from headstone to headstone until I have a clear view.

The sight of him there, bare-arsed and immobile, fires me forward. And before even pulling the dirk from my pocket, I rush up at him, beer sloshing, and fling the flagon and its contents into his face. He falls backwards to the ground, groaning.

But then, with a look of horror, he sees me.

'Fliss?'

The fear in his eyes tells me how much I must look like my sister.

'Aye!' I shriek. 'Fliss has her revenge at last!'

'I thought you dead!' He croaks.

'I am. Thanks to you.'

I lean over him, my hand fumbling between petticoat and riding-skirt for my dirk, my spittle spraying across the beer-soaked stubble of his mouth and chin. But then, despite the breeches around his ankles, Daniel leaps up. In his watch-coat he towers over me like a bear. I grasp, heart racing, for the dirk and finally, my hand closes on the bone handle. Pulling the knife from its loop, I aim the point to the indent of bare skin at his throat and launch myself on him with a howl that contains all of life's unfairness. My only desire is to see Daniel Bragg's blood.

'Jesus!' Daniel yelps. 'What the devil..? And then recognition drills into his eyes.

But my short knife has already met his collar bone. Blood spurts, and I draw back, unnerved.

Pain gives Daniel strength and with a yell he lurches forward grabbing my wrist. Far stronger than me, he holds on and shakes until there is a sickening, twisting crunch of sinew. I scream and drop my dirk to the ground.

'Bastard!' I cry.

Ignoring the blood, Daniel keeps hold of my wrist with one hand and with the other lunges for my neck. Under the full weight of him, I topple to the ground.

His breeches are still around his calves but he pins me down, flattening my stays into my chest. Blood drips from his throat-wound into my eyes making me cough and gag against the pressure of his hand and the smell of his blood, sweat and shit. I try to call out but the men nearby are too engrossed in their own bowels and survival to come to the aid of a girl.

'You!' Daniel's face glistens above mine. He leans harder into my chest. 'You use your dead sister as your disguise? Loathsome creature!'

'Loathsome?' I squeak. 'It's you who killed her!'

'Me? I was miles away.'

'But you forced a child into her.'

'What?'

He jabs hard at my throat but then eases off. Even in my frenzy, I can't overlook the unfeigned outrage in his eye. After a moment, his hand leaves my neck and goes to his own.

'Who else could it have been?' I cry, loudly though with less conviction.

'Not me.'

'You lie.'

'No.'

'You do. You're a liar, liar, liar…'

'No, you simpleton. She was already with child when I returned on the *Swallow*.'

A weight drops inside me.

'What..?' Though even as I say it, my body has already sensed the truth. I start to shake. 'What do you mean?'

Releasing me from the last of his weight, he stands and pulls up his breeches buttoning the flap beneath his coat.

'Are you deaf? She was already with child by someone else. That's why I left Whitehaven forever. Idiot.'

Seething, I claw at the frosted grass around me, feeling for the dirk. 'I won't believe the filth and lies you spout. As you always did.'

Daniel presses his neckcloth against the wound at his throat then looks at the bloodied linen. The flow is already easing. He throws me a glance of pure scorn.

'What ignorance you spout. As you always did.'

He says this last in a simpering imitation of me. The years roll away, and even though my rage boils, I fear I may cry. Much as I hate to, I find myself believing Daniel Bragg's words about Fliss. But if not he, who... ? I can't bear to imagine.

On the other side of churchyard wall, there is a commotion of panicked shouting and instinctively, Daniel looks round though there's nothing to see but damp bricks and mortar.

I stand up, blinking and stupid. 'I won't believe you. You're a liar and a thief.'

He shrugs. 'It's the truth, whether you believe it or not.'

'No, it's not.' I cast around for reasons not to trust him. 'You stole a bill of exchange for three hundred and twenty five pounds from my father. That's the real reason you left Whitehaven.'

Daniel stiffens and his eyes narrow. 'Is that what your father said?'

'And you murdered Captain Power,' I go on, all my indignation returning.

Daniel darts closer, grabbing my collar and putting his face in mine. 'Power went over the side in a storm, right? And then Riddle did so much thievery there were no pickings left even for the rats.' He screws his eyes for a second and shakes his head. 'I pray to God I never again in my life set foot upon a West Indiaman.'

'So it was just coincidence that made you run off to Bristol, was it?'

And I see from the baffled look in his eye that indeed it was. For a moment we are both silent, eyes almost level, he holding my coat, I clutching Fliss's riding-skirt. Then Daniel glances down.

'What's that you have on?'

The yellow petals of the wedding waistcoat peek from under my coat.

I pull back. 'You might have worn it as her bridegroom, if you'd treated her right.'

He snorts. 'It was never meant for me.'

I wonder what he means but am too proud to ask.

For a long moment Daniel stands still, his eyes shifting from the wedding waistcoat to the bloody rag in his hand. 'What happened to her?' he asks, at last. 'I only heard from a cotton merchant that there'd been an inquest.'

I hang my head. 'She was found in the sea by Tom Hurd Rocks.'

Briefly, his eyes close. 'What was the coroner's verdict?'

'Accident.'

His voice wavers. 'Was she still with child?'

I nod.

'Then that was no accident.' He stares at the ground and shakes his head.

'Why do you say that?'

He glances up. 'You don't know anything, do you?'

'Tell me, then!'

He turns up the collar of his watch-coat. The look on his face is fierce and terrible. 'Ask your father.'

'How would he..?'

But at that moment, the air is suddenly alive with high-pitched whistling. Not far off in the churchyard, there is a punch into the ground like a pounding from God's fist. A fountain of mud shoots up. When the earth settles, there is a silent second when the dry-leaved branches of oaks rustle. Then, from all around us, comes a thunder of shouting and screams and musket fire.

Without another look my way, Daniel Bragg grabs his gun

and, wound forgotten, runs off. I see a last flap of his watch-coat into the alley alongside the Tithe Barn that leads to the Town Walls. Then he is gone.

Wrist throbbing, I stand up, pinioned by confusion. Have I been wrong all this time? Has Daniel Bragg, liar though he is, spoken the truth? Beside my foot, a flash of white reveals my dirk's handle in the soil. Right hand throbbing, I pick it up with my left and wipe dirt from the blade. Daniel Bragg has not gone far. There is nothing to stop me running after him and screaming *liar!* as I thrust the blade into his eye. But my belief in his guilt is shattered. Someone else is to blame for Fliss's ruin and I am horribly sure that only my father can tell me who.

Before knowing what next to do, another boom and a crack of stone, hurls me to the ground. My face is pressed into mud, or worse, as clods of wet earth rain down from above. When the pounding briefly stills, I raise myself, spitting out muck, and look around. Within my reach is a freshly erupted dirt-pit. White sticks and rags protrude from its earthen sides. The ground, as I touch it, seems to move under my hand in a writhing magotty mass.

Seized by horror, I try, dizzily, to stand. A dull rushing plugs my ears as I drag my eyes away from the gruesome detritus that litters the muddied ground. The sky has lightened to a dangerous wintry paleness. And from it, with terrifying regularity, iron balls are falling.

Cowering and covering my head with my good arm, I lope toward the Tithe Barn. Metallic thumps and panicked tumults of shouting and gunshot are muffled by the ringing in my ears. I push the dirk into my pocket and cradling my sprained wrist with my good hand, run toward the Sallyport.

Beyond the barn, figures scurry between the firing places on the Town Walls. There is another gut-churning crack of metal against stone and the rush of an unnatural breeze. Then there is a second of silence before a screeching of gurgled screams.

More than one man has been hit. Dust and cordite hang heavy in the shrieking air.

Another shout starts up. It is further away but soon drowns out the cries of the wounded as soldier after soldier takes up the same call. *Hold fire! Hold your fire!* It seems no more than a minute before the air stills and the shouts fade. The guns have stopped. In the quietening sky, crows caw.

I edge against the barn wall until I can peer at the track that runs alongside the West Walls. Cobbles are smashed. The gutter is puddled with blood.

Warily, I peer around the building. Further down the Town Walls, Daniel Bragg is there, unmistakable in his dark watchcoat and surrounded by men with blue and white ribbands on their sleeves. He is holding a pike while one of his comrades fastens a length of white cloth to the bladed end. Then Daniel Bragg hoists the pike into the air and waves the white sheet from side to side. All along the walls, voices rise up into the same cry. *Surrender! Surrender! Surrender!*

And from where I cower by the Tithe Barn I can see that beyond the Town Walls the fields are full of soldiers, some in buff-trimmed red coats others in blue. But all are pointing bayoneted rifles our way and crouching low as they swarm ever nearer across the thawing grass.

the third chapter

All through my imprisonment in Carlisle's castle and on the long, cold trek that followed, Daniel Bragg's words festered in my brain. Could it be that my father was the cause of all my mother's woes, and those of my sister too? As our sorry band of prisoners tramped closer to the mountains, the greater grew Henry Ravenglass's wrong-doings in my memory. And by the time Skidda Hill loomed ghostly from the grey mist, I was convinced of my father's guilt.

Rumours about our destination swirled, but I never had any doubt that fate was leading me home. And on a darkening January afternoon, a familiar whiff of coal-smoke confirms my intuition. The women around me gasp as we descend Bransty Hill and Whitehaven comes into view. The town is lamplit and wintry-white with snow-covered rooftops and a black sea beyond. My own gaze strains to locate the roof at the far end of Queen Street that was ours. Is my father still living in that house with Aunt Ravenglass and Poll just as I had left them? My head tells me that this cannot be, and that I should rejoice if my father is dead or living in wretchedness. But a corner of my heart refuses to accept how completely my old life has disappeared.

Near the bottom of the hill, the salt-works chimney is black against the snow-clouded sky and the windows are dark. I realise in this moment that there's no face I'd rather see in my home town than that of Hannah Salkeld. Yet even if she still lives in Whitehaven, seeing her whilst I call myself Jane Mathewson, seems impossible.

Nearing the House of Correction, the stone archway and small-windowed walls are exactly as I remember. And a glance across the street still shows BRAVERY hanging over the door like an exhortation. But in the parlour window of Nathaniel Bravery's Nautical Academy, illuminated by an oil-lamp, stands a young woman in a pale gown. Watching us from her hip is a child in infant skirts that disguise its sex. With a cramp in my stomach, I think of my mother. Yet this is no ghost. Perhaps the woman is Natty's wife, an idea outlandish enough to be true. And as I am marched under the arch of the House of Correction, I sense, more keenly than I ever have how swiftly and completely a person's fortune can change.

Three rebel women, myself, Peg Strachan and a Highlander called Ann Layread, are housed together in a small cell. Our charge of High Treason by way of Rebellion is the same as that laid before the hundreds of Manchester Regiment men in Carlisle but being female, we have been moved with the weakliest men to a less fortified gaol. A square platform topped by a straw mattress serves us all as a bed.

Ann Layread spoke little English but Peg seemed fluent in the Highland tongue. As they jabbered together, I would often ask what they talked of, especially if they laughed. I didn't always trust the explanations that Peg gave and suspected they talked a great deal about me. The pressure of Ann's gaze in my direction became daunting.

'How can I continue in this garb?' I whisper to Peg as I lie that first night between her and the wall. 'I no longer look anything like a woman.'

'Hush, lamb,' she replies putting her face nearer to mine. 'I cannae say what they'll do to us but I have nae doubt it will be far worse for the men than the women. Keep in those skirts as long as ye may.'

I sigh, but know she is right.

Perhaps due to the special charge against us, we weren't

allowed out of the cell and saw little of our neighbours, the vagabonds, dissolutes and felons awaiting trial. We heard them, of course. And through all the days except Sundays came a thump, thump of wood against wood from somewhere nearby. Peg asked if I knew what caused this sound and I explained about the labour of inmates who beat hemp and old rope with mallets. I didn't tell her that I knew this from my time at a nearby Nautical School for Boys.

Peg was full of questions about Whitehaven. Our barred and shuttered window faced toward Brackenthwaite Hill, so even by standing on the bed she could see little of the town.

'It's a big, grand place, is't not?' Peg asks, trying to see out of the window. 'Aberdeen seems no much bigger.'

I shrug, not knowing what manner of place Aberdeen might be. Having now seen more of the world, I began to realise how little account I used to take of Whitehaven's pleasantly wide streets and sweet-aired setting between green hills and sea. How I longed to walk those streets again!

Sometimes I had an overwhelming sense that my father was passing alongside the House of Correction and I would jump up at the window straining to see. My hand would always go to my breast and to the dirk that I still carried hidden inside my stays. I would picture myself pressing the point against the skin of his throat, forcing him to tell me, at long last, the full truth of his part in the deaths of my mother and sister. His eyes, in these fancies, always flit about in terror as he gapes awestruck at the strength and quick-wittedness of his once-despised son.

Did he ever think of me? Perhaps he thought me dead or had put me forever from his mind. But my growing passion to confront my father sometimes made the lime-washed walls of the cell feel as if they were closing in upon me. Only Peg's comforting presence stopped me falling into mania.

In those first weeks as a prisoner the only person I saw apart from Peg and Ann, was Mrs Whiteside, the Keeper's wife who delivered our rations and took away the bucket for emptying. Despite my yearning to see a familiar face, I was thankful I didn't know this woman and could have some confidence that she didn't recognise me.

Mrs Whiteside said little to us as she went about her business. But her manner was not unkind and the rations she supplied, though plain broth and gruel, seemed to us like a royal banquet after the filthy victuals we had lived on since the siege. Then a week or so after we arrived at the House, Mrs Whiteside came to us in the middle of the afternoon with a pail of water, some wash-balls and a pile of fresh linen.

'I am to tell you that these things come from a benefaction for Women's Cleanliness,' she says and hands them out. 'And that this benefaction was made by Captain Littlewood who wished to be known as the Female Prisoner's Friend.'

'Is he dead, then?' I ask before I can stop myself or disguise the gratification in my voice.

Mrs Whiteside looks at me with suspicion. 'I have no idea. The instruction to say those words came along with the money. Do you know the man?'

'No, no. I am merely curious.' I fluster.

Mrs Whiteside's frown deepens. 'Are you the one called Jane?'

I nod. 'Jane Mathewson.'

'You're not Scotch, then?'

I shake my head.

A screech and sudden banging in a nearby cell makes her look around and purse her lips. 'Aye well.' She bangs closed the cell door and turns the key. 'I'll be back to collect your dirty slops presently.'

I vow to keep my speech minimal in her presence from now on.

Due to the tight space, we take it in turns to undress and wash ourselves. Ann goes first. Peg helps to unpick the ties on her stays that have greased into tight knots. I wonder when she last took them off. I have not changed my own linen since Carlisle. But

Ann, Peg tells me, was with the Pretender Prince's army all the way to Derby and back. She may not have washed since Edinburgh.

With much oooing and ahhing at the feel of cold water and clean linen, the women wash themselves beneath shifts and petticoats and I prepare to join in with the same modesty jig of undressing that I perfected in the bedchamber at the Luckenbooths.

So used have I become to the odours of unwashed female bodies and unlidded easement buckets, that the scent of the wash-balls, cheap and lardy though they are, is like the perfume of a summer garden.

'Do ye need help wi' yer strings.' Peg asks giving me a long sideways wink that Ann does not see.

'Thank you,' I say and finish unbuttoning the wedding waistcoat. When it comes to my stays, Peg stands in front of me unlacing and so blocks my front from Ann's view. The stays have become so moulded to my body that pulling them away from me feels like the extraction of my ribcage.

'Ah!' I exhale but with dismay more than relief.

'Feels queer, does it not?' says Peg laughing. Then her smile fades. 'But what's all this?'

I look down. As the stays are lifted away, the tattered pages of Dorinda's Gift fall out.

'Oh,' I say, 'it kept me warm… and shapely.' I add a titter that seems to come from Stella.

From where she sits, Ann cannot see that my whole bosom was formed by the pages of an almanack for ladies.

'Well, it's nae use for much now,' Peg says. Then she shoots me a look as she sees, wrapped inside the crumbling paper, the bone handle of my dirk. I wedge it swiftly under the straw mattress.

The prognostications of Dorinda's Finger of Fortune lie in a shredded heap and their ink has leached into my already filthy shift. I shake my head at how trustingly I believed in Dorinda's declaration that A WOMAN shall save you from misfortunes. If that WOMAN was Stella, she may have saved me from the

Navy, but she brought me misfortunes perhaps more dreadful.

'Some bits are no too bad,' says Peg gathering up squares of paper from the floor. 'Shall I try to keep them for ye to read?'

'Not to read,' I say, 'but let's pile them beside the necessary bucket and they might serve our convenience very well.'

'Aye, that they would,' Peg smirks. 'We'll keep our new petticoats clean for Captain Littlewood should he come round to inspect them.' She winks as she re-ties my stays over the fresh shift. 'Are ye sure ye dinnae know that good man?'

'Good he most certainly is not,' I snort.

'Well, I'm grateful to him for my new linen. And I'll think of him each time I wipe my arse.'

In spite of the heaviness inside me, I laugh aloud and Ann asks in her tongue what is funny. I doubt Peg's reply tells her.

Through the coldest weeks of the winter our breath froze on the thin blankets and the bucket became solid with our piss. We never left the cell. I wondered how long they could keep us in such close confinement. We might be here all through the summer. Maybe even for years. But we would at least be alive. Any commencement of judicial proceedings would likely end with a punishment too dreadful to contemplate.

Thinking on all this, my numbed fingers go to my chin where the new beard growth feels whiskery. But I can't use the blade of my dirk to shave without revealing my maleness to Ann.

Not many days after, when the morning light comes early through the close-barred window, I awake to Ann's Highland chatter. She sounds angry and is looking at me. Peg's soft tones try to soothe her. For a nightmarish minute, I wonder if I have done something offensive in my sleep. With a flush of shame I feel between my legs but all is dry.

Peg turns to me and smiles but there is concern in her face.

'Is something amiss?' I ask rising from the bed to go to the bucket.

'Oh no,' says Peg and turns her back to give me privacy.

When one of us three needed the bucket, the others' unspoken routine of modesty involved the turning of backs and chattering as if nothing were happening. Skirts covered whatever functions the squatting produced.

But on this morning, Ann's voice rises through her Highland whishing and whooshing into a vexation that seems heightened by the sound of my piss.

'Peg?' I ask when I am finished.

'Oh dinnae worry,' she hesitates, 'but Ann has noticed…'

'Noticed what?'

'…mainly yer chin.'

My stomach flitters. 'Does it look bad?'

'No, no. Dinna worry yersel'.'

'Peg…' I sit on the bed and let my face sink into my hands. 'I don't know what to do.'

The weight of everything that has happened, the pressures of my life as a female, the abuse done to me, my grieving for Fliss and the unknown fate that lies ahead, all toll suddenly down on me like a hammer on a bell. From nowhere, a sob racks my chest.

'There, there, lamb,' Peg puts both arms around me and hugs me to her. 'It's no that bad!'

Her hand pats on my back. But this motherly heartbeat only sharpens my pain. My breaths quicken to pants. My heart races. Cries suffocate before they reach my mouth. I turn to Peg gasping for words.

'Help me… Peg… I can't breathe.'

'Oh lamb! Calm yersel'.'

I want to tell her about my mother, how she too was imprisoned in this place and so hopeless that she ended her life here, but all I can do is pant and moan. Both of my hands clamp against my chest to quell the pounding inside it. My face contorts as I huff and blow. Blackness closes in.

Peg says, 'Gi'me yer shawl and lay yersel' down.'

Heaving for air, I do as she says. And as my head goes to the mattress, Peg covers me with the maud blanket and pins it down over my face. The choking woollen heat seems to starve me of life but Peg's pressure on my face does not lift. Was this how my mother felt, in this very place, suffocated by the cord about her neck?

Then, Ann says something quietly and Peg answers. The back and forth of their unknown words rush like water in a hillside beck. Romack, romack, they both say. And I realise that my heart has slowed and my breathing is deeper.

'What is romack?' I croak when Peg pulls back the blanket from my face.

'It means beardy woman.' Peg sighs. 'I've telled her that ye have the embarrassment of a female condition that causes hair to grow where it shouldna.'

'Oh.'

I turn to the wall. My lungs are steady now but every part of my body aches with worry. How can I continue to live as a woman whilst my body ages into a full-grown man?

I don't rise from the bed that day until the light outside starts to fade. Going to the high window, I stand on my toes and the sails of the Brackenthwaite windmill come into view. Closing my eyes, I conjure my last visit to that place with Jossy. Spread below us are scenes of my youthful delight and disgrace. King Street where I paraded proud and stupid as the Fell Faery. The bowling green that held Lammas Fair. The Bear Mouth. The Custom House. Tom Hurd Rocks.

That night, I'm so awake I can't imagine ever sleeping again. Staring through part-open shutters at window bars against the moonlight, I begin to understand, with fatal certainty, the final thoughts that must have passed through my mother's mind. In a cell like this one. Perhaps on this exact spot. Because I see now how she must have engineered her end. With a strip of torn petticoat tied through the highest window bars and then around her neck. It would not be difficult. Peg and Ann are now asleep so deeply that I could easily do the same.

And my situation is not so different to my mother's. After what she'd done, she could never return to her home or family. Her life, she knew, could only end on the gallows or in the mad-house. Happiness existed only in her past.

Even if I were freed from gaol tomorrow, there would be no happy future. Inhabiting the body of a man after so long striving to be female seems impossible. Yet how can I have conviction in myself as a woman without Stella? I shall be caught between the sexes, an embarrassment to anyone who ever loved me. My name will become as unspeakable as that of Verity Salkeld.

As the blackness behind the bars grows ashen, I rise softly from the bed I stand below the window. The draught blows soft as a mother's breath on her baby's head. Quietly, I raise my skirt and untie the strings of the prison petticoat. The linen is cheap and loose-woven and it is easy to tear with my teeth. I cast a glance at Peg and Ann as I rip a band from the hem, but they snore on. Then, standing on my toes, I reach up to push back the shutter further and loop the linen behind an iron bar.

There, my pet, the draught seems to whisper, there, there. Is it my mother calling me to her? Silent tears slip down my cheeks and I wipe them with my noose. Again, I feel the growing beard on my face and know what I must do. My hands reach up to tie a slip knot into the linen…

But then, a flap of blackness slams against the bars and I jerk back, heart jumping. Something feathery and clawed is on the sill. Through the shutter's opening, a black eye glistens.

'Get you gone, foul pyet,' I breathe.

But this is no magpie. A fearsome hooked beak beats against the bars and powerful wings flap. Every inch of this creature is coal black. I stare up, unblinking and horrified. A raven.

'Shoo,' I hiss, 'be gone!'

But the bird only twists its neck the better to view me. And then lets out its strident, throaty cry. Kaaark, kaaaark.

Behind me, Peg stirs.

'Leave!' I cry out, louder.

The raven fixes me with its glinting eye. Then it flies off.

'What're ye doin' pet?' Peg is propped up on one elbow squinting into the new grey light. She sees, then, the noose at the window. 'Oh, no, no, no!'

Leaping forward, she grabs me into a tight embrace. 'What are ye thinkin' darlin'? Never that, promise me, never that.'

My head falls to her bosom.

Later, when the light is full, Peg takes the petticoat band untied from the bars and gives it, with some Highland words to Ann.

Ann nods. Then, with her teeth, she splits away two long linen threads and twists them to a loop.

'Ann says she's sorry for doubting ye,' Peg says, stroking my hand. 'She says she can see ye are a good person whichever way ye care to dress yersel'.'

Ann moves her light grey gaze from Peg's face to mine and nods as if she understands what has been said.

'Ann says she has a cunning way wi' whiskers,' Peg goes on, 'if ye will not mind to put yer head on her lap.'

Too weak to enquire what is meant, I do as the women say. With one end of the looped thread in her mouth, Ann brushes the twisted linen over my cheeks and chin. Prickles of pain tell me that she is riddin me of my whiskeriness, and the water it brings to my eyes mixes with tears gratitude to these Highland women for saving me from myself.

'There!' Peg says, when Ann is done. She strokes my smooth cheek. 'Ye're a bonnie lassie again!'

the fourth chapter

Our days of confinement went interminably on until, toward the end of April, there came a night in the cell when none of us could sleep. The noises began early on a bright afternoon with the ringing of the old church's bells for much longer than seemed right. Soon, the low *don-don* of King George's Church bells chimed in. Cannon fired from the coastal battery. Six booms, one quick after another. Then, like a nearing swarm of bees, came the massed sailors' *huzzah*s.

On into the evening the bells did not cease and as the sun dipped, a glow of bonfires on the hill-tops lighted our window. When Mrs Whiteside brought in our food for the day, I asked her why the bells continued to chime.

''Tis a rejoicing for the great victory.' Her smile is smug and I guess what is coming. 'Your lot are beat once and for all,' she beams. 'Thanks be to God, King George and the Duke of Cumberland!'

Peg's hands fly to her mouth.

'Is the Prince dead?' I manage.

'Prince?' Mrs Whiteside snorts. 'The Young Pretender I suppose you mean. It'll not be long till they catch him. All the rest of his army is killed or captured.'

Peg translates quietly and Ann makes the sign of the cross on her chest.

That night, when it is dark but the bells continue to ring, we three women stand at the window and stare at the glow of bonfires. Occasional whooping drifts up from drunks in the street below. Then, from the innards of the House of Correction comes a low but tuneful humming. Peg goes around the bed and puts her ear to the door. She nods and then quietly sings along as the male voices swell.

'But all's to no end,
For the times will not mend,
Till the King enjoys his own again,
Yes, this I can tell
That all will be well,
When the King enjoys his own again.'

Peg turns to me, her face bathed in tears. We suspected that male rebel prisoners had been brought to the House of Correction, but not until now how many. I recognise this song for it was sung often on the march from Edinburgh, but I can no longer bring myself to sing it.

The defeat of the Pretender Prince and his rebel army filled us all with doom but it seemed to cause an improvement in our circumstances. A day or two after the victory, Mrs Whiteside announced that we would be allowed, though separately and under close supervision, go outside for some air. I supposed that now the rebellion was over, we posed less danger. Mrs Whiteside said that a female turnkey would come for each of us the following day.

So long had it been since we'd left this small room that next morning we all stand readied and eager as if for an outing to a Pleasure Garden not the outer yard of a gaol. At the sound of a key in the lock, I squeeze Peg's hand and, for the first time since the news of the rebels' defeat, she smiles.

But when the cell door opens and I see who is to lead us forth, my blood sinks to my feet. And as I meet the turnkey's gaze, her eyes seem as shocked as my own. But her voice is steady.

'You,' Hannah Salkeld says, nodding in my direction, 'will

be first.'

Hannah leads me in silence along close corridors and down a stone staircase. Her figure is fuller but she has the same upright gait. Once we're in the open air, she stops by a locked gate and lifts the heavy ring of keys tied to her belt. Her skin, though still pale, has the flush of good health.

I lean against the wall, my muscles weak and shaking. Not taking her eyes from me, Hannah clanks the gate open and signals for me to go through. Then she turns the key behind us.

The yard is surrounded on three sides by the high wall and on the fourth by the windowless gable of the House of Correction. Long scrubby grass covers the ground by the back wall and the rest is foot-beaten mud and stone. It is a miserable place. But to me, so long confined, the rain-cooled air is sweet and heady as a glass of cold wine.

I glance up at the gable wall then at Hannah.

'No-one can see us,' she says, 'but keep your voice low.'

'I'm that glad to see you...' My voice trembles and I cover my mouth with my hand.

'I thought you dead.' Her eyes, clear and interested, move from my face to my skirts and back to my face. 'Everyone does.'

'Do they?'

'Aye.'

I stand, swaying, as I try to take this in.

'You should walk,' Hannah says and leads me in a circuit of flattened ground. Slowly, my legs feel stronger. I glance at Hannah who keeps a little way apart from me.

'My father,' I whisper. 'Does he think me dead?'

She shrugs.

'But he is alive?'

'Aye. Though very reduced from what I hear.'

'Reduced? How do you mean?'

'He lives in a back-house in Tangier Row and mends nets for a living.'

I laugh. The prospect is so outlandish.

Hannah frowns. 'You don't believe me?'

'You always speak truth, I know that.'

I think of her standing by the salterns telling me of my mother's crimes. And at the inquest accusing my father.

She shrugs. 'I speak as I find. Why do otherwise?'

We have reached the grassy patch by the wall and I stop to catch my breath. The ground here is pocked with undulations. Two clear rows of them. Each coffin-shaped raise in the earth is marked with a flat stone.

'Graves,' I say and fold my arms across my belly. 'Is this where my mother lies?'

Hannah nods.

'Where, exactly?'

She shakes her head. 'They don't mark the plots. The ground is not consecrated.'

I find myself suddenly unable to move but Hannah takes my arm.

'Come, Kit,' she whispers. 'Keep yourself moving.'

At last, she holds my elbow as together we slowly circle the yard. There is tenderness in the warmth of her touch.

'What have you been about, Kit?' she asks. 'Are you really a Jacobite?'

I take a breath. 'I don't know what I am any longer.'

'And have you lived all this time as a woman?'

I nod.

'Will that continue?' The question sounds measured, as if either answer would be perfectly reasonable.

'I've no wish to live like any of the men I've known.'

'You must decide, though, before your trial.'

'When will that be?'

'I don't know.'

I glance up again at the blank stone gable and drop my voice to a whisper. 'Will you tell me, Hannah? When you hear what they mean to do with us?'

She gives a single quick nod.

'And you? Have you been at this turnkey business long?'

'A while. I don't have to curtsy and scrape like I would as some merchant's maid. And it's more regular pay than the saltworks though I still labour there sometimes.'

'Do you still need to?'

'I'm saving. For…' Her voice drops so low I hardly catch the word. 'America.'

'Oh,' I say.

This news once voiced seems inevitable, but it brings a tightening in my throat.

During that warm summer, Hannah came to us rebel-women every week to give us exercise and to impart me with news. She told me of my Aunt Ravenglass who'd set up a physick shop in Ulverston with Mrs Arnott the apothecary's widow. This news shocks me almost as much as my father's lowly situation. My aunt, a shopkeeper? And with Mrs Arnott? Though when I thought on it, I could easily picture my aunt dispensing medicines and instructions, and casting as she does so a wry smile to Mrs Arnott, a woman who looks so like her that Ulverston folk will perhaps think them sisters. Of Poll Fairchild, my nurse, Hannah had no news but said she would ask about.

She told me also, in whispers of the crushing defeat of the Young Pretender and all his army that had caused such bell-ringing jubilation in Whitehaven. At a place called Culloden, thousands of rebels were killed or captured in only an hour of combat with the Duke of Cumberland's battalions. Afterwards, every Jacobite stood down and fled. The Pretender Prince himself had disappeared and, though some said he was dead, no one could say for sure. There was a rumour he'd disguised himself in female clothing to escape. I gave a bitter laugh at that.

The castle at Carlisle was overflowing with rebel prisoners sent south from Scotland for trial because King George did not trust Scottish judges to find them guilty.

In July, came the first executions and Hannah told me of them in grisly detail. Colonel Towneley, the commander of the Manchester Regiment at Carlisle, was hung until almost dead. Then he was cut down and his manly private parts sliced off and burnt before his eyes. After I'd swallowed down my disgust to hear her out, my thoughts went straight to Daniel Bragg, but I would not have wished such a dreadful fate even upon him.

In August, Hannah told me of a new Act of Parliament outlawing tartan cloth and Highland dress. When I tell Peg of this news she struggles to believe it.

'How will they live?' She asks, and her face is blank with bafflement as she explains what I have said to Ann.

I think of the Highlanders on the march south and how their long tartan plaids served not just as their apparel but as also their blankets and indeed their homes.

'*Chan eil!*' cries Ann, weeping.

Then toward the end of August, we were awakened just after sunrise by a commotion outside our cell window. There were shouts of *fare ye well!* and *God save the King!* Though which King was not said. Together, Ann and Peg lifted me up to better see what was going on and peering sideways, I spied a column of about twenty male prisoners being shepherded through the stone gateway between the same number of red-coated soldiers. It seemed that after near eight months in Whitehaven House of Correction, the first Jacobite rebels were being sent for trial.

On my next bout of exercise in the yard, Hannah confirms that this is so.

'They have gone to Carlisle,' she says, more agitated than I have seen her. 'And already there are heads spiked above the Scotch Gate.'

How I wish she might sometimes mince her words.

'Are there any women amongst them?'

She shakes her head. 'But that is why the Keeper has gone

with the rebel men. Mr Whiteside means to ask at Carlisle what is to be done with his female Jacobites.'

'Oh.'

We have reached the long grass of the House's graveyard and Hannah steps a little closer to me.

'The person you asked about, Poll Fairchild…'

'Have you found her?'

Hannah nods. 'She works as maid and companion to a mason's widow in Church Street.'

'Thank God!'

'She will help you, I think, and this may be your best chance.'

'For what?'

Hannah leans in toward me. 'Escape.' Her lips hardly move as she says the word.

For a second, I am dumb. Then with a sigh, a great weariness moves through me. I shake my head.

'I haven't the strength for more pretence.'

'If you go far enough away, you may live as you like.'

'What do you mean?'

She takes hold of my hand. 'Will you come with me, Kit? To America?'

I blink stupidly, unable at first to take in the idea. Then, as I look into Hannah's eyes that are so like my sister's, I see that this is what I must do, and that this escape will include my chance, perhaps the only one I will have, to find my father and avenge all that he has done.

the fifth chapter

Ann, Peg and I are awaiting a key in the lock but the clank still makes us jump up and squawk like pheasants from a hedge. We clutch at each other's arms as the door opens but Hannah comes in, as she said she would, bringing new clothes for me and the promise of freedom for us all.

She puts a finger to her lips as she pushes the door behind her and lays out the clothes on the bed. I have Poll to thank for them, I know. The suit is not new but the light grey coat and breeches are of good Exeter broadcloth and show little wear. Without a word amongst any of us, Peg helps me to undress from the riding-skirt and I put it in a pile with my old coat, flannel petticoat and maud blanket. Then I push them all toward Peg and Ann. Whatever value is left in my womanly apparel, they are welcome to it. I only wish I had more to give.

I had told Peg and Ann of the plan only that morning once Hannah said all was arranged. It would be a risk I explained, but if they too wished to try a seaward escape, there was a Scottish tobacco barque, *Greenock Bess,* in the harbour. Should the master take pity, they might be fortunate enough to procure a working-passage home. As Peg relays this to Ann, I can see by the look in both of their eyes it's a gamble they're ready to take.

Hannah slips out to the corridor as I change. First, the breeches go on. I button the flap under cover of Littlewood's charity linen but once I let the petticoat drop to the floor, the women gasp. Though still wearing my stays, the breeches alone have made me into a man.

Peg reaches up then to help me with the stays. I should take them off, I know. But through everything that's happened, Fliss's stays have been my armour and I need them more than ever.

'Leave them on me,' I say, putting a hand on Peg's arm. 'And pull the laces tight.'

She shakes her head but does as I ask. And so, beneath the generous, fresh-laundered shirt, my shape remains feminine. This hidden structure allows Fliss's old wedding waistcoat to sit, smooth and slender, beneath the frocked coat that flares out from my hips.

Once I have gartered the red stockings and buttoned my breeches at the knee, the plain prison cap that has for months been tied under my chin comes off. My hair reaches below my shoulders and Peg gives me her red ribband to tie it in a bow that rests on the back of my collar. A plain black cocked hat gives me the commanding height of a man.

Ann shakes her head and mutters. My stomach twists. I still I cannot be sure what she thinks my true self to be, but then neither, as yet, can I.

'What does she say, Peg?'

Peg bites a lip. 'That ye look the image of our Bonnie Prince.'

Again my stomach twitches but I nod my thanks. Ann, with her reverence for the Young Pretender, could pay me no greater compliment.

A key in the lock signals Hannah's return. Before the door opens, I feel under the straw mattress for my dirk and slip it into my coat pocket without any of the women seeing. The knife's closeness brings a sudden sweat inside my neckcloth. The risks of absconding from gaol seem slight compared to the dreadful project on which I am intent.

Hannah leads us along the cramped corridor lined with locked doors. The light has almost gone from the staircase. But because of the lateness of the hour and the general emptiness of the cells, we escape the House of Correction by simply walking out of the main door and under the stone arch into a mild September evening.

I set off through Whitehaven for the last time with the point of my hat low over my eyes. My legs feel weightless without the dragging burden of a woman's skirts. Across the street, *BRAVERY* is still there urging me to keep to my sworn purpose of revenge on Henry Ravenglass.

We turn away from the town and go by way of Brackenthwaite Lane down to the strand where Hannah points to the *Greenock Bess* at the outer Quay. With tears and hugs I bid farewell to Ann and to Peg, both of them giving me blessings in the Highland tongue.

My passage to the Delaware River is to be on the *Sally and Susan Galley*, a name that stirs a flicker of memory though I can't think why. Hannah says the brig lies at the Merchant's Bulwark and will set the sails before dawn. And, she says, my passage is already paid.

I shake my head. 'I won't go under indenture,' I tell her. 'I'd rather hang here than be in bondage in America.'

Hannah shakes her head. 'We're both to travel as passengers and will be free to disembark as soon as we dock in Philadelphia.'

'Have you paid for me, Hannah?'

'I have not.'

But more than that she would not say.

Hannah knows of my desire to see my father before we leave, but not my darker intent. At the rear of Tangier Row, she nods me toward the warren of overcrowded back-houses and lean-to's behind the street. I turn around to tell her I'll be quick but she is already hurrying away.

These lowest quarters of the town churn with paupers like maggots in a dead cat. But I have no difficulty finding my father. Even the drunkard crouched against the easement-shed knows the name Ravenglass.

At the door of his shanty-room, I pull my unsheathed dirk from my coat-pocket and listen. The smell on this grim landing is worse even than the House of Correction, but I am hardly breathing. A spate of manly coughing tells me that my father is within. Heartbeat racing, I thrust open the door.

He sits on a mess of sacking in one corner and is picking at a pile of hemp with a long bone needle. He looks up blearily and his eyes struggle to focus on the intruder before him. But then he speaks.

'Christopher?' he says. 'My boy!'

His cheeks are slack and his eyebrows almost white. Grey bristle coats his bare head. He is dressed in little more than a ragged hessian apron and gives off an odour of seaweed amidst the general paupery reek. In my mind I've rehearsed again and again the scathing lines to use at this moment, but for several moments I can say nothing.

'Our Kit,' my father spreads his hands as if in welcome. 'You are a gentleman!'

The word inflames me. I'm certain of little about myself, except that a gentleman is something I have no wish to be. My grip on the dirk stiffens.

'I've come only for a reckoning.'

'But you've come. That's all that matters.'

'I'm here on my sister's behalf.'

'Our Fliss?' His eyebrows shoot up as if she might be somewhere still alive.

'I know her death was no accident,' I go on. 'And I know that you had some secret part in it. Tell me…' A whiff of cheap rum creases the air and stiffens my resolve. 'Tell me truly what that is, or I swear I'll get it from you by force.'

My heart is beating so fast I hardly hear my words.

'There's no need for force, boy.' His eye goes to the blade in my hand.

'Tell me, then.'

He shakes his head and slumps to his elbow on the rag bed. I step closer and tower over him as if I am the man and he a child. He starts to mutter.

My voice hardens. 'Tell me, Father. How did she die?'

His hand goes across his mouth then falls to his side. 'I found her strung up in the ware-house. She had threaded a thin rope through a gap in the beams and stood on a barrel. I saw that her neck was in such a state that there would be little doubt of the verdict. But I'd have died myself rather than have our Fliss, our beautiful Fliss, treated in death as her mother was.' He sighs so heavily I wonder if he will be able to continue. Then he says, 'I hoped the sea would be her friend. And it was.'

'So it was you…' my heart is beating louder than my words. 'It was you carrying her that night, on the Steer?'

'Aye,' he breathes.

Hannah had spoken the truth.

'And even now,' he goes on, 'the recollection of her funeral and her fine headstone give me comfort. I thank God, if he exists, that I lost my daughter before I lost my fortune.'

I bite my lip, overcome by fury and grief. I don't ever want to see Fliss's expensive stone in King George's Churchyard. My grip on the dirk falters and I press a hand against my waistcoat to feel the firmness of the stays beneath. Only the thought of Fliss lets me continue.

'Why did she do it? Why?'

He only sighs.

'But you could have helped her, Father. You must have known of her condition.'

He shakes his head. 'If she had told me …'

An imagining leaps up that is so horrible I have not, until now, given it space in my mind. I take a furious step towards him.

'Father, were you to blame for her condition?' Suddenly aflame with rage I thrust the dirk toward his face. 'Was it you?'

'What, lad?' He doesn't flinch. 'What are you saying?'

'Daniel Bragg swore to me the child was not his.'

'Daniel..? He looks confused. 'When..?

'Answer me, Father.' My spittle rains down on him. 'If not Daniel Bragg, then who?'

Understanding at last, he gives a mirthless laugh. Briefly, his eyes close. 'Before she left for Ulverston, your aunt told me Fliss had been sweet on a sailor.'

'A sailor?' The idea is preposterous. 'Who?'

My father shrugs.

Bitterness stokes the anger inside me. He must know more. And I will not let him keep the truth from me any longer.

'You are a liar!' Again, I jab the dirk toward him.

'No!' The old anger flashes in my father's black eyes. 'I'm many things, son. But not a liar.' And his words are so full of quiet passion that, in spite of myself, my face is suddenly wet with tears.

Weakly, I hold the dirk out in front of me. But my father pays it no heed.

'Fliss… was so like your mother.' He sighs and picks up a strand of hemp running it idly in and out of his fingers. 'Perhaps your sister felt, in her melancholy, that she was saving her child from torment…'

My hand, and dirk within it, fall to my side. 'Will you tell me of my mother's end? Why she did what she did?'

He winces. 'It's not something I can speak about, lad. Even if I wanted to…' His breath stutters. 'I found her, you see… I wrested the knife from her…'

For a moment, neither he nor I cannot speak for imagining that dreadful scene.

'And do you say you had no part in causing that tragedy either?'

His head drops. 'No. I cannot claim that. But I still think she was wrong in her views.'

'My mother? Wrong about what?'

'Why, the African trade.' He looks up at me wide-eyed as if this should have been obvious all along. 'My whole purpose was to provide a good life for her. I was sure that she would come round to my way of thinking in the end.'

He snorts and runs a hand over the bristle of his scalp. 'But instead she…' the hand covers his eyes.

'Tell me, Father. Please.' I get closer but dare not touch him. 'If not you, who else can?'

His hand falls to his mouth and he meets my stare for a long moment. And then, he lumbers to his feet. Going to a dim corner of the room, he fumbles at a wooden box before turning to me and holding out a folded paper. The brown-spotted document is tied with a black ribband and sealed with a nub of grey wax.

'Your mother left me this,' my father says quietly. 'Now that you are a man, you should have it and do with it as you please.'

I look once again at that faded word '*Husband*.' The seal is still unbroken.

'But you haven't read it.'

He blinks and rubs his eye. 'I could never bear to.'

I take the letter from him. My father nods. He cannot see the irony that long dead though she is, he still will not listen to his wife. And as I study his careworn face, I understand how little effect my father's pursuit of manliness has had upon his character. At heart, he is a coward.

Perhaps I am one too, for I put the dirk with the letter in my coat-pocket. My vow to avenge my sister by murder had dissolved with my first sight of my father's face.

'Good-bye, Father,' I say and turn my back on him. 'Only God can forgive you.'

the sixth chapter

The light has near gone by the time I approach the first vessels at the Bulwark. Air fills with wafts of briny wood, tar and wet sails that stir a mix of foreboding and excitement within me. I look all around the quay for a sign of the *Sally and Susan Galley* knowing I cannot ask for directions, for if there is anywhere in Whitehaven I'd be recognised, it's here at the harbour.

Then, from the shadow of a wood stack, a shawled figure comes toward me. Too short to be Hannah, I hesitate and my gut twists. Could this be Mrs Whiteside, on my trail? But then she lowers her hood.

'Poll!'

I rush over and at the lip of the quay, we cling together. She pushes me to arms' length. Her face in the dim light is lined and her hair wiry beneath her cap.

'Christopher! Pet.' She looks me up and down.

I clasp her arms. 'Poll! I'm that grateful to you for this suit of clothes, and for my passage. I'll send you full recompense for all you've spent. I promise.'

She gives a laugh. 'Nay, lamb. The suit was Mr Bell's and passed on freely by his widow as a favour to me. The passage I know naught of.'

'I don't believe you, Poll.'

'It's the truth, pet. I swear. You must ask Captain Stewardson about who paid your passage.'

'Captain Stewardson?'

'The master of the *Sally and Susan Galley*.'

'Oh, of course!'

It comes back to me then that master of this brig is the father of my old school-mate, Neville Stewardson, alias Stew-breath, the little burper.

Poll is still holding my hands and she squeezes them tight. 'Take good care, Kit, won't you, on the seas?'

I nod.

'And when you are in America, will you write me that all is well? To the house of Widow Bell in Church Street. Remember. Tell me how you fare. I was in such a state when you left us before… not knowing how you were.'

'I'm sorry, Poll. I should've written.'

'Why did you go? And where?'

I shake my head. 'I can't explain it all now. But I will one day.'

'Do you promise?' She gives me a smile, full of mischief, that brings back so much of my childhood.

I squeeze her hand and nod. 'Aye, Poll.'

And I know that, one day, I will.

'Poll?' I press her hands tighter. 'There's something I must ask you before I go, about Fliss.'

Poll's face creases. 'What is it?'

'Who was the father?'

She shushes her hand to my lips. 'There's naught to be gained from such talk.'

'There is though, Poll. I was sure it was Daniel Bragg but… but if you know, please tell me.'

Poll takes my face between her hands. 'It doesn't matter now. And even at the time, no-one could have saved her. The darkness of melancholy came down upon her, as it did on your mother.' Poll's voice falters. 'There was naught any of us could do. She'd gone beyond help.'

'My father has spoken of her and a sailor…'

'Kit,' Poll's hand moves to smooth my cheek. Her fingers are rough from years of wash-tubs and needlery, but her touch is gentle. 'Think on all you saw, and you will know.' Then she kisses me full on the mouth like a mother and points the way to the *Sally and Susan Galley*.

The plank from the Bulwark is in place and I ask the lad standing watch to direct me to Captain Stewardson.

'Master's below deck,' he says and jerks his head at the hatch.

The brig is so similar to the *Swallow* that despite only lantern-light, I find my way easily to the master's cabin and knock at the door. When it opens, I stand for a moment of blank staring. Captain Stewardson should be a man of my father's age but the face that greets me is no older than mine. And despite the passage of years, it's one I know well.

'Kit?' he says.

'Aye, aye it is,' I reply laughing as I put out my hand.

For the master of *Sally and Susan Galley* is young Stewardson, Neville Stew-breath, my only friend at Natty's Nautical Academy.

'Well, I'm heartily glad to see you safe and well,' he says, pumping my hand. He has grown burly and almost as tall as me. 'And I'm pleased indeed to welcome you aboard the *Sally*.'

'I expected your father,' I say, entering his neat berth.

His smile wanes as he slides the door. 'He died last year. But was so well thought of that the owners saw fit to put another Stewardson in his place.'

'Wise folk.'

'I know I'm young, but I made the crossing many times with my father and our crew are the best in the harbour.'

'It's my great honour to be aboard.'

'And my pleasure to host you.'

He inclines his head and my heart skips as I realise who is my benefactor.

'Is it you Captain, who has covered the cost of my passage?'

'It is. You're my guest.'

'No, Neville. It's too much, I...'

He puts up a hand. 'Your cousin told me of your predicament and to tell you the truth, I'm more than glad to help you as it will ease my conscience.'

'Your conscience? What in heaven for?'

He makes a sound between a cough and a chuckle. 'That awful May Morning, do you remember?'

'The Fell Faery?' I start to laugh. 'How could I forget?'

'I should have spoke up for you. In fact, my mouth opened to tell Natty that the boys had cruelly tricked you into dressing up, but I was too cowardly to speak. I've felt guilty for it ever since.'

'Nay,' I shake my head, laughing. 'I was so eager to wear a skirt, I let them dupe me.'

'But you got a terrible hiding for it. And even now I feel remorse whenever I hear the word fairy.'

'Well, you need feel it no more. And I now owe the Fell Faery a great debt!' I go again to shake his hand and we laugh together. 'But as I'm trained for the sea, let me work my passage, at least.'

And as I say this, I have a sudden urge to climb, fast and barefoot, to the highest cables of the topgallant yard and there to feel the full swell of the sea.

Captain Stewardson nods. 'Thank you, Kit. But only if we have a need of more hands.' He smiles but for a moment is quiet. 'Is that what I should call you? Kit?'

His eye is wary. No doubt he saw desertion notices for '*Christopher Ravenglass*' put up by the impress men of the *Prince of Orange*.

I think for a moment. Who am I? The name I was born with seems dead to me. But so does Stella. Even Jane Mathewson is a name that belongs to a fugitive. Then I remember the dreadful night in the cell when a bird saved me from death.

'I think, from now on,' I reply, 'I'll be called Raven.'

'Raven?' He frowns, considering. 'Raven what?'

'How about... ,' a name springs to my mouth, 'Bravery?'

Stewardson pats a hand to my shoulder and winks. 'Raven Bravery. Aye, it flows very well.' Then we fall together into laughter.

As I laugh, I'm glad that my friend didn't ask me whether I shall be Mister or Mistress Bravery for I still do not know. But my new name will ensure that however I live, I'll never be a coward.

At first light, Hannah stands with me aboard deck as the *Sally and Susan Galley* is rowed out of Whitehaven harbour on a high tide and a fair breeze. We both put our faces toward St Bees Head and don't look back.

The captain treats my cousin Hannah with particular civility, though if he recognises her as the thin barefoot girl who went into the Bear Mouth at Lammas Fair, he does not say.

The journey through the Irish Sea passes easily and in less than a week we have cleared English waters. After a final stop for provisions at Cork, we are soon in open sea, too late for any second thoughts about returning to England, and all of us now dependent upon the seamanship of Captain Stewardson and the soundness of his Whitehaven brig.

Next morning when the air has a first bite of winter, I go early to the top deck with every button of my coat fastened and a muffler that the captain has lent me wrapped around my face. The mate touches his hat as I pass by and I bid him good morning. I don't think he notices the quiver in my voice, for I'm about to read my mother's final letter to my father.

Once at the furthest part of the bow, I plant my feet steady on the scrubbed boards. All around me, as I crack open wax seal, is the rolling, unfathomable heave of the ocean.

Ravenglass

Husband,

The world will condemn me for what I am about to do. And you will too, as you must. But amongst all the People of the Earth only you will understand. For have I not entreated you a hundred, thousand times, Husband, to desist from that business to which you have lately put the Resolve? It is written in Deuteronomy that where gain arises from Violence and Oppression, the land shall be polluted with Blood. And in my eyes the streets of Whitehaven run red with the getting of Africans and the selling them as trade.

You have pointed me many times to Friends who not only stay silent about this foulest of Trades but even profit by it. I cannot act as they for I feel the Afflictions of these stolen Africans as if it were my own. The misery of those aboard the Resolve might as well be mine or my children's.

Well you know that my children are dearer to me than the Light of my own soul. The protection of their eternal Life is my own life's purpose. And my terror for the peril of their souls thrusts me into a tunnel as black and suffocating as a sea-covered mine. This tunnel leads only one dreadful way. I cannot suffer to be in it for another single day.

I know you will reply, as you have a hundred, thousand times, that we all live in bondage of one sort or another and so perhaps we do. But you and I and our children are growing rich from the infliction of terror, misery and death upon innocent strangers. I can no longer suffer my children to live from this foul sustenance. Their souls will never have safety if I do. And so I must place them in the Refuge of the Lord.

I pray that mine Eyes will this day see the Creator. And I pray that my actions will cause you to give up the Trade, repent and ere long join the rest of us with God.

Your wife,

Verity Salkeld

My eyes are dry as they find the line where grey clouds meet greyer water. Verity Salkeld does not sound mad. From a Christian woman such as she, the words have a keen logic. Yet I cannot square her thoughtful, compassionate voice with the hanging-ballad horrors that came after this letter was sealed.

Above me, gulls wheel around the masts screeching their last at the *Sally and Susan Galley* before heading back to land. Underneath my buttoned coat is Fliss's waistcoat, so lovingly made but unused at any wedding. Beneath that, her stays keep me rooted to the windblown deck as I drop our mother's words into the waves. The letter soon sinks. And the departing gulls cry back to me, ever more distant, until they are swallowed by the great grey sky.

letter from Philadelphia

this 17th day of January 1766
The Temple of Manly Fancy
Spruce Street
Philadelphia

Dearest Poll,

Forgive me, I beg. I once promised you a letter and only now, near twenty years later, am I writing your name.

I have no excuse. I should have picked up my pen as soon as I'd disembarked from the Sally and Susan Galley. But even on that first walk through its streets, this city that is named for 'brotherly love' filled my thoughts and consumed my every sense. A wondrous array of faces, English, African, Spaniard, Lenape and Nanticoke crowded the thoroughfares. The city was a little world in itself. And though the houses were more close-packed than Whitehaven's, the plumb-straight grid of streets fronted by a mast-tangled harbour felt at once both foreign and familiar. I knew even then that I would make this place my home.

I will not try to explain all that has occurred since that homecoming. You will have reading enough in the document here enclosed. Suffice it to say that I have shared my life with Jeremiah Balsam, a freed man and time-served tailor who is my dearest companion. Together we have established this city's first emporium of masculine fashion, and we are as outwardly respectable a pair of shopkeepers as you might find anywhere. Some of the more sober townsmen may scoff that our Temple is an establishment only for fops and Macaroni men. But as they pass our window, they cannot help but turn their faces toward our displays of the fanciest cravats, costliest buckles, most feathery hats and highest masculine heels on this side of the great ocean.

Despite my silence, you were often in my thoughts, dear Poll. Many times, I tried to compose you a letter but I knew I could explain my actions only by retelling the whole of my early life. And as you will see, that is, at last, what I have done.

Why now, after so long? Partly because of the death of my aunt, Patience Salkeld, last spring. In Hannah's correspondence back and forth across the Atlantic occasioned by this sad demise, I learned with a fierce mix of emotions that my father was long dead but that you dear Poll, were living in Lowther's Almshouses on Duke Street.

We still miss Patience sorely but give thanks that she lived to enjoy Hannah's happy marriage and the childhoods of her American grandchildren. She was gratified too to play her part in the growing campaign against slave-keeping. She worked tirelessly in this cause and paid for many pamphlets exhorting Christian folk to desist from all connection with the heinous practice. Even those who abhor slavery, often find it convenient to look the other way when slave-goods benefit their pocketbooks. Patience did not care whom she offended by her writings. She told me that she treasured this work not only for its moral rightness, but also because it was done in memory of my mother. My aunt, however, being a Quaker, would not go as far as joining the radicals who have supplied small arms to rebelling plantation-dwellers. Jeremiah and I have no such qualms. Slavery is pure violence and only violence can destroy it. More general talk of Liberty seems trivial until this great outrage of human bondage in our land is ended.

It is not just my aunt's passing that has made me in recent months begin to dwell on the past. For not long after Patience was interred in the Quakers' Burying Ground on Third Street, our shop-door bell rang and a ghost entered. It was a Naval gentleman requesting to return in person some long-held property of mine. Perhaps you will already guess who he was.

Through my years in Philadelphia, I'd given little thought to Josiah Bone. My own Jeremiah soon supplanted all others in my heart, and I never saw again nor heard of the object of my first affections once he had marched away with impress men on Newcastle Town Moor.

But when he entered The Temple on that May afternoon, the years fell away. I could hardly speak for surprise, but Jossy smiled as he placed a cotton-wrapped package on the counter.

'I promised you I'd return it,' he says.

When I open this package, my tears well. Even a first glimpse of the tooled-leather cover tells me it is Fliss's book, Love in Excess. And suddenly I am seventeen again and sitting beside him below the windmill on Brackenthwaite Fell, with Whitehaven spreading out beneath us and my heart full of grief and fear.

Perhaps embarrassed by my tears, he turns away from me to make a purchase from the shop. And though already impeccably attired in his lieutenant's dress, Jossy selects a tall, buckled hat costing near two guineas. Perhaps this is a gesture of apology for abandoning me at Newcastle races all those years ago. Or maybe he just likes the hat. I take his money (he insists), and hastily explain myself to Jeremiah. Angel that he is, Jeremiah nods his assent to the private conversation he knows I must now have.

And so, still full of emotion, I ask Lieutenant Bone to take a turn with me in the open air. We walk, side by side, through the noise of the city, out beyond the tight streets, past the gardens and orchards and into the fields toward German Town. As we walk, we talk without pause.

'How did you find me?' I ask.

'By a glance into your inviting shop window. We are docked in the harbour here.'

'But not the Happy Endeavour? I would have known.'

He smiles and shakes his head. 'I have for several years now, been an officer aboard the Gazelle.'

'And you recognised me? Despite my… my changed appearance.'

'To me, you look the same. And you still put me in mind of Fliss.'

'Fliss…' All is now without question. 'You were her sweetheart.'

And, of course, he was.

We talked then for hours of those long-gone days on the far side of the sea. When was it, I ask, that he first thought himself in love with my sister? Was it that summer I worked with him on his letters?

'Oh no, much before that.' Jossy smiles ruefully. 'I needed little help with reading, as you might have guessed. I would have done anything to be nearer to Fliss. I loved her from when I first saw her.'

I frown, thinking back. 'You mean the night of the Assembly?'

He nods. 'She smiled at me. Just once. That was enough.'

Years later, they had exchanged some friendly words when he brought me home, injured from the Swallow. But before Daniel Bragg left for Africa on that same re-purposed vessel, before even the ball-game betrothal, Jossy came across Fliss one day going up to Saltom cliffs. Disturbed by her demeanour, he asked if she needed assistance.

'When she looked up at me, something seemed to clear from her vision,' Jossy says, his own eyes misty. 'You're Kit's friend? she asked me. And though I sensed that she already knew well the answer, and I told her with feeling that I was.'

Then began their long intercourse of walking, talking and a summer or two later, of loving. Each of the lovers felt that no-one before had ever listened so well to their story nor cared so closely for what they both, in their different ways, had endured. Their conversations brought them together as neither could have imagined ever being bound to another.

'Our precious hours were snatched on empty fell-tops or at the shore by Tom Hurd Rocks…' Jossy shakes his head and looks away. 'I see her there still.'

'Did she never love Daniel Bragg?' I ask, my cheeks wet.

He sighs. 'She did at first but he used her cruelly. His only true love, she said, was profit.'

I tell him of meeting Daniel during the Jacobites' rebellion and Jossy asks if I know what became of him after. Though many rebels of the Forty-Five were executed, some most foully, others were punished by transportation to the West Indies to labour under indenture on sugar plantations for the term of their natural lives. And, as I discovered from an old copy of the Newcastle Courant that found its way to Philadelphia, one of those transported convicts was Daniel Bragg.

The convict-list described him as a Captain in the Manchester Regiment and a Cotton Merchant. He was tried at Carlisle in September 1746 just as I was boarding the Sally and Susan Galley. I tell Jossy that it would be fair retribution for his part on a slaving voyage if Daniel's journey to Jamaica was on the lowest bilge-swilled deck and that the term of his natural life was short. Jossy nods, though not with satisfaction.

I stop us then in the midst of a vast meadow, more perfect in its lush, green flatness than any British field. The nearby river is wider too, the trees taller, and the American sky more blue.

'Did she tell you of the child?' I ask, trembling.

Jossy stops and kicks the toe of his polished shoe into the dirt. 'She did. And I begged her to flee with me, to London or Portsmouth, where we wouldn't be known and where married couples such as us are not unheard of. I knew the chances of success for us were slim but I would've tried anything. She wouldn't countenance the idea, though. By then her melancholy had become too deep. How could she be a mother at all, she would wail, when her own mother had provided such a wicked example?'

'That was not so!' My tears drip into the dirt. 'Fliss didn't know the full truth of our mother's story.'

Jossy shakes his head. 'Any truth would have made no difference. Toward the end, your sister's eyes had become dull and blank. Death seemed already upon her. Do you remember? No one could reach her.'

His words, dear Poll, seemed so profoundly to echo your own that I put my arms about him. Then, Jossy and I held each other for a long time in a brotherly embrace. And if my sister had lived, Jossy might indeed have become my brother, in law as well as in spirit.

On the road back, he told me of his regret that during his last summer with Fliss he'd had to keep me at arm's length for fear I should discover their clandestine love. He told me also about his wife and children in Portsmouth. And I'd lay The Temple in a wager that his wife is tall and slender and as fair as he is dark.

Later, I addressed a package to Lieutenant Bone on HMS Gazelle enclosing a love token, though not one from me. Inside the package was an old-fashioned long-fronted waistcoat adorned with garlands and arabesques, all embroidered in threads of still-shining gold.

Owing my Jeremiah an explanation of all this, I tried to recount the Ravenglass story but found it too full of emotion to be spoke aloud. So, casting back my memory two score years and more, I took up my pen to write. And now it is your turn to read. Some pages of this history may shock you with truths about the times I have lived through, and the entirety of my true self laid bare, a self that is depicted in the likeness here enclosed, drawn by Jeremiah. But please, dear Poll, before you judge me, read my words. And then it will be your privilege, as my reader, to form your own opinion about the person I have become.

Ever Your,

Raven

Acknowledgements

On an early spring day in 2020, before anyone had yet heard the word 'lockdown', I had an incredibly long pub lunch with Dr Julie Farguson of St Hilda's College, Oxford. Julie brought the world of the early Georgians brilliantly to life with her talk of ship owners, naval prizes and the politics of fashion. The writing of *Ravenglass* was immediately thrust into full sail and the following empty months became filled with a wonderfully escapist project. Thank you, Julie. Historical inaccuracies, intentional or not, are all my own work.

Thanks also to; Hannah Weatherill, Elizabeth Counsell, Steven Mair, Lisa Gooding, Caroline Fox, Lorna Gentry, Sally Kirby, Eileen Milner, the astonishing team at Northodox Press - Amy Leacy, James Keane and Ted O'Connor, my amazing publicist - Ana McLaughlin, and most of all, as always and for everything, Paul Kirby.

For information about my books and upcoming events, please visit www.carolynkirby.com